DESIRED B

"Please forgive me," M
it is for me to indulge in su

Silverton laughed softly.
his voice whispering like silk across her skin, "sometimes
a strong display of emotion is precisely what the situation
calls for."

He closed the distance between them and slid a hand up her
arm to caress the bare skin of her shoulder. Tiny shocks sparkled
along the path traced by his fingers. Meredith looked up into his
eyes, and this time she did gasp, completely undone by what she
saw in them.

He looked ready to devour her, his gaze so incredibly fiery as
it roamed over her face that her dazed mind imagined it might
actually leave a mark on her flesh. She no longer harbored any
doubts that he wanted her, and he wanted her very badly. . . .

Mastering The Marquess

Vanessa Kelly

ZEBRA BOOKS
Kensington Publishing Corp.
http://www.kensingtonbooks.com

ZEBRA BOOKS are published by

Kensington Publishing Corp.
850 Third Avenue
New York, NY 10022

All Kensington titles, imprints, and distributed lines are
available at special quantity discounts for bulk purchases for
sales promotion, premiums, fund-raising, educational, or insti-
tutional use.

Special book excerpts or customized printings can also be
created to fit specific needs. For details, write or phone the
office of the Kensington Special Sales Manager: Attn. Special
Sales Department. Kensington Publishing Corp., 850 Third
Avenue, New York, NY 10022. Phone: 1-800-221-2647.

Zebra and the Z logo Reg. U.S. Pat. & TM Off.

ISBN-13: 978-1-4201-0654-1
ISBN-10: 1-4201-0654-6

First Printing: April 2009
10 9 8 7 6 5 4 3 2 1

Printed in the United States of America

This book is dedicated to my husband,
Randy,
and my father,
Phil.
They are the finest men I know.

Many thanks to the three wonderful women
who first read my book:
Anne, Barb, and Kate.

Many thanks to my sister,
Patricia,
who is always there for me.

Many thanks to my friends and mentors in ORWA,
especially Teresa, Elizabeth, and Ellen.

Many thanks to my agent,
Margaret Hart,
and my editor,
John Scognamiglio,
for getting me on the path.
And special thanks to Julianne MacLean,
who pointed me in the right direction
in the first place.

Last but not least,
a bushel full of thanks to
my angel posse.
You know who you are.

Prologue

Meredith Burnley hated spring. All the bad things in her life happened to her on beautiful April days like this.

She stood on the edge of a dirt path, staring at bluebells that swirled into the dense woods encircling her family's manor house. Sunshine peeked through the overhanging branches, sparking a patchwork of blue petals and young green grass into a living mosaic of light-dappled color.

It really was lovely, she thought gloomily.

With a resolute sigh, she thrust painful memories into the dark corners of her mind and resumed her brisk pace through the trees, wanting to return to the house before Annabel awoke from her afternoon nap.

Her half sister's mysterious ailment had returned with a vengeance these last few months. Although Annabel had seemed much improved last year, a strange decline had now taken hold, in spite of treatment by a specialist, Dr. Leeds, from Bristol. Meredith couldn't understand it, and anxiety for her sister shadowed every waking moment.

She emerged from under the ancient copper beeches, catching sight of the pale stone gables of the Jacobean manor that had been her home since she was a little girl. Swallow Hill had been a welcome and necessary refuge for as long as she could remember.

But as she approached the house, Meredith drew in a startled breath at the sight of a groomsman leading a curricle and pair away from the front door. They were not expecting visitors, and only the doctor ever called without notice. She lengthened her stride, cutting across the lawn in her hurry to reach the front steps. The old fear clutched at her heart— had Annabel taken a turn for the worse?

The soles of her half boots rang on the shallow marble steps as Meredith dashed through the oak doors standing open to the warm April weather. The stooped figure of her butler emerged from a doorway at the back of the entrance hall, his wrinkled face creased in a benevolent smile.

"Good afternoon, miss," said Creed. "How was your walk to the village?"

"My walk was fine." Meredith yanked her gloves off, tossing them onto a side table by the door as she struggled to repress her impatience with the elderly retainer. "Do we have visitors, Creed?"

"Yes, miss. Your cousin, Mr. Jacob Burnley, has just arrived from Bristol."

"My cousin!" She frowned, slowly untying the ribbons of her bonnet. "Aunt Nora didn't mention he was due for a visit."

"No, Miss Burnley, she did not."

Meredith turned on her heel at the sound of the drawing room door opening behind her. Jacob Burnley sauntered out, still dressed in his caped greatcoat and boots.

"Well, little cousin," he drawled, "it's been months since I've seen you. Why you bury yourself in the country all the time when you could come to Bristol for a bit of fun is beyond me."

Meredith greeted him with a smile. "Jacob, how are you?"

She extended her hand but was stunned when he grabbed

her shoulders and yanked her to his chest, lowering his head as if to kiss her on the mouth. Meredith shied away, feeling his moist lips press against her face. He laughed softly as her cheeks flared with heat.

"Come now, Cousin," he murmured in a low voice. "You don't have to be so squeamish. Aren't you happy to see me?"

She pushed herself out of his arms. "Of course I am, but that doesn't mean you have to maul away at me, Jacob!"

Something ugly flashed across his face, surprising her.

"Pardon me, Merry," Jacob said. "It's been quite a long time, and I'd forgotten what a very fine woman you are." His eyes raked over her figure with a look she had never seen before.

"Oh, now I know you are teasing." Meredith laughed uncertainly but took a few steps away from him.

She cautiously eyed the man who had always treated her with an affectionate but casual regard, never displaying any evidence he was attracted to her. In fact, although they had once been close, they had drifted apart over the last several years. Jacob had developed into a stocky, strongly built man with blunt features and thick, dark brows. Meredith secretly thought his character had grown coarse as well, which made her feel guilty and disloyal.

She retreated a few more steps, her mind seized with the unwelcome possibility that he might be flirting with her.

Jacob rolled his eyes and chuckled. "Lord, Cousin, you look like a dunce standing there, staring off into nothing. Been out in the sun too long?"

Meredith shook her head and smiled. That sounded more like the Jacob she knew. "No, no, I'm fine. I'm just surprised to see you. I thought that with Uncle Isaac away from the mill, you would not be able to visit Swallow Hill this spring."

"Oh, things are quite in hand in Bristol! No need to worry about that. Wouldn't think of missing time with the family."

His manner was hearty, but he refused to meet her eyes. She had a strong suspicion he was being evasive. Normally, Isaac

Burnley was adamant that either he or his son be present at the wool factory throughout the year. Meredith had been dismayed when her uncle and his wife had moved some months ago to Swallow Hill, but it seemed even more unsettling now that Jacob had suddenly appeared.

As she strove to identify exactly what bothered her about the situation, a piercing voice rang out from the upper gallery.

"Jacob! My darling boy, here you are at last."

Aunt Nora's high-pitched, nasal tone had its usual grating effect on Meredith's nerves. Jacob also winced.

"Yes, I'm here, Mama. There's no need to screech so loudly," her son responded irritably.

"I'm just so happy to see you!" She hurried down the wide oak staircase. "Meredith, is it not lovely to have the whole family together again?"

"Yes, lovely, Aunt Nora."

Even at her most charitable, Meredith still could not think of the thin, pinched-faced woman standing before her as part of the family. Her uncle's wife had never shown her or Annabel the least bit of affection.

"Meredith, have you greeted your cousin properly? Does he not look handsome in his driving rig? I vow, Jacob, it is no wonder you are quite the most popular bachelor in Bristol. I'm sure all the young ladies must be devastated by your absence. Don't you agree, Niece?"

Meredith struggled to keep the amusement from her voice. "Yes, Aunt Nora." She glanced at her cousin, knowing he would be annoyed by the inane flattery.

"Don't be such a fool, Mama." Jacob glared at his mother.

Aunt Nora's thick brows snapped together. She sucked in an angry breath as she prepared to embark on what would, no doubt, be a tiresome lecture on her son's manners.

Meredith hated these scenes between mother and son, so she quickly intervened. "Pardon me, Aunt Nora, but I must see

Annabel before I change for dinner. I know you will not want me to be late, especially with Jacob now here to stay."

Aunt Nora's jaw locked for a moment, but then she tried to compose her crabbed features into a pleasant expression. She failed miserably.

"Of course, my dear," she said, displaying her yellowed teeth in what passed for her as a smile. "If I may, Meredith, I'd like to stop in for a chat before dinner. It will only take a moment, but I have something most particular I wish to discuss."

Meredith couldn't imagine what that might be but simply nodded her head and escaped up the polished oak stairs to the open gallery that led to her sister's bedroom. When she reached the top, she glanced back down to the foot of the staircase. She almost tripped over her feet, stunned by what she saw there.

Aunt Nora appeared to be studying her, her narrow features twisted into a bitter expression of anger and contempt. But Jacob's face gave Meredith an even greater shock, for he looked at her with a ravenous and strangely desperate gaze, as if he would devour her whole.

"He wants to do what?"

Meredith's jaw dropped open, the impact of her aunt's words reverberating through her. Her hands froze in the process of removing her walking dress, as she briefly lost all sensation in her body.

"Don't be a ninny! You heard what I said. Jacob intends to ask for your hand in marriage this very evening. I certainly hope you have the good sense to accept his proposal. You have been on the shelf for so long, it's a miracle he would choose to marry you at all. Certainly no one else wants to."

Meredith ignored the insult, dazed by the notion of marrying her cousin. She hoped for a wild moment her aunt was making a jest at her expense, but the other woman seemed to be unnervingly serious.

"Forgive me, Aunt Nora, but why should my lack of offers require me to marry my cousin?"

"Meredith, your father died three years ago. Until your uncle and I came here to stay, you had only that old governess to lend you the appearance of propriety. It's simply unreasonable to expect us to give up our life in Bristol just to play chaperone to you and your sister."

Meredith almost exclaimed that she had never asked them to give up anything, but she bit her tongue before the hasty words could escape. Aunt Nora would only berate her for her lack of gratitude.

"Your uncle and I have given up much to be at Swallow Hill," her aunt continued. "It would relieve us greatly if you would accept Jacob's offer. You must do something, Niece. You cannot continue in this fashion any longer."

"What fashion?" asked Meredith, completely bewildered by the strange conversation.

Aunt Nora stood in front of a chest of drawers, her restless fingers fidgeting with the various toiletry items and jewelry boxes laid out on top. She spun around, her voice rising to a shrill pitch.

"Two unmarried girls living together, with no wedding in sight for either of them." She cast a contemptuous gaze over Meredith, lips curling into a sneer. "When was the last time anyone even looked at you with interest? You should be grateful such a fine young man as Jacob would consider taking you as his wife."

Her aunt's vulgarity shocked her, but Meredith knew the unfeeling words held an element of truth. She *had* been pursued by a fair number of admirers when she was younger, but nothing had ever come of it. Unfortunately, her reserved manner seemed to intimidate potential suitors. Meredith didn't mean to offend people, but she was impatient, and sometimes the idiocies of courtship were just beyond her.

"You know how much I care for Jacob, but I have never looked at him as anything other than a dear friend and relation," she finally blurted out. "Jacob has a very"—Meredith frantically searched her mind for the words to refuse him in a way that would not offend her aunt—"robust personality, while I have—"

"Be quiet!" her aunt snapped. "You must get ready for dinner. Your uncle does not like to be kept waiting. Take off that dress, and I will help you to change."

Meredith let the gown slide to the floor and turned to face the mirror of her dressing table as her aunt came up behind her to retie the laces of her stays.

"There is another matter your uncle wishes to discuss with you," Aunt Nora said, tugging the laces as tightly as she could across Meredith's back. "It's obvious that Annabel's condition is deteriorating. We have discussed the matter with Dr. Leeds, who agrees her recovery while living here at Swallow Hill is most unlikely. He advises that Annabel be placed in a private asylum, where she can be properly attended."

Meredith gaped at her aunt's sallow face reflected in the mirror. "What in heaven's name are you talking about?" she managed to ask.

Aunt Nora gave another vicious tug on the stays. "Your uncle and I will be returning to Bristol very soon. Annabel can no longer stay here with you. She must go to a private asylum where she will receive proper care, or . . ."

A cunning look spread across the older woman's face. Meredith waited, dumbstruck by what she was hearing.

"Or you could marry Jacob. Both you and Annabel would then be under his protection, and you could take your sister to Bristol with you. The city has many fine doctors who could treat her."

Meredith watched the blood drain slowly from her reflection in the mirror. Lightheaded, she sank into the low chair in front of the dressing table.

"Oh, my dear," cooed Aunt Nora, her face smug with satisfaction, "I must have laced your stays too tightly. Please forgive me. Let me loosen the strings so you can catch your breath."

Aunt Nora's lips parted in a ghastly leer as she finished adjusting Meredith's stays. "There, that's better. After all, you must look your best for your cousin tonight. Sometimes men do need a little encouragement, you know, to express their affection. Not that Jacob has ever had any problem with the ladies."

A wave of nausea swept over Meredith, forcing her to swallow a hot rush of bile in her throat. The thought of Jacob touching her in that way sickened her—he had always been like a brother. How could this be happening?

Standing up, Meredith fought to regain her composure and steady her uneven breathing. When she turned to face her aunt, she struggled to speak in her usual controlled fashion.

"I'm sorry, Aunt Nora, perhaps I have misunderstood you. Are you saying that my uncle will confine Annabel to an asylum unless I marry Jacob? Surely that is not what you meant to say." In spite of her intention to remain calm, Meredith's voice rose, and she spoke more forcefully than she wished.

Aunt Nora's false smile disappeared, replaced by a barely concealed anger.

"Meredith! Your uncle is Annabel's guardian and wants what is best for her. Your sister is very ill and needs the care of good physicians in a quiet and secluded place. You have been used to having your own way for too long. If you will not submit to the guidance of those who know better, then matters will be taken out of your hands. Whether you marry Jacob or not, you and Annabel will not be allowed to go on in this scandalous manner."

Meredith reached out to grasp the post of her bed, each word a blow that threatened to drive her to her knees.

Her aunt looked at her with open contempt. "I suggest you wear your prettiest gown this evening. Jacob could marry any girl in Bristol or Bath. You should be grateful he has decided to have a woman no other man wants."

She stalked out of the room, banging the door shut behind her.

Meredith sank in a boneless heap to the floor, trying to fathom what had just happened. What possible reason could Uncle Isaac have for wanting to confine Annabel to a private madhouse? Yes, the girl was sick, but clearly not insane. And why in heaven's name did her sister's safety depend on her own marriage to Jacob?

She glanced out the window at the beautiful April afternoon. A tiny corner of her mind dispassionately acknowledged the fact that spring was here and, yet again, disaster had befallen her.

A quiet tap sounded on the door. Meredith slowly pulled herself up, stiff and cold in spite of the day's warmth. With shaking hands, she smoothed her crumpled undergarments and went to open the door. Her maid bustled in, tut-tutting at her mistress's state of undress. Meredith barely noticed as the girl tied her gown and finished combing her hair. Her thoughts ran in circles as she tried to formulate arguments to change her uncle's mind. For once, she was grateful Annabel rarely joined them for dinner.

Soon set to rights, Meredith could no longer delay joining the others in the drawing room. She trudged along the upstairs gallery and down the wide stairs, feeling as if she were being forced to attend some freakish and ghastly trial.

Coming to a halt outside the drawing room, she listened to her uncle's harsh voice demanding to know what the devil was keeping her. Aunt Nora began to argue with her husband until Jacob interrupted his mother with a callous disregard. Meredith's heart constricted as the rough, unfeeling voices washed over her. For a moment, she was tempted to turn and flee back to her bedroom. Instead, she gathered her courage, expelled the breath she suddenly realized she was holding, and walked into the room.

Her relatives turned as one to stare at her in silence. She looked at their faces: her uncle's cold and unyielding, her aunt's disfigured with open hatred.

But Jacob's hot gaze alarmed her the most. A prickling flush spread up her neck and over her face. Meredith felt as if he had stripped the clothes from her body, leaving her completely exposed and at his mercy.

As a sense of paralyzing fear swept through her, only one coherent idea began to form in her mind. *Escape,* she thought frantically. *We must escape.*

Chapter One

London, 1815

Stephen Rawlings Mallory, fifth Marquess of Silverton, felt a familiar sense of resignation and boredom creeping over him. Of course, no one observing him would have known that he wasn't listening attentively to his uncle. Silverton had exquisite manners. He would never commit an act of rudeness unless the recipient of such an act deserved it.

"Are you listening to me, Silverton?" snapped General Stanton. "Have you even heard a word I said?"

"Of course I have, sir. You know how much I value your thoughts on this and any subject you may care to discuss."

"Don't try to pull the wool over on me, boy. I'm not your aunt or your mother, and I know you bloody well don't care what I have to say about you," his uncle retorted. "You're nothing but a popinjay who don't give a damn about what he owes to the title or to his family!"

Silverton's young cousin, Robert Stanton, had been sitting quietly in the corner, displaying uncommon good sense in keeping his mouth shut during his grandfather's tirade. But the unjust attack on his mentor and idol proved to be too much of a provocation for Robert, and Silverton could see he was about to come to his defense. He shook his head slightly, willing Robert to silence, but the young man either failed to see or to understand the small gesture. Silverton sighed inwardly, lamenting the fact that his cousin had neither the wit nor the sense of self-preservation to avoid bringing his grandfather's wrath upon himself.

"No, really, sir, that's just not fair. Stephen, a popinjay!" exclaimed Robert. "You must know he is one of the best sportsmen in the country, not to mention having some of the finest horseflesh and hounds in all of England. Really, Grandfather, to compare him to a dandy is just too much!"

The general's head swiveled around to his grandson, iron gray eyebrows bristling with irritation as he trapped his next victim in his sights.

"No, you young jackanapes! That honor in the family belongs to you. Look at you. You can barely turn your head in that ridiculous neckwear. You look like a stork peering out of its nest. And all your poetic airs and lamentations! It is enough to drive me to an early grave. No, you are indeed the dandy in the family, and just as useless when it comes to finding a wife and doing your duty to your name."

Robert turned bright red, sputtering a confused defense that he was still too young to get married. He was easily cowed by his grandfather and particularly sensitive about both his appearance and his literary aspirations. The lad did not actually write any poetry but firmly believed that he only awaited the arrival of his muse to unleash what would undoubtedly be his artistic genius. In the meantime, he read Byron, spent an inordinate amount of time on his clothes, and generally comported himself in a harmless manner with several fashionable young men whose families the Stantons had known forever.

Silverton understood, however, that General Stanton would no longer tolerate this harmless but idle life. He deemed it time to intercede before the squabble developed into a full-out row.

"Now, Robert," he interjected in a soothing voice. "Uncle would never call me a dandy, and I'm sure he appreciates my horseflesh as much as the next person. But you can't blame him for wishing to see us settled, although I do agree you are a bit young to be pushed into the parson's trap."

"Not at all," exclaimed the general. "I was only nineteen and your aunt only seventeen when we tied the knot. I'm sure she has never had any cause for complaint since that day."

"Perhaps we should ask her," muttered Robert.

The general whipped his gaze back to his grandson. "What was that?" he growled.

Silverton hastily intervened. "Yes, well, be that as it may, God knows it's not easy to find a woman with Aunt Georgina's qualities. You must admit, sir, you were exceedingly lucky to snag such a prize so early in life."

General Stanton grunted his reply, mollified as always by the thought of his wife. Silverton knew that in spite of the gruff response, his uncle was inordinately fond of Lady Stanton and cherished her in his own inarticulate manner. He also knew his uncle was dismayed that he and Robert did not seem the least bit interested in settling down and starting families of their own.

The three men sat in the library of General Stanton's richly appointed townhouse in Berkeley Square, shortly before noon on a warm April morning. Silverton thought it much too early in the day to endure a dressing-down, but ignoring his uncle's summons would only have postponed the inevitable. He was, after all, almost thirty-five, and it was indeed high time he took himself a wife.

For many years now he had allowed his mother and aunt to drag him to Almack's, and from one subscription ball to another, in the hopes of finding a woman whom he could imagine living with on a permanent basis. He had met many charming young ladies and enjoyed several delightful flirtations. But over time his willingness to be pleased had evaporated, replaced by a cynical amusement with the relentless machinations of the marriage mart.

The fault lay not with the numerous debutantes thrown his way, who were as trapped by the subtle yet unbending rules of the ton as he was. In fact, in his more generous moments he even felt sympathy for the girls whose parents drove them to hunt him like a prized stag. Mostly, though, he felt irritation and contempt, and not much else.

Silverton had come to the conclusion long ago that he was by nature a cold person or, at the very least, lacking in strong feelings. He enjoyed many things—his horses, his dogs, and his friends. He was fond of his mother and adored his Aunt Georgina. But he could never seem to muster any real attraction toward the fluttering girls paraded before him and honestly had no desire to feel otherwise.

When he thought of marriage at all—which wasn't often— it invariably left a dull, faintly sour taste in his mouth. But Silverton knew it was only a matter of time before he must resign himself to a suitable alliance. Duty required him to marry, and marry he would, but he had no expectations for his own happiness.

Silverton listened absently while his uncle berated Robert. Since it didn't really seem to matter whom he married, he had compiled a list of eligible candidates in his head to present to the general for discussion and approval. Now seemed as good a time as any to make the decision.

He was about to open his mouth when he heard a commotion out in the hallway and the raised voice of Tolliver, his uncle's excruciatingly correct butler. The door to the library flew open and Tolliver exclaimed, "No, no, miss. Wait! You cannot go in there!"

All three men turned their heads toward the door and were met with the astonishing sight of an unknown young woman striding into the room. When she found herself confronted by their shocked gazes, she stopped in her tracks. Tolliver followed closely behind and only just managed to avoid barreling into her.

Silverton rose slowly to his feet. Robert seemed paralyzed, but he finally remembered his manners and sprang to attention. For one long moment, they all remained trapped in a stunned silence before the general finally found his voice.

"Who the devil are you?"

The intruder's eyes quickly surveyed the room, skipping Robert and coming to rest on Silverton. Their gazes locked on each other. He felt as if he had been nailed to the floor, so captivated was he by the sight of the feminine whirlwind who had swept into their midst.

A tall, long-limbed creature, her shiny black hair curled out from under a sturdy country bonnet. Although she seemed no more than twenty-one or twenty-two, her self-assurance in confronting a roomful of strangers suggested she could be older.

But more than anything, her eyes captured him by surprise. They were extraordinary: large under straight, determined brows and framed by thick black lashes. It was their color, however, that had caught his attention so forcefully. They were gray, but not the insipid, neutral color one associated with the term. No, they reminded him of a winter rainstorm— turbulent, untamed, and full of secret depths.

He stared at her, dimly aware he was probably making an ass of himself, but it seemed impossible to look elsewhere. She, too, seemed unable to break away, her eyes widening as a faint flush bronzed her cheeks and the bridge of her nose. For just a second, he thought the darkness in her gaze transmuted into something lighter, a brief flash of silver in the deep. Silverton could not seem to assemble his thoughts into a coherent order, but it occurred to him that she looked like a young goddess, magnificent and full of righteous anger.

Then she blinked, the spell broke, and she turned to face his uncle.

"I am most sorry, General Stanton," said Tolliver, who wrung his hands in distress over this astounding breach of etiquette. "I tried to tell this young . . . woman that she could not disturb you, but she waited until my back was turned and then . . ."

He trailed off into silence, too distraught to even finish his sentence.

The general impatiently waved his hand at the butler. "Yes, yes, well, you may go, Tolliver. I'll deal with this situation."

"Yes, sir." The butler tottered out of the room, clearly shattered by the disturbance to his well-ordered household.

General Stanton focused his gaze on the young woman standing before him.

"Now, miss," he said, "perhaps you will be so good as to explain your extraordinary behavior."

Silverton again saw the faint flush color the woman's pale complexion, but it was apparent by the way she held her ground that the general's irascible demeanor failed to intimidate her.

"I am Meredith Burnley, sir," she replied in a quiet voice. "My stepmother was your daughter, Elizabeth, and your granddaughter, Annabel, is my half sister."

Another stunned silence fell over the library. If she had shot a cannonball through the room, the shock could not have been any greater. Silverton grimaced, bracing himself for the inevitable explosion as General Stanton confronted the stepdaughter of his bitterly estranged and long-dead child.

The old man was, indeed, turning an alarming shade of red as he rose from his chair to contend with this obviously unwelcome spectre from the past. In fact, he appeared on the verge of an apoplectic fit. Silverton cast about for a way to divert his uncle's attention, but his mind at the moment felt approximately as agile as a snail crawling through two feet of mud.

"How . . . how dare you enter this house?" General Stanton finally managed to blurt out. "By God, woman, what right do you have to disturb my peace after your father ruined my daughter's reputation and her life? A tradesman's son to marry my child! Her mother and I have spent many years trying to forget our loss. And now, after all this time, you dare come here . . . to my home!"

The general shook with rage, his hands clenched into white-knuckled fists. "He ruined her life, I tell you, and it broke her mother's heart!"

For a few seconds, General Stanton glared at the silent young woman before turning his back on her. Miss Burnley staggered under the impact of the old man's wrath, swaying a bit as if she might faint. Repressing a curse, Silverton moved quietly across the thick Aubusson carpet until he stood behind her. He could think of no other response to his uncle's shocking outburst, but at least he could catch her if she swooned.

Fortunately, Miss Burnley remained on her feet.

"I am here, sir," she replied in an unexpectedly sharp voice, "because I have no choice. I wrote to you after our father died, hoping you would realize how much your granddaughter needed the protection of her family. You chose to ignore us, and she has been forced to submit to the direction and guardianship of a man who does not have her best interests at heart. I have imposed myself only to implore that you intervene on Annabel's behalf to prevent a most unhappy fate from befalling her."

Miss Burnley struggled to maintain her composure. She clamped her arms tightly against her sides, attempting to subdue the tremors shaking her body. Silverton felt an oddly powerful impulse to take her in his arms and soothe her. He fought the unfamiliar urge as the young woman deliberately straightened her spine and cocked her elegant chin. Instead of retreating, she stepped closer to the desk, leaned into it, and fixed her implacable gaze on his uncle.

"General Stanton, I must insist that you listen to me. If you do not, Annabel likely will not survive this threat to her well-being. She is very fragile."

The general finally looked at her, hostility etched in every line of his face.

"You must help her," she implored again. A note of faint panic seemed to thread her voice. "I would not have disturbed you if there had been any other way to save Annabel. I cannot lose her. She is all I have."

Her voice caught, and she fell silent. Miss Burnley clutched her reticule in a tight fist and turned away from the general as if embarrassed by her loss of control. She gasped when she discovered Silverton standing so closely behind her, taking a hasty step back to regain her balance.

Grasping her elbow, he gently steered her to one of the leather club chairs to the side of his uncle's desk. "Miss Burnley, won't you sit down? You may tell us everything you need to regarding your sister, but I insist you have some refreshment first."

Silverton glanced at his cousin, who was glued to the spot, mouth hanging open and eyes popping from their sockets. "Robert," he admonished, "do stop catching flies and ring the bell for some tea."

The lad snapped his mouth shut and hurried over to yank vigorously on the bell cord.

Silverton returned his gaze to Miss Burnley, who sat bolt upright on the edge of her chair, eyes lowered as she grasped her handkerchief in a death grip. Taking a deep breath to steady herself, she looked up to meet his eyes.

"Thank you, sir. I should be most grateful for a cup of tea." Her soft mouth trembled into a tentative smile.

He blinked as the force of that shy smile lanced through him. The unexpected jolt of emotion was both surprising and irritating.

General Stanton forcefully cleared his throat, jerking Silverton out of his momentary reverie. After briefly examining Miss Burnley's pallid complexion, he crossed to a mahogany sideboard holding a collection of decanters and crystal glassware. Silverton poured a small glass of sherry and returned to her side.

"Yes, tea will be just the thing, but I fancy you could use something a bit more fortifying while we wait."

"No, I'm fine," she protested. "I don't need that." She took another deep breath, folding her hands carefully in her lap.

"Yes, you do," he replied in a firm voice, willing her with his eyes to take the drink. "Come, Miss Burnley, I insist."

She looked at him doubtfully. He nodded his encouragement, and she again offered him that painfully sweet and tentative smile. Miss Burnley took the glass and sipped, casting her gaze up as if seeking his approval. Silverton found himself riveted by the luscious tremor of her full pink lips and the burnished silver of her amazing eyes.

Under the circumstances, his reaction was obviously most inappropriate.

He mentally shook his head at the day's unexpected turn of events. He had reluctantly dragged himself to Stanton House this morning to meet his uncle. Completely unawares, he had been pitched right into the middle of what his mother called the Great Family Scandal. No one spoke of the estrangement between the general and his daughter. It had always seemed like ancient history to Silverton, especially since Elizabeth Burnley had died so many years ago. But part of that ancient history had come back to life today, and with a vengeance.

He looked thoughtfully at the striking young woman perched on the edge of her seat, cautiously drinking her small glass of sherry. In spite of the obvious distress of all the parties in the library, Silverton had to admit this was much more fun than talking about his impending immolation on the matrimonial altar.

Especially when one of the parties involved was Miss Meredith Burnley.

* * *

Several minutes passed in silence as the anxious Miss Burnley sipped her sherry. His uncle continued to fume behind his desk, and Robert fidgeted in the corner. Silverton, however, decided to disregard his relatives until she recovered herself. He was pleased to see the color finally returning to her cheeks.

"Miss Burnley, if you are quite recovered," he said, moving to stand over her, "perhaps you might explain to us why you need the general's help."

Her brows drew together in a worried frown. "I would be happy to, sir, but it is a private family matter and I don't know . . ." Her cheeks turned bright pink as her voice trailed off.

Silverton nodded his head in sudden understanding. "Of course. You don't know who we are. I am the Marquess of Silverton. General Stanton is my uncle. The unnaturally silent young man in the corner is Robert Stanton, the general's grandson and your sister's cousin."

Unfortunately, this information did not appear to assuage her doubts. Her eyes earnestly searched his, and from the expression on her face, he could tell she was trying to decide what to do.

"Come, Miss Burnley." He arched his eyebrows at her hesitation. "I assure you, my cousin and I are quite able to keep our own counsel. We cannot possibly assist you until we know the nature of the problem."

Silverton ignored the murderous look cast his way from behind the massive desk. He also decided to ignore the desperate-sounding squeak that came from Robert's corner.

Miss Burnley paused a moment longer before bowing her head in agreement. She placed her sherry on the red lacquered side table next to her chair and began to speak, hesitantly at first but more strongly as she went along.

"As you may or may not know, my lord, my sister and I have been almost alone in the world since the death of our father three years ago. I achieved independence a few years before that, but Annabel was only fourteen when our father died. Because of the estrangement between our families"—she paused and cast a wary glance at the general—"my father's will stipulated that Annabel fall under the guardianship of his brother, Isaac Burnley. That guardianship also includes control of her fortune, which she inherited on the death of her mother, Elizabeth Stanton Burnley."

"Aye, and that money was the cause of all this misfortune and trouble in the first place!" General Stanton burst out. "Without it she would never have been able to run off and leave her own family."

Miss Burnley's cheeks turned an even brighter shade of pink than before. She and the old man glared at each other, and it seemed that open warfare would break out any moment between the combatants.

"Uncle!" Silverton uttered only the one word, but the warning in his voice was clear.

The old man grumbled something under his breath before settling into his chair.

Silverton turned back to the young woman. "Please continue, Miss Burnley."

She nodded. "As I was saying, this guardianship includes control of the fortune bequeathed to Annabel by her mother." She paused to glance cautiously at the general before continuing. "Which also includes the management of our estate at Swallow Hill. Until quite recently, my uncle was content to leave Annabel's welfare to me, as he and my aunt live in Bristol and were much occupied with their own affairs."

Her features were suddenly infused with a look of anguish as her eyes glittered with unshed tears. Silverton wondered what the devil could plague her to bring such despair so easily to the surface. She looked so beautiful and so lonely that his heart, not easily touched by the emotion of others, began to feel a reluctant tug of empathy.

"Annabel has always been frail," she said, looking at him

earnestly, as if willing him to understand. "When my father died, she suffered greatly, and I have been forced to safeguard her carefully ever since. Last year her health was improving. But lately, well, her spirits are much depressed again."

She stopped, and Silverton watched with dread as tears began to well from her eyes. He wasn't really afraid of weeping females, but this situation was so bizarre he was uncertain how to respond to her.

Fortunately, she blinked away the offending moisture and resolutely carried on.

"A few months ago, my aunt and uncle decided to join us at Swallow Hill. Uncle Isaac has finally asserted his guardianship over Annabel, which has included decisions about her illness. These decisions, I believe, have been very detrimental to her well-being. I'm convinced that her recent decline is the result of this interference, but I'm powerless to stop it."

Miss Burnley paused again, as if collecting herself for what came next.

"Just a few days ago," she explained, staring at Silverton as if her life depended on it, "my uncle made what could surely be called a threat to Annabel, a threat I fear will destroy her completely. We had no choice but to flee our home and throw ourselves on the mercy of Annabel's family."

She twisted in her chair to face the general.

"Please, General Stanton," she implored, "if you have any charity in your heart toward Annabel or toward the memory of her mother, you must help her. I believe you are the only person who can defy my uncle and prevent him from doing what he clearly intends, and which I am certain will be the death of her!"

Miss Burnley's eyes blazed with a desperate determination as she pleaded with the general. The old man looked stunned, shifting uncomfortably in his leather chair.

Silverton had always prided himself on his understanding, but he couldn't imagine what could lead an obviously well-bred young lady to make such an impassioned statement. He was used to his mother's domestic dramas and occasional histrionics, but Miss Burnley did not strike him as a woman given to hysterics. Quite the contrary, he was willing to bet she would be as levelheaded a woman as one could meet.

The situation was rapidly spinning out of control. His uncle was struck dumb, and Miss Burnley seemed unwilling to provide any more clarity to a story positively gothic in nature. Obviously, he had to try and get to the bottom of this before it got any murkier.

"Miss Burnley." Silverton forced his voice to remain gentle. "If you could reveal the exact nature of this threat, it would help us to better understand your sister's predicament."

Her shoulders slumped in weary resignation against the back of the club chair. "My uncle wishes to confine her in a private lunatic asylum."

Silverton felt his temples begin to throb as he realized what would happen next. He bit back a curse as he looked at his uncle, who was doing a passable imitation of one of Congreve's rockets about to explode. Any amusement he had felt toward the day's proceedings had just gone up in a puff of smoke.

"A madhouse?" The general practically levitated out of his chair. "Do you mean to tell me the girl is insane?" His face mottled with fury as he pointed a shaking finger at Miss Burnley. "This is what comes from marrying inferior blood! I won't have it, I tell you. I won't have a madwoman in my family. *Your* family obviously carries the taint, and *your* uncle must deal with it as he sees fit. You will leave the Stantons out of it."

Silverton, dimly aware of Robert gulping like a stranded fish in the corner, felt paralyzed both by Miss Burnley's words and by his uncle's furious outburst. If she didn't swoon now, it would be a miracle.

She did appear stunned, but her shock was rapidly displaced by a growing wrath. Her hands clenched into fists, and her face turned ghostly pale but for two patches of red flying high on her cheekbones. Silverton watched, reluctantly fascinated as she flexed her hands and wrestled her anger under control. She stood, drawing herself up to her full and imposing height. In spite of the awfulness of the situation, he couldn't help but think that Miss Burnley looked absolutely magnificent, with her generous bosom heaving and her silver eyes luminescent with fury.

"General Stanton," she said in an icy but surprisingly well-modulated voice, "you will note the only person in this room lacking control is you. Your behavior is, I think, quite mad! I must conclude that if there is a taint of insanity, it resides in your branch of the family, not mine. As you can see, I am perfectly rational and in control."

As if to prove her point, she folded her hands in a ladylike clasp and sat primly back down in her seat.

"Perfectly rational, perfectly rational!" roared the general. "By God, I'll have you thrown out into the street before you insult this family again."

Silverton managed to recover the movement of his limbs, stepping hastily forward to stand between Miss Burnley and his uncle's desk.

"You'll excuse me, sir, but I hardly think this discussion will benefit either you or Miss Burnley. I urge you to sit down. You do not look well."

The general opened his mouth as if to argue the point, but he looked truly overcome by the events. He bobbed his head once and sank back into his chair.

"Miss Burnley," Silverton said, swiveling his head to capture her attention, "I would take it as a great favor if you would refrain from insulting my uncle any further."

"But . . . ," she began to protest.

"No, Miss Burnley," he said in a quietly lethal voice.

She glared at him, but he simply returned her torrid gaze with a cool and steady regard. Somewhat to his surprise, she gave a stiff nod and dropped her eyes. She sat with her back ramrod straight, staring at the floor as she struggled to rein in her temper.

Silverton turned to his uncle and lifted an eyebrow. The general was muttering to himself again but did not seem inclined to launch back into the fray.

"Thank you," Silverton responded to no one in particular.

Now that he had established a fragile peace, he took a moment to study the two angry faces before him. The thought crossed his mind that Miss Burnley and his uncle were remarkably alike. How odd that they weren't even related, Silverton reflected. They might have been taken for father and daughter.

He shook his head, crossing to the mahogany sideboard to pour himself a glass of port. Robert sidled up to him and hissed in his ear, "Damn it, Stephen, what do we do now?"

As Silverton pondered the answer to that question, the door to the library opened behind him.

"My goodness!" exclaimed a gentle, feminine voice. "What is happening in here? Arthur, what are you yelling about now?"

Silverton repressed the inclination to roll his eyes up to the ceiling. God only knew how his Aunt Georgina would react to the unexpected resurrection of the Great Family Scandal.

Chapter Two

Meredith almost collapsed with relief as she followed Lady Stanton from the library. Her legs were shaking so badly she wondered if she could walk at all.

She had been so angry with the general she'd been tempted to slap him. That was mortifying enough, but her response to Lord Silverton had been even more appalling. One kind word from him and she'd practically melted into a sticky puddle at his feet.

Never in her life had she reacted that way to a man, and Meredith had the awful impression he'd sensed exactly how she felt. Even worse, she suspected he'd found the entire horrid scene more annoying than anything else. She groaned inwardly, recalling the arrogant arch of his brows when he'd practically ordered her to tell him about Annabel. Having to reveal her darkest family secrets to a man like him made her want to crawl into a closet and never come out.

Lord Silverton was, quite simply, the most perfect man she had ever seen in her life. When Meredith had stormed into the library, she hadn't noticed anyone but the general, so intent was she on her mission. But then she turned and saw *him* and thought she had stepped into a fairy tale or an ancient legend.

Her overactive imagination had decided on the spot that the golden-haired man looked exactly like a valiant knight of old.

He was tall, broad shouldered, and had the powerful physique of a sportsman. But it was his classically handsome face that had stopped her in her tracks. Her artistic sensibilities had compelled her to mentally trace the sharply defined cheekbones, aquiline nose, firm mouth, and strong chin. His eyes were incredibly blue—cobalt set against the faint bronze of his tanned complexion. His thick, wheat-colored hair had reflected the sunlight shafting through the library windows, brushed back from a widow's peak before falling in soft waves to his collar.

And although she had been too upset to notice many details of his attire, she had been aware that he carried himself with a masculine power and grace she had never encountered before.

Most disturbing of all, when he had finally allowed himself to smile, her knees had actually wobbled.

Meredith shrugged her shoulders impatiently, irritated by her own foolishness. Then again, she reflected, perhaps it was the strain of the last few weeks that had made her so susceptible to his potent male charm. She *had* been very anxious about meeting the general and the rest of Annabel's family, which might explain her odd reaction to the situation.

That and the fact that Silverton was the most dazzling man she had ever met, she thought dryly. In all fairness to herself, however, handsome London noblemen were actually rather thin on the ground in her part of rural Wiltshire.

Meredith studied the back of Lady Stanton's upright figure as she climbed the imposing central staircase behind the older woman. Glancing around, she noted the high ceilings and marble columns gracing the front hallway of the Palladian-inspired townhouse. The footman who had opened the front door stood impassively at the foot of the stairs, but she had little doubt he too thought her a lunatic for pushing her way into General Stanton's inner sanctum.

What a commotion she had caused! She had gambled everything on her ability to convince her sister's family they must come to Annabel's rescue. If the general's response was any indication, their future seemed increasingly dependent on the goodwill of her cousin Jacob. Her heart shriveled at the thought, and she gave a despondent sigh as she trudged behind Lady Stanton. Her ladyship cast a look over her shoulder, her lips parting in a generous smile.

"Not much farther, my dear. Then you will be able to have a nice cup of tea and explain how I can help you."

At those gentle words, Meredith's heart began to lift, and for the first time in days she allowed herself to hope she had found an ally in her battle to keep Annabel safe.

The butler, who had preceded them up the stairs, now opened the door to Lady Stanton's sitting room, bowing to his mistress and then escorting Meredith through it. A footman carrying a large silver tea service followed them through the doorway. He placed the tray on a low table in front of a divan at the far end of the room.

"Thank you, Tolliver," said Lady Stanton. "That will be all."

The butler bowed once more before he and the footman left the room.

Meredith inhaled deeply, pausing to take stock of her surroundings. In truth, she needed a few moments to compose herself, and looking around the room gave her that much needed opportunity. As she gazed at Lady Stanton's particular retreat, she suddenly experienced a disorienting wave of longing for Swallow Hill.

They were in a smallish, narrow room that ended in a set of graceful bay windows overlooking the gardens at the back of the house. The walls were a delicate shade of pale blue, set off by gray trim and elaborately detailed white plastered ceilings. Floral-patterned Oriental carpets covered the polished floorboards. The furniture looked both comfortable and cheery, upholstered in soft fabrics that matched the gold and cerulean shades in the carpets.

In spite of the small space, the effect was one of airiness and light. Although it looked completely different, the colors and sense of calm that pervaded the room reminded Meredith of her stepmother's bedchamber. She found herself blinking back tears at the unexpected, bittersweet memory.

Lady Stanton examined her with a look that managed to be both shrewd and kind. Seating herself on the richly padded silk divan, the older woman indicated the matching armchair placed on the other side of the low, deeply polished table.

"Come, Miss Burnley, do sit down. You have nothing to fear from me." She smiled invitingly at Meredith. "You see, I have been expecting your visit for quite some time."

Meredith was about to sink into the chair, but she froze, stunned by Lady Stanton's remark. "I don't understand," she replied slowly. "None of your family has been in communication with mine since my father and stepmother were married."

Lady Stanton again waved her hand at the chair. Meredith sank down into the soft cushions as the older woman prepared two cups of tea. She was taken aback by her ladyship's comments but squashed the impulse to demand an immediate explanation, not wanting to offend the one person who seemed most willing to help her—even after Lord Silverton's terse explanation of events in the library a few minutes ago. So Meredith waited, trying not to fidget, as she studied the woman across from her.

Her ladyship was slight of figure, but had a graceful, upright carriage. Her hair was silvery white, and something about her suggested frailty, but her fine-boned face was unlined and her kind blue eyes, though faded, were sharply observant. Those eyes watched her now with a combination of acumen and sympathy that made Meredith want to squirm in her seat. Her patience finally ran out.

"Pardon my impertinence, your ladyship, but could you please tell me why you've been expecting my visit? The general"—she hesitated, not wanting to offend Lady Stanton—"the general certainly did not appear to be anticipating my call."

"My husband does not know I was in regular communication with my daughter from the time of her marriage to the time of her death."

Meredith almost dropped her teacup.

"Everyone supposes that all contact between us ceased after your father and my Elizabeth were married," Lady Stanton continued calmly. "I would not allow that to be so. I knew, however, that the general would not countenance a correspondence between us. As much as it pained me to deceive him, I kept it secret. It was my impression Elizabeth did not want to appear disloyal to your father, either, so she kept our correspondence secret from him as well."

Lady Stanton smiled wryly at Meredith, who knew she looked as stunned as she felt.

"You are, perhaps, shocked by this. We knew the situation was not ideal, but my daughter and I were very close. The thought of never communicating again was not something either of us could bear."

Suddenly, Lady Stanton looked very weary and much older than she had a few minutes ago. She closed her eyes and took a sip of tea, as if to revive herself.

Meredith reached over and fleetingly touched her hand. "I can only imagine the grief the separation must have caused you."

Lady Stanton carefully set her teacup into its saucer, the look of melancholy on her face gradually softening with relief. "Thank you, my dear. She loved you very much, you know. My Elizabeth took just as much pride in your accomplishments as she did in Annabel's. And you, I believe, were very close to her as well."

There was a hint of a question in Lady Stanton's voice.

Meredith's throat tightened as she recalled those long-ago days when she had felt safe and loved.

"Yes, my lady. She was the best of mothers. You must understand that I was quite wild when she took me in hand. My own mother died in childbirth, and Papa was a very indulgent father."

Meredith shook her head as she thought of how defiant she had been when Elizabeth Stanton had exerted her gentle control over her errant stepdaughter. "I owe everything to your daughter, ma'am, and I revere and miss her every day of my life."

"She would be happy to know that," replied Lady Stanton. "I know she would be very proud of you for taking such good care of your sister. When we have time, you must tell me about your life together."

Her ladyship set her teacup on the table with a little clatter.

"Now to the business at hand. The reason I have been expecting you is that I wrote to your father after Elizabeth's death, offering him any assistance he might need for you and Annabel. He never replied, but I have always held out hope that you or my granddaughter would someday find your way to me."

Meredith thought for a moment she had not heard correctly. How on earth could Papa have neglected to tell her something this important! Immediately she felt guilty. Her father had been so broken by his wife's death, he had barely been able to care for his own children.

"I wrote General Stanton after my father died," Meredith replied slowly. "I thought he would want to know. I was sure you both would want to see Annabel—perhaps ask me to bring her to London. But he never replied."

A shadow of bitter regret flitted across the older woman's face. "I'm sorry, my dear. I never knew. My greatest fear has always been that you and your sister resented the estrangement and had no desire to ever contact me. If I had only known."

She shook her head in exasperation, obviously frustrated by so many lost opportunities.

The tension that had gripped Meredith since entering Stanton House began to ease. It seemed she had an ally after all. The only question remaining was whether Lady Stanton would defy her husband and agree to help her granddaughter.

"You know we need your help." Meredith's heart pounded erratically. "Annabel will be lost unless your family intervenes. I have no rights of guardianship, either to her person or her fortune. My uncle is a determined man, and I know that only someone more powerful will be able to stop him from confining Annabel to an asylum."

Meredith could hear her voice starting to tremble. The other woman reached across the table and took her hand.

"There is no question, my dear. Annabel is safe now. Her family will take care of her, and you may rest assured I will never let her uncle harm her, or you."

It was too much for Meredith. All the pent-up emotion could no longer be contained. She broke down and wept as Lady Stanton rose from the divan and hugged her. For the first time in years, she had someone older and wiser to lean on.

Lady Stanton stroked Meredith's face with a soft hand and dried her eyes with a napkin.

"Come, my child. There is no need for any more tears. My granddaughter has finally come home, and we must see what we can do to help her."

Meredith struggled to regain her composure, taking a sip of tea in an effort to clear her throat. It was rather tiresome, she admitted to herself, to act so continuously like a watering pot.

Lady Stanton swished gracefully back to her seat, an engaging twinkle lighting up her eyes. "I suspect you already have a plan, and you simply need me to put it into motion."

"Yes, my lady. I have given the matter much thought," said Meredith, dabbing at her runny nose with a napkin. "What

Annabel needs is a Season. In fact, what she really needs is a husband."

For just a second, Lady Stanton looked astonished. Then she began to laugh with delight. Meredith felt dizzy with relief at the other woman's evident approval.

"Brilliant, my dear! I wish I had thought of it myself. If Annabel marries, then her guardianship and control of her fortune passes to her husband. Your uncle will never be able to touch her."

Meredith nodded thoughtfully, relieved Lady Stanton's thinking confirmed her own. There was, however, one thing still troubling her. "My greatest fear is that we will never be able to get my uncle to agree to her marriage," she confided. "I would hate for Annabel to have to elope to Scotland."

Lady Stanton waved her concern away with an airy gesture. "Special license," she said succinctly.

Meredith hesitated, unwilling to disagree with her ladyship, but her doubts must have been clearly written on her face.

"Don't worry, my dear," Lady Stanton said dryly. "We know the archbishop."

The crushing fear that had weighed so heavily on Meredith began to dissipate. Elation replaced despair as she realized all the risks she and Annabel had taken just might have been worth it.

Lady Stanton rose from the divan, her quick movements belying her age. She walked briskly to the bell pull and tugged on the cord. "Now, my dear Miss Burnley, with your permission I should like to visit my grandchild." An exultant expression suffused the older woman's features. "I have been waiting a very long time for this day to arrive."

The door to the sitting room quietly opened and Tolliver stepped in. Lady Stanton swung around to face him.

"Tolliver," she exclaimed in a commanding voice, "my carriage. Immediately!"

Chapter Three

Meredith sat bolt upright in the elegant, burgundy-colored landau, trying to ignore the assault on her senses as the carriage threaded its way along the busy street. The midday chaos that surrounded them gave her a headache—an unwelcome distraction as she struggled to compose her turbulent emotions. Much to her surprise, she hated London. The noise, the dust and dirt, the myriad of smells that to her were mostly unpleasant, made every trip from their small set of rooms an experience to be endured rather than enjoyed.

Her sister's reaction to the city had been completely the opposite. Annabel reveled in the events that, to her, seemed an adventure rather than an escape. The girl was more animated and healthier than Meredith had seen her in months.

Annabel had eagerly accompanied her on the few errands that had been necessary since their unexpected arrival four days ago on the doorstep of Miss Noyes, their former governess. Meredith, unfortunately, struggled to contain her fears every time they left the sanctuary of the house. She constantly looked over her shoulder, expecting any minute that Uncle Isaac would track them down and drag them back to Swallow Hill.

Closing her eyes on the bustle surrounding the carriage, she recalled their flight from the only home they had ever known. Meredith still couldn't believe they had managed to do it. Annabel had displayed real fortitude and unexpected physical endurance. With the assistance of Creed and their old coachman, John Ruddle, they had slipped away to catch the night mail from the neighboring town of Cross Keys. Ruddle had stayed with them, refusing to leave his young mistresses unprotected. Meredith's concern for the old family retainer was just one of the many worries that haunted her sleepless nights.

But now she found herself ensconced in the Stantons' luxurious town carriage, which smoothly conveyed them through the city to the modest but genteel neighborhood of Hans Town. Meredith sat opposite Lady Stanton, who maintained an entertaining flow of chatter as she pointed out the various landmarks that might interest a newcomer to London. Young Robert Stanton trotted beside them on a beautiful bay mare.

And sitting next to his aunt, taking up far more space than Meredith liked, was the Marquess of Silverton.

After coming downstairs from her ladyship's sitting room, Meredith had inwardly groaned when she saw Lord Silverton exit the library, pulling on his gloves as he watched her through narrowed eyes. He had handed Lady Stanton into the landau and then turned with a cool smile to assist her. Meredith had blushed hotly and dropped her eyes, silently berating herself all the while for acting like a foolish schoolgirl.

Now Lord Silverton lounged at his ease next to his aunt, his golden hair curling out from under the brim of his rakishly tilted hat. His eyes gleamed with obvious interest as he studied her. Meredith found it extremely annoying that he inspected her so carefully, almost as if she were some exotic species of insect under glass.

She stole a peek at him from under her lashes, deciding that Silverton reminded her of a cat. A giant, golden cat—sleek, contained, and supremely self-confident. She even wondered for a moment if he was going to purr at her.

She suddenly realized that Lady Stanton looked quizzical, waiting for her to respond to a question she had just asked her. Dragging her mind away from the glorious and altogether disconcerting male animal before her, Meredith smiled apologetically to the other woman.

"I beg your pardon, your ladyship. I still find myself somewhat distracted by all the bustle of the city. Did you ask me a question?"

The older woman smiled kindly. "Yes, London does tend to overwhelm if one is not used to it. You will become accustomed sooner than you think. I was asking, my dear, how you traveled from Hans Town to Stanton House today?"

Meredith frowned, surprised Lady Stanton would care about something so trivial. "My coachman fetched me a hired hack."

Her ladyship hesitated, her aristocratic brows drawing together in a frown. "Miss Burnley, did you not think to have your maid come with you to Stanton House? Or, failing that, have your coachman accompany you and wait outside? It concerns me that you were traveling in a public conveyance without an escort."

Meredith jerked her head back, stung by the implied criticism. For many years she had been managing her own life and the lives of those who depended on her. Then her aunt and uncle had bullied themselves into her household, forcing her to submit to their will. And although Lady Stanton clearly meant well, Meredith was tired of people telling her what to do.

"I don't require a maid to accompany me," she said, more abruptly than she intended. "I am far from being a schoolgirl and have been managing my own affairs, as well as Annabel's, for years."

Meredith glanced at Lord Silverton, who regarded her with an impassive expression on his face. She bit her lip in vexation, ashamed at how ungrateful she sounded. Lady Stanton gave her a small but uncomfortably astute smile.

"Forgive me, my dear. I have no wish to offend or interfere where it is neither desired nor necessary. You must please yourself, of course." Her pleasant expression grew serious. "I would imagine, however, that my daughter, Elizabeth, would have viewed the matter differently."

Meredith blushed as she thought of Elizabeth Burnley. Her stepmother had drummed into her head all the rules of propriety that would protect her daughters from the kind of gossip and scandal she had been subjected to. As a child, Meredith had been defiant, her will clashing with Elizabeth's gentler, but immovable, force of character.

Those early years had been trying for Meredith, and both mother and daughter had shed many tears. But the lessons were valuable, and Meredith knew she would need to adhere to them even more strictly if her sister had any hope of making a good match. The ton had a long memory, and one scandal in the family was quite sufficient.

She smiled ruefully as she met Lady Stanton's shrewd gaze, aware the older woman had masterfully backed her into a corner. "Yes, my lady, she would have agreed with you."

Lady Stanton rewarded her with a warm smile. "Come, Miss Burnley, you speak of yourself as if you were an aging spinster, which I know you are not. I do not believe you are more than four and twenty. Is that not correct?"

Meredith again became intensely aware of the golden-maned lion sitting opposite her. She felt a burning flush heat her cheeks. How mortifying to be forced into such an intimate discussion in front of the self-possessed Lord Silverton. Was there not one humiliation to be spared her this day?

He observed her carefully. Lord Silverton must have read her thoughts, for he smiled at her in that dazzling way that made her knees turn to pudding.

"Don't mind me, Miss Burnley. After all we have been through today, you must surely consider me as part of the family."

He leaned forward, his cobalt blue eyes narrowed slightly against the sun. His voice dropped a notch to a low, seductive timbre that seemed to curl its way up her spine. "You should know that my aunt has been managing all of us for as long as I can remember. I assure you, it is pointless to resist."

Meredith looked at the pair of them sitting next to each other, so different yet remarkably alike in their self-assured, engaging, and thoroughly aristocratic manner. She sighed and gave up.

"I am almost five and twenty, my lady."

Lady Stanton laughed. "My dear child, you are in your prime. You must not be so eager to climb onto the shelf. You haven't even had a Season in London, which is something I know my daughter intended for you."

Meredith froze, wondering for an awful moment if the older woman was joking. She cast a doubtful look at Lord Silverton, but he didn't seem to find the remark amusing, either. In fact, he studied his aunt with an intensity that Meredith found a bit unnerving.

"A Season! Surely you must be joking, ma'am." Meredith gave an uncertain laugh. "I am nothing but a wool merchant's granddaughter from Bristol. I have no acquaintance in London, only my half-sister's family. You may be gracious enough to acknowledge Annabel, and indeed, I am eternally grateful for that, but who would sponsor a nobody like me?"

Lady Stanton's eyes sparkled with a mischievous gleam. "Well, Miss Burnley," she gently retorted, "as far as I am concerned, you are a part of this family. And as to who will sponsor your Season, there is simply no question. I will."

Meredith found herself speechless once again—a condition that, as far as she was concerned, had struck her all too frequently this day. She breathed a sigh of relief when the carriage slowed to a stop in front of a small house.

A groomsman let out the steps of the carriage, and the marquess took one long stride down to the pavement. He extended his hand to Lady Stanton to assist her. Meredith was next. Lord Silverton squeezed her hand slightly as he helped her down, startling her with what seemed to be an expression of support.

She hesitated on the stoop of the house, glancing back at the dignified old woman leaning on her nephew's muscular arm. Taking a deep breath, Meredith knocked on the front door. Almost immediately it swung open, and Miss Noyes's young housemaid, Agatha, ushered them into the cramped hallway. The girl's eyes popped wide as she took in Lord Silverton's polished magnificence. She dropped a hasty curtsy and rushed ahead to open the doors to the small sitting room.

Lady Stanton advanced into the room, tightly clutching Lord Silverton's sleeve. Her face was pale, and Meredith could see her fine-boned hands were trembling.

Annabel sat next to Miss Noyes on a shabby couch at the other end of the simply furnished room. She had obviously been trying to distract herself with some needlework. The poor girl gripped the material so tightly Meredith was amazed it didn't shred in her grasp. Annabel blinked anxiously at her grandmother, her pretty face a bleached white except for a faint blush high on her cheekbones.

Lady Stanton suddenly looked decades younger, her care-worn expression replaced with one of beaming joy.

Annabel came slowly to her feet, her eyes starting to shimmer with tears. "Grandmamma?" she asked softly, taking a small step forward.

Tears began to course down Lady Stanton's cheeks. She dropped her hand from Lord Silverton's sleeve and, without uttering a word, opened her arms wide. Annabel flung aside her embroidery and ran across the room, throwing herself into her grandmother's embrace.

No one spoke. The only sounds in the room were the sobs of the young girl and Lady Stanton as they clung to each other, the older woman reaching up to stroke her granddaughter's vibrant auburn hair.

Meredith stood in the doorway and let their happiness wash over her as she fought to hold back the tears constricting her throat.

And just like that, all the years of grief and worry finally came to an end. Meredith and Annabel were no longer alone.

Meredith sighed as she surreptitiously blotted her nose with her already tear-dampened handkerchief. Little doubt remained that today's events had turned her into a watering pot.

Annabel and Lady Stanton were still locked in a tight embrace, and no one witnessing the scene could remain unaffected. Miss Noyes wept into her handkerchief, and young Robert shuffled his feet and rubbed his eye as if a cinder had lodged itself there. Even Lord Silverton had lost his guarded and rather hard expression. The corners of his sculpted mouth curved into a genuinely charming smile, surprising Meredith with its warmth. The reunion, by any measure, seemed to be a complete success.

But even as Lady Stanton petted and soothed her, Annabel continued to sob dramatically. Meredith began to worry her sister was on the verge of hysterics. She stepped forward and placed a hand on Annabel's shoulder.

"Come, darling, you mustn't cry so hard. You will make yourself sick. Why don't you and Lady Stanton sit together on the sofa while we wait for tea?" Meredith pointedly nodded her head at the maid, who hovered nearby with a look of eager curiosity on her face. Agatha reluctantly bobbed a curtsy and backed out of the room.

"That is a very sensible suggestion, Miss Burnley," said Lady Stanton, her voice reedy with emotion. "It will do us all a great deal of good to sit and rest for a few minutes." The old woman led Annabel to the sofa. Miss Noyes pulled a handkerchief from her enormous tatting bag and offered it to Lady Stanton.

"Don't weep so, darling. All will be well," Lady Stanton murmured. Annabel leaned against her grandmother's shoulder and allowed her to dry her tears.

Meredith turned to Lord Silverton and Robert. "My lord, Mr. Stanton. Please do be seated." She cast a doubtful glance around the sitting room, acutely conscious of how small and shabby it must appear to their guests. Miss Noyes barely had enough furniture to seat everyone.

But if Lord Silverton was offended by the modest nature of their accommodations, he didn't show it. He bowed gracefully to Miss Noyes, smiling kindly at the flustered woman. "Good afternoon, ma'am. I am Lord Silverton, and this is Robert Stanton. We have the honor of being Miss Annabel's cousins."

Meredith swallowed a groan, conscious that her manners had once again gone missing. "Do forgive me, gentlemen, Lady Stanton. Allow me to introduce our former governess, Miss Noyes. She has most kindly given us shelter since we arrived in London."

"Yes, Grandmamma," Annabel hiccupped. "We don't know what we would have done if she hadn't taken us in."

Lady Stanton smiled graciously at the governess. "Then you will always have my gratitude, Miss Noyes, for taking such good care of my granddaughter and her sister. You must be sure to tell me exactly what I can do to help you."

"Oh, no thanks are necessary, your ladyship! There is nothing I would not do for my dear girls. I mean . . . of course, I . . . for Miss Burnley and Miss Annabel."

Miss Noyes was a gentle mouse of a woman, painfully shy at the best of times, and Meredith feared so many visitors all at once in her tiny sitting room would provoke a spasm. She searched her mind for an errand that would allow Miss Noyes to escape the room.

"Miss Noyes," Lord Silverton said, unexpectedly taking

charge of the conversation, "I noticed you and Miss Annabel were engaged in needlework when we entered. That is certainly a very fine piece of embroidery my cousin is sewing. I presume you taught her the skill when you were her governess?" He sat next to Miss Noyes, picking up Annabel's work and inspecting it as if it were a fine piece of art.

Meredith watched in amazement as the nervous little woman visibly relaxed and began to extol her former student's talents. As their governess pointed out the beauty of Annabel's small stitches, Lord Silverton looked up to meet Meredith's gaze. His eyes flashed with mischief, and the brief dazzle of his smile left her breathless. But he immediately returned his attention to Miss Noyes, leaving Meredith to wonder if she had imagined his teasing glance.

She sighed, irritated by her foolishly overactive imagination. Turning back to Annabel, Meredith was pleased to see the young girl drying her eyes, allowing herself to be comforted by Lady Stanton's gentle embrace. Robert carefully sat down on a spindly cane chair next to the marquess, and Miss Noyes, encouraged by the two men, proceeded to embark on a detailed description of her methods for teaching female students.

Meredith thought it was the strangest afternoon she had ever spent in her life.

With a rattle of dishes, Agatha hurried through the door with the refreshments. The sturdy maid hoisted a large tray across the room and plunked it with a loud clatter on an ancient gate-leg table by the sofa.

"Will there be anything else, ma'am?" Agatha barely glanced at Miss Noyes before turning her gaze to Lord Silverton, clearly transfixed by his masculine splendor. His eyebrows moved up a notch when he noticed the maid's admiring stare.

Meredith winced. "No, Agatha," she interjected before Miss Noyes had a chance to respond. "That will be all."

"Yes, miss."

The girl smiled broadly at Lord Silverton as she retreated

from the room. Meredith caught the amused look on his face and resigned herself to a day of apparently endless humiliations. She hurried to the tea table, eager now to get on with the business of settling Annabel's living situation. The sooner her sister could move to Stanton House, the better. Meredith would miss her terribly, but there was no help for that.

"Your ladyship," Meredith said, once she had served everyone a cup of tea, "please forgive me for being forward, but I would like to discuss Annabel's living arrangements."

"Not at all, my dear. It is why we are here."

All at once, the atmosphere in the sitting room became very serious. Annabel sat up straight, staring anxiously at her grandmother. Lord Silverton looked enigmatic, while Robert stared avidly at Annabel.

Meredith frowned, startled by the young man's demeanor. Now that she thought about it, Robert had been gazing at Annabel with just such a look of fervent admiration ever since he had entered the room.

"Please continue, my dear," prompted Lady Stanton.

Meredith yanked her attention back to the older woman, trying to collect her scattered wits. "Forgive me, your ladyship. I will get right to the point. I have given the matter a great deal of thought, and I believe it would be best for Annabel to move into Stanton House with you and the general."

Lady Stanton and Lord Silverton glanced at each other, their expressions similarly inscrutable. Robert jerked his head away from his contemplation of Annabel and gave a startled snort.

"Oh, I say! Bad idea, that."

"Robert," Lady Stanton admonished, "please mind your manners."

The young man flushed and ducked his head. "Sorry, Grandmamma." He grinned sheepishly at Annabel, who surprised Meredith by giggling back at him. Meredith stared at her sister for a moment before switching her gaze back to Lady Stanton.

"I'm sorry, your ladyship," she continued, puzzled by the lack of enthusiasm for her suggestion. "Is this not what you would advise? She would be safe from our uncle at Stanton House, and it is the logical place from which she could make her debut."

"And where would you stay, Miss Burnley?" inquired her ladyship.

"Here with Miss Noyes, of course."

Annabel squirmed, pulling herself from Lady Stanton's embrace. "No, Meredith! I won't leave you."

"Darling, it would be for the best." Meredith tried to be encouraging, even though her heart ached at the thought of separation from her sister. "We could still see each other almost every day. Besides, you will be so busy with your grandmother, you will hardly miss me."

Annabel shook her head, a mutinous frown wrinkling her youthful brow. "I won't leave you, Meredith." She turned to Lady Stanton. "I'm sorry, Grandmamma. Not even for you will I allow myself to be parted from her."

"Of course not," her ladyship replied calmly. "You and your sister must take a townhouse in Mayfair, close to Berkeley Square. I hope Miss Noyes can be prevailed upon to act as chaperone until a more permanent situation can be arranged."

Meredith's jaw almost dropped open at the shock of Lady Stanton's suggestion. Before she could raise any objections, however, Miss Noyes launched into the conversation.

"Oh, my lady, what a wonderful idea! I can be ready at a moment's notice to assist the dear girls in any way I can. As long as they need me, I will be happy to stay. No sacrifice will be too great!"

Meredith hastily broke in. "Surely this is not necessary, your ladyship. Annabel will be quite happy to live at Stanton House, once she has grown used to the idea. In any event, I would not be able to support a household in Mayfair on my income. And you know we cannot touch Annabel's fortune."

Why wouldn't they understand? Annabel needed more protection and guidance than Meredith could provide. She glanced at Lord Silverton, who looked as if he were trying not to laugh.

Meredith gritted her teeth and stubbornly carried on. "I believe Annabel should be with her grandparents. That is clearly the best solution to our problem."

Lady Stanton wrinkled her nose in gentle dismay. "I'm sorry, my dear, but that is just not possible. You saw how strongly the general reacted to your visit this morning." Annabel peered at her grandmother, who patted her hand reassuringly. "While I have no doubt my husband will accept Annabel into our family, he is not amenable to sudden changes in the household."

She paused delicately. "It would be better, for the moment, if you were to set up your own establishment. There will be no difficulty in keeping you safe, I am sure. You cannot stay here if Annabel is to have a successful Season. And since we are speaking so frankly, my dear Miss Burnley," Lady Stanton continued dryly, "you must know the Stantons are well able to support both you and your sister in the appropriate style."

Meredith sighed. In all the excitement of the last hour, she had forgotten her ladyship's intention to launch her into society.

"Excuse me, ma'am," she said politely but firmly, "but as I said in the carriage, there is no reason for me to have a Season. I must reiterate that I do not wish it."

Her ladyship cheerfully waved away her attempts at refusal and began to discuss townhouses in Mayfair with Lord Silverton and Robert. Annabel chimed in excitedly, and even Miss Noyes ventured to make a few hesitant suggestions. None of them even glanced at Meredith as they debated the merits of possible living arrangements and how soon they could move from Hans Town. She had the distinct and unpleasant impression she had somehow become invisible.

"Silverton." Lady Stanton smiled at her nephew. "I would be most grateful if you could take this in hand and find the girls a suitable house."

Meredith felt ready to shred her bonnet in frustration. Obviously she had lost the battle to settle Annabel at Stanton House, but to be further indebted to Lord Silverton didn't bear thinking about. He was so dangerously attractive, the less she had to do with him, the better.

"Lady Stanton," she exclaimed, "I am most grateful for all your kindness, but it isn't necessary for his lordship to put himself out on our behalf. I will make suitable arrangements for Annabel and myself."

Lady Stanton glanced at Lord Silverton, lifting one brow in a question. He briefly returned his aunt's look before sweeping an imperious gaze over Meredith.

"There is no need to worry, Miss Burnley." Meredith could swear she heard a faint note of mocking laughter in his voice. "My secretary, Mr. Chislett, will be the one to suffer the inconvenience, since he will conduct the search, not I."

That silenced her, as she could think of no polite way to respond to such irritating condescension. Since Meredith had not the faintest idea how to go about renting a house in London, she grudgingly supposed she must bow to the inevitable and do it with as much good grace as she could muster. In any event, she didn't have the energy to wage another battle today.

Lord Silverton must have read her thoughts, for his cynical mouth curved into a lazy and seductive smile that scattered her wits like buckshot. She felt as if she had just toppled off a cliff, a sensation she found both disconcerting and extremely annoying.

Meredith repressed a sudden and childish impulse to box Lord Silverton's ears as she wondered how a man she had met only a few hours ago could so easily bring out the worst in her.

Chapter Four

Silverton lifted a hand in farewell to the Burnley sisters as they stood on the front stoop of Miss Noyes's tiny house, their arms wrapped securely about each other. Annabel looked like a child beside the statuesque Meredith. She was slender and pretty, carrying herself with a sylphlike grace that would attract bachelors like flies to sugar water. Meredith would also attract her share of suitors, he knew, but for entirely different reasons.

The woman was, quite simply, the most physically captivating female he had met in years. Her extraordinary eyes and ivory complexion, her glossy black hair—all those things painted a most fetching portrait. But it was her superb figure that would stop a man in his tracks. She had a beautiful body, with generous breasts and rounded hips that flared luxuriously from a slim waist. Even more compelling, Meredith exuded a subtle yet powerful sensuality that promised a myriad of delights to the man lucky enough to bed her.

Yes, Silverton had thoroughly enjoyed studying Meredith's lush beauty, even though he knew his attentions had made her shift uncomfortably in her seat.

The afternoon—for many reasons—had proven to be as diverting as he had hoped it would be. He had, of course, been truly touched by Aunt Georgina's meeting with her granddaughter and delighted to see them united. And he was genuinely pleased to meet his newfound cousin Annabel.

But the real fun had come from teasing Meredith. Silverton had been unable to resist. Despite her masterful ways, her naïve assumptions had made it difficult for him not to laugh at her. To expect that Annabel could move directly to Stanton House, especially after the general's reaction this morning . . . Well, in spite of all her self-assurance, Meredith was obviously a babe in the woods. The scandal of Elizabeth Stanton's elopement had been enormous, and although the gossip had faded years ago, the ton had a very long memory. The appearance of the long-lost grandchild would cause a great deal of chatter, something General Stanton would surely loathe.

Aunt Georgina was right. The sisters needed a quiet house in Mayfair and a gradual introduction into society. Annabel's debut would be difficult enough, but the obstacles facing Meredith were even greater.

His aunt's insistence that Meredith also be launched on the marriage mart had startled him. Silverton honored her for doing it, especially since the general would no doubt react with fury to the idea. After all her sacrifices for Annabel, Meredith deserved more than a solitary life as a country spinster, and her respectable fortune should be able to attract the attention of at least a baronet or a knight. Her beautiful face and form would do the rest.

Silverton moved restlessly on the plush velvet cushions of Lady Stanton's landau, frowning down at his hands as they suddenly clenched into fists. It struck him rather forcefully that he didn't much like the notion of other men courting Meredith.

"Well, Stephen, what do you think?"

Silverton blinked. He had almost forgotten his aunt's presence in the carriage.

"I'm sorry, Aunt Georgina," he apologized with a smile. "What do I think about what?"

She glanced from the open carriage to Robert, who rode next to them on his bay mare. Aunt Georgina obviously didn't want the lad to overhear their conversation.

"What do you think about your cousin Annabel, Stephen?"

"She seems a perfectly delightful girl. I'm very happy you have found each other."

His aunt's joyous smile practically blinded him. "Thank you, my dear. And thank you for coming with me today. I appreciate your assistance, especially since the general did not wish me to visit our granddaughter."

"No thanks are necessary, my lady. You know that you have only to command me." Silverton meant every word. Aunt Georgina had been the touchstone of his life for as long he could remember, and he would do almost anything for her.

Her eyes narrowed as she studied him. "Hmm," she murmured. "I wonder . . ."

"I beg your pardon?" He straightened in his seat, startled by the intensity of her gaze. He had seen that look before, and it always meant trouble—trouble for him, anyway.

"Annabel is very pretty, is she not?"

"Yes, my lady. Very pretty."

"And she seems to have a very sweet character—loving, loyal, and kind." Her voice was deceptively bland.

Silverton cautiously nodded his agreement, certain now that his aunt was up to something.

"And such a large portion, too—at least ten thousand a year that her mother inherited from my sister, Regina."

He was familiar with the history of Annabel's inheritance. Regina Compton was the oldest daughter of a very wealthy earl, and had never married. When she died at the age of forty-five, she left her entire fortune to her favorite niece, Elizabeth Stanton. Elizabeth's financial independence had allowed her to defy General Stanton's wishes and elope with Thomas Burnley, the handsome son of a wool merchant from

Bristol. That fortune, after the death of both her parents, had eventually come to Annabel.

"Such a generous portion will make her vulnerable to fortune hunters," Aunt Georgina mused, her eyes darting over the busy street as if she were searching for something.

He sighed. "My dear ma'am, what exactly are you trying to say?"

She fidgeted with her reticule. The small movement alarmed him; his aunt never fidgeted.

"The girl needs a husband, and soon."

Prickles of warning rippled down his spine. "So I understand," he replied slowly.

"And you, my dear nephew, are in need of a wife."

Silverton bit back an oath. Surely his aunt could not be serious. Either that, or the shock of meeting Annabel had caused her to lose her wits. "I hope you aren't proposing me as a candidate, my lady."

She looked imperiously down her nose at him. "Stephen, that is exactly what I am suggesting. She is a delightful girl, as you said yourself, and would make you a perfectly lovely wife."

"My dear aunt, she is just a child!"

"Who will soon grow into a beautiful young woman. You know as well as I, these types of alliances can greatly strengthen the bonds in a family like ours. The general and I are second cousins. As you know, our parents arranged the match, and it was of great benefit to both of us."

Silverton's amazement grew. "Good lord, Aunt Georgina, surely you are not comparing Annabel and me to you and my uncle. May I remind you, I'm thirty-four and she is barely seventeen. I'm almost old enough to be her father. Forgive me, but the idea is simply ludicrous, and I'm sure my cousin would agree."

His aunt lifted her eyebrows in a polite but incredulous expression. "Really, Silverton, I have little doubt you could make Annabel love you, once you set your mind to it. In any event, it's not the least unusual to see such a disparity in age between husband and wife, and you know it. I begin to wonder if there is some other reason, besides her age, why you don't wish to consider my suggestion."

Silverton was beginning to ask himself the same question, but he hardly felt inclined to discuss a possible explanation with his aunt.

The silence between them lengthened. Aunt Georgina continued to study him with an enigmatic expression. He sighed inwardly, knowing how determined she could be when she had the bit between her teeth.

"Stephen," she eventually said, "you know very well it is long past time for you to start a family. I don't believe that waiting any longer will make a whit of difference to you. No woman in your past has ever come up to scratch. At least," she paused meaningfully, "none since Esme Newton."

Silverton jerked his head back, astounded that his aunt would dare to broach that particular subject. He clenched his teeth against the quick surge of anger and wounded pride that flowed through him at the painful reminder of his youthful infatuation.

Several heartbeats later, he had himself under sufficient control to respond in a suitably bored voice to her insightful but unwelcome remarks. "My dear ma'am, surely you have not forgotten that even the lovely Esme failed to come up to scratch." He met Aunt Georgina's eyes with a steady but defiant gaze, silently daring her to contradict him.

She stared back with a veiled expression on her face, but her lips were compressed into a thin line.

"You are the Marquess of Silverton. You have a duty to your name and estate. This would be an excellent match and would heal the wounds that have festered in our family for many long years. Annabel needs a powerful man to protect her, and you need a wife who is worthy of you. The marriage would be of great benefit to the entire family."

She sighed, worry lines reappearing on her brow and around her eyes. "And you know as well as I that we can only do so much to protect Annabel. Isaac Burnley is her legal guardian. He could make our lives very difficult if he chose to do so."

Silverton had to acknowledge the truth of that, as well as the urgency of the situation. He nodded reluctantly, even though he hated every word she said.

Lady Stanton finally relented. "My dearest Stephen, you are not a boy like Robert. You are a man who must make his own decisions, ones that are appropriate and honorable. All I ask is for you to spend time with Annabel. Perhaps you will find courting her not as difficult as you think."

Silverton grasped her hand and raised it to his lips. "Of course I will consider it, Aunt Georgina. I never want to disappoint you, or my family."

She smiled gratefully at him and turned the conversation, perhaps sensing that further discussion would only increase his resistance. Silverton lapsed into thought as he tried to imagine what it would be like to court Annabel, perhaps even wed her.

But another image—an incredibly compelling image—pushed its way into his mind, and he feared it would come to haunt him in the days ahead. Only one woman interested him now, and she was, both by his and the ton's standards, completely unsuitable.

That woman, God help him, was Meredith Burnley.

Chapter Five

Meredith heard Annabel's silvery laughter drift down the hallway a full minute before her sister entered the room. She marveled again at the girl's seemingly miraculous recovery since reaching London. Meredith couldn't begin to describe her own sense of relief, but she still puzzled over the extraordinary changes in her sister's behavior.

Why had Annabel been so ill at Swallow Hill? Their uncle had maintained that she would never regain her health at home, and Meredith grudgingly admitted he was right. But she also had no doubt that committing the girl to a private asylum would have killed Annabel. Clearly Dr. Leeds was sadly mistaken, and Meredith had no regrets she had fled with her sister to London.

Annabel skipped into the breakfast room, waving several brightly colored fabric swatches in her hand. "Meredith, Miss Noyes wants you to come to the drawing room and pick out the new draperies for that room and the dining room. She says so many choices are likely to give her a spasm if someone doesn't help her." She laughed again.

Meredith's chest constricted with an almost painful love. The girl looked so delicate and beautiful in a dainty primrose morning gown, her fashionable new haircut swept back off her neck with matching ribbons. She, in contrast, was wearing her oldest gown and had pulled her hair back into a simple knot at the nape of her neck in order to keep her hair out of her face as she worked.

There were times when her sister's youth and beauty forcibly reminded Meredith of her own rapid advance into spinsterhood. Annabel meant the world to her, but never had she felt so keenly the differences between them.

She put down her basket of linens and forced herself to smile. "Yes, darling. Tell Miss Noyes I'll be with her in a few minutes. I just need to organize the mending and give Cook the shopping list for the next few days."

"All right, Meredith, but please don't be long. You promised we could go for a walk in the park this afternoon. It's been ages since we've been able to go outside."

Annabel whirled around and dashed out of the room, her eager steps fading down the hallway to the front of the house. Meredith shook her head at the girl's exuberant energy, contrasting it with her own sense of exhaustion after the tumultuous move to their new townhouse near Berkeley Square.

She hated to admit it, but Lord Silverton had found exactly what they required. Discreetly situated on a quiet street, removed from the noise and bustle of the city, the house afforded them the privacy and security they needed until Annabel was ready to make her debut.

Meredith turned a critical eye on the small, cheerful breakfast parlor situated at the back of the house. It was flooded with sunlight for a good part of the day and just far enough from the other main rooms to be private. She had decided to convert it into a studio where she could paint and Annabel could draw and read her novels without being disturbed by the rest of their small household.

She inspected the contents of the wooden chest beneath the south-facing window. Meredith grimaced at the meager collection of brushes and paints she had managed to acquire in the mad rush of the last few days. It had pained her greatly to leave her supplies and sketchbooks behind when they had fled their home. And she didn't even want to think about what her aunt and uncle might do to her work—the precious paintings that had given her so much comfort during the dreary years after her father's death.

In the depths of her soul, Meredith was an artist. She knew she had talent. As a child, her father and stepmother had always encouraged her, allowing her to spend hours on end in a tiny, makeshift studio next to the schoolroom. But although they had approved of her passion for her art, they had often deplored the subject matter.

Meredith sighed as she reflected on the fate of one of her favorite pictures. Just before her father's death, she had completed a large canvas that depicted the birth of Athena, springing full-blown from the head of Zeus. Miss Noyes had screamed when she saw it, and her father had claimed it gave him the headache. It had been banished to the attic, along with a number of other works that had suffered a similar fate.

Since they had come to London, Miss Noyes had gently suggested she turn her mind to more cheerful subjects, encouraging her to paint a portrait of Annabel. Perhaps she would. It would be lovely, she mused, to capture her sister in such happy spirits.

Meredith closed the chest of art supplies and shoved it back under the window. She picked up the overstuffed linen basket and lugged it down the cellar steps to the kitchen as she mulled over her instructions for the new cook. It was remarkable how quickly they had acquired their kitchen staff. Another testament, she supposed, to the efficiency of Lord Silverton's secretary.

As she thought of the marquess, a faint but disconcerting heat flushed her limbs. Lord Silverton had intruded much too frequently in her thoughts these last few days. Meredith had vowed repeatedly to squash what was rapidly becoming a ridiculous schoolgirl crush.

Her uncomfortably warm feelings for him had surprised her, since more often than not she had found him to be arrogant and condescending. Besides, she reminded herself, it was most unlikely that a man like him would feel any kind of attraction to an aging spinster like her. Meredith simply refused to be any more foolish about him than she already was.

A distant knock echoed down the hallway just as she pushed through the door into the kitchen. Puzzled, she set the basket down on a stool by the door and automatically smoothed her hair back from her face. Who would be calling so early in the day?

The new cook, Mrs. Biggs, up to her elbows in flour, kneaded pastry for the apple tart she was preparing.

"Well, it seems as if you've got your first visitors already," she exclaimed as she wiped pastry crumbs from her beefy hands onto a towel. "Now, Miss Meredith, you just give that list to me and I'll take care of the shopping as soon as I finish my pies. You best get that apron off and give your hair a brush before you go see who's calling so early in the day."

Meredith smiled at the woman's warm, homespun manner. Mrs. Biggs had come highly recommended, and, more importantly, Meredith had liked her immediately. She removed the list from the pocket in her gown and handed it to the cook.

"Very well, Mrs. Biggs. I will speak to you later this afternoon."

She shook out her skirts before hurrying to the stairs, determined at least to brush her hair before joining her sister and Miss Noyes in the drawing room. Their former governess should be able to maintain a polite conversation for a few minutes, and it would do Annabel good to be forced to play hostess without Meredith constantly hovering in the background.

As she climbed the stairs to her bedroom, she heard an

angry masculine voice coming from the drawing room. Meredith froze, then turned around and rushed down the stairs. Agatha came running down the hallway, casting a frightened glance at Meredith before stumbling to a halt in front of her.

"Oh, miss!" she cried. "You must come right away. Some bad men forced their way into the house. One of them is yelling at Miss Annabel!"

Meredith's heart kicked into a gallop as she realized her uncle had found them. She grabbed the maid by the shoulders and shook her slightly to get her full attention.

"Agatha," she rasped, hardly able to overcome the dryness in her mouth, "you must run immediately to Lady Stanton's house and tell her my uncle has come to take Annabel away. You must make sure she gets the message. Don't leave until you know someone will come to help us, understand?"

The girl nodded her head. Miss Noyes had obviously told her about their situation, and she needed no further instruction.

"Yes, miss, you can be sure I will bring help."

Agatha's skirts flew as she raced for the front door. Meredith hurried to the drawing room, sick with fear. What a fool she had been to think they were safe from discovery in this quiet little house. But how had her uncle found them so quickly?

She could hear Isaac Burnley's guttural voice berating Annabel. Suddenly her fear evaporated, replaced by a rage that made her jaw lock and her stomach clench. She flung open the door and charged into the room.

The small group before her froze into a horrid tableau. Her uncle loomed over her sister and the governess, who were huddled against the fireplace screen at the end of the room. Annabel looked scared to death, but her posture was erect and Meredith was amazed to see her standing squarely in front of Miss Noyes, as if to protect her. The poor little woman trembled so badly the ribbons on her cap fluttered.

Jacob Burnley stood beside the door. Meredith's rattled mind registered that her cousin looked uncomfortable, his shoulders hunched up around his ears as if he were embarrassed. At the sound of the door opening behind him, Isaac wheeled around and stared at her, an expression of ferocious satisfaction on his face.

"Well, there you are, Niece. Run to ground at last," he snarled. "You thought you could defy me and make fools of us all. We'll see how clever you are after you feel the back of my hand on your face."

His nostrils flared as he took a slow step toward her, his large hand curling into a massive fist. Meredith gasped with horror as she realized he actually intended to strike her. Miss Noyes shrieked, and Annabel cried out as she tried to pull from her governess's arms to come to her sister's aid.

"No, Annabel!" Meredith commanded. "Stay where you are."

She closed her eyes as she tried to prepare herself for the blow. If she could draw all his anger, then he might leave Annabel untouched. Meredith could bear the pain if it gave them more time before help arrived.

"Father, stop!"

Meredith's eyes flew open at the sound of Jacob's voice. He lunged in front her, shielding her behind his own body. Father and son glared at each other, Isaac red-faced with rage.

"Get out of my way, boy. She needs to be taught a lesson," he growled.

"Not this way," Jacob replied, shaking his head.

They were both large men, but Jacob was bigger and in superb condition. Meredith had no doubt he could stop his father from hurting her.

Isaac's huge fists opened and closed as he stared at his son. For a moment, Meredith thought he would try to force Jacob out of his way to reach her. Instead, he slid his furious gaze over her once more before sharply nodding his head and dropping his hands to his sides. He moved back toward the fireplace and Annabel.

Meredith slid by her cousin, taking a wide berth of her uncle as she crossed the room. She knew her only chance now was to delay Isaac—do anything to prevent him from taking Annabel before help could arrive. Meredith had to hope that Jacob's obvious discomfort with his father's behavior would give them the time they needed.

"How dare you come into our house and threaten us," she challenged. "Your authority may extend to Annabel, but it does not extend to me. This is my house and you are not welcome here."

Meredith felt her resolve ebb as her uncle's face again darkened with rage. But as Annabel's icy little hand slipped into hers, she realized how much she loathed being intimidated by Isaac. Meredith looked down her nose with as much contempt as she could muster, surprised to hear her voice cold and steady as she addressed him.

"I have no doubt General Stanton will take whatever action is required to protect his granddaughter from your cruelty. He is on his way here at this very moment to see Annabel and, if necessary, remove her to his own household."

As soon as Meredith saw the vicious grin on her uncle's face, she knew she had overplayed her hand. His harsh laugh ground across her frayed nerves like glass shattering against pavement.

"If Annabel is under his protection, then why is she here with you instead of with him? No, girl, I've had enough of your nonsense. You and your sister will go pack your bags now, or I will drag you both out of this house so fast your heads will spin off your necks."

Meredith felt Annabel jerk against her. As she looked at her uncle's sneering face, a cold rage swelled in her chest.

"What kind of man are you that you would threaten defenseless women?" she retorted. "You sicken me! Annabel and I will never go willingly with you. You will have to drag us out onto the street for all the world to see what kind of monster you truly are."

"Meredith, don't be a fool," Jacob blurted out, clearly exasperated by her defiance.

Isaac Burnley bared his teeth in a ghastly smile. "As you wish, Niece. I am only too happy to oblige." He moved across the room, large hands outstretched to grab them.

As Meredith shrank back against Annabel, she heard a clattering from the hall. A flustered Agatha materialized in the doorway. Casting a frightened glance about the room, she bobbed an unsteady curtsy and announced in a breathless voice, "Lord Silverton is here, miss, and Mr. Robert Stanton, too!"

Chapter Six

Meredith stared at Agatha, who stood panting in the doorway, her hair tumbling out of her now-askew cap. She heard a firm, masculine tread out in the hallway and almost collapsed with the sheer relief that help had arrived so quickly.

Silverton appeared in the passageway behind Agatha. He gently placed his hands on the maid's shoulders and moved her as he stepped into the room, followed closely by his cousin Robert.

"Thank you, Agatha," he said, his eyes fixing on Meredith. "You may go now. Please shut the door behind you."

"Yes, my lord." Agatha bobbed again, backed out of the room, and shut the door quietly behind her.

Silverton stood silent and motionless, but his eyes moved from Meredith and came to rest on Isaac. His cobalt gaze turned wintry, and his patrician features grew haughty as he returned the older man's glare.

"Who the devil are you?" growled Isaac. He planted his big fists on his hips, his stance both aggressive and insolent as he confronted Silverton's obviously aristocratic presence.

The marquess leisurely reached for his quizzing glass, raising it to his eye and deliberately perusing Isaac from head to toe. The older man's face mottled a bloody red.

Silverton dropped his quizzing glass and looked at Meredith, a hint of a smile touching his hard mouth.

"Miss Burnley," he said in a bored tone of voice, "please forgive me if we have interrupted a private family discussion. Perhaps you will be so good as to introduce us to your guests."

She gaped at him in astonishment. One of his eyebrows quirked up, and the smile that played around his lips grew genuinely amused. That look finally galvanized her into action.

She walked swiftly across the room, her arm outstretched to return his greeting. Silverton took her hand in a strong clasp and squeezed it slightly before letting it go.

"Lord Silverton, I am most happy to see you." She smiled tremulously at him and then glanced at Robert, who stared grimly at her uncle, a look of murderous intent on his normally boyish face.

"And you, too, Mr. Stanton. Indeed, your visit is most welcome."

She turned to face her uncle, who had moved across the room to stand by his son.

"This is my uncle, Isaac Burnley," she said, hardly able to contain her anger. "And this is my cousin, Jacob Burnley. Jacob, Uncle Isaac, these are Annabel's cousins, Lord Silverton and Mr. Robert Stanton. They have been most helpful in assisting General and Lady Stanton to place us in our present situation."

She glared defiantly at her uncle, feeling infinitely more secure now that Silverton stood by her shoulder. Meredith didn't know why she felt that way, given the gravity of the situation, but she was absolutely sure the marquess would allow no harm to come to her or to Annabel.

Isaac ignored the introduction as he scowled at the unwelcome visitors. Jacob, however, threw a cautious glance at Meredith and sketched a small bow in Silverton and Robert's direction.

"My lord, Mr. Stanton," he said. Silverton acknowledged the greeting with a remote nod of the head.

A quiet sob snapped Meredith's attention back to her sister and Miss Noyes. Annabel was still dreadfully pale, but she bravely stood her ground, her arms wrapped around the small governess, who wept into her handkerchief. Meredith crossed the room and led the two women over to the sofa, murmuring encouragement as she gently pressed them to sit.

She glanced at Silverton. His mouth thinned with displeasure as he observed the scene through narrowed eyes. Meredith took a deep breath.

"Lord Silverton, we are in need of your assistance once again. My uncle is insisting that Annabel and I leave this house immediately and move with him to Swallow Hill. I have tried to explain we are under the protection of General and Lady Stanton, but my uncle refuses to acknowledge that we are perfectly safe here and that he must abide by the wishes of Annabel's family."

Isaac spun around surprisingly quickly for a man his size.

"Don't get impudent with me, girl. Annabel is under my command, and if I wish her to come with me, then come she will. I have the legal right of her and that is the end of it."

He sneered and took a step forward, as if he meant to grab her sister and make good on his threat. Annabel shrank back against the sofa cushions and Miss Noyes wept harder than ever.

As Meredith braced herself in front of her sister, Silverton's voice whipped through the room like a lash, causing her uncle to halt in his tracks.

"I would advise you to stay where you are, Mr. Burnley, or you may well regret the outcome of your actions."

The marquess walked slowly toward Isaac, but the way he held his body was anything but relaxed. Meredith became aware, not for the first time, of how very tall and muscular Silverton actually was. He also exuded a subtle but commanding force of presence that made the other men in the room look smaller than they were.

Isaac stared incredulously at Silverton. He laughed harshly at first, but his brow furrowed with anger when he perceived the look of cold disdain on the other man's face.

"I don't know who the hell you think you are to order me around," her uncle growled, "but I can assure you, I have the legal right to take the girl with me now. She is under a doctor's care at home and will come with me immediately."

Robert, quiet until now, uttered a smothered oath and stepped hastily forward, apparently ready to charge across the room and attack Isaac.

Silverton's hand shot out and grabbed the boy's wrist in a tight grasp, locking him by his side. Robert started to protest, but his voice died when he looked at his cousin's face. Silverton's gaze remained fixed on Isaac.

"I'm sorry to disappoint you, Mr. Burnley," he replied, not sounding disappointed at all, "but neither Miss Annabel nor Miss Burnley will be leaving this house or London until they choose to do so. They are under my uncle's protection and, by extension, mine as well."

He glanced over at Meredith and Annabel, and his eyes grew even colder.

"It is obvious that you have distressed the ladies enough for one day. I suggest that you and your son remove yourselves immediately. If you wish to talk about their situation in greater detail, you may accompany me to my house, where, perhaps, we can discuss this as civilized men."

Isaac's beefy hands clenched into fists. Meredith closed her eyes, sick with fear that a terrible brawl would erupt right in the middle of her sitting room. At least, she thought desperately, that might give her the chance to get Annabel out of the room and out of the house.

Her eyes snapped open and she grabbed her sister's arm, ready to drag her out to the hall as soon as the fighting began.

But the mayhem failed to materialize. Much to Meredith's surprise, Jacob suddenly gripped Isaac's arm.

"Father." He uttered only the one word, but the warning was clear in his voice.

Isaac impatiently tried to shake the restraining hand from his arm. Jacob tightened his grasp and refused to let go, willing his father to meet his gaze. Isaac finally switched his attention from Silverton to his son. For a few moments they simply stared at one another as an unspoken communication passed between them.

Meredith darted a glance at Silverton, who stood calmly in the center of the room, continuing to hold Robert's wrist in a light clasp. In spite of herself, a hysterical urge to laugh bubbled up within her. Silverton was utterly serene in the face of her uncle's frightening behavior. In fact, she thought as she peered at him, he was beginning to get that increasingly familiar look of boredom on his face. She almost expected him to extract his snuffbox and inhale a pinch, simply for lack of anything better to do.

The tension in her body began to ebb.

Isaac finally shook his arm free of his son's hold. He glowered at Silverton but had obviously given up the idea of resorting to fisticuffs.

"You may be unaware, my lord," her uncle spat the title out with contempt, "but I am Annabel's legal guardian and have full control over both her person and her assets. Do you care to dispute that in a court of law?"

Silverton dropped Robert's wrist, his eyes suddenly gleaming with amusement.

"By all means, Mr. Burnley," he responded affably. "I know several magistrates at the Court of Chancery who will be happy to see us, if I make such a request. You will be relieved to hear that I have a personal acquaintance with many of them. I am sure I can arrange for the particulars of this situation to be heard without any further delay."

He paused, and Meredith couldn't quite believe her eyes when he actually did extract a snuffbox from his coat pocket and flip it open, availing himself of a tiny pinch with an elegant flick of his wrist.

"Of course," he mused thoughtfully, "I will feel it necessary to inform the magistrate—Sir Reginald Phillips comes to mind as one who might be available—that you intend to incarcerate your niece in a madhouse when she is quite obviously not a lunatic."

Meredith glanced warily at her uncle, who looked as if he wanted to wrap his fleshy hands around the marquess's throat and throttle him.

Silverton returned his snuffbox to his pocket. "If you are ready, Mr. Burnley, perhaps we can adjourn to the Inns immediately. I fail to see the point in letting this unpleasant situation go unresolved any longer. If you care to follow me, then we can just step up the street and hail two hackneys."

Silverton continued to stare impassively at Isaac, although a slight smile softened the edges of his mouth. "I will be sure to give the hackney driver exact directions so that you will not get lost driving through the city," he finished helpfully.

Guttural noises emerged from Isaac's throat. He spun around and glared at Meredith and Annabel.

"This isn't over. You may think you have the high and mighty to protect you now, but the law is on my side. And you," he said, sneering at Meredith, "you will find that you don't belong here. They will run you out, just like they did your father, and then who will you have to come to?"

Meredith could feel what little blood was left in her face drain away. "Not you, Uncle," she managed to gasp out around the catch in her throat. "It will never be you!"

She turned from Isaac, her legs trembling as she finally gave in to the weakness she had kept at bay as long as Annabel was in danger.

"Mr. Burnley," said Silverton, and the affable tone was now

replaced by one that was glacial. "Either avail yourself of my invitation to see the magistrate or leave immediately. I will not repeat myself."

A small frisson tingled up the back of Meredith's neck at his threat of implied violence. It occurred to her that the soft-spoken marquess would make a powerful enemy to anyone who dared to cross him.

Her uncle spun on his heel and strode out of the room, brushing by Silverton as he did so. The marquess simply shrugged his shoulders. He looked inquiringly at Jacob.

"Mr. Burnley, do you intend to join your father, or is there something you wish to add to this discussion? An apology for his behavior, perhaps?"

Jacob threw him an impatient glance. "In a moment." Looking at Meredith, he seemed to hesitate before clearing his throat.

"Meredith, it wasn't my idea to come here like this today. You know I would never hurt you or Annabel."

Silverton's eyebrows shot up and he opened his mouth, but Meredith lifted a hand to stop him from responding. He clamped his lips shut, frowning his displeasure with her un-spoken request.

"Jacob, I am grateful you prevented your father from hurt-ing us," Meredith said, "but why would you come with him and force your way into my house for the sole purpose of taking Annabel from me?" She stared at him reproachfully.

He took an eager step forward, his hand outstretched to take hers, but stopped when she shrank away from him.

"Cousin, you must not be afraid of me. I came to London to prevent my father from acting so rashly. You know what he is like. He would have come regardless, and I thought to pre-vent him from taking you once we got here. Merry"—he looked earnestly at her—"you know I'm your friend. You must believe I wouldn't let him hurt you."

Meredith studied him, trying to read his mind in his

countenance. These last few weeks had seen her world thrown into chaos, and she hardly knew whom to trust anymore. But she had known Jacob all her life. He had always been her companion and protector, rescuing her from any number of childhood mishaps.

As Jacob held her gaze, Meredith was forced to admit he had rescued her that last terrible night at Swallow Hill, as well. When Isaac had turned his wrath on her, Jacob had intervened, insisting that his father leave her alone. He and Meredith would, he had told his parents, discuss any pending nuptials in the morning, after she had rested.

That conversation, of course, had never taken place, since she and Annabel had fled their home that very night.

"Meredith, did you hear me?"

She started as Jacob's voice abruptly recalled her to the drawing room.

Silverton was still scowling at her cousin, his eyes glittering with an unspoken but obvious challenge. Jacob ignored him, looking impatiently at her as he waited for an answer to his question.

"I'm sorry, Jacob. What did you say?" Meredith tried to gather her scattered wits, suddenly aware that everyone else had fallen silent while they waited for her to reply—except, of course, for Miss Noyes, who continued to sob into her handkerchief.

"I said," Jacob frowned at her, "that I'll be back in London on business in three weeks. It would please me greatly if you would allow me to visit you when I'm in town." His expression softened. "I give you my word I will not allow Father to accompany me or bother either of you again."

She glanced at Silverton to gauge his reaction. His mouth had thinned into a hard, skeptical line. Obviously he disapproved, but Meredith couldn't really believe her cousin had any desire to hurt her or Annabel. Jacob was a gruff man and could be callous, but she felt certain he disagreed with his father's actions. She trusted him when he said he would try to protect her and Annabel from Isaac's anger. Whether he could do so was another matter entirely.

Exhausted and numb, Meredith wished everyone would go away and leave them alone. She didn't want to make any more decisions today. Unfortunately, Jacob looked to be growing irritated, and Silverton seemed to be on the verge of opening his mouth, no doubt to argue with her cousin. Perhaps she was a coward, but she simply couldn't bear any more upsets.

She forced herself to smile at her cousin.

"Yes, Jacob, you may call when you return to London. I shall be happy to see you."

Some of the tension seemed to drain from Jacob's body.

"Thank you." He reached out and lightly touched her shoulder. "Write to me in Bristol if you need anything at all, Meredith. And don't worry about Father."

He nodded brusquely to Silverton and, without another word, strode out of the room.

Meredith allowed herself to collapse on to the sofa, next to her sister. At the same time, Miss Noyes finally gave full vent to the hysterics she had been trying to suppress for the last half hour.

Chapter Seven

Silverton forced himself to unclench his teeth as he studied the three women huddled on the sofa. Miss Noyes wept uncontrollably. Annabel threw herself on the floor in front of her, stroking her hands and murmuring quietly as she attempted to soothe the overwrought woman.

Meredith seemed completely detached from the little scene playing out beside her. Her shoulders were slumped, and her hands had dropped loosely into her lap as she stared absently out the sitting-room window. She looked to be in a state of shock.

Not surprising, Silverton thought, after what she had just been subjected to. Now that the immediate danger had passed, all the courage and defiant determination she had displayed in the face of her uncle's wrath seemed to have drained out of her.

He also realized that Annabel's attempts to calm her governess were singularly unsuccessful, as the mousy little woman grew ever more hysterical.

There were few things in life Silverton loathed more than copious displays of weeping, having been subjected to them by his mother for as long as he could remember. Unfortunately, all attempts to soothe Miss Noyes apparently made it worse. Meredith seemed oblivious to the commotion —extraordinary, given the wails coming from beside her.

Sighing, Silverton turned to Robert, who, once again, was frozen in place like the proverbial pillar of salt. What was it about the Burnley sisters that threw his young cousin into such a state of paralysis?

"Robert," he prompted. The boy did not respond, and Silverton noticed that he was fixated on Annabel's graceful figure kneeling on the floor.

"Robert," he repeated, more loudly this time. His cousin jumped with a guilty start.

"Oh! Sorry, old fellow. Did you say something to me?" He grinned apologetically at Silverton.

"Yes, dear boy, I did. Will you please ring the bell and see if we can get some assistance for Miss Noyes?"

"Oh, of course! How stupid of me not to have thought of it before." Casting a lingering look at Annabel, he rushed over to the corner of the room and rang the bell pull.

Silverton crossed the room to Meredith. He went down on one knee so that he could look directly into her face.

She was pale and her eyes were unfocused, her pupils dilated so much that her gray eyes appeared almost black. He reached out and took her cold hands gently between his own, keeping his movements slow and steady so as not to alarm her.

"Miss Burnley, how are you?"

She did not respond. His concern grew as he chaffed her fingers in an attempt to give her some warmth and comfort.

"Miss Burnley," he repeated gently. "Is there anything I can get for you?"

She sighed, a wavering exhalation of breath that quivered just on the edge of a sob. The sound of it wrenched at his heart, and he involuntarily tightened his grasp on her hands.

That small movement seemed to bring her back to herself. She sat up straight, her eyes finally resting on his face. Meredith stared back at him for a moment before blushing to a rosy hue. She carefully tugged her hands out of his grip and reached shaking hands up to smooth her disheveled hair.

Not wanting to embarrass her any further, Silverton stood and stepped back from the sofa.

"No, my lord. Thank you. I am quite well." Meredith attempted a trembling smile. Pushing herself to her feet, she turned to her sister and the still-weeping governess.

"Annabel, my love, perhaps it would be better if you took Miss Noyes up to her room so she could get some rest."

Surprisingly, Annabel rolled her eyes at her sister, as if annoyed by the suggestion.

"Yes, Meredith, that would be best, but I can't seem to get her to listen to me. I think it would be wise to ring for Agatha. She will know what to do."

Silverton swallowed a laugh at Annabel's tart rejoinder. It would seem the girl had more backbone than her sister gave her credit for.

"I have just rung for her, Miss Annabel. She should be here momentarily," Robert piped up eagerly from the corner of the room.

Annabel threw him a grateful smile before returning her attention to Miss Noyes. Silverton couldn't help but notice that Robert continued to stare at his fair cousin with an expression of dazzled adoration on his face.

Before he could think about that further, Agatha appeared in the doorway. Standing behind her was a remarkable-looking creature—a large, florid-faced woman covered in flour and clutching a rolling pin in her massive hand.

"Ah, Agatha, there you are," said Silverton as he stared uncertainly at the other woman in the hallway. "Your mistress would appear to be in need of some assistance."

Agatha hurried across the room, pulling a vial of smelling salts out of her pocket. "Yes, my lord. I was afraid something like this would happen."

She dropped to her knees next to Annabel, opened the vial,

and began to wave the salts under Miss Noyes's nose. "The poor lady is prone to upset, and I thought those horrible men were like to kill us if you hadn't come when you did."

"Yes, and we shall see what happens if they dare to show themselves in this house again," exclaimed the flour-covered woman as she waved her rolling pin menacingly. "I didn't spend ten years following the drum to put up with the likes of those hooligans. If I had known what was happening I would have been in here in a trice. Bullying my poor young ladies!"

Silverton blinked at the outburst. "I'm sorry, madam, I don't believe I know you."

"Oh, forgive me, Lord Silverton." A flustered Meredith spun around, skirts swirling. "This is our new cook, Mrs. Biggs. Your secretary recently hired her for us, and she has been most helpful in setting up our establishment."

Mrs. Biggs dropped an awkward curtsy, impeded as she was by her rolling pin.

"And I'm honored to meet your lordship, seeing as how you rescued the young ladies. You can be sure the next time those ruffians appear on the doorstep, I'll vouch for it that they won't touch a hair on my ladies' heads." She shook her flour-covered rolling pin with an exaggerated flourish, as if to illustrate exactly what she would do to anyone who threatened Meredith or Annabel. Tiny bits of pastry scattered on the polished floor.

Silverton was dazed by the image of Mrs. Biggs beating Meredith's uncle about the head with a baking implement. He silently reminded himself to commend his secretary for finding such a remarkable character. Struggling to compose his face, he nodded gravely to the cook.

"I have no doubt you would be successful in protecting the ladies, but I feel confident that Miss Burnley and Miss Annabel are no longer in danger. Mrs. Biggs, would you please bring some tea? I'm sure your mistresses could both benefit from the refreshment."

"Oh dear! I beg your pardon again, Lord Silverton." Meredith actually wrung her hands as she cast him an anxious glance. He thought she looked adorably apologetic.

"Yes, Mrs. Biggs, please bring tea and some refreshment to the drawing room as soon as you can. Anything simple will be fine."

"Nay, miss, don't you worry about simple or not. I knows how to put together a proper tea tray, and I'll be back with it in a twinkle. You just let Agatha get Miss Noyes up to bed and I'll fetch her a cup of tea, as well."

Mrs. Biggs looked thoughtfully at Miss Noyes, whose hysteria, thankfully, was beginning to abate. "Mayhap a splash of gin in her cup will do the poor soul some good."

Silverton almost laughed out loud as he heard Meredith smother a groan.

"Yes, Mrs. Biggs," she agreed hastily. "Thank you very much. I'm sure that will be most helpful." The cook bustled from the room.

Annabel and Agatha managed to get Miss Noyes to her feet. The maid looped a sturdy arm around the little woman's waist and practically carried her from the room. Silverton couldn't help but wince sympathetically at Miss Noyes's ignominious exit. Mostly, though, he was just grateful.

A profound silence fell over the room. Those left behind stared uncertainly at each other, as if they couldn't quite believe all the turmoil had finally come to an end.

Silverton looked enquiringly at Meredith, who dropped her eyes to the floor as she bit her lower lip.

"My lord," she began. Her voice trailed off, as if she could not think of a single thing to say that would explain the mortifying events of the afternoon.

"Good Lord, Miss Burnley," Robert burst in, clearly unable to contain himself any longer. "Pardon me for saying so, but you do seem to have the most appalling relations."

Meredith flushed a bright pink as she turned her face away,

obviously unable to deny the truth of his tactless statement. Annabel glared at Robert and moved swiftly to her sister, wrapping an arm protectively around her waist.

Silverton studied the two girls standing side by side—so physically dissimilar but tied to each other by a devotion forged through years of emotional hardship and solitude. He turned to Robert and raised his quizzing glass.

"Too true, dear boy, too true," he said in a tone of withering sarcasm. "It's one of life's greatest misfortunes that we must be saddled with relatives we would rather not have to acknowledge. Take me, for instance. Lord only knows what social crime I have committed to be saddled with an overdressed, inconsequential fribble such as yourself for a relation."

His cousin gaped at him and then looked embarrassed enough to cut his own tongue out of his mouth. Annabel peeked over her shoulder and began to giggle.

"Oh, curse you, Silverton," Robert exclaimed. "You're right, as always." He bowed gracefully to the girls, a rueful smile tugging at the corners of his mouth.

"Miss Burnley, Miss Annabel, please accept the apology of a witless dolt. I had no right to make any kind of judgment on you or your family. Please forgive me."

He was rewarded with a brilliant smile from Annabel, which brought a flush to his cheeks as he stared bemusedly into her pretty face.

Meredith turned around to look at Robert, her eyes sparkling with unshed tears.

"No, Mr. Stanton. It is I who should apologize to you for subjecting you and his lordship to such a disgraceful scene," she replied in a husky voice. "I cannot, however, regret your timely intervention, and Annabel and I can never begin to express our deepest gratitude." She walked slowly over to Silverton.

"Indeed, if you had not come I suspect things would've ended very badly for us," she said softly, eyes like burnished silver gazing earnestly into his. "I can never thank you enough for your kindness."

The intensity of those amazing eyes tugged at something located in the vicinity of his heart. For a moment they stared at each other, and then Silverton busied himself with polishing his quizzing glass.

"Your thanks are not necessary," he replied brusquely. "I acted only as my aunt would have wished. Lady Stanton would have expected nothing less."

Meredith stole a bit closer as she reached out and fleetingly touched his arm.

"Nevertheless," she murmured, "I shall always be grateful for your assistance."

He realized with a slight shock that she was gazing at him with an expression of fervent admiration on her pale but lovely face. It startled him. It should have made him nervous. But if he were honest with himself, Silverton had to admit it was remarkably pleasant to bask in the glow of her approval.

Even more strangely, though, it made him feel, well, amorous. All he wanted to do right now was find a dark corner to pull her into, push her skirts up, and explore all those lush curves and velvet skin with his mouth and hands.

Good God, he thought irritably, he was becoming positively deranged. Perhaps he was the one who should be committed to a lunatic asylum.

Silverton hated feeling so out of control. From the moment he had entered the drawing room he had been flooded with a wash of extreme emotions. First, he had wanted to pummel Isaac Burnley into a bloody pulp, especially when he had turned on Meredith and mocked her common birth. Then, when her cousin Jacob had insisted on seeing her again, Silverton had been overcome by a violent wave of jealousy. He had wanted to pummel Jacob, too. And now, when Meredith looked at him with that achingly sweet expression on her face, he could barely keep his hands off her. He needed to master these idiotically primitive instincts, and soon.

Especially since the purpose of this visit had originally been to visit Annabel. What a tangle the entire situation had become.

The door opened and Agatha reappeared in the room, laden down with a large and very full tea tray. Struggling under its weight, she carried it to a small table by the sofa and deposited it with a less than graceful thump. Meredith hurried over to assist her.

"Thank you, Agatha. I don't know what we would do without you." She smiled kindly at the girl as she helped her unload teacups and plates onto the table. "How is Miss Noyes?"

"She's resting, miss. I mixed up some of those sleeping powders the doctor gave us the last time she was feeling poorly," Agatha exclaimed cheerfully. "Gin doesn't really agree with Miss Noyes, in spite of what Mrs. Biggs might think."

"Yes, well, thank you, Agatha. That will be all for now," Meredith replied in a faintly horrified voice. "Lord Silverton, Mr. Stanton, please be seated. You, too, Annabel. I'm sure we have all been standing about long enough."

Robert hurried across the room to sit next to Annabel on the sofa. His cousin seemed to be developing a marked taste for the girl's company, Silverton thought, and that was a complication he really didn't need.

He sat down in an overstuffed floral armchair, murmuring a quiet thanks when Meredith brought him tea but declining an offer of a thick slice of plum cake. Both Annabel and Robert enthusiastically accepted plates loaded with cake and scones topped with thick-clotted cream. Clearly, the distressing events of the last hour had done little to dampen their youthful appetites.

Stirring his tea, he stared thoughtfully at Meredith as she served the others.

"Miss Burnley," he began, after she had taken the seat next

to him, "it occurs to me that you're in rather desperate need of a footman, preferably one who is both large and able-bodied. You must allow me, or, rather, Mr. Chislett, to find you one immediately."

Meredith toyed with her teacup for a moment before replying in an apologetic but firm tone of voice.

"I'm sorry, my lord. I don't think that is possible. As you know, we intend to live modestly and quietly. Agatha is more than capable of answering the door and running any necessary errands. I'm quite certain that we don't need a footman."

Her tilted chin suggested resentment that she had been forced to admit they could not afford the extra help.

"I feel certain my aunt would think it improper for you to be without a footman to take on those duties," he persisted. "You need someone who is capable of turning away unwelcome visitors from your doorstep."

Meredith's sweet mouth pursed stubbornly at his refusal to drop the subject.

"We do have Mrs. Biggs," she blurted out defensively.

She did have a point, but Silverton doubted even the masterful Mrs. Biggs could subdue both Isaac and Jacob Burnley at once.

"As capable as Mrs. Biggs is, I still believe it's not fitting to have no male servants in your household to assist you," he replied dryly.

She brightened at this last comment.

"Oh, but we do, Lord Silverton," she exclaimed as she unleashed a dazzling smile in an obvious attempt to placate him. "Our coachman, John Ruddle, is normally about to assist us with anything we might require. I simply needed him to conduct some business in the city today. That is why you don't see him."

Silverton squashed a growing sense of irritation. Clearly the lady was used to ordering the household in her own way and did not take kindly to any interference. Especially, he suspected, of the masculine variety.

Of course, it was rather puzzling that he seemed compelled to direct her living arrangements to his own satisfaction. He felt vaguely uneasy as he tried to reason out the answer to that question, until he remembered he might be a candidate for Annabel's hand. Surely that gave him the right to ensure the girl's safety, and that of her sister.

"John Ruddle," he finally replied. "Is that the elderly man we saw at Miss Noyes's rooms in Hans Town last week? The one with the slight stoop and the arthritic limp?"

Meredith frowned down her elegant nose at him. "John Ruddle has been with my family since I was a child. He is both loyal and extremely dedicated. In fact, we wouldn't have been able to escape from Swallow Hill without his assistance."

Silverton drummed his fingers against the arm of his chair. "Perhaps you can enlighten me as to how loyalty will enable an elderly man to keep your various unworthy relations from forcing their way into this house."

He found it immensely annoying that Meredith could be so naïve. Did she not understand how vulnerable she and her sister were, given the uncertainties of Annabel's legal situation?

Meredith glared at him, her eyes narrowing in a mutinous gaze. He had seen that expression before, in his uncle's study. How was it that only a few moments ago she had been gazing at him with a look of adoration and now she appeared ready to box his ears? She really was one of the most irritating women he had ever met in his life.

Meredith thrust her elegant little chin up defiantly.

"Lord Silverton, not everyone can afford vast fleets of servants who can be deployed in response to their master's every momentary whim," she said in a frosty voice. "Some of us are required to make do with the economies that have been forced upon us by circumstances. It is entirely unnecessary for you to trouble yourself with our domestic arrangements."

She positively glowered at him. "But I thank you for your generous concern," she finished in a politely clipped tone that utterly failed to disguise her vexation.

Robert and Annabel, who had been chatting merrily away in the corner, had fallen silent and were now staring uncertainly at their elders. It occurred to Silverton they must appear to be out of their minds to be arguing over servants, and he suddenly started to laugh. Meredith looked at him with surprise, but as he continued to laugh, her mouth grew thin with disapproval.

Silverton threw up his hands in a gesture of mock surrender. "Miss Burnley, I suggest we cease this discussion before we fall into an unseemly brawl. Surely we can come to some kind of arrangement that will satisfy both my concerns for your safety and the demands of your pocketbook."

He leveled his most compelling smile at her, the one that never failed to render young women totally compliant.

"You know Lady Stanton will be most alarmed by this day's events. If not for your own sake, then think of her feelings at the thought of her granddaughter left so unprotected."

She continued to frown at him, obviously immune to either his smile or his reasoning.

"Meredith," Annabel interjected in a hesitant voice.

Meredith pulled her gaze reluctantly away from Silverton to look at her sister.

"I must confess that I would feel better with a proper footman at the door. It is, perhaps, not fair to ask Agatha or John to be so responsible for our safety," Annabel finished softly.

Meredith thawed immediately. She cast a guilty look at Silverton, blushing in that enchanting manner he was beginning to find insidiously captivating. Biting her lip, she paused for only a moment before responding.

"Annabel is right, of course," she said, smiling apologetically at him. "Please don't think I'm not grateful for all you have done for us. We are already so obliged to you and Lady Stanton for all your many kindnesses."

"There is no obligation, Miss Burnley."

He didn't want her to feel indebted to him, Silverton realized with a jolt. He wanted her to be so taken with him that she would do whatever it was he wanted her to do. That thought finally alarmed him. He could feel himself sliding into very dangerous territory.

"I feel certain we can come to a satisfactory arrangement," he continued, making a point of smiling at Annabel. "Let me speak to Lady Stanton about what I feel is necessary to safeguard you and your sister."

"Thank you, my lord. Whatever you think is necessary." Meredith reached for his cup to pour out more tea. He gently waved her off.

"No more for me, I thank you. Robert and I have imposed on you long enough," he said as he rose to take his leave.

His cousin reluctantly stood up from the sofa, staring wistfully at Annabel for a moment before moving to stand by Silverton. Robert was about to make his bow to Meredith when he smacked himself on the forehead.

"I completely forgot what I wished to say to you," he exclaimed. "Miss Burnley, Miss Annabel, the purpose of my visit this morning was to invite you to accompany me and my sister, Sophia, to Green Park. I have told her all about you, and she is most eager to meet you. We were on our way here to extend the invitation when Agatha came racing up the street to fetch help. That's why we were able to respond to your summons so quickly."

Meredith cast a speculative glance at Robert, and then to her sister, who was clapping her hands in pleasure at the unexpected invitation.

"Oh yes," cried Annabel, her eyes sparkling with joy at the idea of finally getting out of the house. She was practically bouncing up and down in her seat with excitement. "May we,

Meredith? I'm sure we'll be perfectly safe with Robert and his sister."

Meredith hesitated. Silverton could tell she didn't want to ruin Annabel's fun but was reluctant to expose her sister to any unnecessary risk. The words were out of Silverton's mouth before he had a chance to think.

"Miss Burnley, I will be happy to escort you and your sister to the park with Robert and Sophia, if that will ease your mind."

The worried frown on her face disappeared, replaced by a grateful smile.

"If you wouldn't find it too irksome, my lord, we should be pleased to see you." She turned to Robert. "And delighted to meet your sister."

Robert and Annabel grinned at each other. Just like silly puppies, thought Silverton with a trace of irritation. Why he had agreed to be part of what would surely be a tedious family outing was beyond his understanding.

Oh well, he thought with resignation, at least he could spend some time with Annabel. That would make Aunt Georgina happy.

But as he watched his cousin chatting eagerly with Annabel and her beautiful sister, he chided himself for being a fool. He knew exactly what he was doing and why, and it had everything to do with a certain obstinate, countrified spinster whom he couldn't seem to shake out of his mind.

Chapter Eight

Meredith stole a glance at Lord Silverton as he pointed out to Annabel the small herd of milk cows clustered by the picturesque dairy. Her sister clung lightly to his arm, and his head bent gracefully as he made some, no doubt, charming remark that caused her sister to giggle. They made a very handsome couple, she realized with an unexpected stab of jealousy.

Appalled by the wayward direction of her thoughts, Meredith tried to think of something more pleasant. Unfortunately, dark images flooded her consciousness all too frequently these days—the result, she was sure, of the nightmarish encounter with Uncle Isaac.

She also found herself jumping at the slightest sound, and looking over her shoulder whenever they left the safety of their small house on Hill Street. Meredith knew that it was ridiculous to be so nervous. She had given her overactive imagination any number of scoldings, but with little positive effect. Only when Annabel was safely married could she afford to let down her guard.

"Meredith! Do come see these sweet cows. The milkmaids are just about to bring them in, and Lord Silverton says we can even have a fresh cup of milk."

"Yes, dear. We're coming," Meredith called to her sister.

"I say, Miss Burnley, your sister seems to be having a bang-up time today, doesn't she?"

Robert gazed eagerly at Annabel while offering his arm to Meredith. As they walked over to join the rest of their party, he dropped his voice to a whisper, turning his head slightly away from his sister, Sophia.

"No ill effects from the other day, I hope? Shocking incident! Truly shocking to treat a lady so cruelly!"

"I thank you for your kindness, Mr. Stanton," Meredith answered him in a low voice. "Annabel and I are both quite well."

"Robert! Whatever can you be muttering about? Don't you know how rude it is to whisper?"

Sophia frowned at her brother in mock anger, but her expressive hazel eyes gleamed with mischief.

"Oh, hang it, Sophie," Robert grumbled. "You don't have to know every little thing that goes on in the world, do you? What a busybody you are."

"Dear brother, you know for a fact that I do need to know everything about absolutely everyone. And if you don't want to tell me what you are whispering about now, then I shall winkle it out of you later when we are alone. You know that you can never keep anything secret from me."

Robert muttered something uncomplimentary about sisters under his breath, and both Sophia and Meredith burst into laughter.

Sophia Stanton was as friendly as her older brother, and her lively manners had immediately put Meredith and Annabel at ease. A slender girl of medium height, Sophia had an abundance of curly auburn hair, and almond-shaped eyes set under delicate brows. Her face was fine-boned and elegant, and the artist in Meredith fancied that she looked like an angel in a Botticelli painting.

Unfortunately, she also had poor eyesight and usually wore a pair of thin, gold spectacles. That had surprised Meredith, as she had never seen a woman so young wearing spectacles. But Sophia seemed to be completely unaware of her looks, and her lack of vanity was a quality that made her even more attractive. She was just the kind of girl Meredith wished to be friends with Annabel.

As their small group caught up with the others, Annabel dropped Lord Silverton's arm and skipped over to join Meredith.

"Is this not the dearest little park that you could ever have imagined? I never dreamed there would be a real farm in the middle of the city. Please, Meredith, can we go to the dairy to see the maids milk the cows?"

"Darling, we can do whatever you wish."

Annabel whirled away to join Robert and Sophia, and the three young people marched up the gravel path to the small barnyard and dairy situated in the middle of the park.

Silverton smiled at Meredith and offered her his arm.

"Shall we accompany the children on their rustic adventure, Miss Burnley?"

She hesitantly placed her hand on his sleeve, unable to ignore the acceleration of her own heartbeat as she felt the hard strength of him through the luxurious material of his finely tailored coat.

Meredith had never known a man like the Marquess of Silverton. He was so handsome and so elegant that just looking at him made her feel bedazzled. As they followed along behind the others, her eyes involuntarily dropped down along the length of his body. She couldn't help but notice the long, powerful legs tightly sheathed in breeches and top boots, corded with hard muscles that he must have developed from hours spent in the saddle.

Meredith yanked her gaze back to the gravel path, mortified by the inappropriate and unladylike thoughts that seemed to invade her mind whenever she was with him. And even, she was sorry to say, when she was not.

Meredith sighed, finally acknowledging to herself that she was completely fascinated by him. Her new feelings both troubled and excited her.

Never once in her nearly twenty-five years had she experienced even a schoolgirl infatuation for any man. Not one of her former suitors—not that Lord Silverton could be considered a suitor—had ever evoked any feeling in her other than mild affection or, more rarely, respect.

She had always been frustrated by this, and wondered if she lacked some vital component most other women seemed to have. One after another her friends in the country had married, and all had seemed content. Only she remained a spinster, and during the past few years loneliness had grown inside her like a bitter weed.

Meredith ached to know, just once, what it was like to feel genuine passion.

Now it appeared that her wish had finally come true, and she couldn't think of a more inappropriate target for her unruly affections than the elegant and worldly Marquess of Silverton. She devoutly prayed that she would be able, at least in his presence, to preserve a calm demeanor so that neither he nor anyone else would ever know how foolish she had become.

"Your sister seems to have remarkable recuperative powers." Silverton studied Annabel closely as she chatted gaily with her cousins. "It seems impossible she could have been so ill only a short time ago."

"I assure you, my lord," she exclaimed, startled by the implications of his comments, "Annabel was very ill only a few short weeks ago. Indeed, I have no explanation except to say that the change of scenery and her reunion with her grandmother must have spurred her recovery."

"Forgive me, Miss Burnley. It was not my intention to criticize you or cast doubt on your sister's behavior. I am sure she was as ill as you say she was. It does seem strange, however, that her health should improve as a result of moving from the country, which is surely a more healthful environment, to the dirty air of London."

A teasing smile lifted the corners of his well-shaped mouth.

"I suspect that you would agree with me, Miss Burnley. You do not seem as fond of the city as your sister does."

"I hate it!" Meredith blurted out and then grew warm with embarrassment when he started to laugh.

"That is to say," she added hastily, "I have not yet grown used to the noise and the crowding. You must understand that Annabel and I led very quiet lives at Swallow Hill. I am sure, in time, I will come to enjoy London as much as my sister apparently does."

"Do not apologize, Miss Burnley. I find London to be a vastly entertaining and stimulating city, but any reasonable person will find it occasionally taxing to the senses."

"If you say so, my lord," she replied politely. Meredith found it difficult to imagine that someone like Lord Silverton could ever be content to live a peaceful country existence.

They lapsed into silence while they strolled over to the dairy.

"Miss Burnley," Lord Silverton began, but then paused. She was surprised to see him frown.

"Yes, my lord?" She wondered what made him look so serious.

"I have no wish to offend, but I hoped I could prevail on you to explain the exact nature of your sister's illness."

She gazed at him, unsettled and puzzled by his persistent questions regarding Annabel's state of health. Why would he be interested in something like that?

Some of her bewilderment must have shown on her face, because he briefly pressed the hand that clasped his arm.

"I assure you, my curiosity is neither idle nor vulgar. I wish to understand why your uncle is so adamant that Annabel be treated with such extreme measures."

Meredith found she had to resist the urge to tell him everything. But she was uncertain that she should expose Annabel's intimate history to anyone other than Lady Stanton.

He waited patiently, not seeming the least bit troubled by her reluctance to speak.

As Meredith pondered how to respond, she realized that his assistance and protection required her to answer most any question he might care to ask. More than that, in the short time she had known him, she had already grown to trust him. Like most men of the ton Lord Silverton probably led a life devoted to the pursuit of masculine pleasure, but he had stood beside her as a friend when she most needed one.

Meredith lifted her face to the warm afternoon sun. She closed her eyes as her mind drifted back to the events of three years ago.

"After my stepmother died—she succumbed to a fever seven years ago this spring—my father and sister became inseparable. They were much alike, and enjoyed spending hours together in the woods on our estate. My father was a devoted bird-watcher and he liked to take Annabel with him, especially in the spring when the birds were nesting."

She glanced nervously at him, her stomach beginning to twist as the memories came flooding back. Silverton listened calmly, with a detachment that she somehow found reassuring.

"Three years ago this month they were out for a morning ramble, not far from the house but deep enough into the woods that they could not be seen or easily found. I was in my sitting room, going over the menu for the day with our housekeeper . . ."

Her voice faded as the terrible images of that day cascaded through her mind.

"Yes?" he gently prompted.

"It was a warm day and the windows facing the woods were open. I heard a shot and then a horrible scream. It took me a few seconds to realize the cry was Annabel's. She continued to scream for several minutes, the sound unlike anything I have ever heard in my life, and I hope never to hear anything like it again."

She shifted her gaze to her sister and her companions as they disappeared into the artfully pretty dairy covered in tumbling rose vines.

"The sound of Annabel's screams allowed us to find them. I ran from the house, as did our butler and footmen, and the men working in the stables. We found them in a small clearing. A poacher had shot my father in the chest. It was obvious he died instantly."

She fought back the anguish, which was almost as powerful now as the day it had happened. Gritting her teeth, Meredith resumed speaking in a voice that was clipped and unfamiliar even to her own ears.

"By the grace of God, Annabel was unharmed. But she had thrown herself across my father's body and was covered in his blood. I tried to pull her from him, but she would not let go. It took three of us to disengage her. By the time she was carried to the house, she had stopped screaming. In fact, she said not another word and barely made a sound for a fortnight after that. I was afraid she would never speak again. She was only fourteen years old at the time."

A cold heaviness invaded her limbs, as it always did when she recalled her father's death. Meredith felt paralyzed by a familiar darkness that threatened to overwhelm her, and drag her down to the hollow and dreary place deep within.

A pair of large, strong hands settled on her shoulders. Silverton turned her gently around and away from the gray emptiness. Meredith looked up into his eyes. They reflected bright sunlight and an emotion she didn't recognize.

In that moment he looked like summer to her—glorious, golden, and full of heat. Meredith drew in a shuddering breath. The chill that had seeped into her body faded away, replaced by a warmth that curled through her stomach, down her legs, and out through the soles of her feet.

"But she did speak again, and you have cared for her and nursed her back to health, have you not?"

Meredith nodded, unable to look away from the compelling eyes that drove away the icy despair. Silverton placed her hand back on his arm, gently urging her down the path to the dairy.

"What happened next?"

"Annabel fell into a profound melancholy for over two years. She rarely left her room and slept many hours each day. Our local physician counseled patience, that Annabel's natural youth and vigor would eventually reassert itself and that she would recover from the shock of our father's death. He was right. Last year, her spirits began to return, and I was so hopeful she would be herself again. But then—"

Meredith broke off, puzzled as always by Annabel's strange relapse a few months ago.

"But then?"

"But then my aunt and uncle came this winter, insisting that Annabel be treated by a new doctor. Her illness returned in force and has not abated until these last few weeks in London."

She shook her head in frustration at her inability to understand her sister's condition.

"Do not misunderstand me, my lord. I am grateful beyond measure that Annabel has recovered. But I can never be quite easy. I cannot rid myself of the fear that she might become ill again. More than anything I wish to understand the nature of her malady, and what I can do to prevent a relapse."

They strolled down the path, Silverton gazing thoughtfully into the enclosed meadow by the dairy.

"Thank you, Miss Burnley," he said after a minute. "I know how difficult it must have been for you to tell me. You may be certain I will preserve both your and your sister's privacy."

His serious expression lightened with an easy smile. "And now I suggest we join the children, who must surely be wondering why we have dallied."

Meredith gratefully let the subject drop. As they strolled down the path to the dairy, she peeked at him from under her lashes. He had listened to her gruesome story so calmly—sympathetic, but without any uncomfortable expressions of pity or distaste. In fact, she was amazed by his casual acceptance of her family's lurid history. Meredith hated telling people how her father had died. Most were shocked and strangely fascinated, and all too curious to know details that were incredibly painful to relate.

But Silverton had just listened, and that simple act had somehow made the burden that Meredith carried all these years seem lighter. She decided to let go the memories of the past, at least for now, and try to savor the beauty of the warm afternoon.

As they approached the dairy, Meredith couldn't help but think how odd it was to encounter a working farm so close to St. James's Palace. She was fast realizing that her limited experience of life had left her woefully unprepared for the eccentric complexities of London and, most particularly, of its upper class inhabitants.

As a child, she had always longed to visit the city. Now that she was finally here, she couldn't wait to return home to the country. Her response surprised and frustrated her, especially since Annabel had embraced their new life with courage and enthusiasm.

Meredith knew her reaction was unfair, since they had barely begun to sample the delights of London, or the diversions of the Season. Unfortunately, thinking about the balls, routs, and musicales they would soon be attending only depressed her. She knew she had little chance of success among the glittering sophisticates of London's elite and shrank at the thought of making her debut. All of her hopes were for

Annabel. The sooner her sister found an eligible suitor, the sooner Meredith could return to Swallow Hill, where she belonged.

"Why so quiet, Miss Burnley? I sincerely hope you do not find my company tiresome, although I am afraid your heart-felt sigh sadly indicates just that."

Meredith gave a guilty start. What a peagoose she was to forget herself in Silverton's presence. She had been completely distracted by her gloomy reverie, one that he had obviously been too polite to disturb.

"Oh, no, my lord, how can you think it? I was simply trying to fathom the purpose of an ornamental dairy and farm in the middle of London. It is yet another aspect of the city I find most amazing and difficult to explain."

His eyes widened in mock astonishment. "Do you mean to tell me that you do not understand the function of a decorative farm in the middle of London? Why, Miss Burnley, surely you know that Green Park is our own Petit Trianon!"

He made a sweeping gesture to draw her attention to the royal palace at the other end of the park.

"In the days when our unfortunate king was in residence, the ladies of the Court used to toddle over to the farm to watch the cows being milked. In fact, some of the fair ladies even delighted in playing dairymaids themselves. It has been said that Beau Brummell first met the Prince of Wales when His Royal Highness escorted the Marchioness of Salisbury on a visit to the dairy."

His lips curled in a sardonic smile. "O happy day for the Prince."

Meredith blinked, thunderstruck by the bizarre image of members of the royal family trotting off to a farmyard to milk a cow. She caught his sly smile as he anticipated her reaction. Her own lips twitched in response as she struggled to contain a laugh.

"Isn't that just the sort of thing that cost the Queen of

France her head?" she asked dryly as she observed the absurdly bucolic scene before her.

Silverton burst into laughter. "Fortunately, Miss Burnley, the English peasantry seem to be much more enlightened than their continental counterparts."

His intensely blue eyes gleamed with amusement as he grinned at her. Meredith's heart skipped a beat, and she suddenly felt as if her lungs had ceased to function. She forced herself to breathe out as she followed Annabel and the Stantons toward the dairy.

"Of course," Silverton mused, "if Prinny had been their king, one could hardly blame them for wanting to chop off his head."

Meredith gasped at the seditious remark.

"I've shocked you, haven't I?" He looked like an unrepentant schoolboy caught in the midst of a prank.

Meredith wondered how many women had lost *their* heads when confronted with the devastating sensuality of his charming smile. It suddenly made her quite cross to think of him flirting with other women.

"I assure you," he continued, obviously unaware of the tumult in her brain, "when you meet the Prince and, indeed, most of the members of the Royal Family, you will understand exactly what I mean."

Meredith frowned at his easy assumption that she would be presented at Court as part of Lady Stanton's plan to bring her out. The unwelcome reminder was like a slap in the face with a cold cloth.

"I very much doubt, my lord, that I will have the opportunity to meet the Prince or any other member of the Royal Family," she said in a clipped voice. "I will, however, be both happy and grateful to see Annabel presented at Court one day. That will be satisfaction enough for me, I assure you."

His handsome face suddenly looked shuttered and remote.

Compared to the way he had grinned at her just a few moments ago, it was like the sun had moved behind a cloud.

"I stand corrected, Miss Burnley," he drawled in what she had come to think of as his bored voice. "Shall we join the children now?"

"As you wish, my lord."

Silverton's affected and haughty manner never failed to irritate her, but she was really angry with herself. He had been nothing but kind, and she had responded by biting off his nose. For the life of her, Meredith did not understand why he often made her feel so defensive and argumentative.

Since she had no answer for that, she allowed him to lead her into the dairy, silently castigating herself for failing to control her lamentably unguarded tongue once again.

Chapter Nine

Silverton wanted to curse. He had made a mull of things with her, once again. Every time he managed to convince Meredith to confide in him, he invariably said something that put her back up and prompted her to retreat behind a prickly exterior. In so many ways the blasted woman plagued him, and he wondered why he simply couldn't leave her alone.

But as he glanced down at her elegant profile, framed by her untrimmed poke bonnet, he recalled her steadfast courage in the face of her father's appalling death and Annabel's illness. He had wanted to do more than just listen while she related the awful series of events, but sensed that any overt expression of sympathy would make her uncomfortable. Instead, he was forced to resist an unfamiliar and powerful surge of protectiveness that made him want to wrap her in velvet and silk and never let anything hurt her again.

It wasn't, however, just her defiant vulnerability that appealed to him. She also made him laugh. Meredith's reaction to the history of Green Park had been all that he hoped for. Her quicksilver eyes had glimmered with intelligence and amusement, while her beautiful, laughing face had made his whole body tighten with a heavy desire.

Which was an entirely different reaction from the one he experienced in Annabel's company.

Silverton admitted to himself that his little cousin was sweet, lively, and very pretty. But she was young, so young that he felt a vague sense of distaste at the thought of her in his bed. Of course, men his age married very young girls all the time. He just knew with a depressing certainty that he didn't want to be one of them.

Suppressing an irritated sigh, he glanced at the woman whose slim fingers rested so lightly on his arm. She was fast becoming a puzzle that he felt compelled to decipher.

Meredith's resistance to Aunt Georgina's plans surprised him. He suspected she was shamed by her common birth, and now he also knew that she longed for her old life in the country. Even so, most girls would leap at the chance for a Season sponsored by one of the most powerful women in the ton. Meredith obviously didn't want it, and that was just one of the things that made her completely different from any other woman he had ever known.

She was a beauty, too, and that disturbed his peace of mind more than anything else. Her cherry red velvet spencer shaped her generous breasts and framed her hips to perfection. He wanted to stroke her all over, run his fingers through her glossy black hair, over her womanly curves, all the way down to her elegantly shaped feet encased in sensible half boots.

Clearly, it was time to get a grip on his wayward imagination. He had promised his aunt that he would seriously consider courting Annabel, and he meant to do just that.

Silverton ushered her through the double barn doors into the ridiculously pretty and tidy dairy. Robert sat in a stall, straddling a low stool as he attempted to milk an obviously unhappy and uncooperative cow. Annabel and Sophia were doubled over, clutching their sides as they shook with helpless laughter. A long-suffering dairymaid stood at the cow's head, patiently trying to explain the proper technique for extracting milk without harming either the animal or the man.

"No, sir, do not yank on the teat like you was trying to rein in a horse!" she exclaimed, nervously eyeing the cow as it stamped its very large back hooves.

"Well, I say! If the silly beast would just stay still for a moment then I wouldn't have to keep trying to grab hold of the blasted thing every time it slips out of my hands!" Robert declared loudly.

His frustration set the two girls off into more peals of laughter, and Silverton could see the dairymaid was reaching the end of her tether. More to the point, it was clear that the cow's patience was waning also, and Robert was in imminent danger of a nasty kick.

"Robert, do stop torturing that unfortunate animal," Silverton ordered. "If you continue on as you are, we will be taking you home on a stretcher!"

Robert looked up, gratitude and relief evident in every line of his face and body.

"Well, you two certainly took your time getting here," he grumbled, leaping up from the stool and away from the cow. "I've been left alone to amuse these two horrible girls, and they both insisted I try to milk the silly beast, because everyone knows how easy it is to milk a cow!"

"Annabel, how perfectly awful of you," cried Meredith, although Silverton could see that she was trying not to laugh. "You know how difficult it is to milk a cow."

"You do?" Robert stared at Annabel with a stunned look on his face. "Well, I say, Miss Annabel, you could have said so before Sophia insisted I make a complete cake of myself."

"Oh, but it is easy," Annabel giggled at him. "Look, I'll show you."

She sank gracefully down onto the stool, looking as comfortable as if she had been sitting in her own drawing room.

"Are you sure you want to have a go at this, miss?" the dairymaid asked doubtfully.

"Oh, yes. I know exactly what I am doing."

She murmured quietly to the restless animal, petting it soothingly before placing her hands under its belly. In a moment, she was quickly and efficiently drawing milk from its teats into a large copper pail. The cow lowed contentedly, swished its tail, and leaned gently into Annabel's shoulder as she continued to milk.

"Well done, miss!" cried the dairymaid, releasing the cow's head and coming around to watch.

Robert's eyes popped out of his head, and Sophia laughed again, clapping her hands in appreciation for Annabel's skill.

"I say, Miss Annabel," Robert exclaimed, "I'm beginning to think there isn't anything you can't do!"

Silverton had to laugh. If Sophia had bested her brother in the milking competition, the boy would have been mortified. "Your sister is a constant revelation to me, Miss Burnley," he said. "She does seem to act in the most unexpected ways for such a shy and retiring girl."

Meredith nodded as she watched her sister with a strangely wistful expression on her face. "Swallow Hill is a small but very self-sufficient estate. My stepmother was very proud of her dairy and home farm, and Annabel and I were allowed to spend a great deal of time there when we were children."

She looked at him, her eyes soft as mist as they reflected the memories of those clearly happy times.

"Annabel loves all living creatures. She was constantly bringing home sick animals to nurse back to health—baby birds that had fallen from the nest, injured rabbits, stray dogs. And they never tried to bite or escape, either. I have even seen her put her hand down on wasps and never get stung. It's almost as if they know how much she loves them."

Meredith inclined her head toward him, speaking softly so that only he could hear her.

"Now that you know her a little, perhaps you can understand why I worry so about her. Annabel is an extraordinarily sweet and sensitive girl, and I would do anything to protect her."

Silverton nodded thoughtfully as he looked from Meredith's earnest face to the petite, unaffected girl sitting on the stool. He believed her, having already seen the lengths that Meredith would go to in order to guard her little sister. He was also coming to realize he would probably do almost anything to help her achieve that goal.

This urgent protectiveness he felt toward Meredith and her sister startled him, unused as he was to feeling such powerful emotions, even toward his own family. Then again, he had never before been forced to worry about the safety of anyone he cared for.

Silverton couldn't imagine how someone as young and sheltered as Meredith had carried on for so long—and all alone, too. Well, he thought grimly, that was going to change. He would convince her that she and Annabel were no longer alone, and that he and his aunt would do everything in their power to help them.

He turned his back to the others, wishing no one but Meredith to hear him.

"Yes, I do understand why you worry. And I swear to you, Miss Burnley, you and your sister are safe. I will not allow any harm to come to you, and neither will my aunt."

Her eyes flew to his face.

"I swear it," he repeated in a quiet but firm voice.

A rush of pink sped over her cheekbones, and she closed her eyes against a sudden sparkle of tears. She took a deep breath and opened her eyes. It was like daylight breaking free of the smoky mists of a winter morning.

"I believe you, my lord," she whispered in a husky voice. "And thank you most gratefully for your friendship to us both."

Out of the corner of his eye, Silverton noticed that Sophia was studying them, her expressive face signaling surprise and curiosity. Annabel had finished milking the cow and now chatted merrily to the dairymaid. Robert stood next to her, staring at her with what Silverton suspected was a burgeoning affection.

It was obviously time to go.

"Robert, if you are finished playing Farmer George, perhaps you could compensate the dairymaid for her patience and we can be on our way."

Robert extracted a few coins from his tailcoat. "Capital idea, old fellow. If I never see another cow again, it won't be a moment too soon."

Silverton offered his arm once again to Meredith, although he knew he should take Annabel by his side instead. He appeased his guilty conscience by swearing to himself that he would take his young cousin for a drive in Hyde Park very soon.

"Now, Miss Burnley," he said as he led the party from the building, "I thought you and Miss Annabel might like to visit Sir Thomas Lawrence's studio on Bond Street. I understand he is currently working on an interesting portrait of the Prince Regent. You can see for yourself if I exaggerate the Royal defects."

"Oh, yes, my lord! I have read about Sir Thomas's studio and have always longed to visit. You are much too kind, sir, to both of us."

Her eyes were alight with enthusiastic approval and warmth. It was a look he found himself growing addicted to, despite knowing that he played with fire by encouraging her innocent admiration.

Silverton knew he was being selfish, but right now he wanted to be her knight in shining armor. He would worry about the future later.

"No, Miss Burnley," he murmured in reply, leading her down the gravel path toward Piccadilly. "I am anything but kind."

Chapter Ten

Meredith smiled politely at Lady Bellingdon. The countess had been expounding for several minutes on the benefits of mustard poultices as opposed to other, apparently useless, remedies for arthritic complaints. Her small audience listened with rapt attention—not surprising, since they were all quite old and seemed to suffer from a variety of joint ailments themselves.

Meredith wondered, not for the first time, how she invariably found herself in the company of aging spinsters, dotty widows, and elderly bachelors. She sighed to herself, supposing that fate had already ordained the course of her life, which apparently dictated a future spent with the likes of Mr. Bolland.

"Fenugreek tea, Miss Burnley!" that worthy gentleman had declared just moments ago. "It is the only reliable beverage for the treatment of gaseous stomach disorders."

The occasion for all this gaiety was their first foray into polite society, at a very select dinner party at Stanton House. The guests were all highly influential members of the ton and, Lady Stanton assured them, extremely loyal to the family. A great deal of time and effort had gone into choosing just the right sort of people.

Although still early in the evening, Meredith was already wracking her brains for suitable topics of conversation besides her health. She had withdrawn completely from society after the death of her father and Annabel's subsequent illness, so her party manners had grown exceedingly rusty. And other than the Stantons, she didn't know a single person in the room.

She couldn't help but feel relieved, then, when Silverton finally appeared in the doorway, his eyes roaming over the ornately formal salon in search of his aunt. He strolled toward Lady Stanton, pausing to acknowledge the greetings of his acquaintances but steadily making his way through the small crowd. Bowing first to General Stanton, he took his aunt's gloved hand and brought it to his lips, smiling gently into her upturned face.

Meredith covertly studied the openly affectionate expression on his countenance as he greeted Lady Stanton. She had never met a man so self-assured in demonstrating his fondness for his family. Sometimes, as in the case of Robert, it manifested itself as a teasing camaraderie. To his uncle he was respectful but never obsequious, and the women were treated as gently as if they were made of the finest Chinese porcelain.

No wonder she found him so attractive, Meredith thought ruefully. A woman would have to be blind or deranged not to notice and desire that kind of attention.

Over the last several days she had been forced to admit she was in the grip of a dangerous attraction. She also forced herself to admit that Silverton likely treated her no differently than any other woman he knew. In fact, he often paid a great deal more attention to Annabel than he did to her. That was only natural, she supposed, since her sister was part of his family. Whereas she, well, she didn't even count as a distant relation, no matter what Lady Stanton said.

Still, her stubborn imagination couldn't help but recall that day in the park and the way he had looked when he promised to protect her and Annabel. His expression had been anything but distant. Rather, the heat in his gaze had ignited a corresponding warmth in her chest, which had spread like wildfire to her limbs.

Meredith took a deep breath. Better not think about that now or she would never be able to carry on a rational conversation with him—or anyone else, for that matter. Especially since he looked so handsome in his severe but beautifully tailored black coat and slim-cut trousers that covered but could never disguise the masculine power of his sportsman's physique.

Appalled by the direction of her wayward and uncomfortably warm thoughts, Meredith decided to stop thinking about Silverton at all. She turned deliberately in her seat and focused on Annabel, perched beside her on a red lacquered chair, chatting with one of Lady Stanton's oldest friends.

Meredith's heart swelled with pride as she listened to her sister easily deflect Lady Delfort's pointed questions.

"Oh, yes, my lady," Annabel said cheerfully, "General Stanton has been kindness itself since we have arrived in London. He and Grandmamma have done so much to make us feel welcome. In fact, just yesterday my grandfather invited Meredith to make free with his library and take home as many volumes as she desired."

Meredith almost laughed out loud at Annabel's look of sparkling mischief. Nothing could be further from the truth. The general had vociferously objected to the notion of her taking even one book from his precious library. Only the prompt intervention of his wife had prevented yet another row between them, something that had grown to be a fairly regular occurrence at Stanton House.

Oh well, thought Meredith with a tiny sigh, at least he had stopped threatening to throw her out on to the street. And, she acknowledged, he had easily accepted Annabel's presence into his household after only a token resistance.

"Miss Burnley, why is it that every time I see you, you feel compelled to emit a heartfelt sigh? If you are not careful, you will begin to wound my confidence, and I fear that I shall fall into a decline."

She jumped slightly in her seat and looked up to meet Silverton's quizzical smile. Meredith quickly recovered, extending her hand to take his in a friendly handshake. To her surprise, he raised it to his lips and dropped a light kiss on the back of her hand before returning it to her lap. She felt the hot rush of blood to her cheeks.

"Why, my lord," she said, making a determined effort to rally, "I was convinced that no weapon could ever pierce your formidable armor. Perhaps I have confused you with someone else."

He laughed as he sat beside her on the ivory-striped silk settee.

"You wound me to the quick, Miss Burnley. Believe me, my vanity is just as sensitive as the next man's, especially when it comes to the ladies. One cutting look from your keen eyes is all that is necessary to slay my pretension. I will then be forced to rusticate in the country for months to recover from such a deadly blow."

"Come now, Lord Silverton," she responded in the same playful spirit. "I begin to think that you confuse me with Mr. Brummell or some other member of the dandy set."

"I assure you, madam, there is no chance of that. The Beau is not nearly as interesting as you, and after years of close acquaintance, one has grown weary of his particular brand of wit."

"Do you know him well, sir?"

"All of London is acquainted with the Beau."

She hesitated for a moment because he seemed to be displeased by the turn in the conversation.

"I have heard that one must still make a favorable impression on Mr. Brummell if one is to be accepted in the ton."

His brows lifted in surprise. She arched her own eyebrows in return.

"My lord, even in the wilds of Wiltshire we have heard of the influence of the great Beau Brummell on polite society."

A faintly cynical smile lifted the corners of his aristocratic mouth. It made him look even more handsome, if that was possible, but also both proud and untouchable.

"Fear not, Miss Burnley, your sister's beauty and innocent character, combined with the support of her grandparents, will be all that Annabel needs to assure her success on the marriage mart. That, and her considerable fortune," he finished dryly.

Meredith smiled gratefully at him, her misgivings over Annabel's future easing considerably at his reassurance.

"Oh dear, are you two speaking of Beau Brummell?"

Annabel had finally escaped Lady Delfort's interrogation.

"I have heard continuously that we must seek his approval at all costs," she said, rolling her eyes. "That, and the patronesses at Almack's, if we are to have any hope of receiving a voucher to that holy of holies."

Silverton gave Annabel what Meredith thought was a strangely stiff bow. "I have no doubt you will charm all the patronesses, Miss Annabel. You will likely receive your voucher as soon as you make your appearance at the Countess of Framingham's ball next week."

"And Meredith, too," insisted the young girl, a note of defiance in her usually sweet voice.

Silverton hesitated and glanced from Meredith to her sister, clearly trying to weigh his next words.

"Now, Annabel," Meredith smoothly interjected. "You know we have discussed this. Given my parents' lineage it is extremely unlikely, if not impossible, that I will receive a voucher to Almack's. Nor, may I add, do I desire one."

Annabel's pretty eyes narrowed ominously.

"My dear." Meredith forestalled her sister's interruption. "You know I am right. There is no use to wish for something that cannot be attained. Lady Stanton has explained the situation, and we must acknowledge her experience in this, as in every other matter, is superior to ours."

Annabel looked mutinous for a moment longer. Then her eyes widened and she let out a frustrated sigh.

"Yes, I know," she grumbled. "But it is so unfair. Don't you think so, my lord?"

The girl's eyes pleaded with Silverton to agree with her.

"Yes, Miss Annabel, it is unfair. I know the exclusion must grieve you, but I believe that Lady Stanton is correct in her assessment. The patronesses are very unlikely to extend their approval to your sister. But," he said, dropping his voice as he leaned across Meredith toward Annabel, "you must remember it is all a game. An important one, but a game nonetheless. Your sister's worth is not diminished because she lacks the approval of a small group of arrogant women who would not recognize true character if they fell over it."

Meredith once again felt a blush prickling across her cheeks, both at his nearness as he leaned over her and at his seemingly heartfelt praise. She didn't know how to respond, so she fastened her gaze rather desperately on Annabel, who smiled approvingly back at Silverton.

"You are right, sir. I am a selfish creature, and I want her to be there with me for my own sake."

Annabel darted a sly glance at Meredith.

"If truth be known, my lord, Meredith would rather eat gruel for a week than go to Almack's. I think if she did receive a voucher she would probably fall into a panic and lock herself in her room."

Meredith frowned at her sister with pretend outrage.

"Really, Annabel, you will give Lord Silverton a very poor idea of my courage. I do not wish to go to Almack's because I have heard that the refreshments are barely tolerable and the entertainment boring. I would much rather stay at home with Miss Noyes than spend the evening trying not to trip over my own feet or those of my unfortunate and usually much shorter dance partners."

"Almack's! Lord, you don't know how lucky you are to avoid it, Miss Burnley," Robert exclaimed as he joined them. "It's the most boring evening you could imagine. Why anyone needs the approval of that old group of dragons is beyond me!"

"Why, Mr. Stanton," Annabel replied with a saucy tilt of her head, "you know how important it is that I don't disgrace the family name by forgetting my dance steps."

"Lord, no chance of that, Miss Annabel. You and your sister are the epitomes of grace and deportment."

Annabel laughed outright, her eyes sparkling at the young man.

"I suspect our dancing master may have something to say about that," Meredith responded tartly. "I'm sure the poor man has been driven to desperation by our inability to comprehend the basic figures of the quadrille and our uncanny genius for running into each other despite his direction."

Robert blew out an exasperated breath. "Oh, hang the man. I've never met such a mincing, pompous fool in all my life! It's appalling, really, to have a French caper-merchant ordering you about for half the day."

Silverton extracted his snuffbox and offered a soothing pinch to his aggrieved cousin.

"I wasn't aware that you were taking dancing classes, Robert. Surely that is one skill you have already mastered?"

"I should say so, my dear fellow. I am simply assisting Miss Burnley and Miss Annabel in their lessons at Stanton House. Grandmamma insisted, and, I must say, I do think it's rather good of me to spend hours prancing around the drawing room."

He cast a swift and apologetic glance at Annabel. "Not that I'm not delighted to help in any way I can. Enchanted, I assure you."

Meredith waved her finger at him. "Please don't apologize,

Mr. Stanton. If not for your support, I fear that Monsieur Renault would have decamped back to France long ago."

She glanced at Silverton, who was observing her with an amused expression on his face.

"I'm afraid the poor man is terrified I will crush his feet. After all, he is at least three inches shorter than I."

They all burst into laughter as Meredith sadly shook her head.

"You must be sure to save me a waltz at Lady Framingham's ball," said Silverton.

"A waltz! My lord, Monsieur Renault has not yet been able to force himself to make the attempt. He says that first we must cease stomping about the room like a tribe of savages before he will even consider doing so."

"Meredith, you are a beautiful dancer," cried Annabel. "You know that I am the one who can't stop laughing long enough to follow his instructions."

"Well, who can bear to listen to that intolerable mushroom!" Robert sprang to Annabel's defense.

Meredith laughed, touched by Robert's fierce loyalty to her sister.

"Well, Mr. Stanton, I suppose I should be grateful I will be spared the rigors of Almack's. On the night of Annabel's debut there, I will think of you all with a great deal of pity as I pass a cozy evening at home with Miss Noyes and a good book."

"You display your usual excellent sense, madam," said Silverton. "I only wish I could join you."

As he gazed at Meredith, the laughter in his brilliant blue eyes slowly transmuted into something deeper, more intense.

"And I have no doubt, Miss Burnley, that if given half the chance, you would cast every other woman at Almack's into the shade."

His voice slid up her spine like a piece of brushed velvet. Her eyes locked on his face, and she couldn't look away.

Awareness sharpened to a pinpoint as she saw only him and the heat of his gaze that trapped her so completely.

At that moment, and with a frightening sense of inevitability, she understood that what she felt for him was not a schoolgirl's crush or a spinster's foolish infatuation. After all these years, and with a finality she knew spelled her doom, Meredith realized she had fallen madly and irrevocably in love.

Chapter Eleven

"Come closer, my dear, and let me get a proper look at you."
Lady Stanton, dressed in a lacy wrapper, reclined on a silk
chaise in the small but elegant sitting room attached to her private suite of apartments.

The old woman looked pale and exhausted. Clearly, the
bustle and excitement leading up to Annabel's debut had worn
her out. General Stanton, always worried about the frail state of
his wife's health, had insisted that her physician examine her
this morning. Much to everyone's dismay, Dr. Gates had ordered
her to remain at home for several days of strict rest.

Meredith quailed at the thought of attending the Framingham
ball without Lady Stanton by their side, but nothing could be
done to remedy the situation. She and Annabel would simply
have to muddle through it on their own.

Lady Stanton had sent round a note earlier in the day, asking
Meredith and Annabel to wait on her before the ball. Meredith
suspected she wanted to give them a few discreet words of
advice, now that the day of reckoning was finally upon them.

"Oh, my darling girl," Lady Stanton cried softly as Annabel
rotated slowly in front of her. "You look beautiful. Your mother
would have been so proud of you."

The girl was truly lovely in her gown of pale green net over a white silk underdress. Her hair had been cut in the latest style and swept into a shiny mass of curls on top of her head. Strands of delicate seed pearls threaded her auburn locks, completing the ethereal look that so well complemented Annabel's petite figure. Meredith was convinced that no other girl would appear to greater advantage than her sister did tonight.

"Meredith, step closer, please. I want to get a good look at you as well."

She obediently crossed the room to Lady Stanton. Meredith's hopes for the evening were all pinned on her sister, but she could not deny the pleasure she had felt when putting on the new gown. It had been a long time since she had worn anything so lovely, and she had dressed with extra care. She had even made Agatha pull down her hair three times until she was certain that her new coiffure suitably matched the understated elegance of the dress.

"That gown is wonderful, my dear. It perfectly suits the color of your eyes."

Meredith carefully inspected her appearance in the large pier glass mounted on the wall. Her gown was made of pearl gray gauze, with pink satin trimmings under the low bodice and on the tiny sleeves. She wore matching pink dancing shoes and long, gray gloves made of the finest kid on her arms. Agatha had woven silver ribbons through her glossy locks, and a few black curls tumbled artfully around her neck and shoulders.

After a long and critical look, she decided that any flaws in the picture were the result of her own defects and not of the gown or her coiffure.

"You are both astonishingly beautiful, and I have every expectation that by the end of the evening all the men in London will be paying court to you." Lady Stanton's eyes twinkled with merriment. "You must be careful not to break too many hearts your first night out."

"Oh, Grandmamma, now you are being silly. I only hope I

have enough partners for the evening. I simply dread the idea of standing about in the corner while everyone whispers behind their hands at the dowdy country wallflower." Annabel peered around Meredith to stare at her own reflection in the glass, patting her curls into place for at least the tenth time since she had entered the room.

Meredith could tell by Annabel's voice that she was very anxious. They were both painfully aware of how important this evening was to the young girl's future.

"Annabel, my dear, I assure you, there is absolutely no chance of that. Simply be yourself and everyone will love you." Lady Stanton smiled reassuringly at her granddaughter. "I know you are not used to this kind of event, and that you are experiencing some apprehension, particularly since I cannot be with you tonight."

Annabel nodded solemnly, her hazel eyes grown wide with appreciation for the import of the occasion.

"If you have any questions or doubts about anything, do not hesitate to ask Lady Silverton for advice. She may be a very silly woman in some respects, but there is nothing she knows so well as the ton, and how to move through it. Her sponsorship and my nephew's escort are all you need to make an initial good impression."

Meredith's stomach fluttered at the thought of spending the evening in such close proximity to Silverton. He and his mother were arriving shortly at Stanton House to drive them to the ball. His presence, she finally admitted to herself, was the real reason she had dressed so carefully tonight.

She squashed that thought immediately. Her ridiculous feelings for Silverton did not matter; only Annabel's success did.

"My cousin, Lady Framingham," continued Lady Stanton, "has been most gracious in inviting us to use her annual ball as the opportunity for your coming-out. She will do whatever she can to assist you, but she will be very busy and cannot look after you. If Lady Silverton is not by, then you may also rely on

Robert and Sophia's mother for guidance. Her judgment can be depended on completely."

Lady Stanton raised her eyebrows pointedly at Annabel.

"I know you are excited, my dear, but please remember that you must not talk across the dinner table, no matter how interesting you find the company on the other side."

Annabel giggled. She had a lamentable tendency to forget the strict rule of conversing only with those seated right next to her at dinner.

"Yes, Grandmamma, I promise."

"Meredith, I expect you to keep a watchful eye on your sister. She is very young, but I know you are sensible enough not to be dazzled by a lot of handsome young men and their flattering ways."

No, thought Meredith with a stab of guilt—just one charming and virile marquess.

"Yes, my lady," she replied, simultaneously swearing to herself that she would not let Annabel out of her sight all night.

"Well." Lady Stanton sighed. "I've done all that I can. The rest is up to you. Annabel, my love, would you please go to the library and say good-night to your grandfather? He is waiting to speak to you."

Annabel dropped a kiss on her grandmother's cheek and hurried from the room. Meredith lifted an enquiring brow at Lady Stanton, who clearly wished to speak to her in private.

"Meredith, I know you are nervous about tonight, and I am very sorry that I will not be with you."

"My lady, please don't worry. I will keep a strict watch on Annabel. I know how important this evening is to her future."

"Yes, my dear, it is important. But try not to reflect too much upon it. Annabel will be loved wherever she goes, and I have no doubt she will attract her fair share of admirers tonight."

Lady Stanton rose from her chaise and wandered over to

her dressing table. She cast an enigmatic glance at Meredith, who felt a frisson of foreboding trickle down her spine.

"And even if Annabel doesn't find an eligible suitor in the next little while, you must not worry."

Meredith wrinkled her brow. "Why is that, my lady?"

"Because I believe that an excellent match can be made for Annabel within our own family. We need not depend on the vagaries of the marriage mart to secure her future."

"Do you mean one of Annabel's own relations?" Meredith's sense of foreboding grew even stronger.

Lady Stanton nodded.

"Do you mean Robert?" She had noticed in the last few days that Robert had become quite attached to Annabel.

The older woman broke into a pealing laugh.

"Goodness, no! Whatever the general thinks, Robert is still too young to get married. No, there is someone else in the family who would be a fine husband for Annabel. But since he must first make the decision for himself, I will say no more. I only wanted to tell you that you must not worry so much. Our family will see to Annabel's future, no matter what happens tonight."

For an interminable moment, Meredith's brain refused to function. She heard a buzzing sound in her ears, and the floor tilted under her feet. *Silverton*, she thought. *She means Lord Silverton*.

"Meredith, is something wrong?" Lady Stanton's voice cut through her daze.

"No . . . no, my lady. I'm fine." Meredith struggled to compose herself, even though her whole world had just been spun around like a top.

Could this really be happening to her? Could she really have fallen in love with a man whose family intended him to marry her sister? What else had her foolish infatuation blinded her to?

"Are you sure, my dear? You look very pale." Lady Stanton's sharp gaze studied her.

"I'm simply thinking about Annabel and her future, that's all," she hastened to reassure the other woman. Panic ripped through her chest. *Oh Lord, please don't let anyone realize how I feel!*

"Well, don't think too much. All will be well. Now, go join your sister, and say good-night to the general."

Meredith somehow managed a credible curtsy and blindly reached for the doorknob.

"Oh, and Meredith . . ."

She looked over her shoulder at Lady Stanton, wondering bleakly what other revelations might be forced on her tonight.

"Don't forget to have a good time."

Meredith nodded and escaped from the room. She managed to make her way to the library, although she had no recollection of doing so until she stood outside the door. Before she could even catch her breath, the footman opened the door and bowed to her across the threshold.

"Ah, there you are," rumbled General Stanton in his gruff voice. "I thought you had changed your mind and decided to stay at home like a sensible woman instead of running all over town with my silly granddaughter."

Silverton leaned against his uncle's desk, the height of masculine elegance in his impeccable attire.

Meredith almost stumbled when he turned and smiled at her. His gaze swept over her body, and the naked intensity of that look stoked a reluctant heat that curled down from her stomach to the top of her legs.

How could he look at her that way if he planned to marry Annabel? Perhaps, she thought, with a faint dawning of hope, she had misunderstood Lady Stanton. Perhaps her ladyship intended someone other than Silverton for Annabel.

"Really, Arthur," exclaimed Lady Silverton from her perch on one of the leather club chairs. "How can you be so old fashioned? Annabel is over seventeen and Miss Burnley is well past the regular age of making her debut. It is more than appropriate they should be going out into society."

"Age has nothing to do with it," retorted the general. "Damned disrespectful to be carousing all over the place, what with the Monster on the loose again in France."

"You are right, of course, Uncle," interjected Silverton. "But the war has been going on for so many years that one cannot expect society to come to a complete halt. We can only hope that Wellington and the allies will soon be able to stop Bonaparte's advance across the continent once and for all."

Lady Silverton ignored the general completely as she rose to greet Meredith.

"Well, Miss Burnley, you look very nice this evening. And Annabel, I am in transports over your gown! You are to be commended on your excellent taste. I have every confidence that you will be the most beautiful girl at the Framingham ball."

Annabel smiled with relief at Lady Silverton's effusive praise. She got on extremely well with the dowager marchioness, who treated her with a careless affection.

Her treatment of Meredith was an entirely different matter. Lady Silverton was very high in the instep, and Meredith knew she would have preferred to grant her sponsorship to Annabel alone. Although never rude, whenever she talked to Meredith the cool reserve in her manner suggested a faint but clear disapproval. In spite of herself, it stung her to realize that Lady Silverton thought so poorly of her.

"Are you ready Miss Burnley? Miss Annabel?" Silverton's engaging smile encompassed them both as he draped his mother's spangled gauze scarf over her shoulders.

Meredith busily arranged her own light shawl, and Annabel flitted around the desk to drop a kiss on her grandfather's cheek. He murmured gruffly into her ear, but his concerned gaze followed her slender figure as she joined the others by the door.

"Take care of 'em, Silverton. They are both too green to look after themselves, and I daresay they'll get into trouble if someone doesn't keep them under a close watch."

Silverton glanced at Meredith, his cobalt eyes almost black in the flickering candlelight. A smile quirked the corners of his mouth, almost as if he were enjoying a private joke.

"No need to worry, Uncle," he replied, a hint of laughter in his well-bred voice. "I won't let them out of my sight."

Meredith barely heard a word at dinner. The elderly gentleman seated to her left was a cultured baronet with a passion for Renaissance art. Once he discovered that she painted, he proceeded to lecture her on the merits of the Flemish School versus the Italians. She tried to pay attention, but the interminable meal with its astounding number of courses passed in a complete blur.

Fortunately, Silverton sat at some distance from her, giving her the opportunity to recover from the short but nerve-wracking journey from Stanton House.

He had remained silent for the entire carriage ride, observing her intently as his mother and Annabel chatted amicably. Even in the dim light of the carriage lamps his eyes had seemed to pierce her, and there was an unfamiliar stillness about him that set her nerves on edge.

At one point Meredith saw the marchioness study her son through narrowed eyes, a slight frown creasing her brow. A peculiar frozen expression had crossed Lady Silverton's face when she noticed him watching Meredith so closely.

On their arrival in Grosvenor Square, the Countess of Framingham had swept them all into a large group and Silverton had not come near her again.

But dinner was now over, and their hostess had risen to lead the guests from the dining room. Meredith sighed with relief as she saw Silverton walk ahead of her, deep in conversation with a handsome, dark-haired man. She hoped he would be too busy with his friends to take much notice of her for the rest of the evening.

As she strolled with the elderly baronet up the wide marble staircase to the ballroom, she suddenly realized that Silverton would surely ask both her and Annabel for at least one dance.

She swallowed a startled gasp as butterflies took flight in her stomach. Part of her longed for his attention, although it provoked a terrible sense of yearning she knew could never be appeased. A man like him—one of the highest peers of the realm—could never be with a woman like her.

Even worse, how could she allow herself to feel this way if there was any possibility that Annabel might have to marry him? And how did Annabel feel about him? Although certain that her sister knew nothing of her grandmother's plans, Meredith could easily imagine Annabel falling in love with Silverton.

"Is there a problem, Miss Burnley?" Meredith had come to a stop near the top of the staircase, the baronet waiting patiently by her side.

"Goodness, no, Sir Phillip," she replied hastily. "I was simply admiring the beauty of this magnificent staircase and the unusual frescoes on the ceiling."

Fortunately, her elderly companion saw nothing odd about this explanation. Instead, he launched into an enthusiastic description of the types of Italian marble that had been used in the construction of the grand staircase and imposing entrance hall. Breathing a sigh of relief, Meredith allowed him to guide her to the entrance of the ballroom, where Annabel eagerly awaited her.

Her sister stood in the doublewide doorway, her eyes as round as dinner plates as she gazed into the brilliantly lit room. Meredith halted next to Annabel, amazed by the ostentatious and riotous splendor of the Countess of Framingham's ballroom.

The huge space was lit with several gigantic crystal chandeliers and a dozen gold candelabras placed on large alabaster side tables. The walls were covered in panels of burgundy velvet surrounded with white satin damask, the whole then bordered with burnished gold moldings. The draperies were scarlet silk lined with snowy white taffeta, trimmed with numerous gold fringes and tassels. An elaborate frieze scrolled across the ceiling, displaying a veritable jungle of painted foliage.

And on either side of the doors were two gigantic stone lions, carved so as to appear ready to spring on the unsuspecting guests.

To complete the fantastical effect, large pier glasses hung on those parts of the walls not covered in velvet, reflecting the glittering throng in an endless profusion of light and color.

It was vulgar and absurd, but the artist in her could not help responding to the stimulating nature of such an overwhelming spectacle.

Annabel began to laugh. Meredith smiled, her troubled heart soothed by the girl's amused delight.

"Oh, my goodness!" Annabel exclaimed as she reached over and grabbed Meredith's hand. "This is going to be fun!"

Chapter Twelve

Silverton brooded. He leaned against a massive gilt column in the corner of Lady Framingham's ballroom and brooded. He never brooded. He never crossed his arms over his chest and scowled moodily at his friends when they tried to talk to him.

But when Nigel Dash had sauntered up to say hello, Silverton had practically bitten his head off. His old friend had beaten a hasty retreat, but not before uttering a smothered laugh.

Silverton knew he was acting like a madman, but as far as he was concerned she had driven him to it.

The source of his uncharacteristic behavior was currently gliding across the dance floor with her latest partner. Meredith's delicate gown of silky gauze whispered over her body, clinging lovingly in all the right places. Her luscious white bosom rose above her low-cut bodice, displaying what he considered an unreasonable amount of smooth, tempting flesh.

She looked like a princess, although in this particular version of the fairy tale her highness was not a demure innocent but a voluptuous and bewitching woman.

He did not, however, feel like the prince to Meredith's fairy-tale princess. Silverton knew he was really the big, bad wolf, and he wanted nothing more than to snatch up his prey, throw her over his shoulder, and carry her off to some secluded corner of the garden where he could devour her in peace.

He snorted at the absurdity of the image, and at this ridiculous struggle to control his baser instincts. But that was how she made him feel—base and primitive. He had never felt primitive before in his life, not even at Eton when he had been forced to pummel the occasional tormenting older classmate into submission.

Since that moment when Meredith had drifted on a silver cloud into his uncle's library, he had felt overcome with a ravenous hunger. He had already danced with her twice, but if he didn't get his hands back on her soon, he would go insane with jealousy and frustration.

Silverton frowned when he thought about her response to him during those dances. When he claimed her hand, she had risen from her chair with friendly anticipation, smiling rather shyly as he led her onto the floor.

But once there, she had acted like a skittish colt whenever his body brushed hers as they moved through the intricate figures of the dance. Her hands had trembled through her fine kid gloves, and he had seen a hectic flush come and go across her clear skin. When the dances were over, she had seemed as eager to return to her chair as she had been to leave it.

Now all he could do was watch as one man after another eagerly led her onto the dance floor.

Of course, he had no business playing the jealous fool. He should be glad for Meredith's success tonight. Her beauty and intelligence would surely attract at least one man who might come up to scratch as a husband. Since he couldn't marry her, why should he begrudge her the opportunity to find an eligible suitor?

But as far as Silverton was concerned, there wasn't one man in the room worthy to kneel at her feet.

He also forced himself to acknowledge that he was doing his best to ignore a nagging sense of guilt. He should be talking to

Annabel, not mooning over her sister like a love-struck calf. The young girl had already danced a quadrille with him, and he knew he should solicit another dance before the ball was over.

But Silverton didn't care about Annabel, or any other woman in the room for that matter. He cared only about Meredith.

He sighed with relief as the violins scraped out their final notes and the cotillion finally came to an end. Meredith curtsied to her partner, the Earl of Trask, who led her from the floor to rejoin Annabel and Robert.

When the earl's hand moved up to rest lightly on Meredith's back, Silverton felt a sudden urge to throttle him. He pushed away from the column and stalked across the room to join the others.

"Ah, Silverton, here you are." Trask welcomed him with a friendly smile. "I was wondering where you were hiding yourself."

"I'm sure you weren't wondering at all, since you were draping yourself all over the prettiest woman in the room," Silverton retorted.

Meredith's eyes opened wide. Trask's left brow shot up as the smile froze on his face.

As Silverton glared at his oldest friend, he reflected briefly on the fact that Trask was one of the few completely reliable people in his life. But at this particular moment he had strong doubts that he could depend on the earl's reliability. He saw the way Trask looked at Meredith. He knew what it meant, and it made him want to haul the man outside and draw his cork.

Silverton bitterly acknowledged that it didn't get much more primitive than that.

The two men eyed each other for a moment longer before Trask grinned and moved slightly away from Meredith.

"Good God, man," exclaimed the earl, "what the devil is wrong with you? You look like you want to pound someone into the dance floor. Is your mother trying to force you to make the usual round of hen-witted debs again?"

Trask's dark eyes gleamed with mischief. Meredith glanced uneasily between the two men, a slight blush staining her ivory cheeks.

Silverton ground his teeth together to hold back the scathing retort his friend so richly deserved. "Trask, I haven't a clue what you are talking about."

The earl rolled his eyes but held his tongue, clearly deciding it was time to sound the retreat.

Before the situation could deteriorate any further, the orchestra struck up the opening chords of the first waltz of the night. Trask swept a graceful but careless bow over Meredith's hand.

"If you will excuse me, Miss Burnley, I am promised to Lady Randolph for the waltz." He nodded at Silverton and strolled away to find the voluptuous countess who all the gossips claimed was Trask's latest mistress.

Meredith peeked at Silverton, her cheeks still flushed with a charming shade of pink. When he met her eyes, she bit her lower lip and turned quickly to speak to Robert.

"Mr. Stanton, since we must sit out the waltz, I hoped to prevail upon you to escort me to the punch bowl."

Robert immediately offered his arm. "I should be delighted, Miss Burnley."

Meredith smiled at Annabel and made a point, Silverton thought, of avoiding his gaze. It annoyed him that she appeared so eager to leave him alone with her sister.

He glanced at Annabel. She stood quietly by his side, tapping her little shoe as she stared wistfully at the dancers gliding through the waltz. She caught his eye and laughed.

"Yes, I know I shouldn't be so envious, but it does look like such fun, doesn't it?"

"Yes, most vexing, isn't it," he agreed amiably. "But as soon as the patronesses of Almack's give you permission, you may waltz to your heart's content. And when they do, your sister will be able to join you without any reservation."

Annabel nodded, looking up at him with a perfect, innocent trust. "I am sure you are right, my lord, as you always are."

Silverton felt another stab of guilt lance through his chest. Annabel really was a beautiful, sweet girl, and he hoped like hell she wasn't falling in love with him.

He turned his head and scanned the room, searching for her sister. Silverton knew he should be concentrating on Annabel, but Meredith was a lodestone that drew all his attention. He easily picked out her tall, graceful body from the colorful swarm that surrounded her.

Silverton noticed that several other men seemed to be aware of Meredith, too, following her progress down the room with open interest. His jaw tightened in response, and a faint red mist appeared around the edges of his vision.

"Meredith looks to be enjoying herself, doesn't she?"

Silverton jerked his head back to Annabel, who studied him with a merry twinkle in her eye. He smiled ruefully back.

"Yes, she certainly does."

"I'm so glad. It worries me that Meredith is sacrificing so much on my account. She misses our home in the country, even though she never says a word to me about it."

"I'm sure that you both do. But, in any event, it's not possible for you to be at Swallow Hill for some time to come. You are safer here, and that is what is most important to your sister."

"Yes, I know." Annabel looked solemn, following her sister and Robert with her eyes as they made their way to the refreshment table.

They both lapsed into silence. Silverton couldn't think of a single topic of conversation, so he decided to ask her a question that had been bothering him for several days.

"Miss Annabel, I hesitate to bring up an unpleasant topic, but have you heard at all from or had any dealings with your uncle or cousin? I hope you would tell me immediately if you did."

She shook her head vigorously. "We have heard nothing from Uncle Isaac, thank God. I believe that Jacob will be calling sometime next week, but you already know that. I am sure Meredith would send for you immediately if she had any fears."

"I am glad to hear it."

Actually, Silverton had several questions about Isaac Burnley's bizarre and vicious behavior. He had been reluctant to broach the subject, particularly when the sisters were readying for their debut. But as time passed, he felt a growing urgency to have a thorough conversation with Meredith about her family. Perhaps he might do so when her cousin Jacob came to town. Now that he thought about it, he just might insist on being present for that particular interview as well.

He was racking his brains to think of a way to question Annabel about Meredith's relationship with Jacob when the music came to an end. Glancing over at the refreshment table, he noticed that Robert and Meredith were now talking to Sophia. Trask, who had apparently abandoned Lady Randolph, strolled up to join them.

Silverton was gripped by a sudden desire for watered-down, pink punch.

"Miss Annabel, would you like to join your sister for a cup of punch?"

Annabel dimpled at him. "That would be delightful, my lord."

They made their way slowly around the edges of the packed ballroom, joining the others just in time to interrupt an argument between Sophia and Trask.

Silverton couldn't help grinning at his young cousin as she gently poked her slender index finger into the earl's massive shoulder. Having known Trask since childhood, Sophia apparently felt no discomfort in lecturing him, even though he was a good nine years her senior.

"Really, my lord. Your aunts are longing to see you. It has

been months since you have been to Bath, and they are all too aware of every passing week that you fail to do your duty by them."

"Oh, hang it, Sophie," grumbled Trask. "Why can't you mind your own business?"

"I should be happy to mind my own business if you would mind yours," she replied in a pretty voice that did little to disguise her iron will.

Trask glared at her, but Sophia ignored him, smiling in the vague way she did when she wasn't wearing her spectacles. Robert grimaced sympathetically at the earl when his sister turned away to speak to Meredith.

"Beastly girl, ain't she?" he said in the most affable tone imaginable. "Best to do what she says or you'll never hear the end of it."

"You're her older brother, Stanton," growled Trask. "Why don't you keep her nose out of other people's business?"

"I've tried, Lord knows I've tried." Robert casually shrugged his shoulders. "But she doesn't listen to anyone, including Mama."

"Well, someone should have the schooling of her," Trask exclaimed testily.

"Feel free to try, my dear fellow. Just don't get your hopes up."

"Hallo, Trask, haven't seen you in an age." Nigel Dash strolled up and clapped the earl on the back. "What's the matter, old fellow? You look like you've swallowed a wasp."

Silverton and Robert burst into laughter.

"Maybe I have," muttered Trask.

Nigel looked befuddled for a moment, then shrugged and turned to address the ladies.

"Miss Sophia, you are looking in prime twig tonight. And I must say, Miss Burnley, Miss Annabel, you are both looking first rate, too. And Miss Annabel, I saw you dance the quadrille.

You were the most graceful lady on the floor. Don't know how you two managed to pull all this off in so short a time."

Meredith smiled at Nigel as she gently waved her silver and lace fan. "You are kind, Mr. Dash, but the credit belongs to Lady Stanton. I know the general is the military strategist in the family, but her ladyship's campaign skills and organization are worthy of Wellington himself. We could not have come so far in so short a time without her able guidance."

Meredith glanced mischievously at Silverton from under her thick black lashes. That simple look was all it took for the blood to heat up in his veins.

"And," she continued, amusement lighting up her smoky gray eyes, "when her ladyship issues a command, we are all compelled to obey. Is that not correct, Lord Silverton?"

Silverton struggled to collect his wits, which had seemed to evaporate under the impact of her bewitching gaze.

As the violins began to play the opening bars of the next waltz, he forced himself to look away before he made a complete fool of himself. Fortunately, Sophia and Trask were arguing again, providing the distraction he needed to pull himself together.

"My lord, going to visit them in Bath every six months is not enough!" Sophia put her hands on her hips as she peered at the earl.

"Oh, Sophie, please stubble it," Trask retorted. "Maybe getting you out onto the dance floor will silence you."

"I doubt it," mused Robert as Annabel giggled beside him.

Ignoring Robert and grabbing Sophia's hand, the earl dragged her out onto the dance floor.

"But I can't see a thing without my glasses!" she cried as he led her away.

"You won't need to," Trask growled in reply. He pulled her into his arms and swept her down the length of the ballroom.

"I say, Miss Annabel, since we can't waltz, perhaps you

would care for a stroll around the room?" Robert gallantly offered his arm to his cousin.

"Oh, that would be most refreshing!" Annabel blew her sister a kiss and strolled off with Robert in search of entertainment.

Silverton switched his attention back to Meredith. She stared longingly at the dancers as they circled the floor in a swirl of shimmering fabrics and glittering jewels. A small, wistful sigh escaped her lips. Suddenly, he couldn't stand it a minute longer. He had to hold her now or he would surely go mad.

He gently slid his gloved hand down Meredith's arm and took her hand. She shivered at his touch.

"Lord Silverton," she began, but her voice trailed off when she saw the expression on his face. For a long moment she gazed at him, her breath escaping much too quickly from between parted lips.

"Miss Burnley." He smiled down at her as he held her hand in a possessive grip. "May I have the honor of this waltz?"

Her mouth dropped open with unladylike surprise. Silverton wanted to laugh; he seemed to have a knack for making her forget her manners. But his amusement faded as her pink tongue slipped out and dampened her lower lip with a nervous flick.

"I . . . I . . . ," she stammered, her eyes jumping around the room.

Nigel, who had been leaning idly against the wall, straightened up. Concern replaced the usual good-natured expression on his face.

"Stephen, old man," he began.

Silverton just looked at him, and Nigel's next words died on his lips. Silverton turned back to Meredith, whose entire body seemed rigid with tension.

"Well, Miss Burnley, shall we throw caution to the winds?" He smiled coaxingly at her. "How bad can it be? After all, you are no green debutante like your sister."

Something vivid flashed in her eyes, an expression that almost looked like pain. Her chin tilted up, and for a charged moment she met his gaze with what he could have sworn was defiance. But then her face softened with longing and a sweet vulnerability that made his heart thump in his chest. Her lips trembled into a dazzling smile as she stepped confidently into his arms.

His body blazed to life at the touch of her silky warmth, and he pulled her against him as he circled smoothly through the first turn. She breathed a small but voluptuous sigh of satisfaction, her eyes dreamy and unfocussed as she allowed herself to relax into the dance. Everything faded away but the sensations of holding her so closely—the soft swish of her gown as it wrapped itself around his legs, and the gentle pressure of her hand resting lightly on his shoulder.

Without warning, Silverton had a vision of that slender hand curled tightly around his neck, her naked body lying beneath him in the huge mahogany bed at his estate in Kent.

He blinked in surprise. Of course, it was entirely reasonable he should be having lurid fantasies about Meredith. But what startled him was the absolute clarity of that image of her in the family's venerable old marriage bed.

Right then and there, Silverton knew he could never marry Annabel, no matter what Aunt Georgina might have to say about it.

He inhaled a sharp breath. Meredith looked up, her eyebrows raised in an unspoken question. Silverton realized he was holding her much too tightly, so he eased his grip as they swept slowly down the room. He searched for an innocuous comment to break the physical tension building relentlessly inside him.

As they rotated through a turn at the bottom of the room, he caught a glimpse of Annabel leaning on Robert's arm, laughing gaily as she looked up into the young man's face. Meredith followed the direction of his gaze.

"Annabel is having a wonderful time," she exclaimed. "I have never seen her as animated as she is tonight."

Silverton stared at his two cousins as they strolled through the crowd. How odd that he'd never really noticed before how happy Annabel and Robert were in each other's company. In fact, they seemed to positively sparkle with life whenever they were together.

"So is Robert," he replied thoughtfully. "It's funny, but whenever he's with Annabel he acts as if he's been knocked on the head. What little wit he has seems to pour straight out of his ears and onto the floor."

An arrested expression crossed Meredith's face, as if the thought had never occurred to her. She twisted around in his arms to stare at the young couple before looking up at him doubtfully.

"Truly?"

He nodded solemnly as he struggled to keep the smile off his face. "Dicked in the nob, poor boy. I begin to suspect that he is completely mad for your sister. Don't forget, she did convince him to milk a cow."

A great surge of relief coursed through him as he realized that Robert just might be the solution to Annabel's problem of finding a husband. After all, one cousin might do just as well as the other.

Meredith looked shocked, but then she tilted her head back and broke into laughter. She had a full, throaty laugh—not the simpering titter of a nervous miss—and he gloried in the husky sensuality of her response. Several heads swiveled to look at them, but Silverton didn't care. He tightened his arms around her as he swung her into the final turn of the waltz.

As the music ended, he brought her to a gentle halt. Her cheeks were flushed with exertion, and her eyes sparkled with an enjoyment he rarely saw in her. He slipped her hand through his arm and escorted her back to where her sister stood with Robert. Annabel chatted with Sophia and her mother, who had just joined them. Nigel was also there, engaged in a whispered conversation with Trask, who glanced at Silverton with a startled expression on his dark face.

"Oh, my dears, there you are!" exclaimed Mrs. Stanton. "I didn't realize you were waltzing. I must say, Stephen, you surprise me."

Robert and Sophia's mother was both doting and kind, and she readily extended her affection to her children's friends. At her gentle admonition, a look of dismay dimmed Meredith's happy expression.

"The fault was mine, Aunt Agnes," Silverton interjected smoothly. "You know that I can never resist a waltz."

"That's right, Mama," Robert agreed hastily. "No point in making a fuss about it."

"Oh, my dear children," Mrs. Stanton protested. "I wouldn't dream of making a fuss! It's just that . . . well, never mind. It's time for supper, and we really should be going down if we wish to secure a table. Lady Framingham always invites so many people that it's a miracle we don't all get trampled underfoot."

They moved through the crush of bodies toward the doors leading to the supper room. Meredith and Annabel, who had linked arms, were suddenly jostled by the crowd and pressed against an older gentleman and his companion, a formidable-looking woman with a severe expression on her face. Silverton froze in his tracks when he realized the woman was Mrs. Drummond-Burrell, the coldest and most judgmental of the patronesses of Almack's.

"Oh, I beg your pardon!" Meredith smiled at the stern-faced woman. "I do hope I didn't step on your foot."

The gentleman seemed about to reassure her when Mrs. Drummond-Burrell's piercing voice rang out clearly above the chattering throng.

"Such manners! I really wonder what the world is coming to when the Countess of Framingham allows a vulgar shop-girl to attend an affair like this. Whatever could be next, I wonder? I vow, I do not understand how General Stanton can bear to have the forward creature in his house."

The crowd around them fell silent. Then someone laughed, and the chattering resumed at an even louder pitch as the callous remark passed quickly around the room. Silverton's lips drew back in a snarl, and he began to push his way through the mob toward Meredith. She and Annabel were stricken into immobility, their faces pale with astonishment and wounded pride.

Silverton looked at Mrs. Drummond-Burrell's cruel, self-satisfied expression and wanted to kill her. The intention must have been evident on his face because Trask suddenly materialized by his side and grabbed his arm.

"Try not to be a complete fool," his friend hissed in his ear. "You've done enough damage for one evening. Let Nigel and Robert take the girls to supper and we'll follow behind."

Nigel gently took Meredith's arm and led her away, conversing cheerfully as he hurried her through the supper-room doors. Annabel followed behind, Robert and Sophia flanking her in a protective stance.

Trask gave Silverton's arm one last warning squeeze before releasing him.

"Well, old man, shall we follow the ladies down?" the earl enquired in a jovial voice, as if nothing had happened, as if Meredith's world had not just come crashing down around her ears.

Silverton's eyes swept the crowd. He could already see and hear the malicious gossip cresting like a foul wave. There was no choice but to ride it out. Later, when the black rage in his head had subsided, he would figure out exactly how to bring Meredith and Annabel back to safe harbor.

Returning Trask's steady gaze, Silverton forced himself to adopt the attitude of cool self-possession that had served him so well during his years in the haute ton.

"Lead on, my dear Trask," he said calmly. "Lead on."

Chapter Thirteen

Meredith was blind, deaf, and dumb. The noise, the suffocating press of people, the chaotic colors that swirled around her, all faded away into a gray and soundless fog. The only thing she could hear was the beating of her heart as it pushed the blood through her veins in an angry, hectic surge.

When she had seen the look of shock in Annabel's eyes, seen her turn pale as if she had been struck, Meredith had experienced a flash of rage so strong it had made her dizzy.

Lady Stanton had warned her. She had told her the ton would be callous, that nothing pleased them more than the cold barbs and destructive gossip that seemed as necessary to their existence as food and drink. But until she had heard the cruelly uttered words drop like venom from the lips of the stern-looking woman, she had never understood it for herself.

Perhaps she and Annabel had been too sheltered. Everyone they had met so far had been, if not kind, then at least correct and courteous. She realized now that it was for Lady Stanton's sake she had been treated so carefully. It had all been a polite ruse, and the first time they had ventured out without the older woman's protection their hopeful little fantasy had been sliced apart with the precision of a stiletto blade.

Her fantasy, at least, if not Annabel's. What a fool she

had been to allow Lady Stanton to convince her to come here tonight.

As cruel as these people were, what stung her most was that the evening's debacle was her own fault. She had let her guard down. Meredith had permitted herself to be lulled by the beauty and gaiety of the evening, and by the deceptive charm of the magnificent surroundings.

Worst of all, she had let *him* lure her in. For one glorious moment, she had permitted her feelings for Silverton to swim to the surface, for him and all the world to see. Meredith had lost herself in the blue heat of his eyes, and she had allowed herself to believe it had all really meant something.

And for one brutally stupid moment she had let herself imagine that she could actually have a life with him. That it was her he wanted, not Annabel. When he had clasped her against his powerful body and spun her across the dance floor, she had believed that anything was possible.

She would never make that mistake again.

"Miss Burnley, please sit down."

Nigel's soothing voice penetrated the daze permeating her brain. "Allow me to fetch you and your sister some refreshment."

Meredith forced herself to smile as he guided her to a spindly gilt and fruitwood chair. Inhaling a quavering breath, she finally looked around for Annabel. For her sister's sake she must brave the public humiliation that made her want to flee London and never look back.

Annabel had followed closely behind into Lady Framingham's formal salon, which had been converted into a supper room for the several hundred guests. Sophia's arm circled Annabel's waist as she murmured quietly into the girl's ear. Her sister looked strangely blank as she joined Meredith at the little table placed near a Chinese screen and several large potted ferns.

Nigel had chosen well; they had as much privacy as they could under the circumstances.

Meredith took her sister's hand. "Are you all right, dearest?" she asked, trying to keep her worry for Annabel out of her voice.

Annabel's gaze focused sharply, and the strange expression in her eyes blazed into furious passion. When she spoke, she carefully enunciated each word.

"I want to kill that woman for what she said about you. If I had a pistol, I would shoot her myself."

Meredith gaped at her sister, a sudden spurt of hysterical laughter welling up as she returned the fierce look. She forced herself to swallow it and tried to answer Annabel with her usual calm.

"No, darling, you must not be so upset. I don't care what she said about me. I only care how this will affect you. Try not to worry. Lady Stanton will know what to do."

Annabel blinked rapidly as she nodded in agreement, her body vibrating with the effort to maintain her composure. Guilt burned through Meredith like a flaring torch. If her sister suffered a relapse because of the events of this evening, Meredith would have only herself to blame.

As she patted Annabel's hand, she noticed Mrs. Stanton speaking in a restrained but urgent manner to Robert. Her son nodded, cast a troubled glance at Annabel, and then left the room. Meredith surmised that his mother had instructed him to order their carriage. As far as she was concerned, deliverance from this awful little drama could not come a moment too soon.

"My dear girls," Mrs. Stanton said kindly, "we will only stay a few minutes longer. Robert has gone to arrange for our carriage. You will both have a cup of punch while I speak with a few of our acquaintances, and then we will leave."

The older woman gently touched Annabel's cheek.

"Please, my child, try to compose yourself," she encouraged.

"The best thing for us to do right now is to appear as unconcerned as possible. Mrs. Drummond-Burrell is not universally admired. She is abominably high in the instep, and there are many who find her conduct capricious and cruel."

With those comforting words, she hurried away.

Meredith was both surprised and impressed by Mrs. Stanton's able handling of the situation. In the last few minutes, she had come to realize that Lady Stanton's assessment of her sister-in-law's character was justifiably accurate. Now that she had a few moments to reflect on the situation, she realized that Mrs. Stanton's conduct was in sharp contrast to that of Lady Silverton, who seemed to have disappeared. Given that the marchioness had agreed to be their chaperone, Meredith found it alarming that she had abandoned them.

She sat with Sophia and Annabel in troubled silence until Nigel returned, followed by a footman carrying a tray holding glasses of champagne punch.

"This will make you feel much more the thing," he exclaimed heartily.

Meredith forced herself to take a sip of the iced punch even though her throat was so constricted she could barely force it down.

When she glanced up to thank Nigel for his kindness, she spotted Silverton and Trask making their way through the crowded room to their table. Her heart, which had only just started to regain a steady rhythm, kicked painfully in her chest and began to race.

To the casual observer Silverton looked as collected and cool as ever, seemingly unaware of the numerous glances and whispered exchanges that followed his steady progress across the room. Meredith wished fiercely that she possessed his talent for unflappable self-control.

But as he neared their table she caught sight of his eyes; they glittered with a barely repressed fury, their gaze locked right on her.

Her vision blurred, her stomach twisting with a cold anxiety that made nausea rise in her throat. She had been so worried about Annabel she had not yet thought of his reaction to the events of the evening. Not only had she humiliated herself, her inappropriate behavior had obviously embarrassed him, too.

Meredith didn't know why he had asked her to waltz, and he should not have done so, but the fault was hers for succumbing so readily to temptation. She had promised Lady Stanton she would see to Annabel's good conduct, and yet her own behavior had been thoughtless and improper. Because of her weakness, Silverton must endure the gossip and slander right along with her. She was certain that he must be as disgusted with her as she was with herself.

Meredith turned away and desperately fastened her gaze on Annabel. She could not look at him, could not bear to see the disapproval in his eyes that she knew must be there. More than anything, that would shatter her fragile composure.

There was nothing to be done but gather the tattered shreds of her dignity and wait as patiently as she could for this terrible night to come to an end.

So she waited, and a few minutes later Robert and his mother came to fetch them all and finally take them home.

Silverton stared at the back of the Stanton's town coach as he struggled mightily to conceal his growing frustration from his mother and her friends. The look of anguish on Meredith's white face as he had tried to assist her into the carriage had struck him like a blow. Even worse, she had jerked her hand from his as if stung by an insect. She was building a wall around herself, and he couldn't believe how swiftly their growing intimacy had evaporated into the cool night air.

He stifled a groan. Only an hour ago her warm body had snuggled in his arms as he swept her in lazy circles across the ballroom floor. Silverton had poured all his charm and energy into pleasing her, and he had succeeded beyond his wildest expectations. Meredith had melted against him as if she were made just for him—lithe, supple, and infinitely responsive to the slightest touch of his hand. He had reveled in the sound of her laughter, a simmering slurry of intoxication pouring like honey through his veins. She had a courtesan's laugh, full and throaty, and it made him think of all the ways he wanted to possess her.

Silverton had noticed the heads of other dancers swiveling around to stare at them, but fool that he was, he hadn't cared. He had focused completely on her, and all of London could have burned to the ground as long as Meredith remained in his arms.

"Stephen, our carriage is here."

His mother's voice pulled him abruptly back to his surroundings. He placed a hand under her elbow, helping her into the plush interior of their coach. As he climbed in after her, he felt worn down and impatient beyond measure with the dreary absurdity of his social life. He settled heavily into his seat, prepared to brood silently for the duration of the short ride home, while his mother engaged in her usual gossipy prattle about the evening's events.

Silverton closed his eyes and tried to ignore her, but her mention of Meredith's name yanked him out of his gloomy reverie. He listened with growing consternation to his mother's unexpected and pointed criticism of Meredith and, by extension, his own outrageous behavior.

"Really, one cannot be surprised by Mrs. Drummond-Burrell's remark. Annabel is a very sweet girl, but I find that Miss Burnley's manner is quite forward and rather fast." She tittered maliciously as she restlessly arranged the gold bangles bunched around her wrists.

"I vow, one can practically smell the shop on her. Stephen, how ever could you bring yourself to dance with Miss Burnley three times, much less one? I was ready to die on your behalf. I shudder to think what your friends must say about it."

His mother sighed dramatically as she slid an assessing gaze to where he sat so silently. "How unfortunate for Annabel, indeed for us all, that we should be burdened with such an unfortunate relation."

His temples began to throb as he listened to the spiteful undertones in his mother's normally light and breathy voice. She never criticized him, at least not directly. And it infuriated him to hear her denigrate Meredith, who was so obviously a lady in every way that mattered.

The marchioness's face was just visible in the intermittent gaslight that spilled through the carriage's windows. A small, cruel smile touched her lips. She looked at him with an air of smug satisfaction that captured his attention more forcefully than her words.

The evening had developed into a series of revelations, and the most surprising one right now was his mother's reaction to Meredith. He was ready to kick himself for his unthinking behavior.

As he stared at his mother through narrowed eyes, he tamped down the anger that flared within him. Silverton never lost his temper with his mother. Exasperation was an emotion he felt frequently in her company, and, occasionally, frustration. But never anger. Her petty cruelty toward Meredith, however, tested the limits of his patience.

As he watched her fuss with her jewelry, it dawned on him that her response was likely to be duplicated by almost every other person at the ball, especially the grande dames.

Silverton closed his eyes and shook his head. He had been so absorbed by his own emotions and so distracted by Meredith's distress that he had failed to adequately observe the ton's reaction to their tawdry little scene. His mother's words made it abundantly clear that Meredith was in a great deal of trouble.

He cursed inwardly as he realized how unfair he had been

to both Meredith and Annabel. He was so used to the world ordering itself to suit his needs and wants that he rarely gave a thought to the consequences of his own behavior. *Their* situation was precarious, however, and they would be the ones to suffer for his arrogance.

He was an ass, Silverton thought grimly, and he must do something to correct his mistake before Meredith and Annabel were ruined. He wasn't sure yet how to accomplish that, but he could stop his mother, at least, from fueling the incipient scandal.

"The fault was mine, Mother," he said, ruthlessly interrupting her silly chatter. "Miss Burnley was merely being polite when she agreed to dance with me. Her sister's long illness and their difficult domestic situation have made it impossible for them to move in polite society. Any faux pas they make should be entirely understandable."

His mother's eyes widened with uncertainty. He returned her look with an unforgiving stare.

"I hope," he continued in a cold voice, "you will be charitable enough to overlook any small errors on their part. One could suppose, in fact, that since you were their chaperone tonight, any whispers of scandal might possibly attach to you."

He felt a grim surge of satisfaction as she bit back an exclamation of dismay.

"In addition, Mrs. Drummond-Burrell is not the kind of woman I would wish my mother to emulate. She is insufferably arrogant, mean-spirited, and boring. I avoid her company whenever I can. Correct me if I'm wrong, but I always thought you did, too."

He lapsed into silence, holding his mother's gaze as the carriage moved swiftly along the deserted streets of Mayfair. Silverton could barely make out the expression on her face, but he could guess how surprised and dismayed she was by the unexpected reprimand. He always treated her with an affectionate respect, but now he deliberately made his voice and manner both frigid and distant to shock her into complying with his wishes.

It worked.

"Oh, of course, my son," she fluttered anxiously. "I have all the sympathy in the world for those poor, dear girls. You can rely on me to scotch any gossip that may arise from this evening's events. You are absolutely right. It was most unseemly of Mrs. Drummond-Burrell to make such a fuss about nothing. After all, it was a private ball, and it's not as if the waltz has not been danced at Almack's these last two years. It's too ridiculous!"

"Thank you, Mother," said Silverton, allowing some warmth to creep back into his voice. "I knew I could depend on you."

She quickly switched the conversation to another topic. He barely listened. Silverton again felt a surge of weariness and frustration overwhelm him. He leaned back into the velvet cushions and turned the night's events over in his head, wondering how, exactly, he was going to make everything right again—for Meredith's sake.

Chapter Fourteen

Meredith hadn't wanted to get out of bed this morning. In fact, she wished she could lock herself in her bedroom and not come out for a week. Her night had been miserable and restless, and she had risen late with bleary eyes and an aching head. She had just made her way to the breakfast parlor of their little townhouse in Mayfair when the imperative summons from Lady Stanton arrived.

Now she and Annabel were back in her ladyship's dressing room, but the mood was very different from what it had been last night.

Meredith leaned her head against the window in the bay alcove, sighing as she looked out into the garden. The cool glass soothed her pounding temples. Annabel murmured gently to her grandmother, but Meredith couldn't find the energy to pay attention to what her sister was saying. Besides, there was nothing she didn't already know, and nothing that could be said to cast the situation in a more favorable light.

The truth was, she had made a complete fool of herself. She had embarrassed her family, exposed her feelings to a man who would never be able to reciprocate them, and jeopardized her sister's chances on the marriage mart before they even began.

Even worse, Meredith was now sure that Annabel would have to marry Silverton, whether she wanted to or not. If the scandal was as bad as it seemed to be, it might be impossible to find a husband for her sister as quickly as they needed to. Meredith's unthinking behavior could either precipitate Annabel's marriage to a man she might not love or place her at further risk from Uncle Isaac.

And although Meredith could bear anything if Annabel were safe, her heart broke at the thought of Silverton as her sister's husband.

She sighed again as she turned away from the soothing image of Lady Stanton's rose bushes to face the questions she hardly knew how to answer. London was a foreign country to her, and she despaired of ever being able to decipher its opaque and unforgiving social codes.

And she had no idea how to explain her own actions without revealing her feelings for Silverton to his aunt. Meredith prayed that she would have the self-control to justify her behavior in some kind of rational manner. She could not and would not betray the Stanton family's trust in her by acting like a foolish and besotted girl.

Annabel fell silent. She gave Meredith a tiny smile, much calmer now that she had unburdened herself to her grandmother.

Actually, Annabel's response had been the biggest surprise of the entire affair. After her initial outburst in the supper room last night, the girl had reacted with much less fuss to the unpleasant events than Meredith had expected. She had slept well, and seemed at ease and even cheerful this morning, more concerned for her sister than for herself. Meredith marveled at Annabel's newfound ability to shrug off something that only a short time ago would have devastated her.

Lady Stanton smiled at Meredith as she patted the seat of her chaise lounge in an invitation to sit next to her.

"You needn't say anything more, my dear," she said as

Meredith sat beside her. "Your sister and Mrs. Stanton have told me everything."

The older woman took her hand and held it in her lap. She gently stroked it, as if she were comforting a frightened child. Meredith found the soft touch infinitely soothing.

"I'm so sorry that you had to be subjected to such callous and cruel behavior." Her ladyship's faded blue eyes glittered with righteous outrage. "Mrs. Drummond-Burrell is an extremely haughty woman who fancies that only she knows who is socially acceptable and who is not. But as Mrs. Stanton explained to you last night, she is not universally admired, and I feel sure we can weather this little storm with a minimum of fuss."

She glanced over at her granddaughter, who watched them intently.

"Meredith, I know you never expected to receive a voucher to Almack's."

"No, your ladyship. I neither expected nor wished for it. I only hope I didn't ruin Annabel's chances to receive one."

Lady Stanton chuckled, and gave her hand one more pat before she let it go.

"I don't think we need worry about that. Lady Cowper is a dear friend of mine, and she has quite a talent for smoothing over disagreements among the patronesses. I know she will want Annabel to receive a voucher. And truth be told, Mrs. Drummond-Burrell has always had a soft spot for the general. I'm certain he can be convinced to help change her mind."

Annabel's eyes widened in surprise, and Meredith almost laughed at the idea of General Stanton engendering softer emotions in the forbidding woman she had seen last night.

Lady Stanton shrugged her shoulders at the irony of it. "I know it sounds absurd. It is because they are both such high sticklers. She does not, of course, have the general's kind heart."

Despite her misery, Meredith again felt the urge to laugh, but did not dare to under Lady Stanton's perceptive gaze.

"How will Grandpapa be able to help?" Annabel tilted her head in curiosity.

"Never mind for now. I must think on it some more, but I'm sure we can manage this unpleasant affair to our complete satisfaction. I forbid you, my dears, to waste any more time worrying about it."

Annabel grimaced, clearly wanting to ask more questions, but evidently Lady Stanton had finished with the subject. The older woman walked over to her granddaughter and patted her cheek.

"Now give your grandmother a kiss and go down to the general in the library. He is waiting for you. I want to speak to your sister for a few minutes."

Annabel hesitated, her brow creased with concern as she looked at Meredith.

"Go on, Annabel," Lady Stanton ordered in a gentle voice. "Meredith will join you shortly."

"Do go down, dearest," urged Meredith. "There are a few things I would like to discuss with her ladyship. Everything will be fine."

Annabel stared suspiciously at them for a moment longer and then reluctantly capitulated.

"Well, don't be long," she said. "You promised we could go to the millinery shop this afternoon, remember?"

Meredith smiled at the obvious warning in the young girl's voice. Annabel adored her grandmother, but she would not allow anyone, even Lady Stanton, to distress her beloved older sister. Annabel's loyalty was a comforting balm poured into the bruised recesses of her heart.

After the girl left the room, Lady Stanton turned her full attention to Meredith.

"Annabel loves you very much."

"Yes, your ladyship. Her affection and loyalty mean everything to me. My life without her would be empty."

Lady Stanton gazed at her for an endless moment, her eyes piercing Meredith with a discomforting shrewdness.

"Yes, I know," she finally replied, sitting once more on her chaise.

Lady Stanton did not invite her to sit with her again. Meredith began to feel as if she were a disobedient child about to be lectured. She clearly remembered standing in her stepmother's bedroom, waiting for a gentle but firm reprimand after committing a childish prank. Her ladyship had the same look on her face as Elizabeth Burnley had on the numerous occasions when Meredith had misbehaved.

The memory of her much loved stepmother, combined with the guilt she felt over her own behavior, overwhelmed her. Tears prickled behind her eyelids, but she forced herself to blink them back. She would not act like a child. She would accept, with good grace, any criticism, and agree to whatever actions were required to rectify her mistakes.

Lady Stanton suddenly laughed. "Meredith, please, you look like a schoolgirl who is afraid she will be sent to bed without supper. I assure you, the situation is not as dire as you think."

Meredith stared at the older woman in surprise, but when she saw the genuine amusement on Lady Stanton's face, the tension in her own shoulders began to ease.

"If you say so, madam." She tried to smile in return, but knew she failed miserably.

Lady Stanton's amusement faded as she shook her head. "It is I who owe you an apology, Meredith. It is truly not your fault. I was not there to watch over you, and, after all, this was your first appearance at a ball. There were bound to be some missteps."

The lines on the older woman's face became stern. "I must say, however, that I'm sadly disappointed in Lady Silverton. From what Annabel tells me, she seems to have abandoned you for the evening. I expected better from her."

Lady Stanton's warm eyes turned a wintry blue. They looked so like Silverton's that Meredith felt briefly disoriented. The same expression had been on his face when he had stalked toward her in the supper room last night. At the memory of it, a tiny shiver trickled down her spine.

She remained silent. Although she could not bring herself to defend the marchioness, the woman was mother to the man she loved, and Meredith would not criticize her.

"What I really can't understand, however," continued Lady Stanton in a musing tone of voice, "is why Silverton asked you to waltz in the first place, since he knew the patronesses of Almack's had not yet given their approval. I find his behavior completely inexplicable, and I intend to ask him why he did it when he arrives here this morning."

Meredith didn't know what she found more appalling: that Lady Stanton would ask her partner in crime why he had danced with her, or that she might have to face him so soon.

"Oh, no, my lady," she gasped, her heart beginning a panicky tattoo, "I'm sure he simply wasn't thinking. We were all conversing and standing about when the orchestra began to play the waltz. It was just an idle and spontaneous request. No harm was meant by it."

Lady Stanton's eyes narrowed suspiciously. Meredith had an overpowering desire to open the window and throw herself down into the rose bushes. A few broken bones would be infinitely preferable to the mortification she felt right now.

"I'm sure he didn't mean to hurt you, but it's quite obvious he wasn't thinking clearly," retorted Lady Stanton. "I have no wish to make you uncomfortable, my dear, but I think it necessary that my nephew explain his actions to my satisfaction."

Meredith started to protest again, then bit her tongue, willing herself to be quiet. She would only expose herself if she continued to make objections that would be ignored anyway.

"Meredith, there is no way to pose this question without

distressing you, so I will just ask. Have you developed an attachment to my nephew?"

Meredith closed her eyes. She should have known she couldn't escape Lady Stanton's keen observation, any more than she had been able to hide childhood secrets from her stepmother. Or else, she thought bitterly, her feelings for Silverton were so obvious that it was apparent to anyone who looked closely enough.

"Lady Stanton," she said, hating the tremor in her voice, "I hardly know how to answer such a question. Both Annabel and I owe Lord Silverton a tremendous debt of gratitude. His friendship means the world to us."

"Yes, yes, I know all that." Her ladyship cut her off impatiently. "You are not a child, Meredith. You know what I am asking. Have you formed an attachment to Silverton?"

If someone had put a pistol to her head, Meredith knew she still would not answer the question. She could hardly explain her chaotic feelings to herself. Besides, her foolish infatuation would never amount to anything, anyway. There was no point in discussing the situation with another soul—not Lady Stanton, not even her sister.

"My lady." She looked the other woman directly in the eye. "Annabel and I will always be grateful for your nephew's friendship."

She sealed her lips, vowing silently that she would never utter another word on the subject.

As Lady Stanton continued to examine her, her brows arched slowly up. Meredith returned her gaze with an impassive expression, determined to hold on to the last few shreds of her battered pride.

Quite unexpectedly, Lady Stanton nodded, seemingly satisfied by her answer.

"Very well, my dear, I will respect your privacy. But as the nearest thing to a mother that you have in this world, I am compelled to give you a word of advice."

"Of course, my lady," Meredith replied as she tried not to grind her back teeth.

"As a general rule, a lady should never reveal her feelings for a man until she is able to ascertain *his* feelings for her. It is the safest way to guard her own heart and to protect herself from unwelcome comment."

Although Lady Stanton looked sympathetic, Meredith wished that the imaginary person holding the pistol to her head would simply shoot her and get it over with.

"I mean this, of course, as general advice and not specifically applicable to you."

"No, of course not," Meredith sighed.

"Well, that is enough on that subject!" Lady Stanton exclaimed briskly. "As I said before, you are not to worry about last night. I will take care of it, and you may be sure that Annabel will come to no harm as a result."

"Thank you, my lady."

Meredith tried to sound appropriately grateful, but all she wanted was to flee the room as quickly as she could. If it were only possible, she would walk right out of Stanton House and keep on walking, getting as far from London and Silverton as she could.

An impatient rap sounded on the door. Her stretched nerves practically snapped at the unexpected noise.

"Enter," said Lady Stanton, looking vaguely surprised.

The door swung open and Silverton strode into the room. He approached his aunt and executed a correct but hasty bow.

"Please forgive the interruption, Aunt Georgina," he said in a clipped voice. "I told Tolliver I would show myself up."

Silverton halted in his tracks when he heard the small, stifled gasp behind him. He spun on his heel, his eyes immediately capturing hers. But Meredith ducked her head and quickly looked away.

That she still refused to meet his gaze made him both immensely frustrated and determined. Enough was enough. He had let her go without a word last night, but today he would make her see that she had no reason to avoid him.

"Stephen!"

His aunt's warning tone recalled him to his surroundings. Without realizing it, he had started to reach for Meredith. Silverton forced himself to turn back to Lady Stanton, whose features were cold with disapproval.

"Forgive me, dear Aunt, I have forgotten my manners this morning." He bent down to kiss the hand she extended.

"Good morning, Nephew. Thank you for responding so quickly to my note. I hardly thought to see you so early."

Silverton reflected on the imperious nature of his aunt's summons. He had already surmised the extent of her irritation from the coldly correct tone of her missive. Now she addressed him as nephew, something she only did when she was seriously displeased. Knowing he was in for a scolding, he only hoped that it would not take place in front of Meredith.

Not that he would blame his aunt one bit if she rang a peal over him. The recollection of his behavior at Lady Framingham's ball had kept him awake much of the night—a good part of it in his library imbibing a generous amount of brandy in the hope that it would help him sleep. That had resulted in nothing but a dull headache. He awoke this morning feeling more restless and irritable than he could ever recall.

Silverton mustered what he hoped was an ingratiating smile; he must have failed miserably, because Lady Stanton continued to scowl at him.

"Dear ma'am, you know that I am always yours to command."

She gave an uncharacteristic and grumpy hrumph, and glanced over at Meredith.

"Stephen, you may bid Miss Burnley good-morning," she ordered.

He walked slowly over to Meredith, who looked ready to escape from the room at the first opportunity. When he stopped directly in front of her, she finally lifted her head. She met his gaze with a resolute and wounded dignity that wrung his heart.

"How are you this day, Miss Burnley?" He had to struggle to keep the roughness out of his voice, because the pain in her eyes made him want to break something.

"I am well. Thank you for your concern, my lord."

Her voice was so soft and distant that he wanted to shake her and crush her in his arms all at the same time. He fleetingly touched her chin.

"I think not," he said. "You look very pale to me."

At the touch of his hand, her eyes slid away and fastened at a point somewhere over his shoulder.

"No indeed, sir," she said very formally. "I am quite well."

He dropped his hand.

"And how is Miss Annabel this morning? I hope she suffered no ill effects from the events of last evening?" The thought of Annabel and her fragile health had been one of the things keeping him awake all night.

She glanced at him, managing a small but genuine smile.

"Annabel is fine," she said. "She is quite herself today, thank God." Meredith inhaled a shaky breath and looked him directly in the eyes.

"Lord Silverton, I wanted to tell you how very sorry I am that I embarrassed you and your mother last night. There was no excuse . . ." Her voice faltered and she stumbled to a halt, obviously too humiliated to continue.

Shame clouded the burnished silver of her beautiful eyes. It nearly broke his heart.

"Miss Burnley," he exclaimed, "you must not fret so. I should apologize to you. You are innocent of any wrong, while I behaved very stupidly indeed. If you remain in this room, you will be sure to hear my aunt give me a thorough and well-deserved trimming."

At his words, the strained expression around her eyes began to ease.

"Do not refine too much on what was a distasteful but insignificant event," he assured her. "All will be well, I promise."

He silently vowed to do whatever he must to keep his promise.

"Meredith, my dear," Lady Stanton's voice gently intruded. "You may go down now and join your sister and the general."

"Yes, my lady," she replied quickly. "My lord."

She sketched a quick curtsy and fled.

He sighed as he watched her hurry from the room. It was indicative of her discomfort that she responded with such alacrity to Lady Stanton's command. Normally, Meredith would do almost anything to avoid the general's company.

He turned back to his aunt, noting the cold expression that had returned to her face.

"I won't ask you to explain yourself," she said. "There is no justification for what you did. It was selfish and irresponsible—conduct most unbecoming in the head of the family."

He didn't bother to defend himself.

"Yes, I know you regret it now," she said, waving her hand impatiently. "That is little consolation, however. Meredith and Annabel are both much too vulnerable. It is your duty to protect them, not injure them."

As far as reprimands went, he had heard much worse from her over the years. But his aunt needn't say any more, and she knew it. Silverton felt exactly as he did when he was seven years old and had pushed his sister into the lake at Belfield Abbey. He hadn't meant to hurt her, but she had almost drowned. It had taken him weeks to recover from the shame and guilt.

"My dear." His aunt's voice had softened. "You know what is best for your own life. But I must remind you that Annabel needs you."

He shook his head in exasperation.

"Aunt Georgina, has it ever occurred to you that Annabel might not want to marry me?"

"Don't be ridiculous!"

"You overestimate my charms," he replied dryly.

"I certainly do not. The girl has a great deal of admiration for you. A little more attention on your part, and I'm sure she would happily fall in love with you."

"And I'm sure she would not."

Although Silverton felt relatively certain Annabel had given her affections to Robert, he wasn't ready to reveal that to his aunt. He wasn't sure how she would react, and he suspected that the budding romance might not survive if Lady Stanton raised objections to it.

"Stephen." His aunt regarded him severely. "You can no longer afford to indulge in meaningless flirtations. This is not a game."

Silverton jerked his head up as if he had been slapped. He crossed his arms over his chest.

"I am aware of that, Aunt Georgina. I assure you, I do not take my responsibilities lightly." In spite of himself, he could not keep the chill out of his voice.

One of her eyebrows shot up as if to express disbelief. A faintly disdainful smile lifted the corners of her mouth.

"I am relieved to hear it," she said in what he privately called her queen-of-the-ruling-classes tone of voice.

He raised a mocking eyebrow in return, imitating her expression so exactly that she finally had to laugh.

"You are a dreadful boy," she exclaimed. "Now, if you are finished teasing your elders, perhaps you could turn your mind to finding a solution to this problem."

"I should be happy to do whatever you think best, Aunt Georgina. But I suspect you have already arrived at the solution yourself."

"You are correct. I believe that Lady Cowper can be of

assistance. I will send her a note immediately and call on her in the next day or so."

Silverton nodded his approval and slowly began to pace the room.

"The entire family must be seen with the girls in public," he mused. "One must never show weakness to the enemy."

Lady Stanton laughed again. "I'm sure the general would say the same. In fact, I have plans for him as well. He has agreed to take the girls driving in Hyde Park this afternoon. You know this is a remarkable concession on his part, since he despises the entire nonsense of the afternoon parade."

Silverton's mouth dropped open in disbelief.

"He did?" He shook his head. "That is extraordinary."

"Yes, I know," she agreed. "But he seems to have developed a grudging respect for Meredith. He remarked the other day that at least she wasn't a lily-livered miss."

Now it was his turn to laugh. "High praise, indeed!"

"Yes, thank God." She smiled in return. "One does get tired of the constant wrangling between the two of them. They really are too much alike."

He grinned at the image of Meredith and the general suffering each other's company as they were trotted out on display for examination by the ton. How he wished he could be there just to see the look on her expressive face.

Silverton glanced at his aunt. She seemed to be studying him very carefully, with a look that set off warning bells in his head. He swiftly composed his features into a bland expression.

"Is there anything you wish to discuss with me, Stephen? Anything of a personal nature?" Her faded but shrewd eyes probed him.

The directness of her question startled him, but he recovered quickly.

"No, Aunt. Except, of course, to discuss where you wish to present the girls in public."

Lady Stanton gave a thoroughly ladylike and dissatisfied snort.

"Have it your own way, my dear, but I would advise you to watch your step. The situation is complicated enough as it is."

He smiled blandly, refusing to take the bait. His aunt rolled her eyes at him, then stood and hurried over to her cream and gilt-edged writing desk.

"Now, as to other places to take the girls," she said, "I have been thinking on that as well. It occurs to me that an evening at the theater might be an excellent place to start."

Chapter Fifteen

Lady Stanton's plan worked perfectly.

Two days ago, the general had driven Annabel and Meredith through Hyde Park in the family's elegant landau. According to his granddaughter, he had nodded and waved regally in response to the slack-jawed reactions of those who assembled every afternoon to gossip, flirt, and, in the general's opinion, act like a flock of bird-witted nincompoops.

Annabel had doubled over with laughter when describing to Silverton the pained expression on Mrs. Drummond-Burrell's face when the Stanton carriage drew up next to hers. The general had genially inquired after the proud lady's health and then made a point of introducing Meredith and Annabel to her as if the events at Lady Framingham's ball had never occurred.

Mrs. Drummond-Burrell had returned a brief but icily correct acknowledgment. As Lady Stanton had predicted, she could not bring herself to publicly cut one of her oldest friends, a distinguished military man who also happened to be descended from one of the most respected families in the kingdom. Mrs. Drummond-Burrell might be high in the instep, but the general was higher.

Silverton was now charged with executing the next part of

the plan. Annabel and Meredith were to be seen at a variety of social events, and the more public those events, the better. When the ton realized that both General Stanton and Silverton stood behind the Burnley sisters, the gossipmongers would grow bored and begin to seek more interesting game.

Lady Stanton had decided that she and Silverton should take Annabel and Meredith to an evening of theater at Drury Lane. No venue was more suited to a public display of familial unity and to illustrate to the fashionable world a casual disregard for mean-spirited gossip.

"You see, girls," Lady Stanton explained as they rode to Drury Lane in Silverton's town coach, "we must be above such pretension and petty jealousies. There is no family in the ton with a lineage as ancient and proud as the Stantons. If the general is willing to acknowledge Meredith, then that should be an end to the matter. Those who slight either of you shall no longer be welcome at Stanton House."

Silverton handed the ladies down from the carriage and escorted them through the melee in the brilliantly lit lobby to the comparative quiet of his box.

The play that evening was Shakespeare, although Silverton doubted anyone could hear a word over the din of the crowd. The theater was a riot of activity as fruit sellers hawked their wares, footmen carried notes back and forth between genteel matrons, and dandies in the pit flirted with high flyers renting boxes near the stage in the hopes of attracting business.

Mrs. Stanton, with Robert and Sophia, joined them at the first interval. The ladies engaged in a flurry of greetings and soft kisses before organizing themselves in the luxurious but confined space.

"Do forgive us for being late, Grandmamma," Robert apologized. "Sophia kept us waiting forever while she finished reading some blasted book! Can you imagine preferring some moldy old history to an evening at the theater?"

"But Robert," Sophia replied with an innocent look, "it was

a history of the fall of the Roman Empire, and I was just getting to the good part."

Robert grimaced at Sophia, Annabel giggled, and Mrs. Stanton gently tut-tutted her son for teasing his sister so unmercifully.

Silverton smiled indulgently at his young cousins. After an uncomfortable few days, he felt remarkably content as he watched his family settle in around him. Mrs. Stanton chattered amicably to Lady Stanton, who listened with her usual quiet dignity. Robert tried his best to be charming and sophisticated in his ongoing attempt to impress Annabel, and Sophia, as always, was ready to be interested in whatever transpired around her.

Most importantly, he was sitting next to Meredith. It had taken some masterful arranging on his part to seat the group to his satisfaction. Now that all was composed to his liking, he prepared to focus his undivided attention on her.

Silverton had spent an inordinate amount of time these last few days thinking about her. His desire for Meredith's company had become a compulsion, and he knew that ought to worry him. It went far beyond physical attraction, although that was fierce enough.

The problem—as he saw it—was that he genuinely liked her.

Liked her! He mocked himself for using such an insipid term. Obsessed with her was a good deal more accurate. He shook his head, wondering how he had gotten himself into this state.

The state of matrimony.

The words seemed to pop into his head out of nowhere. He glanced uneasily around the box, almost afraid that he had spoken the words out loud.

If he were honest, though, he would have to admit the thought had been lurking just beneath the surface for several days. Now that he no longer needed to worry about Annabel— careful observation had convinced him that she and Robert were smitten with each other—he could afford to ponder the very pleasing idea of Meredith as his wife.

The thought of his family's reaction, however, was not so pleasing. His mother would go into hysterics, and the general, despite his grudging respect for Meredith, most certainly would not approve of her as the next Marchioness of Silverton.

Aunt Georgina, however, was another matter entirely. She had made it very apparent the other day she suspected him of flirting with Meredith, and had obviously felt protective toward her. Silverton suspected that as long as Annabel was safely bestowed in a suitable marriage, his aunt would not object to his taking Meredith as a bride. In fact, Lady Stanton could be a formidable bulwark against the censorious reactions of the ton if he did decide to pursue what his social equals would surely consider a misalliance.

He gave himself a mental shake, acknowledging that he was leaping much too quickly into an uncertain future. Nothing could happen until Annabel and Robert were married, so he needed to do everything in his power to encourage their budding courtship.

For now, though, he would push all thoughts of the future to one side and enjoy the evening's entertainment. Shifting slightly in his seat, Silverton angled his body so that he could more easily observe the beautiful young woman sitting next to him.

Meredith looked good enough to eat in the lacy, peach-colored confection that draped her luscious figure. The neckline of her gown gently curved to reveal the swell of her generous breasts, and the tiny, lace-trimmed sleeves accentuated the creamy slopes of her white shoulders and slender arms.

He admired those breasts for a few moments until he noticed they were rising and falling much too quickly, as if she were breathing in a shallow and rapid manner. Surprised, Silverton examined her face, which was very pale. Her right hand gripped the railing of the box so tightly her glove looked like it might tear along the seam.

Glancing around the box, he made sure the others were occupied with their own conversations. He covered her slender hand with his and addressed her in a low voice.

"Is something wrong, Miss Burnley?"

She gasped in surprise and jerked her hand out from under his. "No, no, I'm fine," she blurted out, but the slight tremor in her voice betrayed her.

"Come now, Miss Burnley," he chided with gentle amusement, "you look as unhappy as Robert does when he is forced to spend the entire day with his grandfather. I know very well that something is wrong."

She cast him a troubled glance before turning her eyes to stare into the pit. He leaned slightly forward, draping his arm casually along the back of her chair. She stiffened and blushed an enchanting shade of pink, obviously disconcerted by the feel of his arm so close to her bare shoulders and neck.

"You know you can count me as one of your most devoted friends," he said softly. "Can't you tell me what bothers you? Perhaps I may be able to correct it."

He was riveted by the way she gently chewed on her lower lip as she pondered his words. Her full, cherry-ripe mouth tempted him almost beyond reason. He waited patiently, however, knowing that if he said or did anything more she would withdraw behind her cool, proper façade.

Meredith finally let out a small sigh and met his gaze.

"You will think I'm foolish, sir, but I'm generally not fond of crowds," she admitted, making a small gesture to indicate all the people who filled the theater to bursting. "And all the noise they make, it's, well, very . . . noisy."

Her voice trailed off and she closed her eyes briefly, as if to block out the pandemonium swirling about them.

Silverton felt jolted by an awareness of his surroundings and how they must appear to her, a young woman whose entire life had been spent in near seclusion in the country. He became acutely aware of the heat, and how thick the air was with competing and almost overwhelming odors. The scent of heavy perfume, snuff, and wax candles barely masked the strong smells of sweat and alcohol that emanated from the galleries and pit. The theater shimmered, brightly lit by hundreds of dripping candles casting so much light that the patrons were as exposed as the performers on the stage. The restless movements and excited voices of the crowd ebbed and swelled, but were never less than a dull roar.

It was really quite appalling, he thought, surprised he had never noticed it before. No wonder Meredith looked like she wanted to bolt out the door.

As he studied the sensitive woman sitting beside him, the noise and turmoil faded away, just as it had the night of the ball when he had swept her into his arms. Silverton became almost painfully aware of her, and of how much he wanted to feel her warm, sweet body against his.

She suddenly looked at him, her eyes as beautiful and sad as a winter twilight. Those eyes seemed to capture and possess his soul, and he felt consumed with an insatiable need to possess her in return.

A loud laugh from the adjoining box roused him from his dreamlike state, and the heat and noise flowed back in a rush. Silverton forced himself to smile as he briefly pressed her hands. Releasing her, he picked up his quizzing glass and turned a critical eye on the mob below them.

"Well," he drawled in a sardonic voice, "no sane person could blame you for disliking this particular crowd. A more ill-favored set of mushrooms and toadies I have never seen in my life."

Silverton inspected the crowd disdainfully through his glass. Out of the corner of his eye, he saw a tiny smile begin to form on Meredith's lips.

"And the din they make," he continued in exaggerated tones of disgust, "is enough to drive a saint into a frenzy."

He then spent the rest of the interval identifying various members of the crowd, interspersing his commentary with pointed remarks on his subjects' morals, manners, and dress. He managed to make her laugh twice, although she protested each time that he was encouraging her to act as rudely as everyone else.

Diverted by his observations, Meredith gradually relaxed. When the actors returned to the stage she watched the play attentively and with, he thought, some appreciation.

He couldn't help noticing, though, the numerous stares and pointed gestures directed at her and Annabel from the other boxes. The gossipmongers were making no secret of their interest in them, and the carefully rigid look on Meredith's face told him that she felt their scrutiny, too.

At the next interval, many visitors came to their box. While all were friendly to Annabel, several ladies indicated a subtle disapproval of Meredith by barely acknowledging her presence. Silverton took note of the carefully blank expression on Meredith's pale face as she listened politely to Mrs. Stanton's chatter. Those who didn't know her would think nothing amiss, but he knew how much it cost her to sit so quietly.

Moving across the box to his aunt, he stooped to murmur a few words in her ear. Lady Stanton glanced at Meredith and then nodded her head. She leaned across Annabel to address Mrs. Stanton.

"Agnes, my dear," she said, smoothly interrupting her sister-in-law, "I am feeling quite fatigued. Silverton has graciously offered to escort me home. You may stay, of course, but if anyone wishes to go I shall be happy to drop them on the way."

"Oh my," cried Mrs. Stanton, "of course you must go if you are tired. But I'm sure the young people are having much too good a time to leave. After all, Annabel and Meredith have never been to the theater before."

Sophia, Robert, and Annabel all cast pleading eyes in their grandmother's direction.

"Of course the children must stay." Lady Stanton smiled graciously at them. "I would not dream of ruining their fun."

She looked at Meredith, who was already reaching for the wrap cast over the back of her chair.

"Well, Meredith, will you stay to enjoy the rest of the entertainment, or have you had enough merriment for the evening?"

Silverton almost laughed out loud at the look of dismay on Meredith's face at the suggestion she might wish to stay.

"Thank you, my lady," she said, choking out a polite reply. "I think I've had enough fun for the evening."

Meredith glided past Silverton, casting him a grateful smile as she stepped out of the box. He gave her a bow and a roguish wink in return, pleased to see her eyes widen in surprise as a delicate flush bloomed across her cheeks. She had developed the most charming habit of blushing whenever he embarrassed her, which seemed to be quite often.

She ducked her head, quickly following Lady Stanton along the corridor and down the staircase to the waiting carriages. He prowled closely behind, admiring the sensual sway of her hips and the graceful turn of her head as she bent to listen to something his aunt said to her.

Unfortunately, he was also aware of the rude stares and muttered remarks that followed in Meredith's wake as she passed by the throngs clustered outside the boxes and in the lobby.

Silverton felt his anger grow as he watched the casual display of cruelty, and he had to force himself to plaster a genial smile on his face as he returned the greetings of various acquaintances. Overtaken by a fierce sense of possessiveness, he realized he would like to do a great deal more than just protect Meredith from the harpies of the ton. But for now, all he could do was shield her as best he could from idle gossip.

It nagged at him that he had not yet had the chance to make a full apology to her for his actions at the ball. He felt a driving need to be alone with her—to see if she had really forgiven him. She had been so guarded in his presence these last few days that he found it difficult to read her emotions. And he sorely missed the look of sweet longing that used to shine in her eyes whenever she gazed at him.

Silverton had an almost irrepressible urge to grab Meredith and make her look at him, to force her to see how much he wanted her. But her eyes were fixed firmly ahead as she exited out the front doors and followed Lady Stanton to the carriage.

He stood quietly on the pavement, pondering his next gambit in this increasingly complicated and serious game. It was obvious that Meredith was determined to ignore him as much as possible, at least in public. In private, he thought, it might be a different matter altogether.

He laughed softly to himself, then gave the coachman a tersely worded order before leaping up into the carriage. Meredith glanced briefly at him before looking out the window, her face obscured by shadows in the flickering light of the coach lanterns. Silverton watched her in silence, content to bide his time.

She didn't know it, but he was about to put his next move into play.

Chapter Sixteen

Waves of sensation rippled down Meredith's spine, a restless heat that pooled like honey in the secret places of her body. All was velvet and charged silence in the darkened coach as it rolled through the deserted streets of Mayfair. Her palms grew damp with anxious awareness of the man seated opposite her, his presence filling the unbearably intimate space until she could hardly draw a breath.

The marquess, though, seemed to be his usual cool and confident self. He lounged gracefully on the padded bench, apparently unmoved by either the events of the evening or their conversation during the play.

Meredith, however, could barely sit still whenever she thought about that electrifying moment when his gaze had penetrated deep into her soul. As far as she was concerned, her escape from the theater had not come a moment too soon.

But she had almost gasped out loud when the carriage had pulled up first at Stanton House, and Silverton had quickly jumped down to assist his aunt to alight. Lady Stanton had looked momentarily stunned, but quickly recovered. She had bestowed a soft kiss on Meredith's cheek and allowed her nephew to hand her to the pavement.

Her ladyship and Silverton had exchanged a few terse

words, but Meredith had not been able to hear them. After escorting his aunt to the door of Stanton House, Silverton had returned to the carriage and leapt inside. He had then given her a slow, hot smile that wreaked havoc on her nerves.

Now all she wanted to do was get away from him, and as soon as possible.

Although separated by mere inches, she refused to look at him. But he was so big, and he radiated a seductive power in the small space; she could hear the siren call of his masculine sensuality in every part of her body. Meredith desperately fought the urge to crawl into his lap and curl herself around him, burrowing her face in his neck and inhaling the healthy male scent that affected her so completely.

Inwardly cursing her lack of self-control, she lectured herself for the hundredth time that a lady should be well able to control her physical passions. Unfortunately, her little scold failed to work, which didn't surprise her, because it hadn't worked all the other times, either.

She breathed a heartfelt sigh of relief as they slowed to a halt, the groomsman leaping from his perch to pull down the step. Silverton turned to help her, his long fingers wrapping themselves around her hand in a steady grip.

Meredith gulped, unable to repress a sudden image of that large hand curving over her breast. The very idea of that possession caused the heat in her belly and legs to flare up more hotly than ever before. She pulled her hand away, covering her confusion by rummaging in her reticule for the key to the front door.

After climbing the steps, Meredith spun awkwardly around and gave him her brightest smile. "Thank you, my lord, for seeing me safely home. Please accept my thanks for a pleasant evening."

Silverton ignored her words as he frowned at the key in her hand.

"Why don't you simply knock on the door?" he demanded. "Surely the footman is waiting up for you?"

Meredith almost groaned as she realized Silverton would surely be displeased that she had given Peter the night off.

Their new footman was a burly young man, seconded from the Silverton mansion with clear orders to provide security for their small household. Meredith hated to admit it but Peter's bulky presence was a comfort, even though it chafed her to be in Silverton's debt.

"Since we were to be out most of the evening, I told Peter and the other servants they need not wait up for us," she explained patiently. "I knew that you or Mr. Stanton would be escorting us home."

Silverton's mouth thinned with displeasure. Without saying a word he plucked the key out of her hand, reached past her, and opened the front door.

"Thank you, my lord," she said, trying to control the irritation in her voice. Meredith was about to bid him good-night when put his hand on her waist and gently pushed her through the door, following closely behind.

"Lord Silverton," Meredith protested, "I am grateful for your protection but there is really no need for you to come in. I will wait up for Annabel, I assure you."

He coolly removed his hat and stripped off his gloves, tossing them on the table by the door.

"And I assure *you*, Miss Burnley, there is every need to see you safely inside your house." He bent his golden head close to hers, and his voice dropped almost to a whisper. "I thought we had reached an agreement about this."

Meredith took a hasty step back, all too aware of the force of her attraction for him in the close quarters of the small hallway.

"Yes, well, be that as it may," she stammered, "all is well now, and I will bid you good-night."

"Not yet," Silverton said. "I need to talk with you."

"Now?" she questioned faintly. The thought of being alone

with him in the dark and silent house was almost more than she could bear.

"Now," he responded firmly.

An enigmatic smile played around the corners of his mouth, and the look on his face caused her to turn on her heel and walk to the drawing room with a hasty step. He strolled leisurely after her, but she had the oddest feeling that a wild beast stalked her footsteps. It did nothing to calm her disordered state of nerves.

This late at night, the drawing room was only dimly lit with a banked fire and a single candle under a lamp. She used the taper to light a branch of candles, refusing to look at Silverton until she had done so. He leaned casually against the doorframe, his muscular arms straining the material of his coat as he crossed them over his chest. The intensity of his gaze as his eyes followed her about the room caused her scalp to prickle with a strange mixture of apprehension and excitement.

Straightening her spine, Meredith took refuge in the self-control her stepmother had drummed into her so many years ago. No matter what, she would not allow him to see how greatly he affected her.

"Yes, my lord? What is it you wish to discuss with me?" Her voice sounded wary, even to her own ears.

Silverton pushed away from the door. Crossing to her, he tipped her chin up with his hand and forced her to look directly into his eyes.

The shock of his touch streaked through her like a bolt of summer lightning. Under his steady scrutiny, her cheeks burned with heat.

"My dear girl, you must think me a perfect ogre." His voice was very soft, and his hand caressed her chin for a moment before he let her go. "I simply wanted to apologize for my inappropriate behavior the other night at Lady Framingham's ball. I'm not sure you understand how sorry I am. It was my fault that you and Annabel were exposed in so painful a manner, and I beg you most sincerely to forgive me."

Meredith stared back, stunned that a man like him would feel it necessary to apologize for his actions. In her experience noblemen rarely apologized, especially to someone from a lower social standing.

"Lord Silverton," she exclaimed earnestly, "there is nothing to forgive. My foolishness was entirely to blame for the whole incident. I cannot even plead ignorance as an excuse, since Lady Stanton gave Annabel and me very clear instructions regarding our conduct. It was my fault entirely, and I regret that I have caused such inconvenience and trouble to you and your aunt."

Silverton shook his head. He didn't smile, but his eyes gleamed with a rueful amusement.

"I should have known you would take all the blame on yourself. Miss Burnley, I have never met anyone with such an exaggerated sense of responsibility. It would be refreshing if it were not so alarming."

Much to her surprise, he laughed.

"If only the other members of the ton shared your sense of selflessness. Now *that* would be truly radical. Of course, if such a revolution were to occur, the nobility wouldn't know what to do with itself, since there would be nothing to gossip about and no one to insult. I don't think the Upper Ten Thousand could survive the shock."

Meredith frowned, unable to share in his sardonic amusement. She could only feel anger and resentment as she recalled the whispered cruelties and mocking looks of the last few days. She turned from him, swallowing the bitter words that sprang to her lips.

"You must not be so hurt, Miss Burnley," he added softly. "Believe me, those who have wounded you are not worthy of your notice."

"Hurt!" she cried as she jerked stiffly around to glare at him. "I am not hurt. I am . . . furious!"

She began to pace around the room. "How dare they treat my sister that way? She is the sweetest, most innocent creature that ever lived!"

Silverton watched impassively as she pivoted on her heel to cross the room again.

"I don't understand how you can bear such horrible people. They are petty, small-minded, and cruel!" Meredith flung the words at him, angry that he could be so dismissive of her pain. "They believe their aimless, selfish lives actually mean something, are of value to the rest of us. I see no evidence of kindness or compassion—even tolerance would do—but they lack that quality as well! Sometimes I think that I would like to . . ."

She stumbled to a halt, suddenly horrified by the words she had almost blurted out.

"Like to kill them?" Silverton inquired genially.

Meredith clapped her hand over her mouth, humiliated by her outrageous display of temper. Why did she find it so difficult to control herself when she was with him? All night long she had been tossed on a sea of turbulent emotions. A few moments ago she only wanted to wrap her arms around his neck and cover his cynical mouth with her lips, and now she lashed out at him like a madwoman.

Silverton, however, did not appear the least bit put out by her conduct.

"My dear girl, you must not be embarrassed on my account. I share your contempt for the privileged classes but must, alas, count myself as one of them. It's my hope that when you get to know some of us better, you will not judge us so harshly. Surely we must have a few redeeming qualities. Perhaps if you look hard enough you will find them."

He made no attempt to disguise the laughter in his voice.

Meredith blinked away angry tears, wishing that she were anywhere but here, exposed so completely to his amused regard.

She hesitantly met his eyes, miserably aware of the social and emotional distance between them. No matter how much she yearned for it, she could never be comfortable in his world, nor be the kind of woman he could possibly desire.

Besides, she remembered with a guilty start, she still didn't know what he intended for Annabel. Why was she even talking to him like this? He must think her a complete hoyden.

"I beg your pardon, my lord," she managed to get past the lump in her throat. "You must truly be shocked by my outburst. You know the last few days have been very taxing, which can be my only excuse."

When he didn't answer her, Meredith couldn't hold back a sigh. "Please forgive me. I know how inappropriate it is for me to indulge in such strong displays of emotion."

Silverton laughed softly. "Ah, Miss Burnley," he murmured, his voice whispering like silk across her skin, "sometimes a strong display of emotion is precisely what the situation calls for."

He closed the distance between them and slid a hand up her arm to caress the bare skin of her shoulder. Tiny shocks sparkled along the path traced by his fingers. Meredith looked up into his eyes, and this time she did gasp, completely undone by what she saw in them.

He looked ready to devour her, his gaze so incredibly fiery as it roamed over her face and breasts that her dazed mind imagined it might actually leave a mark on her flesh. She no longer harbored any doubts that he wanted her, and wanted her very badly.

Meredith pressed cold hands to her flaming cheeks, stepping quickly away and stumbling over to the fireplace. She rested her forehead against the cool, marble mantelpiece.

"No, no, you don't understand," she said in a tremulous voice. "What I feel is . . . I can't . . ."

She fell silent. Never had she been so unsure of herself, so trapped in a bewildering tangle of emotions. His desire stunned and frightened her, precisely because she longed for it more than anything else in the world. But how could they ever bridge their differences—differences arising from so many things she couldn't even begin to count them.

And how could she betray Annabel, robbing her sister of Silverton's protection when she needed it most?

He crossed the room to stand beside her and with a light touch on her shoulder turned her to face him. His long fingers stroked her cheek, gently urging her to meet his gaze.

She had to fight against an overwhelming desire to nuzzle her cheek into the warmth of his big hand. He made her feel so vulnerable, and she was both strangely thrilled and appalled by her impulse to surrender to him.

"What is it, Meredith?" His voice was a soft growl that sent shivers down her spine. "What are you afraid of?"

She refused to look at him, shaking her head against his hand, unable to voice her guilt and confusion.

"Tell me," he whispered as he brushed his cool lips against her burning face.

She jumped back, stung by the gentle kiss.

"No," she cried. "You mustn't!"

To her surprise, he seemed more annoyed by her reaction than anything else. His eyes narrowed suspiciously on her.

"Meredith, tell me what troubles you."

She recognized an order when she heard one. His perfect face, so often a mask of casual indifference, blazed with a potent combination of desire and anger, so intense it made the hair stand up on the nape of her neck.

"It's Annabel," she blurted out. "I know Lady Stanton wishes you to marry her—to keep her safe. You must not ask me to stand in her way! I could never hurt Annabel like that."

He stared at her in disbelief and then shook his head, exasperation replacing anger on his features.

"Sweetheart, your sister doesn't want to marry me. In fact," he said wryly, "I think she would find the whole idea revolting."

"But you know she must marry, and soon." Meredith literally wrung her hands, desperate for him to understand what was almost impossible for her to explain.

"She will, darling, I promise," he soothed, as his hand returned to her shoulder. "No harm will come to her. Please believe me."

"But . . ."

"No, Meredith, no more questions." His other hand wound around her waist, and he slowly but inexorably pulled her to him.

Meredith gave a breathless laugh, shivering as a wave of relief and shock washed through her. As she looked into Silverton's ice blue gaze she could swear that his eyes glittered—actually glittered—just like frost on a bright winter's day. He mesmerized her, and she tumbled, heart and soul, into his light.

His lips curved in a knowing smile as he lowered his head toward her mouth. Meredith knew she should turn away, step back from the grip around her waist—do something. But she couldn't move, couldn't deny the yearning to give in to his hunger, couldn't help wanting to appease her own.

And so she stood captive to his slow advance. As his mouth met hers, her eyelids fluttered shut as if her mind had to block out anything that might distract from his touch. At first, his lips gently brushed her, barely kissing the soft bow of her mouth, just feathering the edges of her lips. Then his kiss grew firm, pressing insistently as his tongue slid along her lower lip.

How could something so soft be so hard? Tremors coursed through her body, down her legs, and she was forced to grab his waist to keep from staggering. His powerful arms wrapped around her, his hands on her back pulling her securely against him and more deeply into the kiss.

His tongue felt luscious! It glided over her lips, stroking and coaxing in a gentle but determined manner. Suddenly, Silverton nipped her lower lip, and when she gasped in surprise he surged in, stroking the inside of her mouth and tangling with her tongue. Her heart hammered in her chest, and her limbs turned heavy and oddly weak.

Meredith was stunned. Some small part of her mind registered astonishment that so intimate an act could be so pleasurable. She had a fleeting memory of her cousin Jacob thrusting his thick, wet tongue into her mouth when she was fourteen. It had disgusted her, and she'd kicked him hard in the shins.

Silverton's kiss was velvet, dark, and smoky, and Meredith had not the slightest desire to kick him in the shins.

His long fingers were stroking, moving down her waist and hips, gently urging her body flush against his.

All at once, Meredith felt as if she were going up in flames. Consigning any unpleasant memories to the dustbin of history, she slid her arms around his neck and rose up on her toes, eager to increase the delicious pressure of his lips against her mouth.

Unexpectedly, Silverton lifted his head, and the sudden withdrawal wrenched a whimper of protest from her lips. He cocked his head, apparently listening to something out in the hallway.

As Meredith slowly came back to herself, she realized that she had curled herself around him, still sheltering in his possessive embrace. She finally heard what he did; a light step on the stairs as someone descended toward the drawing room. Cursing softly under his breath, Silverton carefully set her away from him. She stumbled slightly, and he put a hand under her elbow to steady her.

The footsteps came down the hall, and a moment later Miss Noyes entered the room, still dressed but with a large and ridiculously overtrimmed sleeping cap on her head.

"Oh, Lord Silverton!" she exclaimed, her eyes widening in surprise. "I thought I heard voices and assumed the girls had returned from the theater." She cast a doubtful glance between the two of them. "I hope I am not interrupting a private conversation."

Meredith was annoyed to see that Silverton had completely recovered himself, bowing gracefully to Miss Noyes as if nothing momentous had just happened.

"Not at all, my dear lady," he said with an engaging smile. "I was just seeing Miss Burnley safely inside. Robert and his mother will be escorting Annabel home shortly."

"Miss Burnley," he said, turning back to her, "I will bid you good-night."

Meredith found it a bit difficult to breathe, so she decided it best to say nothing at all. She dropped a brief curtsy, but he gently grasped her hand and carried it to his lips. He lingered there for a second or two longer than was absolutely necessary, which made her breath come in even shorter gasps. As he straightened up, she could see the devilish glint of amusement had returned to his eyes.

With a nod of the head, he strode from the room, and a few seconds later they heard the front door click behind him.

"Well," said Miss Noyes, stifling a yawn, "you must tell me all about it in the morning. I'll just go lock the door before I go back up to my bed."

As she turned to leave the room, she paused and looked searchingly at Meredith.

"Are you sure you're feeling well, my dear?" Miss Noyes asked anxiously. "You seem quite flushed and overheated. I do hope you have not caught something at the theater. Such a crowded place cannot be healthy!"

"Dear me, no." Meredith tried for a hearty voice. "I'm sure it's nothing that a good-night's sleep won't put to rest."

She repressed an exasperated sigh, knowing without a shadow of a doubt that the memory of Silverton's kiss would keep her awake for many nights to come.

Chapter Seventeen

Meredith huffed out a breath of relief as the Stanton carriage pulled away from the front step of the townhouse. She could hardly believe it, but Annabel was finally on her way to Almack's with her grandmother.

"Oh my goodness, Miss Burnley," exclaimed Miss Noyes, who stood beside her at the drawing room window. "Annabel looked just like an angel, did she not?"

"She did, indeed," Meredith said with a smile.

Annabel had truly been a vision in a simple but elegant gown of white mull covered with silver tinsel embroidery. The curving neckline of the wrapped bodice and the gauzy puffed sleeves were the perfect complements to Annabel's youthful beauty. Meredith had little doubt the girl would be a smashing success at Almack's.

"It was so romantic," Miss Noyes sighed dramatically. "Mr. Stanton was rendered speechless by her charms."

Meredith laughed. "Dumbfounded, more like it."

Robert had come upstairs to fetch Annabel, practically skidding to a halt when he first laid eyes on her. Silverton was right about Robert's infatuation with his cousin. Meredith needed to think about that and whether it was a positive development. For tonight, though, she could put her worries aside and enjoy the triumph of Annabel's formal debut into polite society.

As she watched the carriage roll away down the street, Meredith couldn't help but feel a pang of regret that she would miss her sister's debut. In spite of her protestations to the contrary, she did feel lonely, and more than a bit like Cinderella. But Meredith knew that even though she had found her Prince Charming, there was little chance the glass slipper would fit on her foot.

She plucked her sewing from her workbasket, determined to be satisfied with a quiet evening beside her own hearth. Now that the scandal resulting from her ill-fated waltz had faded, she really had no cause for complaint. All in all, they were very comfortably established, and Annabel seemed to be adapting to her new life extremely well. Meredith ought to be happy to spend the evening at home instead of traipsing about a crowded and overheated ballroom.

She tried not to think about the real reason she was so restless, but that grew harder with every passing minute.

Almost a week had passed since the night Silverton kissed her. He had not been at Lady Aldring's dinner party three nights ago, though she was certain he had been invited. Then, after the vouchers for Almack's arrived the next morning, she and Annabel were launched into a flurry of activity. There had been no time for visiting Stanton House as they dashed from one shop to the next in a mad rush to prepare for Annabel's debut.

Now Meredith finally had time to catch her breath and think. And all she could think about was Silverton. How wonderful his strong arms had felt about her. How gloriously intoxicating his mouth had felt on her lips. For the last several nights she had awakened from muddled dreams that left her embarrassed and confused. Dreams about him that involved intertwined, naked limbs, rumpled sheets, and his hot mouth trailing wet kisses all over her body.

Meredith had been so flustered by the parade of images that each night she lit a branch of candles and ruthlessly turned her attention to an improving book. One night she had tried Milton, and another Richardson. Neither had proved salutary, since all she could think about—despite her best efforts—were Silverton's intense blue eyes and how the heat in them made her soften like warm butter.

"Excuse me, Miss Burnley."

Meredith jumped when Miss Noyes's voice yanked her out of her evocative daydream. She smiled weakly at the little governess and rearranged her work materials to cover her guilty start.

"No, excuse me, my dear ma'am," she replied. "My wits must be wandering tonight."

"Well, it is no wonder," Miss Noyes staunchly defended. "You have been working your fingers to the bone to prepare Annabel for this momentous event. Perhaps you should retire early this evening. In fact . . ." She paused, looking anxiously at Meredith.

"My dear Miss Noyes," she responded instantly, "you look exhausted. Please go to bed. I shall be fine. There is quite a bit of needlework to go through, and if that fails to hold my attention I can always work on my painting."

"Are you absolutely sure?"

"Absolutely." Truthfully, Meredith would rather be alone than make labored conversation with Miss Noyes for the rest of the evening.

"Well then, I'll bid you good-night, Miss Burnley." Miss Noyes bustled out in a flutter of skirts and tatting material.

The oak and gilt-bronzed clock on the mantel ticked the minutes slowly by as Meredith applied herself to her sewing. She sternly bid her restless mind to cease pining for Silverton or worrying about Annabel's progress at Almack's.

It took a great deal of discipline, but she finally completed the set of table linens she had been stitching for several weeks. She folded the material and stood, pressing her fists into her back to ease the strain from sitting for so long.

Meredith began to wonder if she should go to bed herself, when a loud knock at the door made her start with surprise. Who could be calling this late at night? She hurried to the small pier glass hanging in the corner, smoothed her hair and straightened her wrinkled skirts. A masculine voice rumbled in the hallway, followed by a quiet knock on the door.

"Enter!" she called.

The door swung open and their footman stood on the threshold.

"Your cousin, Mr. Jacob Burnley, to see you, miss," announced Peter, his voice heavy with wariness.

Her heart dropped to her feet. She had forgotten about Jacob's promised visit. Had it already been three weeks since that horrible scene with her uncle? She didn't feel prepared to face her cousin just yet, especially alone, but it appeared she had no choice.

Taking a deep breath, Meredith nodded her head at the burly footman.

"Thank you, Peter. You may let my cousin in."

"Yes, miss."

Peter stood aside, glowering fiercely as Jacob strode into the room. The footman's demeanor radiated suspicion, and Meredith was suddenly very thankful that Silverton had insisted on his presence.

"All right, Peter." She smiled at the young man. "You may go. I'll call if I need you."

For a long moment, Meredith and Jacob eyed each other.

"Hello, Jacob," she finally managed in a polite voice. "It's good to see you."

Her cousin glared at her, his face set in rigid lines.

"Is it?" he demanded. "Is that why you didn't bother to write me, even though I asked you to?"

He stood much too close, looming over her in an intimidating manner. She masked her confusion by stepping away and stacking her needlework neatly in her basket.

"Would you like some tea?" she asked in a calm voice. Meredith had no intention of offering him a brandy, since she could already smell alcohol on his breath.

Jacob muttered a curse. "No, Meredith, I do not want any bloody tea! I want you to come to your senses and return home where you belong."

He began to stalk her across the room, forcing her to retreat behind the sofa.

"My home is with Annabel," she replied, grateful to hear the steadiness in her own voice. "As long as your father continues to threaten her, we will stay in London under the protection of Annabel's grandparents."

Meredith folded her arms and stared back at him, determined to appear strong. Jacob made an impatient gesture with his hand.

"Do you take me for a fool? I would not have come here if I thought Annabel had anything to fear from my father," he retorted. His eyes flickered over her body. The look on his face changed from one of irritation to something much more disturbing.

"You should be grateful to me, Meredith. Father has allowed me to decide what to do about Annabel." He continued his slow stalk around the sofa. "There is no reason to be afraid. I'm sure we can come to an agreement on what is best for everyone."

She started to move away, but his hand shot out and grabbed her wrist. Meredith gasped as he began to draw her closer.

"Don't you want to come home, my girl?" His voice had dropped to a husky growl. "You must miss Swallow Hill. I know how much you love it in the springtime."

The thought crossed Meredith's mind that her cousin really didn't know her at all if he believed she liked anything about spring. But that brief reflection dissipated when he captured her other hand and pulled her toward him.

"I . . . we are very content here in London," she stammered as she tried to wrestle her hands from his grasp.

Jacob laughed contemptuously. "That's hard to believe. You will never be accepted by the fine folk of the ton, and you know it. In their eyes, you're nothing but a shopgirl—fit only to be a fancy piece for their men, not a wife."

His words infuriated her. She fruitlessly yanked her hands away from him again before staring sullenly at the floor.

"Well, well," Jacob said softly, "sits the wind in that quarter, does it? The swells have already let you know you're not good enough for their sons, eh? What a surprise. Did you really think they would?"

Bitterness wrapped itself around her heart, his words resurrecting the ugly memories of Lady Framingham's ball and its painful aftermath. Meredith barely noticed when Jacob slowly pulled her against his chest.

"They don't want you." His mouth brushed against her ear, sending a cold shiver down her spine. "They'll never want you, and you'll never be happy here. But I want you and I understand you—I always have. I know exactly what you need."

Ice water seeped through her veins, and his words pressed on her so heavily she could hardly breathe.

"Enough is enough, my girl," he whispered. "Time to come home." Quite suddenly, he reached up into her hair and pulled her head back, his lips pushing wetly against her mouth.

His touch, so different from Silverton's, shattered her paralysis and she pushed back with all her might. Wrenching an arm free, she slapped his face as hard as she could. Her fingers stung with the force of the blow.

Jacob fell back, stunned for a second, but then his face blackened with rage. Despite his momentary shock, he didn't lose his iron grip on her other wrist. He shifted his hands to her upper arms, clutching her in a punishing hold.

"You'll be sorry for that, Cousin," he snarled.

She struggled to break away but was powerless against his

brute strength. Meredith opened her mouth to scream just as he fastened his lips to hers, trying to force his thick tongue into her mouth. A wave of nausea swept through her and, for a terrible moment, her vision blurred with panic.

As she fought back, trying to free herself, she heard the door open and a firm bootstep cross the room. Jacob was pulled away from her body so forcefully that she staggered and almost fell.

Meredith looked up just as Silverton delivered a powerful blow to Jacob's face, driving her cousin to his knees. The marquess glanced over his shoulder at her, his eyes shimmering with a cold light she had never seen before.

"Are you all right?" His voice sounded as hard as iron, but his hand was gentle on her arm.

Meredith nodded, unable to speak. Carefully setting her out of harm's way, Silverton turned back to her cousin, who was dragging himself up off the floor.

Jacob's nose bled profusely. He pulled a handkerchief out of his pocket and swiped his face, smearing blood across his mottled cheeks.

"I'll kill you, you bastard," he rasped.

"I should be interested to see you try," Silverton responded softly, his hands clenching once more into fists.

Meredith came to life, knowing that she had to intervene before the two men tore each other apart.

"Jacob!" she cried. "You will do nothing of the sort."

Her cousin ignored her, twisting his huge body into a fighter's crouch as he advanced toward Silverton.

Meredith stepped between the two men, raising her hands imperiously in the air.

"Stop!" she commanded Jacob. "There are four here, and only one of you. If you do not leave my house immediately, I will call the night watch and have you taken to Newgate."

Jacob halted and glanced around him, finally noticing Peter and Mrs. Biggs in the doorway of the drawing room.

The servants looked more than capable of wrestling her cousin to the floor.

"I would advise, Mr. Burnley," Silverton added in that voice like iron, "that you take the lady's suggestion to heart while you can. My patience is almost at an end."

Jacob looked ready to explode, but he obviously knew he could not overpower both Silverton and Peter. His gaze swept over Meredith, and the hatred she saw in his eyes froze her deep in the bone.

"You'll regret this, girl," he flung at her. Jacob turned on his heel and stumbled to the door, pushing past Mrs. Biggs and Peter as he left the room.

Silverton cocked his head at the footman. "Make sure the door is locked after him."

"Yes, my lord."

Now that the danger had passed, Meredith's legs began to tremble so forcefully she could hardly stand. Silverton took one look at her and steered her by the shoulders to the sofa. Mrs. Biggs bustled over, her round face crimson with outrage.

"There now, dearie," she exclaimed, flapping her apron in Meredith's face, "I'll wake Miss Noyes and fetch her smelling salts. You just rest here on the couch till I get her."

Meredith practically bolted off the sofa at that suggestion. Silverton pressed her back down.

"No, no, Mrs. Biggs," she gasped. "Please don't wake Miss Noyes—she'll be terrified, and I couldn't bear that tonight. I'm fine, truly."

"I would second that opinion," Silverton opined dryly. "Mrs. Biggs, why don't you fetch some tea for your mistress. I'm sure that will be more refreshing than Miss Noyes's smelling salts."

Mrs. Biggs looked doubtful as she inspected Meredith's face. The cook glanced over at Silverton and then nodded reluctantly, deferring to his authority.

"Right you are, my lord. And mayhap a splash of brandy in

that tea will be just the thing to set Miss Burnley to rights."
She lumbered to the door. "I'll be back with your tea before
you can say jack rabbit."

"What a remarkable woman," mused Silverton after the
cook had exited the room. "I really must remember to thank
my secretary for engaging her."

Meredith let out a tremulous sigh and collapsed into the
cushions. She gazed up at Silverton. He stared back at her, his
face still marked with the residue of his anger.

"If you had not come when you did . . ." Her voice broke.
She blinked rapidly to stem the tears that threatened to fall
from her eyes.

Silverton muttered something under his breath. He reached
out an arm to hook the back of one of the glazed cotton arm-
chairs, pulling it toward him and in front of her. He sat and
took her hands in a comforting grip.

"It's all right, sweetheart," he murmured. "He can't hurt
you again. I won't let him."

Meredith sat up straight and tried to smile back. She
thought her face might shatter from the effort.

"My lord, I fear you must be growing tired of coming to
my rescue. I hardly know how to thank you again."

The ice in his eyes began to melt. "You know I will do
whatever is necessary to protect you and Annabel."

Despite her best efforts, a few tears escaped and rolled down
her cheeks. He released one of her hands and extracted a handkerchief from his pocket. She took it and dabbed her eyes. Part
of her was mortified to be crying in front of him, but another
part felt infinitely soothed by his protective attitude.

"Tell me what happened."

In a halting voice, Meredith told him. As she talked, his
face grew dark and his mouth set with anger, but he refrained
from comment. Just as she finished, a light tap sounded on
the door and Mrs. Biggs entered with the tea tray. Silverton
waved Meredith aside when she tried to serve him, preparing

her a cup himself. He urged her to drink, holding back any questions until she had taken several sips and Mrs. Biggs had left the room.

Feeling more herself, Meredith set her cup aside and frowned.

"What is it?" asked Silverton.

"Well, what I have never been able to understand is why Jacob and Uncle Isaac would act like this in the first place. Neither of them ever expressed any interest in Annabel or her health until just recently."

She raised her eyes to his, and she saw her own concerns reflected there.

"In fact, until three months ago, we never saw Uncle Isaac and Aunt Nora more than once or twice a year. It's a complete mystery to me. And as for Jacob wanting to marry me"—she paused, noting with interest how Silverton's eyes flared with heat—"he never expressed any desire to do so until a month ago."

He leaned forward, resting his forearms on his knees as he stared absently at the polished floorboards. She listened to the quiet tick of the clock, reluctant to disturb his ruminations.

"Meredith," he said abruptly, "I don't wish to pry, but I would like to know how things stand with you financially. I know Annabel inherited a large fortune from her mother. I also assume you have a separate income to support you. Is that correct?"

"Yes, my lord," she answered readily. "Annabel inherited ten thousand a year from her mother. My father left me fifteen hundred a year, which passed to him from my grandfather, who, as you know, established a wool mill in Bristol."

"And the mill is now run by your uncle, is it not?"

"Yes, sir. As the oldest it passed to him. My father had no head for business and never displayed any interest in the mill. Jacob, however, joined his father as soon as he came of age."

Silverton once more lapsed into thought. Meredith hated to

bother him, so she allowed her restless mind to wander instead. After a few minutes, she stole a glance at his handsome but distracted countenance. It finally occurred to her how strange it was that he had come calling so late in the evening.

She started to fidget, all too aware of his muscular leg brushing up against her skirts. He glanced up, his expression alert.

"What is it?"

She hesitated for a moment but couldn't seem to prevent herself from asking the question.

"My lord, why did you come to call tonight?"

Meredith regretted the words as soon as they were out of her mouth. Most likely he was simply being polite, taking pity on her as she sat at home with only Miss Noyes for company. She winced at the idea that he would only come to visit because he felt sorry for her.

She started to turn her head to the side, but he captured her chin between his fingers. His eyes were warm, and she had the feeling he was trying not to laugh at her.

Again.

Meredith stifled a groan, all too aware that she always seemed to amuse him. But the laughter in his eyes died away and became something else—a smoldering gaze that sent heated tendrils crawling up her legs to the junction between her thighs. Now she couldn't help but fidget in her seat.

"I came to speak to you about something of great interest to us both." The dark purr in his voice made her stomach feel strangely muddled. "And I wanted to do so without an audience of curious relatives."

"Is that why you haven't called on us since . . ."

"Yes, sweetheart, that's why you haven't seen me for several days. I didn't think I'd be able to control myself if I were in the same room with you."

Silverton gently stroked her cheek with his big hand. His lips curled in a smile that dazzled her with its sensual fire.

More than anything, Meredith wanted to fasten her mouth on his and draw all that spectacular warmth into herself.

"But I think," he continued as his hand slid around to the sensitive skin at the back of her neck, "that you have had enough excitement for one evening. We will continue this discussion later."

Her eyelids drooped as his head slowly descended to hers. His mouth brushed across her lips, nuzzling her with a tender kiss that still managed to be completely possessive.

Meredith had just started to lean into him, clutching at his shoulders, when he pulled back. His eyes danced wickedly as she fought to stifle a whimpering protest. One last soft stroke of her cheek with his fingers, and then he stood. She couldn't help sighing regretfully as he prepared to take his leave.

"I want you to get some rest, Meredith," he ordered gently. "You must be exhausted. We will continue this conversation soon enough. And when we do, I promise you that we will finish what we started the other night."

Chapter Eighteen

He leapt up the imposing marble stairs of Stanton House in two bounds.

A footman had arrived with the summons just fifteen minutes ago—a hastily scrawled note from his uncle informing him that Lady Stanton had fallen gravely ill. Silverton had practically run most of the way to Berkeley Square, his fear causing him to ignore the calls of several acquaintances as he dashed past them.

Tolliver opened the door, his normally impassive face marked with pinched concern. That was a bad sign. Silverton didn't wait to be announced, hurrying through the entrance hall to his uncle's library.

He paused on the threshold to catch his breath and observe the scene before him.

General Stanton stared in grim silence at the polished surface of his desk. Meredith and Annabel sat together on the red velvet settee in front of the fireplace, clutching each other's hands. Robert stood in one of the window alcoves, anxiously tugging at his waistcoat as his eyes flickered between Annabel and his grandfather.

Meredith looked his way when she heard the door open,

greeting him with a smile that seemed mostly composed of relief. Not surprising, given the level of tension in the room.

"My dear sir." Silverton strode to his uncle's desk. "Please tell me how the situation stands with Aunt Georgina."

"She has caught a lung infection, that is how the situation stands," the general managed in a strangled voice. "I knew all that damned gallivanting about town would come to no good end. And this is the result of it. She is ill, Nephew, very ill!"

Silverton heard a horrified gasp and turned to see Annabel raise a hand to her mouth to stifle a sob, looking absolutely guilt stricken. Meredith hugged her sister close, casting a resentful glance at the general as she did so. Robert rolled his eyes at Silverton, silently pleading with him to manage the volatile situation.

Sighing inwardly, he turned back to his uncle. The general's eyes were filled with anguish, and Silverton's heart was wrung with pity for the stern old man who loved his wife above all else. For the first time in his own life, he understood how a man could feel like that for a woman.

"I assume the doctor has been to see her. What is his prognosis?" he asked in a calm voice. Obviously someone had to keep his wits about him today, and he suspected it would probably be him.

The general's jaw worked mightily, but no words came out of his mouth.

"The doctor is still with her," Meredith spoke up from behind him.

Silverton turned and leaned his hip on his uncle's desk as Meredith released Annabel and rose to her feet.

"Lady Stanton returned home from Almack's last night complaining to her dresser that she felt short of breath. She passed a restless night and was very unwell this morning. The general sent immediately for the doctor, and then sent a note to us. We came as soon as we received it. That is all we know at the moment."

"It was too much for her!" The exclamation was wrenched from his uncle. "I knew I should have ordered her to stay home last night—I could see her fatigue. Stubborn woman will never say so, but you know she ain't strong, Silverton. Fool that I was, I said nothing!"

"Oh, no, Grandpapa," Annabel cried. She sprang from her seat and flew around the desk to the general. The girl dropped to her knees before him and took his hands in a convulsive grip. "It was my fault. Grandmamma was only trying to help me. I'll never forgive myself if anything happens to her."

General Stanton stared in helpless dismay as his granddaughter struggled to choke back her escalating sobs. Silverton pushed away from the desk, ready to pull the weeping girl away from his uncle, when Meredith's steady voice intervened.

"Annabel, my dear, you must try to control yourself. We don't know for sure the nature of Lady Stanton's illness. In any event, falling into hysterics will certainly not improve the situation. Please, get up off the floor. Mr. Stanton"—Meredith glanced at Robert—"will you be so kind as to pull a chair over so Annabel can sit by her grandfather?"

"Of course, Miss Burnley!" Robert responded with alacrity. He hurried to drag a fretted Chinese sidechair over to the desk.

"General Stanton," Meredith continued in the same level-headed manner, "I know you are worried, but the doctor will return soon. Perhaps we should refrain from envisioning grim scenarios until he finishes examining her ladyship."

The general's eyes snapped with anger, but Meredith returned his look with a serene countenance. Much to Silverton's surprise, his uncle did not rip into her. Instead, some of the tension seemed to drain out of his body. Reaching down, General Stanton grasped Annabel's hands and helped her sit in the chair Robert had placed beside the desk.

"That's right, my dear," he said to his granddaughter, patting her hand as she attempted to swallow her tears. "No use letting yourself fall into a flap—it ain't good for your health, either. Dr. Sibley has been taking care of your grandmamma for years. We can depend on him completely."

Annabel gulped as she leaned over to rub her cheek against her grandfather's shoulder. Meredith watched them with a satisfied expression before glancing at Silverton. He lifted his brows, silently expressing his admiration for her adroit handling of the emotional eruption. She bowed her head in acknowledgment before sitting quietly back down on the settee.

She really was a magnificent woman, he thought. No wonder he couldn't keep his hands off her.

They waited in nervous silence until the doctor slipped through the door of the library to join them. Dr. Sibley brusquely waved Meredith aside when she offered to ring for tea.

"No need, young lady. I have a birthing to attend to, and I must return home first to make up a tonic for Lady Stanton."

"Blast you, Sibley," growled General Stanton. "Don't keep me waiting! How is my wife?"

The doctor ignored the old man's bad temper, clearly inured to such behavior after so many years.

"Well, General, she has taken a severe cold. Normally I would not worry, but Lady Stanton's weak heart and chest make her susceptible to fever. She needs careful watching over the next few days if she is not to fall into a decline."

Dr. Sibley didn't need to explain that such a decline could be fatal.

"I will send over the tonic immediately and return later this afternoon. But it's imperative that an experienced nurse attend her constantly over the next few days."

"Her dresser has seen her through several illnesses," said the general. The color had leached out of his face, leaving it a pasty gray. "I'm sure she will know what to do."

Dr. Sibley frowned. "Tillman is not young, and your wife

will need to be watched most carefully at night. If there is no one else to assist, then I shall send over a nurse to help."

Silverton bit back an objection. The last time Lady Stanton had been ill, the night nurse had fallen asleep after taking one too many nips from a flask of gin she had concealed in her apron.

"Absolutely not!" roared the general. "I'll not have another drunken slattern anywhere near my wife."

Annabel flinched at his outburst, while Robert shook his head in consternation. Meredith crossed her arms over her waist and frowned thoughtfully at the floor.

"General Stanton, be reasonable," sighed Dr. Sibley. "Your wife needs someone used to caring for sick people. Tillman cannot possibly watch her day and night."

The general opened his mouth to argue, when Meredith interrupted him.

"I will nurse Lady Stanton," she said.

The doctor tilted his head, studying her carefully as if assessing her fitness for such a task.

"Don't be ridiculous!" snapped the general. "What kind of experience would a girl like you have?"

Meredith raised her eyebrows as the older man bristled at her. "As a matter of fact, General," she replied in a slightly superior voice, "I have a great deal of experience caring for sick people, including your granddaughter."

"Oh, yes, Grandpapa," Annabel said eagerly. "Meredith took care of me for years. You know how sick I was. Dr. Bailey always said he never knew a finer nurse than Meredith. And she was very good whenever one of the servants fell ill, too. She took care of all of us. Please let her help Grandmamma!"

General Stanton glowered at Meredith, his natural suspicion at war with his concern for his wife.

"Miss Burnley," asked Dr. Sibley, "have you nursed someone with an infectious complaint?"

"Many times, sir," she replied in a confident voice. She

stood quietly while Dr. Sibley observed her for a few more seconds. He nodded his head as if satisfied.

"You'll do. Come with me to Lady Stanton's room, and I will give you and Tillman instructions. Work it out between yourselves who will sit up with her at night. She is not to be left alone for a minute until I am certain the fever does not take hold."

"I understand, sir." Meredith followed in the doctor's wake as he walked from the room.

"Wait!" cried General Stanton. Doubt and fear clouded his features. As Meredith visibly struggled to control her impatience, she turned and stepped back to the general's desk.

"Sir, I know we do not always see eye to eye, but I beg you to allow me to help Lady Stanton," she implored in a quiet voice. "Believe me, I know all too well the effects of a violent cold on a weakened system. I assure you I will care for her ladyship as if she were my own mother."

Meredith obviously sought to remind the old man of his own daughter's untimely death. Silverton had to admire her unconventional tactics.

General Stanton gazed searchingly into Meredith's eyes and then finally bobbed his head once in acquiescence. She gave him a gentle smile. Without uttering another word, she spun on her heel and left the room, sparing not a glance for Silverton or anyone else.

Chapter Nineteen

"I love him, Meredith, I really do!"

Meredith gaped at her sister, stunned into immobility by the unexpected declaration. Annabel's eyes were wide and unblinking as she anxiously waited for her sister's response.

"Are you sure?" Meredith managed to croak.

The girl nodded her head vigorously. "Oh, yes. I've known for days now that I will love him forever. He understands me so well, and he makes me feel safe." Annabel's voice dropped to a whisper as she reached out to fleetingly touch her sister's hand. "Meredith, are you very angry with me for not telling you before?"

Meredith couldn't actually find any words to describe what she felt. Fatigue crushed her in a massive fist, and until a few moments ago, her mind had been fully occupied with the details of Lady Stanton's care.

She had spent the last six days in her ladyship's sickroom, nursing the old woman through the illness that had wracked her frail body with feverish chills. The crisis had passed only yesterday, when Dr. Sibley declared the fever had finally broken. Even so, Meredith had spent the night by Lady Stanton's side—as she had the last five nights—and Tillman had come only a few minutes ago to relieve her of her duties. She desperately wanted to crawl into bed, giving in to the stupefying exhaustion that permeated every part of her body.

But Annabel had stationed herself in her grandmother's dressing room, nervously awaiting an opportunity to speak with her. Her sister had pleaded for just a few minutes of time, anxiously clutching her hands in her dainty sprig muslin skirts.

Meredith had bitten back a curt refusal, remorsefully aware that she had virtually abandoned her sister during Lady Stanton's illness. She had dredged up a smile to assuage the wounded look in Annabel's eyes and led her over to sit on the white silk chaise.

And at that point the girl had lobbed the emotional cannonball, blowing Meredith's wits to the four winds.

"Meredith, please say something!" Her sister's eyes shimmered with tears.

Meredith struggled to disperse the wooliness in her brain, forcing herself to pat Annabel's hand in a comforting manner.

"No, dear. Of course I'm not angry with you, just surprised. When did all this happen?"

Annabel perked up, a shy smile lighting her heart-shaped face. "Well, as you know, Robert, Sophia, and I are very close. When Grandmamma fell ill, and you were so taken up with caring for her, we spent even more time together. I tried to be with Grandpapa as much as possible, but sometimes he was too agitated to sit with me." Her voice grew wobbly. "That upset me very much because, well, I don't think Grandmamma would have gotten sick if she hadn't been trying to bring me out."

"Darling, you mustn't feel that way," Meredith exclaimed, her chest muscles constricting with painful guilt. "This is not the first time your grandmother has fallen ill, and she certainly wouldn't want you to blame yourself. I'm so sorry I didn't take the time to explain that to you. It's all my fault that you have been feeling so badly."

"No, Meredith, don't you see?" Annabel responded, bouncing slightly with excitement. "You didn't need to tell me—Robert did! He has been with me almost every waking moment, telling me that Grandmamma will be fine, that I was not to blame myself for anything. And he's been so wonderful with Grandpapa, too. If only you could have seen him taking care of both of us this last week—you would have been so proud of him!"

Annabel's eyes now shone with fervent and wholly committed admiration. Meredith recognized the look immediately. She suspected she displayed the same kind of expression whenever she thought of Silverton.

"Darling." Meredith hesitated. "I don't mean to pry, but has Robert actually asked you to marry him?"

The light in Annabel's eyes now suffused her face. "He asked me last night! And he bought the most beautiful ring, but we agreed I shouldn't wear it until he asked Grandpapa for permission."

Meredith sighed. It had all sounded much too easy. Obviously Robert had not thought to discuss the matter with his grandfather first.

"What's wrong?" Some of the joy faded from Annabel's face. "Please tell me you approve, Meredith. I couldn't bear it if you didn't."

Meredith thought longingly of bed and the escape of deep slumber, but immediately shoved the temptation to the back of her mind. She had to find a way to deal with this situation now.

"Annabel," she said, looking her sister earnestly in the eye, "Robert is a wonderful young man, but you have just begun your Season. Are you sure about this? Are you ready to love him above all others, committing to him for the rest of your life?"

Her sister gazed solemnly back at her with eyes that held a wisdom beyond her years. Although only seventeen, Annabel had endured much in her life, and Meredith knew the girl already possessed a maturity tempered by tragedy and illness.

"Yes, Meredith, I do love him, and I'm ready for a life with him. You must trust me."

She thought about that for a few moments, realizing she did trust her sister's judgment. And, after all, the point of their escape to London had been to find Annabel a husband. Robert was young, but Meredith had little doubt he would develop into a fine man, and he had adored Annabel from the minute he laid eyes on her. If General and Lady Stanton granted their approval, Robert and Annabel's marriage would be the solution to many of their problems.

Unfortunately, Lady Stanton had other plans for Annabel. Plans that included the Marquess of Silverton.

The guilt in her chest tightened another notch, but Meredith decided to hold her tongue. No good would come of telling Annabel of Lady Stanton's plans for her, since nothing would come of them anyway. Annabel loved Robert, and Silverton—well, she knew that Silverton didn't love Annabel. That didn't mean, however, that Lady Stanton would approve of the events that had transpired during her illness.

As for what Silverton's plans were, Meredith hadn't a clue, since they hadn't exchanged more than a few words in the last week. Truth be told, she didn't really know what he thought about her, other than he seemed to like to kiss her. And she had a very strong suspicion that Lady Stanton wouldn't approve of that, either.

She sighed, the muddle in her head growing worse by the second. With Annabel waiting anxiously for her response, Meredith decided she could only deal with one problem at a time. She took a deep breath and forced a smile.

"Annabel, my love, if you are sure of your feelings, then I will do all in my power to support you. But"—she held up a hand to forestall Annabel's attempt to throw her arms around her—"I insist that you and Robert wait a few days before speaking with the general. He will no doubt want to discuss the situation with Lady Stanton, and she must be allowed to rest before he speaks to her about this."

Annabel subsided back onto the chaise. She frowned before glancing at Meredith, her reluctance to comply clearly written on her face.

"Annabel, you must learn patience."

The girl sighed and slumped against the upholstered cushions. "I know. You're right, Meredith, and it's ghastly to be thinking only of myself. I'll tell Robert we must wait for Grandmamma to recover." A mischievous gleam crept into her eyes. "He won't like it, but I think I know a way to keep him quiet."

"Annabel!" Meredith blinked, shocked by the knowing expression on her sister's face.

Annabel laughed, kissed her on the cheek, and danced over to the door of the dressing room. "You're not the only one who knows what it's like to have a beau, you know. The only difference is, some of us don't try to keep it a secret!"

Meredith groaned and rubbed her throbbing temples, wishing she were in bed, with the covers pulled safely over her head.

Silverton stretched his top-booted legs toward the low flames flickering in the cast-iron grate. He swirled his brandy in the crystal glass, sprawling against the pillows of the plush, red velvet settee. The general had just retired to his chambers for the night, leaving Silverton alone to nurse his drink in the library.

He supposed he ought to get his coat and stroll the few blocks to his own mansion, but he couldn't seem to rouse himself from his comfortable position in front of the fireplace.

It was the first time in a hellish week that he could finally relax. The first time since Aunt Georgina had fallen ill that they knew she was really on the mend. And the first time he could think clearly about the night he had rescued Meredith from Jacob Burnley's assault.

Silverton grew cold at the thought of what could have occurred had he not arrived when he did. The bastard was lucky he hadn't killed him.

He shook his head, still puzzled by the aggressive attempts to force Meredith and Annabel back to Swallow Hill. He had his suspicions, but he needed more information about the Burnleys and the state of their finances before he could develop a concrete theory.

Silverton had been forced to postpone any investigation, however, when Lady Stanton had taken ill. The ensuing week had been marked by several crises, as Lady Stanton's infection developed into a dangerous fever. Meredith had spent every night with his aunt, but he knew she had also passed many hours of the day in the sickroom as well. Her devotion and careful nursing had won even the admiration of Tillman, Lady Stanton's long-time, fiercely possessive dresser.

In fact, the entire household had come to depend on Meredith. It seemed a gradual but natural process when the servants began to ask her to resolve a variety of domestic questions during Lady Stanton's illness. She responded to every problem with a quiet, unassuming ability that had won the respect of all the inhabitants of Stanton House, including the general.

Meredith had gracefully risen to every challenge. Silverton no longer harbored the slightest doubt about her ability to function as his marchioness. *She* might not believe she was fit to move among the ton, but in every way that mattered she was more a lady than any woman he had ever known.

Yesterday, Meredith and Dr. Sibley had come to tell the general that Lady Stanton's fever had broken. By this morning, she had improved so much that Sibley declared her out of danger. Annabel wept tears of joy, and his uncle had practically wrung the doctor's hand off his wrist.

"Don't thank me," said Sibley, "thank Miss Burnley. Her expert care made all the difference to your wife's recovery. You should be exceedingly grateful to her."

Silverton had smiled while his uncle hemmed and hawed, still reluctant to express his gratitude to Meredith but fair enough to know he should.

Later in the day, he had sat with his uncle in the library while Annabel and Robert huddled on the settee, their heads together as they perused Meredith's sketchbook. The girl had decided they all needed a distraction after the week's ordeal and proposed that her sister paint a portrait of General Stanton.

"She's awfully good, you know," Annabel explained after fetching the sketchbook from their townhouse. "I'm sure she would be happy to do a painting of Grandpapa. Grandmamma told me she has wanted to get a portrait of him forever, but he will simply not sit still for it."

Silverton smothered a laugh at the appalled look on his uncle's face as he flipped through the sketches. Meredith had talent, but her chosen subjects were not what the general would consider appropriate for a genteel young lady.

A sly grin crossed Robert's face as he inspected a graphic depiction of Theseus slaying the Minotaur. "I say," he said, pointing at the snarling beast Meredith had created, "that does rather resemble the expression on Grandfather's face first thing in the morning!"

Only Annabel's immediate and stern rebuke had saved Robert from General Stanton's wrath.

Yes, everything seemed to be returning to normal. Now he could turn his full attention back to Meredith and the questions tugging persistently at the edges of his mind.

Silverton exhaled a tired breath as he placed his snifter on the low table in front of the settee. Standing slowly, he reached his arms over his head, gradually stretching the knots from his cramped muscles. Despite the brandy his nerves felt raw. He suspected the only remedy for that irritation would be the sensation of Meredith's lush body against his, and the taste of her sweet tongue in his mouth. That was not to be his luck tonight, however, so he might as well take himself home.

Silverton glanced around for the coat he had tossed on a chair earlier in the evening. As he crossed the floor to retrieve it, the flames of the candles suddenly flickered as the library door opened quietly behind him. His senses leapt to full awareness at the sound of a quickly stifled gasp. He pivoted quickly on his heel, knowing precisely who would be standing before him.

Meredith paused just inside the doorway. Her mouth dropped open in startled surprise, and he could see in the reflected light of the candles that her eyes were wide and wary. He slowly but deliberately crossed the room to her.

As he did, Silverton took the time to appreciate that his luck was finally about to change.

Chapter Twenty

Meredith's eyes darted nervously around the room. She took a small step back toward the door as Silverton approached her.

"Forgive me, my lord," she apologized as she touched her hand fleetingly to her hair. "I didn't realize anyone was still in the library."

Silverton held his tongue as he studied her. Although still dressed in the same burgundy silk gown she had worn for dinner, she had released her hair from its pins. The glossy, sable waves tumbled around her shoulders and flowed down her back to her elbows. Her hair was unfashionably long, and for that Silverton was exceedingly grateful. All that glorious, unbound beauty made him think of bed things, and what he would do once he got her into his.

"There is nothing to forgive, Meredith." He smiled down at her as he smoothly crowded her body against the doorframe. The faint scent of violets wafted up from her thick hair, teasing his nostrils with a delicate sweetness. "I'm very pleased to finally have you to myself, if only for a little while."

She blushed and looked doubtfully up at him. He grasped her by the elbow, drawing her gently but inexorably into the room.

"Lord Silverton," she protested faintly as he shut the door

behind her, "I really don't think it proper that you call me by my first name. Lady Stanton would surely object."

"Well, since she isn't here," he replied, "I suggest that we not worry about it."

He quickly turned the key in the lock before guiding her to the settee. Although he could feel the tension in her arm as she tried to pull away, he ignored her attempt to resist him. With an irritated sigh, Meredith reluctantly gave in to his superior strength.

"I take it the general has gone to bed?" She cautiously scanned the darkened room.

"Yes, my dear," he murmured. "You are, for the moment, safe from any criticism or evaluation, artistic or otherwise."

She grimaced at him but acknowledged the hit with a short laugh. Silverton released her arm and nudged the small of her back, urging her to sit down on the settee. She complied, although she threw him a dubious glance as she did so.

"I suppose I should be grateful life is beginning to resume its regular course," she muttered with a sigh, relaxing back into the overstuffed cushions.

Silverton took a moment to appreciate the contrast of her shimmering mane against the crimson velvet of the settee.

"Thanks mostly to you," he said as he crossed the room to the sideboard holding a number of crystal decanters.

Meredith leaned her head against the back of the settee. She closed her eyes and exhaled a long, whispering breath, as if all the week's tension were suddenly flowing out of her.

"Dr. Sibley is an excellent physician." She stifled a yawn. "And Tillman is an experienced and devoted nurse. I don't know what we would have done without her."

Silverton didn't comment. It was in Meredith's nature to be self-effacing, and he knew she would argue with him if he tried to praise her any further. Instead, he poured a small glass of sherry and brought it to her. As he reached the settee she raised her lids, focusing on him in spite of the fatigue that clouded her silvery eyes.

He paused for just a few seconds, carefully studying the face that had become so dear to him. Her pale complexion made the dark smudges under her eyes stand out like painful bruises. His heart wrenched with compassion.

Poor darling. She's obviously exhausted from nursing Aunt Georgina. With a sigh, he consigned his amorous plans to a future time when she was not half-dead with fatigue. He handed her the glass, and unlike before when he had brought her a drink in this very room, she didn't refuse him. She sipped and closed her eyes again, murmuring her appreciation softly in her throat.

Silverton's gaze drifted down to the generous curves of her breasts, which were snugly framed by the shimmering delicacy of the lightweight silk. He could feel the ache in his groin slowly beginning to build, along with the frustration of his continually thwarted desire. If he didn't get some relief soon, he was sure he would end up a cripple.

He muttered a curse under his breath and seated himself at the other end of the settee, careful to keep at least two feet between them. Silverton grabbed his brandy from the table and took a large gulp, hoping the burn of alcohol would somehow cancel out the fire that coursed through his veins.

Meredith slowly opened her eyes and moved her head against the cushions to look at him.

"Did you say something, my lord?"

"It's late, Meredith," he replied abruptly. "You should be asleep by now. I understood that Tillman would stay in Aunt Georgina's dressing room tonight so you could get some rest. Surely it's no longer necessary for you to sit up all night with her?"

She smothered another yawn behind a slender hand. "No, Lady Stanton is much improved. I looked in on her, and she is sleeping peacefully. Dr. Sibley said she should be well enough to travel into Kent in a few days time."

The doctor had advised that Lady Stanton remove to the country for several weeks to aid her recovery. The general and Silverton had decided the entire family would decamp to Belfield Abbey, Silverton's closest estate, rather than to Stanton Park in Yorkshire. The Abbey was an easy journey from London—one that could be accomplished in less than a day, placing as little stress as possible on his aunt.

Silverton again inspected the smudges under Meredith's eyes. She looked like she needed rest as much as his aunt.

"Meredith, you should be in bed," he repeated. *Preferably with me,* he added mentally, but that would have to wait until they were at the Abbey.

"I know," she sighed, "but I just can't seem to sleep. Perhaps I have become too used to being up at this time of night. I did try to lie down, but that only made me feel more awake than before."

She glanced at him, touching her hair again as if embarrassed that he should see her in such a state of disarray. "I only meant to borrow a book from the general's library and take it back to my room."

For long moment they stared at each other. Silverton swore he could feel a lash of heat whip between them. Meredith wrenched her gaze away to stare into the fire, a sweet blush flaring across her cheeks.

"But, somehow," she said, swallowing nervously, "I seem to be much too restless to even read."

Silverton smiled to himself. He slid over to her end of the settee, plucked the glass of sherry from her hand, and carefully set it down on the table. Snaking his arm behind her, he reached his fingers into her hair and gently combed them through the silky mass.

Meredith jumped slightly in her seat, but did not pull away. A myriad of emotions flickered across her face until they settled into one clear expression of mute and almost desperate yearning.

"I . . . I should probably go upstairs now," she stammered as her eyes dropped to his mouth.

Silverton could feel his lips curve into a rapacious smile as he wrapped his other arm around her waist.

"In a minute, my sweet," he whispered before swooping down to capture her strawberry-colored lips under his mouth.

Meredith felt herself opening to him like a flower opens to the morning light. All the fatigue and tension that had dragged on her for days was suddenly blasted away by the exhilarating heat of his kiss. She opened her lips and his tongue surged into her mouth. He devoured her like a man who had not taken sustenance for a week.

She whimpered, collapsing slowly back into the cushions. Silverton answered with a low murmur deep in his throat, and the sound of it was so delicious her stomach clenched with an unfamiliar excitement. Her legs grew so weak she knew she could not escape him even if she wanted to.

Meredith had nearly fainted when she saw him standing in the gleaming light of the fire, his golden hair burnished to the color of flame. He had looked so big and powerful, like an ancient god or spirit who had come to sweep her away to his enchanted realm. Her instinctive self had told her to flee the room before he could dominate her, but her rational mind had argued that she had the fortitude to resist him. She reasoned that no harm could result from spending a few stolen moments in his company.

Now she knew how foolish it was to think she could ever say no to him. And she knew in the depths of her soul that she didn't want to, because Silverton was everything she had ever longed for.

Meredith clutched his arms, digging her fingers into the

soft linen of his shirt. He lifted her hand and placed it around the back of his neck, shifting her closer into his embrace. The tender swell of her breasts brushed against his satin waistcoat, the rasp of her nipples against the fabric like nothing she had ever felt before. Hard and pointed, they tingled with an intensity that was almost painful.

She pressed against him urgently, seeking to ease the delicious agony.

Silverton seemed to know exactly what she needed. As he invaded her mouth with the stroke of his tongue, his hand smoothed over the front of her bodice until he captured her right breast between his long fingers. When he touched her nipple, it beaded even more tightly. That obviously pleased him, because he made a humming noise deep in his throat as he rolled it between his thumb and forefinger.

Meredith pulled back and stared at him, shocked by the stab of sensation that jolted straight to her loins. Silverton's blue eyes had darkened to indigo, and the expression on his face was so fiercely exultant that she quailed before the force of it. He gazed back, his eyes softening as he sensed her trepidation.

"Easy, love," he whispered in her ear. "There's nothing to be afraid of. I just want to hold you tonight—taste you a bit and soothe you so you can sleep."

His hand rested quietly on her breast as his mouth moved in soft kisses over her cheek, her ear, and down her neck. She relaxed under his soothing caress, the tension once more flowing from her body as he cuddled her against him. Her momentary flash of anxiety faded, banished by the feel of his strong arms enfolding her so securely.

Meredith began to breathe in long, slow surges as she slid her hands up his chest. As if they had a will of their own, her fingers unbuttoned his waistcoat, parting the material to stroke the hard muscles through his shirt. Silverton's hand left her breast, reaching up to tug the knot in his cravat, pulling it away from his neck and tossing it on the floor. She slowly walked her fingers to the opening of his shirt and slipped them inside.

Meredith marveled at the coiled strength she sensed in him, at the heat that flowed into her tired body as she nestled in the crook of his arm. She stroked and played, weaving her fingers through the wiry blond hair scattered over his bronzed skin.

He stilled beneath her hands, letting her explore him. Pleasure built inside her as she felt his muscles flex under her sensitized fingertips.

Meredith couldn't resist stretching up and touching the edge of her tongue to the base of his throat. She tentatively licked the rapid pulse that beat there as she whispered an incoherent appreciation for his intoxicating and potent masculinity.

For a long moment he seemed to freeze. Then, in a movement so swift that she felt it before she saw it, he dragged her across his lap, settling her on his thighs. She opened her mouth in a surprised squeak, but he dipped between her lips, ruthlessly capturing her breath and drawing it into him. One hand wrapped hard around her shoulders, keeping her still, while the other grasped her hip, stroking and kneading through the thin layers of her dress and chemise.

Meredith felt as if she were melting, the soft flesh between her legs turning hot and damp. She wanted to writhe against him even as she thought she might collapse into his arms in a heated swoon.

Silverton's kiss tasted like hot brandy. He smelled faintly of the spice of his snuff, and something intangible and yet so wonderful she wanted to burrow against him like a kitten searching for warmth.

She returned his kiss with an eagerness that some dim part of her mind knew she should be ashamed of. But instead of shame she felt only growing excitement and need—a sense that she was about to launch herself off a precipice into a glittering place where every sense would be heightened, every feeling magnified.

Grasping the edges of his open collar, she pushed herself into his kiss, sucking his tongue in a wicked imitation of what he had done to her only moments ago. Silverton pulled back gently and nuzzled her cheek, pushing her head sideways to expose the side of her neck to his questing mouth. He made her shudder with pleasure as he hungrily licked and bit the sensitive flesh beneath her ear.

Meredith let her head fall back, the slide of his wet tongue across her skin so intense that it made her dizzy. Her eyes were shut now, but she could feel his hand move leisurely to her bodice, clever fingers searching, tugging at ties and pulling the delicate silk away from her breasts. She forced herself to raise her lids as something inside compelled her to watch his face as he exposed her body to his gaze for the first time.

He cradled her on his lap, one hand moving up her back to hold her steady across his thighs. His other hand pulled at the ribbons of her chemise, carefully lowering the lace-trimmed garment to her waist.

Meredith couldn't help but moan at the feral expression on his face—a mewling sound that brought his eyes up to hers. His features were as hard as granite, but his eyes shone with a tenderness that made her want to weep. He lowered his mouth to hers, brushing a gentle kiss across her lips as if to reassure her. But he immediately returned his gaze to her breasts, and she understood that he would not be distracted again until he had gotten exactly what he wanted from her.

With an almost painful sense of anticipation, she watched him study her. Meredith was ashamed to admit it, but she loved the covetous look on his face as he gazed at her body. His hand finally moved back to her breast, his fingers stroking upward from the plumpness beneath her nipple. She panted as he teased her, embarrassed that she couldn't control her uneven breathing. His lips parted again in a mesmerizing smile as his fingers circled her nipple, making her wriggle her bottom against his muscular thighs.

She suddenly became aware of his erection nudging against her as he slightly parted his legs so that she rested more heavily against his lower body. Meredith felt the moist heat grow between her legs, and she was afraid he would sense the dampness through the thin fabric of her gown.

But in the next instant he lowered his head to her breast, taking the hard peak of her nipple and sucking it into his mouth. She jerked in his arms, choking back a cry of astonishment at the streak of sensation she felt all the way to the center of her womb.

Silverton raised his head at her smothered shriek, his eyes filled with laughter, an expression of mock alarm on his face.

"Hush, my darling," he exclaimed softly. "You must not cry out so loudly."

"I'm sorry," Meredith gasped, mortified by her lack of control. "I just can't seem to help it."

"I'm depending on that," he murmured before lowering his head back to her breast.

She was about to ask him what he meant when his teeth closed around her nipple. He tugged on her flesh so sweetly that she could swear it plumped more fully into his mouth. Meredith tried to swallow the moans forced out against her will as he licked and nipped the tight bud, stopping occasionally to blow air on it before sucking it back into his mouth. Just when she thought she would lose her mind, he switched to the other breast, swirling his tongue in luxurious strokes that built up the tension in the pit of her belly to almost unbearable levels.

"Please!" she gasped, not understanding quite what she wanted but certain he would know exactly what she needed. "Please!"

Meredith arched her back, deliberately pushing her breast against his rasping tongue. He made a low purring sound, like a giant cat, feasting on as much of her softness as he could pull into his mouth. She writhed in his lap, pressing against an erection that felt rock hard and startlingly large against her bottom.

He lifted his head with a gasp, his face branded with a flush of desire that made her heart pound even harder. Silverton looked into her eyes; his expression was both rampantly possessive and achingly tender at the same time.

Meredith suddenly realized with a bone-deep conviction that he would do everything in his power to protect her. She lay across him, completely vulnerable and open to his touch, completely at his mercy, but feeling safer than she had at any other time in her memory.

"God, Meredith." His deep voice reverberated through her body. "You are so beautiful I can hardly bear it."

The words were almost as good as his touch. Her eyelids fluttered shut when his mouth returned to her lips.

As he slipped his tongue inside, his hand moved under her dress and up her thigh. His touch was not so gentle now, his fingers firm against her leg as if he could barely restrain himself. He moved past her garter to exposed skin, sliding upward until he reached the damp curls between her legs.

She could hardly breathe as she inhaled in ragged sobs, her emotions a dizzying combination of eager impatience and a stunned bashfulness that made her want to shrink from his commanding touch. But Meredith knew he would not stop, nor would she ask him to.

Silverton stroked through her curls and probed carefully, pressing a long finger into tender folds that seemed to melt as he pushed farther inside her. She was no longer a woman of reason and control, but a creature of sensation, and only he could satisfy her spiraling need.

He stroked her sheath, a knowing hand fondling her drenched softness. Meredith trembled under the onslaught, her body straining to understand what his hands were teaching her.

Silverton suddenly withdraw his finger from inside her. At the loss of his touch, she opened heavy lids to look at him. His eyes swept across her, and she felt incredibly wanton as she lay against his thighs and chest. The curls between her legs glistened with moisture, her breasts, tipped with hard pink nipples, still wet from his mouth. A soft growl rumbled in his throat as his eyes lifted to meet hers.

He held her gaze as he deliberately, relentlessly pushed her thighs wider with the hand that still played between her legs. Stroking once more into her curls, he found the most secret part of her, an aching sensitivity hidden in the folds of plump flesh. Parting her once again, his fingers caressed and gently rubbed the swollen bud. She began to shiver deep inside, the sensation both unbearable and glorious.

She couldn't stand it, couldn't take any more. As if he knew, he pushed a long finger back inside her as he simultaneously exerted a steady pressure on the little bud. She arched her back, completely unraveled by the intensity of the pleasure radiating from her very core, rippling out in shuddering tremors through her body.

Meredith parted her lips to cry out just as Silverton brought his mouth down on hers—hard, dominating, taking into himself the sweet, sweet blessing of the astonishing release.

Silverton fell back against the cushions as Meredith collapsed in a trembling heap on his lap. It was a miracle he hadn't come himself, what with her delightful bottom wriggling so sensuously against his cock. He continued to gently stroke her butter-soft flesh, and he kept the bounty of her full breast captured possessively in his hand. Silverton had no idea how he would ever let her go, when all he wanted to do was pull her down on the floor and bury himself in all that satiny heat.

But he wouldn't take her in his uncle's library, especially

not the first time. Part of him couldn't believe he had pushed her as far as he did, but his accumulated frustration had collided with her sweetly offered desire, and his control had melted like ice in a spring thaw. He knew that the next time he held her like this, there would be no holding back for either of them. Still, he reminded himself, it wouldn't help Meredith to be discovered in so compromising a position.

With one more lingering look at her glorious body, Silverton smoothed her dress and pulled her chemise and bodice over her breasts. Meredith, who seemed to be in some kind of floating daze, began to move as she felt him rearrange her clothing. Her eyelids fluttered open and he saw consciousness returning, along with a dawning expression of incipient panic.

She began to struggle against him as she attempted to sit up. He bit back an oath as he clamped her firmly in place.

"Stop struggling, sweetheart." Silverton fought to speak in a soothing voice. "Just rest in my lap for a minute to recover yourself."

She continued to squirm, forcing a groan from him as she pressed down on his aching cock.

"Meredith," he growled, "sit still."

She froze at the sharp command in his voice, a look of consternation spreading across her face. He sighed and sat up higher, easing her into a more comfortable position on his lap.

"I didn't mean to alarm you, my sweet, but if you keep moving like that I cannot be held responsible for my actions."

Meredith frowned, not comprehending the pain she caused him. But then she glanced at his face. Blushing, she dropped her gaze as she clumsily began to tie up her bodice.

"Let me help you, sweetheart," he said, brushing aside her shaking hands. "You need to be still for a minute, give yourself a chance to regain your, ah, poise. After all," he smiled at her, "you just had your—"

"No, no, don't say it," she cried in a flustered voice. "I don't want to know what it's called! Please, my lord, you must let me up." She wiggled against his groin as she attempted to rise.

Silverton involuntarily tightened his arms around her in response. "Meredith," he ground out between clenched teeth, "please stop calling me my lord."

"Well, I don't really know what else to call you, except Lord Silverton," she protested as she pushed ineffectually against his chest.

Hoping to quiet her, he nuzzled his mouth against her neck. For a moment, she did stop squirming. Silverton lifted his head, pleased to see her lips parting as her eyes turned the color of velvet mist.

"You could try calling me Stephen," he murmured. "At least when we're alone."

Her body stiffened as she resumed her struggle to get up. "My lord, we cannot possibly be alone like this again. I shudder to imagine what you must think of me, but I assure you I have never done anything like this before in my life. You must let me up—now!"

He muttered another oath, releasing his grip around her waist and shoulders. Meredith pushed herself from his lap in a tangle of flailing limbs and skirts. She stumbled as she came to her feet, and he reached out quickly to steady her.

Rising, Silverton scowled as she bent to rummage around on the floor for the slippers that had fallen off her feet.

"Meredith, we need to discuss what happened here tonight."

She shook her head vigorously as she yanked on her soft shoes. "No, my lord, we have no such need. This was a mistake. I don't blame you for dallying with me. . . ."

"I am not dallying with you! What in God's name are you talking about?" Try as he might, Silverton could not hold back his resentment that she would think so poorly of him.

Meredith edged away from him.

"I know you meant no harm, my lord." She avoided his

eye, hastily tying up the tapes of her gown. "And I know that you do have some feelings for me. . . ."

"Feelings for you!" he thundered. "Is that what you call it?"

"Keep your voice down," she hissed, looking over her shoulder at the door.

Silverton stalked across the room and grabbed her chin in his hand. He tilted her head up, forcing her to meet his gaze.

"Explain yourself," he demanded.

She stared back at him, her face a study of conflicting emotions. "I know you meant no harm. I know that you even care for me. But it's wrong to indulge ourselves in this way, and . . ." Her eyes slid away from him.

"And what?"

"You must not toy with me," she whispered. "I couldn't bear it."

Silverton felt his mouth gape open in shock. How in God's name had she come to such a wrongheaded conclusion?

Snapping his mouth shut, he released her chin and grasped her by the shoulders. "Meredith, I'm not toying with you. What kind of man do you take me for?"

Her eyes flew up to his face, her gaze wide and startled.

"I want to marry you, foolish child." He could hear the growl in his voice. "I never would have touched you if that were not my firm intention."

She stared at him for a moment. Her lips, still swollen from his lovemaking, parted in what looked like dismay. Before he could stop her, she wrenched herself from his arms and backed quickly to the door.

"No, no, Lord Silverton, you must not—it's impossible. Think of what you are saying! Please, I must go."

He stood frozen to the spot as he listened to her flustered rejection of his admittedly clumsy offer. She fumbled briefly with the key before wrenching the door open in her hurry to escape.

Meredith spun back to face him. As he watched in disbelief, she dropped him a lopsided curtsy.

"Please excuse me, my lord," she exclaimed in a breathless voice. "I will bid you good-night."

She turned and fled the room, leaving him in a state of near befuddlement. In spite of what had just happened between them, in spite of Meredith's obvious mortification and panic, she had still felt obliged to observe the forms of propriety. Although he was beyond frustration, his groin throbbing with an unremitting ache, Silverton couldn't help but laugh. He would cherish her ridiculous curtsy for the rest of his life.

Now he simply had to ascertain what troubled her about their proposed marriage. After tonight he was convinced she loved him, so he suspected her refusal stemmed from the unfamiliar emotions and sensations she had just experienced. The whole situation had obviously overwhelmed her.

Not to mention the fact, he thought ruefully, that his proposal had been as inelegant as it could possibly be. He would have to make amends for that bit of stupidity.

Fetching his coat, Silverton slipped it on and strolled from the library. He let himself out through the massive front doors of Stanton House, knowing that Tolliver would lock up behind him. As he strode down the deserted streets of Mayfair, he began to formulate a plan to pursue Meredith and to assuage any doubts she might have about their union. He looked up at the dusky night sky and laughed softly. First he would get her to Belfield Abbey, and then he would woo her, wed her, and bed her.

But not, Silverton promised himself, necessarily in that order.

Chapter Twenty-One

Feminine laughter mingled with the dainty clink of Sèvres teacups on saucers, drifting across the cavernous space of the drawing room to the large French doors that opened to the terrace. Silverton stood in the doorway, gazing out over the deer park cloaked in the lengthening shadows of the early summer evening.

He caught the occasional snatch of conversation but couldn't make out the thread of any particular discussion at this distance from the main group. The Elizabethan salon was large enough to billet an entire regiment, and he had never been fond of the gilded and intensely overwrought style of its grandiose décor. Why his mother chose the enormous room for such a small party was beyond him.

He supposed that she wished to impress the guests—a few of the local gentry, Sophia and Robert, Trask, and the Earl and Countess of Wrackley and their two children. The latter family was a surprising addition to the group, since his mother rarely went to the trouble of socializing with their closest neighbors.

The Wrackleys' estate ran parallel to Belfield Abbey along the North Downs. The earl held an ancient and distinguished title but was a spendthrift and a poor manager, and his lands had suffered from years of neglect. Everyone knew the family was in the hunt for a lucrative alliance for their daughter, Isabel, still considered a diamond of the first water even after three years on the marriage mart.

As Silverton observed the company from his post by the door, he acknowledged a sneaking suspicion that he was the Wrackleys' chosen prey. His mother's newfound liking for the countess, a woman she normally despised, confirmed this assumption. He also suspected that the source of his mother's odd behavior lay in her disapproval of his discreet attempts to court Meredith. She clearly hoped to distract him from that objective by dangling the beauteous Isabel right under his nose.

He sighed, convinced that his mother's all-too-obvious dislike of Meredith was one of the reasons his sweet girl had proven so elusive. Although they had been living in the same house for almost a fortnight, Meredith had managed to evade any attempt on his part to be alone with her. She had spent most of her time with Lady Stanton, attending to his aunt's needs as she recovered from her illness.

Against every single one of his natural inclinations, Silverton had not pressed her. But he hated that she shied away whenever he approached, likely mortified by her loss of control in his arms that night at Stanton House.

He glanced covertly across the room at her, where she sat on an ebony and purple silk settee conversing with the Earl of Wrackley's young son, Viscount Tuddler.

The memory of Meredith's erotic surrender still had the power to arouse him. It had taken enormous discipline on his part these last few weeks not to pounce on her and drag her off to the nearest bed. Instead, he had waited patiently. Now the excuse Meredith had used so effectively to avoid him was gone—literally. General and Lady Stanton had departed for Brighton this morning. His aunt loved the sea, and the general had determined that a trip to the seaside resort would help restore his wife to health.

Meredith had wanted to go with them, but, much to Silverton's delight, Lady Stanton had insisted she and Annabel remain at the Abbey.

"No, my dear," his aunt had replied firmly when Meredith tried to protest the decision. "You've been waiting on me hand and foot for three weeks. It's time for you to enjoy yourself a little, and the Abbey is delightful at this time of year. There are many lovely prospects and opportunities for both you and Annabel to paint and sketch. I absolutely insist that you remain."

Meredith had seemed to submit with good grace, but she had not been able to stop herself from sliding a nervous glance at Silverton. That shy look had strengthened his resolve to get her alone as soon as possible.

He snapped out of his pleasant musings when he saw Tuddler lean close to Meredith and murmur something in her ear. The youthful viscount had been flirting with her all evening, just skimming the boundaries of acceptable behavior. Silverton wanted nothing more than to grab the pimply faced boy by his absurdly high collar, drag him out to the terrace, and pitch him over the balustrade into the prickly rosebushes below.

Fortunately, Meredith's cool response to the young man's advances managed to allay Silverton's primitive impulses. Right now, she inspected Tuddler as if he were a species of exotic toad that had somehow hopped its way into the drawing room.

"Silverton, do stop making an ass of yourself," Trask brusquely interrupted his murderous fantasy. "The girl is clearly impervious to anyone else's advances but yours."

Silverton grinned ruefully at the earl. "That obvious, am I?"

His friend snorted in derision. They both watched Meredith, who, at that moment, pointedly turned her back on Tuddler to speak to Annabel. The two men looked at each other and broke into laughter.

"For God's sake, man," exclaimed Trask after his amusement had subsided, "when are you going to put us out of our misery and ask Miss Burnley to marry you?"

"I've been trying," grumbled Silverton, "but she won't let me get near her." He frowned as he studied the object of his thwarted affections. "She has gotten the notion into her head that I'm toying with her."

"And what have you done to dispel that notion?"

"Well . . ." Silverton hesitated, fearing he would sound ridiculous. "I'm wooing her."

"Wooing her! What in blazes are you talking about? Any idiot can see you are both well beyond that point. Just tell Miss Burnley how you feel and be done with it."

Silverton shook his head. "I don't think that would suffice. The scandal at Lady Framingham's ball, and its aftermath, deeply affected her. She hates the life of the ton, and I suspect she is having some difficulty imagining herself as the Marchioness of Silverton." He hated to even acknowledge that thought, but his instincts—and Meredith's behavior—told him that he was probably right.

"Well, Tuddler's mother doesn't seem to have any difficulty imagining it," retorted Trask.

Silverton narrowed his eyes as he studied his mother and Lady Wrackley seated together on the other side of the room. They were engaged in a quiet but intense conversation, the countess occasionally glancing with smug satisfaction at her son's efforts to engage Meredith's attention.

"Indeed," murmured Silverton. "That is odd."

"I believe your mother is responsible for that. Lady Silverton has obviously encouraged the countess to see her son's pathetic attempts to flirt with Miss Burnley as a diversionary tactic. If Tuddler can woo her away from you, then the beautiful Isabel will have a clear field to reach her objective. And"—Trask grinned wickedly—"in case you haven't noticed, that objective is you."

"I noticed," Silverton responded dryly.

"I take it that Lady Silverton would object to Miss Burnley as a daughter-in-law?"

"What do you think?"

Trask's lips curled with a subtly expressed contempt. "Permit me to say with all due respect, Silverton, that your mother is a fool."

"Trask, you are stating the obvious. You are aware, however, that as devoted as I am to her, I rarely listen to my mother."

"I'm glad to hear it, particularly in this case. Miss Burnley is a rare prize." Trask's eyes returned to his appreciative study of Meredith. "In fact, if you are not successful in your attempts to pursue her, then perhaps I might be inclined to take up the chase."

"Don't even think about it," growled Silverton, not bothering to hide his reaction to his friend's jest.

Trask rolled his eyes, but Silverton no longer cared that he acted the part of a wild animal protecting his mate. When it came to Meredith, he was long past the point of hiding his possessive instincts.

"Well, in that case," the earl mused, "you clearly need another plan."

"What do you suggest?"

"Why don't you just bed her, and then she'll have to marry you."

"You don't know Meredith," Silverton replied, refusing to meet his friend's eyes.

Trask stared at him for a moment, and then gave a low hoot of laughter. "Come now, Silverton, don't tell me that your vaunted skills have failed to have the desired effect?"

"Can we please change the subject?" Silverton ground out between clenched teeth. "Although you may not believe it, I invited you down here not for the dubious pleasure of your company, but because I need your advice on a matter of some import."

Trask grinned but refrained from any more lewd comments. "I am yours to command."

Casting a quick glance around to ensure their privacy, Silverton launched into a brief recitation of the events that had occurred the night Jacob Burnley forced himself on Meredith. The smile faded from Trask's face as Silverton also related Isaac Burnley's attempt to control the sisters, and his threat to incarcerate Annabel in an asylum.

"What possible reason could he have for wanting to do that?"

"That's what I need to find out," answered Silverton. "The Burnleys are prosperous wool merchants and tradesmen. I believe the uncle is sole owner of a large factory in Bristol. Given that you have investments in the trade, I hoped you could use your contacts to determine the state of the family fortune. The uncle and son, apparently, had no interest in either Meredith or Annabel until a few months ago. Something must have changed to precipitate their rash behavior."

Understanding dawned on Trask's face. "Annabel is a considerable heiress from her mother's side, is she not?"

Silverton nodded. "Ten thousand a year. And although Meredith's income is much less, it would still provide a tidy sum for a business that may be encountering difficulties."

"Leave it with me. I'll be going back to London in a few days; there are one or two people in the city that might be able to provide some answers. In the meantime, I'll write to my contacts in Bath and Bristol. If there is anything to know, I will find it."

Silverton was about to reply when his mother drifted over in a cloud of peach and gold silk. The two men turned politely to greet her.

"You are both very naughty boys," she purred as she wrapped her hand around Silverton's forearm. "My son, you are sadly neglecting your guests. Lady Isabel has most graciously consented to play the pianoforte for us. You must know how accomplished she is, and her singing voice—simply divine!"

Trask pointedly raised his eyebrows. Silverton gave him a sardonic smile in return.

"In that case, my lady, I'll rejoin the others." The earl escaped across the room to take a seat next to Sophia.

"Stephen," Lady Silverton asked with an imperious look on her delicate features, "would you be so kind as to open the instrument for Lady Isabel? You have been ignoring her all evening, and I assure you, the poor girl is most conscious of the slight."

Silverton studied his mother's haughty expression.

"Well, we certainly can't have that." He arranged his features into their habitual social mask and allowed his mother to lead him over to the young lady waiting eagerly by the pianoforte.

Meredith had spent the last two weeks trying to forget the life-altering encounter that had occurred in the library at Stanton House. That, of course, was impossible. Every time she looked at Silverton the memories came flooding back, along with a liquid heat that threatened to melt her from the inside out.

She had done everything she could to avoid him—no mean feat given they were living in the same house—but her bulwark and shield had departed this morning in a traveling coach to Brighton.

Meredith dragged her attention back to the absurdly dressed young man who had spent the evening flirting with her. Viscount Tuddler had been a nuisance ever since the men had joined the ladies in the drawing room after dinner. The murderous glares Silverton directed at the viscount were the only consolation she had for the purgatory of his company.

She cast a surreptitious glance at her host as he stood deep in conversation with the Earl of Trask. Meredith tried mightily to suppress the wistful longing she felt in his company, a longing that had only grown more intense during these last few weeks at his estate.

Imposing and beautiful, Belfield Abbey had appealed immediately to her artistic sensibilities. Meredith would never forget her first glimpse of the manor house. Both she and Annabel had gazed impatiently out the windows of the chaise as it bowled up the long drive through the enormous, lushly wooded deer park. Suddenly, the trees had parted and the Abbey had revealed itself in all the venerable splendor of its Tudor glory.

She spent many secret hours wandering the house and grounds, the majesty and ancient history of the estate exerting a powerful influence on her imagination. Meredith couldn't help yearning for a life here with Silverton, raising children and weaving herself into the fabric of generations that had come before and would continue unbroken for years to come.

But her wistful fantasies must remain just that—fantasies. Whenever she thought about what life would really be like as the Marchioness of Silverton, she was swamped with anxiety and a bitter sense of her own inadequacy. And even though Silverton might not realize how ill equipped she was for the position, his mother certainly did.

Lady Silverton had been icily polite for the past two weeks. The woman's obvious dislike of her too clearly reminded Meredith of the reception she would receive from the ton if she were foolish enough to marry Silverton. She didn't even want to imagine how poorly her ladyship would react if she knew that her son had already proposed marriage.

Fortunately, Meredith would never find out, since she had no intention of accepting his offer. She lay awake at night thinking of little else, and there was no doubt in her mind that if she married him it would only be a matter of time before he grew bored with her. Even worse, she would eventually irritate him with her lack of social polish, an essential quality in the circles in which he moved. He needed a true lady accustomed to the ways of the ton, one who wouldn't embarrass him with repeated social blunders.

He needed someone like Lady Isabel.

Just looking at the elegant young woman made her stomach curdle with resentment. The Wrackleys' daughter was a stunning beauty, petite and slender, with classical features and a tea-rose complexion. Next to her, Meredith felt like a gawky, aging spinster.

Even worse, when Lady Isabel had chatted with Silverton before dinner, Meredith couldn't help but notice what a striking pair they made. Apparently, Lady Silverton thought so too because she had done everything she could to throw them together, including seating the earl's daughter next to him at dinner.

And to make the evening just as horrible as it could possibly be, Meredith also had to suffer the plague of Lady Isabel's encroaching toad of a brother, who clearly thought his tasteless advances were every woman's dream.

"Ah, Miss Burnley," the viscount suddenly murmured in her ear, "the evening air whispers of fragrance and romance! I insist that you join me on the terrace—your dusky beauty will surely outshine even the glorious rays of the setting sun."

Meredith's hands itched to box the side of his head.

"Thank you, my lord, but no," she said firmly, turning her back to him as Annabel came to sit beside her.

"Sophia told me to come over and rescue you," Annabel whispered. "That horrid boy has been nattering at you all night. Do you want me to try to draw him away? I'm sure I could persuade him to come out to the terrace with me, if you like."

Meredith laughed. "No, darling, but thank you. I suspect that if you did, Robert would be very unhappy. He's glowering at us both this very instant."

Annabel glanced over at her fiancé and giggled. "Oh, dear,

I hadn't thought of that. He's really getting terribly possessive, isn't he?"

"Getting possessive?" retorted Meredith. "Really, Annabel, it's a miracle he hasn't locked you in a room by now. He's been devoted to you from the first, but now he's become positively proprietorial."

The two sisters looked at Robert, who gazed at Annabel with a look that managed to be both stern and adoring at the same time.

Meredith chuckled. "Robert seems to have undergone quite a change in the last few weeks, ever since your grandfather gave him permission to marry you. I think he would carry you around in his pocket, if you let him."

A silly grin spread across her sister's face. "Yes, I know. Isn't it wonderful?"

"Yes, darling, it is." She smiled at Annabel, but inside she wrestled with a stabbing pang of regret at the thought of losing her sister so soon.

Much to Meredith's surprise, General and Lady Stanton had given their unqualified approval to the match. Her ladyship never said another word about her plans for Annabel to marry Silverton, apparently content with the young couple's decision. In fact, the relationship between Annabel and Robert seemed to bring a sense of closure to the tragic estrangement that had sundered the family for so many years. Everyone rejoiced in their happiness. Meredith tried to rejoice, too, but she dreaded the years of lonely solitude stretching before her like a blank canvas that would never see color.

Taking a deep breath, she gave herself a sharp little scold, resolving to drive such gloomy reflections from her mind. Annabel was radiantly happy and healthy, and that was all that mattered.

"Attende, everyone!" Lady Silverton stood in the center of the drawing room, gently clapping her hands to silence the quiet chatter. "Lady Isabel has agreed to play for us tonight. I assure you, we are in for a rare treat."

Annabel murmured a swift apology before slipping away to join Robert, who impatiently awaited her return. Meredith sighed, resigning herself once again to the torture of Viscount Tuddler's undivided attention. She wondered how much worse the evening could get.

She had her answer a moment later, when Silverton took Lady Isabel's hand and escorted her to the pianoforte. The young woman murmured something to him and then laughed; it was a delightfully light sound that caused Meredith's chest to constrict with pain. A knowing smile curved Silverton's lips as he gazed down at her, and he said something in response that made her laugh again.

"What a lovely couple they make, don't you agree, Lady Wrackley?" Lady Silverton settled gracefully into the chair next to Meredith.

"Simply charming!" With a flick of her wrist, the countess motioned to her son to vacate the seat on the other side of Meredith. The young man glared at his mamma but took himself off to join his father, who seemed to be happily drinking himself into a stupor.

"Miss Burnley, do you play?" enquired Lady Wrackley as she fussily arranged her draperies.

"No, your ladyship, I do not," Meredith replied quietly.

"Miss Burnley is an accomplished artist, however," said the marchioness, "although some might say that the subjects of her paintings are rather odd, especially for a young lady."

Meredith could hear the undisguised contempt in Lady Silverton's voice.

"Dear me," tittered Countess Wrackley. "How unusual. My Isabel, as you will hear, plays and sings like an angel. She is much sought after for musical evenings in London."

At that moment, the angelic Isabel brought her hands gracefully down on the keyboard and began to play a popular aria by Handel. *Oh God*, thought Meredith, swallowing hard, *she really does play amazingly well.* Even worse, Lady Isabel looked serenely beautiful as she proceeded to dazzle the guests with her musical prowess.

"Isn't she divine, Miss Burnley?" asked Lady Silverton in a stage whisper. "So accomplished, so very much the lady. She is just the kind of woman I would wish my son to marry."

Struck dumb by that comment, Meredith simply nodded her head.

"Her deportment is perfect, and she would make him an excellent hostess. More importantly, she would never inconvenience him. My son hates to be inconvenienced."

"What do you mean?" Meredith inquired faintly. She knew Lady Silverton was baiting her, but she still couldn't stop herself from asking.

Lady Silverton's well-bred laugh trailed shivers down Meredith's spine.

"Surely, my dear, you are aware of Silverton's reputation. He is a notorious flirt who has broken any number of hearts over the years."

In all fairness, Meredith had never seen him flirt with anyone but herself, although what had occurred in the library two weeks ago was certainly a great deal more than flirtation. She looked at him as he stood by the pianoforte, an easy smile on his perfect face as he turned the music for Lady Isabel. All at once, Meredith came to the realization that she had been an absolute fool.

"A man like Silverton cannot be expected to change his nature simply to please his wife. And a young woman like Lady Isabel will never be so foolish as to embarrass him with displays of passion, or intemperate behavior." Her ladyship gave a delicate shudder. "Such displays are, of course, repulsive to any man in Silverton's position. It would make him a laughingstock amongst his acquaintance."

The marchioness inspected Meredith from beneath her

eyelashes. Obviously satisfied by what she saw, she leaned back in her seat, languidly fanning herself as she nodded in time to the music.

Meredith, however, found that she could only stare blindly at the floor as the cold despair inside her effectively turned whatever heat remained into an impenetrable block of ice.

Chapter Twenty-Two

Silverton tried manfully to focus his attention on his land agent's droning voice. Normally, he would have listened with great interest to Peterson's report on the expected yields of the apple orchards this fall. Kent was famous for its orchards, and the fruit from the Abbey provided a lucrative source of income for the estate.

But Silverton's mind had drifted away from the ledger books an hour ago, when he saw Meredith and Annabel emerge from the house and walk down the terrace steps. Through the open windows of his library, he had watched them amble across the lawn on their way to the wooded path leading to the north escarpment.

The sisters had carried baskets full of art supplies. They were followed by two footmen who fairly staggered under their loads of easels, stools, and other accoutrements necessary for a morning of artistic activity. Meredith had turned around to talk to the men, gesturing at the unwieldy burdens each of them carried. Silverton hadn't been able to hear her, but she had obviously offered to help them with their loads.

His servants had declined, of course, shaking their heads vigorously in reply. No wonder his staff had become so devoted to Meredith, he thought. She treated them with a quiet courtesy that unintentionally illustrated the obvious lack of such conduct in Lady Silverton.

He frowned when he thought of his mother and her behavior at last night's dinner party. She had been positively effusive toward the Wrackleys, doing everything in her power to throw their daughter in his path. It had been impossible for him to avoid Lady Isabel. His mother had made sure that any attempt on his part to elude the girl's company would have been perceived by the other guests as an obvious slight by their host.

Even more disturbing to him was the look on Meredith's face during Lady Isabel's performance. His insides had twisted with frustration as he had helplessly watched his mother and Lady Wrackley drip poison in her ear. He could only guess what they had said to her, and the misery on Meredith's face had made him feel wild. It had taken all his willpower to remain at Lady Isabel's side, calmly turning the pages of her music like a trained monkey.

Unfortunately, as soon as the performance was over, Meredith had excused herself and fled the room, evading him once again.

Today was the day, however, that all such evasions would come to an end. Silverton vowed to himself that he would track her down this very afternoon and explain to her in no uncertain terms her future as his wife. He knew Meredith loved him; it was long past time that her doubts about him were laid to rest. His mother would have to be dealt with, of course, but convincing Meredith of his affection and loyalty claimed priority over anything else.

Besides, his primitive self was becoming increasingly unmanageable. He needed to feel Meredith's soft body melting against his, needed to feel the lush warmth of her perfect lips as they gently returned his kisses. That and only that would satisfy the predatory urges he struggled to control.

"I beg your pardon, my lord." Peterson's monotone voice

recalled him to his surroundings. "Have I failed to make myself clear?"

Silverton smiled apologetically at the plainly dressed man who sat on the other side of the old-fashioned, carved oak desk. "Forgive me, Peterson, what did you say?"

Extending his arm across the desk, Peterson indicated a row of figures in the ledger. "If you will compare the numbers in this column, Lord Silverton," he intoned, "to the numbers in the next column, you will see the projected income that will result from the increased crop yields at harvest this year. These projected yields seem to bear out the efficacy of the changes we have made in the management of the orchards on the south estate."

Peterson was an exemplary land agent—honest and thrifty to a fault. But he had to be as boring as any man that had walked the earth since the days of Adam. Today was worse than usual, and Silverton simply could not get his intellect to cooperate with the task at hand.

His gaze drifted again to the view out the window. He came alert when he saw Annabel emerge from the woods and cross the lawn, swinging her bonnet in her hand. She climbed up the steps to the terrace and disappeared into the house.

Meredith was alone at the escarpment.

Silverton was just about to dismiss the land agent when he heard another pair of footsteps on the flagstone walk that led to the kitchen gardens. Rising from his chair, he strolled to the open window. A footman appeared around the corner of the house, carrying a small tray with two glasses and a pitcher full of an iced beverage.

The servant hurried toward the path that Annabel had just returned on. His obvious destination was the escarpment, and, just as obviously, Meredith had no intention of returning to the house anytime soon.

"Peterson." Silverton ruthlessly interrupted the endless recitation of facts and figures.

"My lord?"

"That will be all for today."

"As you wish, my lord."

Peterson methodically gathered up his papers, stacked the ledgers, and solemnly bowed before exiting the room. Sighing in relief, Silverton strode over to the library's French doors and stepped outside.

He turned his face up to the early afternoon sun, absorbing the heat and light that reflected off the white marble of the terrace. Stretching his cramped arms, he pulled in a deep breath, inhaling the humid air scented with the heavy aroma of cut grass and blooming rosebushes.

Silverton never minded the summer heat. He loved the country in all kinds of weather as long as he could be outside—cantering on his roan hunter through the deer park or the woods of the Abbey, talking to his groundskeepers or tenants, riding with the hunt during the season—he loved it all. As much as he enjoyed the tumult and excitement of London, it was here at Belfield Abbey that he found contentment. Even more importantly, he was never bored.

Except, on occasion, with Peterson, he admitted wryly.

He crossed the terrace and ran down the steps that led to the broad lawn ringing the manor house. Striding across the grass, he entered the woods and took the narrow path now used only by the groundskeepers but which had once been the entrance to the magical forest of his childhood.

Silverton had spent endless hours playing in these woods. He had launched countless quests for the Holy Grail or embarked on hunts for treasure hidden deep in Merlin's cave. His childhood innocence had faded years ago, but the dense and shadowed forest with its long ago memories still exerted a subtle pull on his imagination.

He hunted again today, but this time it was a not a game for children, and he knew exactly where to look for his elusive prey.

Deep in the woods, he paralleled the regular path that led to a small meadow on the edge of the escarpment. Although it was after noon, the strong light of the sun only dimly penetrated the thick canopy of ancient oaks. The air was still, the heat having silenced most of the birds and small animals. Silverton heard only the sound of his boots crushing the dried leaves on the overgrown path, and the occasional rustle of a squirrel or vole burrowing through the undergrowth.

Suddenly, he heard loud footsteps pounding down the other path, coming from the direction of the escarpment. Through the trees, he glimpsed a man in footman's livery, running as if he were in a panic. It must be the servant who had brought the drinks to Meredith, but shadows cast by the heavy oak canopy obscured his face.

Silverton frowned to himself, struck by the footman's strange behavior. He froze in his tracks, wanting to observe the servant without alerting him to his presence.

The man stumbled to a halt, turning to stare back along the path to the meadow as if waiting for something to happen. The sounds of his labored breathing echoed harshly through the quiet of the deep woods. Before Silverton could identify him, the footman pivoted and raced back down the path toward the Abbey.

He stood for a moment, watching the servant disappear into the trees. Then he turned and strode quickly through the undergrowth, cutting diagonally from the path in his hurry to reach the meadow. His desire to see Meredith became acute, underscored by an apprehension created by the footman's flight through the woods. He accelerated his pace, the oaks around him beginning to thin as he neared the edge of the escarpment.

Bursting through the tree line, Silverton jerked to a stop as his eyes adjusted to the glare of the midday sun after the gloom of the forest. He blinked, and the meadow slowly came into focus. His gaze swept across the space before him, and he saw her sitting peacefully in the sunshine. He bent over and rested his hands on his knees, catching his breath as a hot rush of relief flowed through his body. God only knew why the footman had acted like a madman—he would have to find out later—but Meredith was clearly fine.

Forcing himself to inhale a slow breath, Silverton willed his muscles to relax before stepping away from the trees to cross the meadow to join her. She had her back to him, perched on a wooden stool before her easel, only a few feet from the edge of the escarpment. Annabel's easel was close by, her empty stool serving as a table for the tray that contained the drinks.

The setting could not have been more idyllic. The meadow, dotted with red and white wildflowers, overlooked the undulating chalk hills of the North Downs of Kent. It was a landscape made for artists, a varied expanse of woodlands, pastures, and orchards, with the occasional church spire rising in the distance.

Silverton walked slowly across the meadow, allowing his boots to rustle in the grass so she would hear him coming up behind her.

Meredith's nose practically touched the canvas, so absorbed was she in her work, but at the sound of his footfall she put down her brush and turned in her seat. A ready smile began to light her face.

That smile faded as soon as she saw him, replaced by a somber expression he found both surprising and annoying. Clearly she had been expecting Annabel. Even more clearly, he was not a welcome substitute.

Silverton smothered an irritated groan. He knew Meredith had been upset when she fled the drawing room last night, but he had hoped a good-night's sleep would have lightened her spirits. Now, instead of enjoying the luxury of finally having her to himself, he would be forced to devote most of his energy to discovering her reasons for avoiding him.

Perhaps, he briefly reflected, he should simply pull her down into the grass and remind her of the heat that had scorched them both that night at Stanton House. But as Silverton observed the firm set of her elegant jaw, he realized that such a decisive strategy would likely meet with limited success. Reigning in his impatience, he forced himself to smile as he sat on the ground beside her.

"Good afternoon, my lord," she said in a tight little voice before returning her attention to the painting.

"Good afternoon, Meredith."

Silverton stretched up to inspect her work. He experienced a shock. Instead of a sunny rendering of the bucolic vista stretched out before them, Meredith had chosen to paint the gently rolling hills as covered in a blanket of snow and ice. It was grim depiction—gray, lifeless, and chill.

Puzzled, he tilted his head in an unspoken question, but she ignored him. He decided, for the moment, to let her do so, leaning back on his arms to give himself a better view of her face.

She carefully dipped her brush into a small pot of paint and leaned forward into the canvas, her brow wrinkling in concentration. Silverton thought she looked adorable, with her hair swept back from her face in a loose knot, her nose crinkling as she pondered the next brushstroke.

He loved the focus and intensity of her gaze, remembering the last time he had seen that look. It had been in the library at Stanton House, when she had lain half-naked and panting across his lap. He couldn't wait to have her in his arms again, when he would unleash all that intensity for himself as he slowly penetrated her silky flesh.

Silverton luxuriated in that delightful image for a few minutes, allowing the silence to stretch between them.

"Meredith," he finally said, letting his eyes roam over her face, "I wanted to speak to you last night but you left the room before I had the opportunity to do so."

Her hand froze in midair. She cast him a veiled glance before resuming her work on the canvas.

"How odd," she murmured, her voice and expression revealing nothing. "I would think you had many opportunities both before and after dinner to do just that."

"Yes. Well . . ." He hesitated, searching for the right words to explain the situation. "You might think so, but the situation was not . . . convenient."

Once again she paused in midstroke, frowning intently at her painting as if she expected it to begin speaking to her. Then she calmly resumed her work.

"I'm not surprised," she eventually replied.

This time he had no trouble hearing the frigid tones in her voice.

"Lady Silverton told me that you never inconvenience yourself for anyone's sake."

"What?" He sat up straight.

"Would you like me to repeat myself?" she asked politely.

"No, thank you," he muttered. This was not the conversation he had anticipated when he had come searching for her. He stared at her, willing her to look at him so he could gauge the intention behind the remark.

Meredith kept her face turned away, concentrating on her work. She seemed almost disinterested in the conversation in general, and in him in particular.

Silverton felt his lips curve in a humorless smile. He had never thought of himself as vain, but her unexpected comment stung his pride. He pulled one leg up and rested an arm on his knee, pondering the situation.

"My family has, on more than one occasion, seen fit to label me as a selfish creature," he said.

"Oh, no," she responded absently, still not looking at him. "Not selfish—spoiled." She leaned back from the easel to inspect the canvas. "There is a difference, you know."

Silverton's jaw dropped open, but he quickly snapped it shut.

He fumed for a minute, irritated not only by her impertinent pronouncements but also by the fact that she still refused to look at him.

"Well," he finally ground out, "what is the difference?"

Meredith carefully mixed another color on her brush and reapplied herself to the painting. He thought her hand trembled a bit, but her voice sounded oddly detached.

"People who are selfish lack generosity of spirit. They are spiteful and mean, and can only really love themselves. You, on the other hand, are a kind and generous man. You care for your family and friends. But because of your position in society and your"—she hesitated, and he saw a blush creep up into her cheeks—"your personal attributes, you have been given everything you could ever desire or need. No one has ever said no to you. You have never really had to work for anything. In truth, no one could blame you for being spoiled, since it is due entirely to the circumstances of your life."

Why doesn't she just drop an anvil on my head, he thought, dazed by her comment. She had delivered a devastating analysis of his character as calmly as if she had been commenting on the weather. No one except his aunt and uncle had ever dared speak to him in such a fashion. He had, of course, endured the vulgar taunts and jests of his friends, but that was different. That was simply how men spoke to each other.

In fact, he had always been comfortable with his place in the world: confidently at the top of the pile. But Meredith made him feel like a callow youth. It astounded him that an inexperienced young woman from the country could make him so bloody unsure of himself.

"You're wrong, you know," he finally replied. He needed her to understand that the social mask he sometimes wore was simply that: a mask. "There are those who have said no to me before, many times. Aunt Georgina in particular has always tried to impress upon me the wisdom of putting the needs of others before my own. Since I am the head of the family, she has always wished me to cultivate a more serious and determined character. I regret you think she failed in that endeavor."

In spite of his good intentions, Silverton felt a twinge of satisfaction when he saw her shift uncomfortably on her little stool. He leaned over and inspected her face, certain now that she regretted her candid remarks.

"In fact," he continued, unable to repress the desire to exact a small measure of revenge, "you remind me greatly of Aunt Georgina. You're so solemn that you sound remarkably like her. Even your countenance has the same stern, disapproving expression."

Meredith bit her lower lip. He watched with interest as her shoulders moved up around her ears.

"Lord Silverton." Her voice sounded tighter than a drum. "Please forgive me. I have grown too accustomed to thinking of myself as a member of your family. I had no right to say what I did. There is no doubt you fulfill all your duties exactly as you should."

He didn't reply, determined to force her to reveal what she really thought of him. Long moments stretched by as Meredith fiddled with her brush.

She cast him a hunted look. "It's just that sometimes you seem to lack . . ." She ground to a halt. Silverton suspected that she was now truly cursing her unruly tongue.

"Lack seriousness of character?" he prompted.

"No," she blurted out. "Seriousness of purpose."

Silverton frowned and leaned heavily back on his hands. He didn't know how to respond, since he was genuinely puzzled by her remark. There was no doubt Meredith had suffered much heartache over the years, but he thought it unnatural that a beautiful and wealthy young woman should hold such a grim view of life. It seemed to him that she actively resisted enjoying herself.

He cocked his head to one side and studied her face, which had turned rosy with embarrassment. "Meredith, considering that we have been blessed with such privilege, don't you think we should try to enjoy ourselves, just a little?"

"You seem to enjoy yourself too much," Meredith retorted. Her eyes flashed with anger before she turned away, as if conscious that she had revealed more than she wanted to.

He realized with a jolt of understanding that he had just found the trail of breadcrumbs through the forest.

"And when do I enjoy myself too much, Meredith?"

She hunched a shoulder at him, refusing to answer.

"Did I enjoy myself too much last night?" he persisted. "Did I enjoy myself with Lady Isabel?"

Meredith jumped up from her seat and began hastily collecting her brushes and wrapping them in rags. Silverton pushed himself up from the grass, eyeing her closely as he brushed the dirt from his buckskins.

After a few moments he gently grasped her arm, taking the brushes from her with his other hand. Meredith froze at his touch, her color coming and going with a hectic flush. He slowly raised her hand to his lips, brushing it with a soft kiss.

"I may sometimes enjoy life too much," he said, "but you, my dear girl, do not enjoy it nearly enough."

She looked up to meet his gaze, her quicksilver eyes reflecting a tumult of conflicting emotions. To Silverton's dismay, those eyes began to fill, tears sparkling on her thick black lashes. Meredith blinked rapidly, turning her head to the side to hide her face. She tugged her arm, trying to escape his grasp, so he forced himself to let her go.

As he watched her grope in the pocket of her gown for a handkerchief, Silverton racked his brains, wondering what he could possibly do to ease a pain that he suspected had very deep roots.

He hated the sight of her tears, and he had never felt so helpless in his life.

Chapter Twenty-Three

Meredith pulled away from Silverton, unable to bear the look of sympathy on his handsome face. She hated it when people felt sorry for her. That it was Silverton made it even worse; he would never feel pity for a woman like Lady Isabel.

At the thought of that dainty beauty and her flirtation with Silverton, Meredith found her emotions suddenly veering off in another direction, rapidly converting to anger. She hastily reached down and retrieved a brush from her basket, plopping back onto her stool. If she pretended to paint, then at least she wouldn't have to directly confront Silverton's aristocratic arrogance when she answered him.

"Tell me, my lord," she exclaimed, "what has there been to enjoy in my life so far? While it is true that Annabel and I are fortunate not to suffer impoverishment, there has been little else in our existence, to this point, to make us happy. I have only two things that give me joy—my sister and my painting."

The tears were welling up in her eyes again, and she blinked hard to keep them from falling onto her cheeks. She cursed inside, having known all along that it would be a mistake to allow herself to talk to him.

Her heart had dropped to her shoes when she saw him striding across the meadow, his long, muscular legs eating up the space between them. Meredith had never expected him to follow her all the way out here, assuming he would eventually grow bored with the chase and leave her in peace.

Especially since the sainted Lady Isabel resided only a short distance away. After last night, Meredith had been sure he would prefer to spend time with someone more suited to the life he seemed to enjoy so much.

Instead, for reasons she couldn't fathom, he had chosen to violate her sanctuary and crash through her hard-fought reserve, just as he always did. And she had responded in the worst possible way, by insulting his character, his way of life, almost everything about him.

Why didn't she just dump a pot of paint on his head and be done with it, Meredith sighed to herself, clenching her brush in her fist. He unfailingly brought out the worst in her, especially after that unforgettable night in the library. She couldn't think of that encounter without feeling hot and restless, and angry at him for making her so uncomfortable with herself.

She glanced sideways and saw that his features were etched with gravity, but his beautiful eyes were softened with a warmth and kindness that soothed her wounded pride. When he looked at her like that she had to struggle against an overwhelming urge to throw herself into his arms, ignoring all the warnings that swirled constantly in her head.

But she couldn't do that, no matter how much she wanted to.

Meredith knew that someday soon she would return to her solitary life at Swallow Hill. Despite his promises to her in the library, she knew how unlikely it was that Silverton really wanted to marry her. And even if he thought he did, she had no doubt his mother would strenuously oppose it. Lady Silverton had made that perfectly clear last night. Meredith also couldn't imagine that General and Lady Stanton would approve of the match, either, not after the pain their daughter— her stepmother—had caused them so many years ago.

No, Meredith knew she must continue to try to ignore him.

Difficult, to say the least, since he would not go away and leave her alone.

"Meredith."

She stifled a gasp. Silverton had moved very close, looming over her as he thoughtfully studied her work. He crossed his arms over his broad chest, head tilted to the side as if he were puzzled.

"Why do you paint such unsettling pictures?"

She blinked at him, surprised that he asked the question so bluntly. Most people danced around the subject, worried they might offend her or, even worse, that she might actually tell them why she did so.

"It's difficult to explain," she hedged.

"Try," he ordered gently.

Meredith glanced up at him, afraid she would see either amusement or disdain on his features. He gave her a steady look in return, and she had the feeling he wouldn't let her go until doomsday unless she made some attempt to answer his question.

"Well," she said, swallowing against a sudden constriction in her throat. Picking up her glass from the other seat, she sipped, grimacing slightly at the bitterness of the drink. She was momentarily distracted by the thought that it was the worst lemonade she had ever tasted.

"Well," she started again, "I don't intentionally select a particular scene in order to disturb anyone. My ideas usually stem from something I am feeling at the time. . . ."

She trailed off, realizing how inadequate any explanation must sound. How could she convey to him the grief and anger that often surged within her when she painted? How to describe the relief she experienced when she allowed that terrible power to flow through her fingers and manifest itself on the canvas? There had been many days when her painting had been the only thing that made her feel alive and capable of going on.

Silverton didn't move or make a sound, obviously determined to wait her out. Meredith bit her lower lip and tried again.

"I know it might seem strange, but I often think of my parents when I paint. Sometimes I feel overcome with sadness, and this is the only way I can seem to express it." She stared into the distance, vaguely aware of the beauty of the rolling hills and the luminescent green of the early summer foliage that covered them. "I suppose it's the grief and sorrow that make me paint this way."

She shrugged and finally looked at him, certain that a man who so thoroughly controlled his world could never understand what she was trying to say.

Silverton met her gaze, the intensity in his searing blue eyes seeming to reflect the hot summer sky. He reached down and gently stroked her cheek.

"My dear girl, is it only the pain you remember? Only the grief and bitterness you keep alive in your mind? Why can't you remember the affection your parents must have felt for you and your sister? There is no doubt in my mind that they loved you very much and that you will be loved again like that in the future."

His words penetrated the icy barriers she had desperately erected around her vulnerable heart. She felt the terrible weight of her yearning for him, a burden she knew she would carry for the rest of her life.

"I don't know," she said softly. "Perhaps I don't know how to do that. I have lost three parents. Losing two is tragic. Losing three is . . . simply absurd."

Meredith lowered her eyes, noticing with surprise that she gripped her brush so tightly her nails dug into the palm of her hand. Taking a deep breath, she relaxed her fingers while struggling to keep from bursting into tears. She hated that he could make her feel so mawkish about her life.

Suddenly, she became immensely annoyed with herself and

with him. Could anything be more ridiculous than whining self-indulgently about the past? It didn't really matter what Silverton thought about her paintings anyway, or about anything else, for that matter.

Not really.

Meredith sat up straight on her stool. "This is what I feel," she said defiantly, looking away from him and returning her gaze to her canvas. "This is what feels true and right to me. It is how *I* choose to remember my life."

Silverton didn't answer, and the silence between them lengthened. Strangely, it did not feel uncomfortable to her. They did nothing for several minutes but listen to the occasional trill of a lark and the buzzing of the honeybees in the wildflowers of the meadow. Meredith felt the tension begin to drain slowly from her body.

She eventually worked up the courage to look at him. He stood quietly beside her, his manner subdued. She arched her eyebrows in inquiry, and his well-shaped mouth quirked into a devastating smile, igniting in her the slow burn of sensual longing that always remained so close to the surface.

"Meredith, has anyone ever told you what a terrifying creature you are? I feel the cold, dread fingers of a miserable fate creeping up my spine at this very moment."

She reluctantly returned his smile, unable, as usual, to resist the pull of his warmth.

"Come," he said. "It's much too hot out here in the sun— you are turning quite pink. Finish your drink, and I will take you for an exceedingly dull and merely pleasant walk through the dovecote garden. Not very exciting, I know, but I feel sure the insipid nature of our stroll will vastly improve the tone of your mind."

Meredith took another cautious sip from her glass, wrinkling her nose at the strange taste.

"As you wish, my lord, but I would prefer not to finish this.

I vow, it is the oddest-tasting lemonade I have ever had. And it smells bitter, too. I wonder if some of the lemons were rotten."

Silverton had just extended a hand to help her up, but he paused at her words and plucked the glass from her instead. He brought the glass to his nose and sniffed. A gasp escaped his lips.

His other hand shot out and grabbed her wrist. "How much of this did you drink?"

Meredith tried without success to tug her hand from an unbreakable grip. She suddenly felt oddly hot, and slightly sick to her stomach.

"Just a few sips. I told you, I didn't like it."

He dragged her to her feet. "Come," he said urgently. "We must get back to the house immediately."

"Why?" she protested, casting a glance at her wet canvas. "I don't understand, my lord."

His manner had changed so quickly that it began to alarm her. She had no choice but to follow him as he towed her across the meadow to the break in the trees.

Silverton glanced down at her face, his mouth set in a grim line. "How do you feel?"

He tried to hurry her along, but Meredith's legs began to feel very heavy and strangely detached from the rest of her body. She stumbled against him.

Silverton stopped, his eyes skimming over her, his expression even darker than it had been a minute ago. A prickling wave of apprehension washed through her.

And her stomach was beginning to churn with a burning nausea.

"Now . . . now that you mention it," she stammered, "I don't feel very well."

She grabbed his other arm and swayed against him. "I . . . I think I need to sit down."

* * *

Silverton fought back the terrible fear rising in his throat. Meredith's face had gone dead white, the pupils of her eyes so large that all he could see was blackness limned with a thin circle of gray. She sagged heavily against him.

"What's happening?" she whispered.

Sweeping her into his arms, he stalked down the path as he held her tightly against his chest. He struggled to contain the volatile mix of rage and fear that threatened to overtake him; he must reassure her, not frighten her.

"The lemons must be rotten," he said, his voice surprisingly steady. "You're obviously feeling the effects of that, and you'll have to rid yourself of the drink before you can feel better."

Silverton couldn't bear to say what he really thought. She had been poisoned. The bitter scent in her glass had told him all he needed to know: someone had dosed the lemonade with cyanide.

"I'm sorry, Meredith." He cradled her gently as he hurried through the woods. "When we get back to the house you'll have to take a purgative."

She whimpered and turned her face into his waistcoat. "I'm going to be sick," she gasped. "Put me down."

He lowered her to the ground and quickly untied the ribbons of her bonnet, which he tossed aside into a pile of leaves. She tried to turn away, and he knew she was mortified at the thought of being sick in front of him.

"Don't be embarrassed, sweetheart," Silverton murmured. "You're not the first person I've seen cast up his accounts."

Meredith leaned forward and retched, her body twisting with the force of the spasm. Liquid spewed from her mouth onto the ground.

Relief surged through him when he saw a fair amount of liquid come up. She continued to retch and gag, bent over double, her hands digging into the dirt with the force of her body's contractions. He held her gently, stroking her hair back from her face as he murmured soothing noises.

Watching her hunched over on the ground, gasping breathlessly, was the worst thing Silverton had ever seen and almost more than he could bear to witness. He wrapped his arm carefully around her chest to give her more support. Her heart pounded like a hammer against him. His own heart, in turn, felt squeezed in the grip of some awful, sympathetic agony, keeping measure with hers in a rhythm of fearful emotion.

She can't die. He repeated it in his mind, over and over again. He simply wouldn't allow it, he told himself as he gently rocked her in his arms.

Silverton knew in that instant that if anything happened to Meredith, his life would be finished. She had become essential to his existence—a meaningful existence, anyway. He would gladly give his life for hers, but for now all he could do was hold her and pray this crisis would pass. Black rage hovered at the edge of his consciousness, but he pushed it back, focusing all his energy on the shivering body clasped in his arms.

After a few minutes her shuddering seemed to ease, and her pulse gradually began to slow to a more normal rhythm. He eased her upright against his chest, letting her lean back against him. Her thick hair fell in a wild tangle around her shoulders. He removed a handkerchief from his pocket and gently blotted her face and mouth.

"How do you feel now, my poor darling?"

Meredith took a tremulous breath and shifted in his arms. She had to swallow several times before she could answer.

"I would be very grateful if you would carry me back to the escarpment and throw me over the edge," she whispered in a hoarse voice.

He smiled and felt the vise around his heart begin to loosen. If she was able to joke, she must be feeling better.

Silverton wrapped his arms more tightly about her and

stood, pulling her with him to her feet. He slipped one arm beneath her legs and swung her up against his chest.

"Just a few more minutes, my love," he murmured in her ear, "and you'll be able to rest."

She was silent, huddled against him as he strode quickly down a side path leading directly to the kitchen gardens, the fastest route back to the house.

As they emerged from the trees, he saw Cook and the head gardener conferring just outside the entrance to the pantry. Cook turned her head and gave a cry, clearly startled by the sight of the master carrying one of the guests. She and the gardener hurried toward them.

"Lord Silverton." Meredith stirred against his shoulder. He bent his head to hear her more clearly.

"Yes, sweetheart?"

"It wasn't just the lemons that made me sick, was it?"

He hesitated, reluctant to cause her any more distress. But she was no fool, and he could not keep the truth from her and keep her safe.

"No, Meredith, I don't think so."

Her head drooped back down. She began to shiver as she absorbed the meaning of his reply. He glanced up. Cook and the gardener would be within hearing any second.

"Meredith," he said in a low, urgent voice. "Don't say anything about this to anyone but your sister. Say that you ate something that did not agree with you. I will deal with this situation, but you must be quiet, for now."

She nodded her head, seeming to shrink into him as he clasped her more tightly against his body.

Silverton struggled to rein his anger onto a tight leash, not wanting to frighten her any more than he already had. But someone would pay dearly for this day's work. Someone would die for almost killing the woman he loved.

Chapter Twenty-Four

"There is no trace of the footman."

Silverton looked up from his letter as the Earl of Trask stalked across the library to the carved walnut trolley holding several decanters of spirits. Trask poured himself a generous glass of brandy and tossed back a healthy swallow, grimacing slightly as he did so.

The earl had yet to change from his riding clothes after returning from the search for Welland, the footman who had disappeared after Meredith's poisoning. Trask looked exhausted after two long days searching the surrounding countryside. His dark eyes were ringed with circles, and harsh lines bracketed his hard mouth.

Silverton pushed back from his desk and walked over to join his friend by the trolley. After pouring a brandy for himself, he waved Trask into one of the comfortable wing chairs placed by the marble fireplace.

"Sit down, Simon. You look as if you've been in the saddle for a week."

Trask threw him a sardonic look. "Well, some of us had to do the dirty work, while others chose to stay home with the ladies."

Silverton smiled briefly, knowing his expression was devoid of amusement.

"I could not leave Meredith or Annabel unprotected," he answered quietly.

Trask gave a tired grunt by way of reply.

"Besides," continued Silverton as he settled into the matching wing chair on the other side of the mantel, "you wouldn't think that if you'd been forced to spend the last few days listening to my mother's litany of complaints. You've no idea how gruesome it's been around here since the whole thing happened. She's reduced half the maids to tears, and Cook even threatened to quit and join her brother at his coaching inn in London. I had the devil of a time persuading her not to do so."

Trask laughed, his countenance lightening for the first time since he entered the room. "I can only imagine the techniques Lady Silverton employed to make her feelings known," he replied, stretching his booted legs out as he massaged the muscles of his thighs. "But interrogating every innkeeper and barmaid within a twenty-mile radius is not an experience I'll remember with any fondness. Chawbacons—the whole lot of them."

"Even the barmaids?" Silverton innocently inquired.

Trask snorted and slumped into his chair. "Especially the barmaids. I heard so many Banbury tales I thought my brain would explode. I hope Peterson had better luck than I did."

Silverton shrugged. "Not by much. He did get a sighting in Aylesford. The keeper of the Hare and Crown said he was almost certain Welland came into the pub a few times, although he wouldn't swear it to a jury. According to him, Welland met two men one afternoon about a week ago. They spent an hour huddled in a corner with their heads together. He remembers because one of the strangers bristled up at his wife when she asked if they wanted any food. Told her to mind her own damned business. The innkeeper said he threatened to toss them out if they didn't keep a civil tongue in their heads."

Trask sat up, looking interested now. "Any descriptions?"

Silverton shook his head. "Not much to go on. One older, one younger. Big men, well dressed. The innkeeper did find it odd that Welland would be drinking with two swells, as he called them."

"Do you think it was Jacob and Isaac Burnley?"

Silverton expelled a frustrated breath. "Yes, although I don't see what good it will do us, at least not yet."

"Do you know why Isaac Burnley would try to poison Meredith?"

Silverton shook his head. "Meredith has not yet left her room, and Annabel has spent most of that time with her. I've been reluctant to question them until Meredith recovers. My first concern has been to keep them safe."

He stared into the small fire that had been lit against the mild chill of the early summer evening. "My guess, though, is that the poison was not meant for Meredith, but for Annabel. I suspect that Welland bungled his assignment, and he knew it."

Silverton thought back to the footman's panicked behavior. The man had likely been shocked on arriving at the meadow to discover that Annabel had already returned to the house.

"As soon as she is able, I will ask Meredith to explain the exact disposition of Annabel's finances," he continued. "In the meantime, I'm writing to General Stanton and asking him to make some inquiries with Annabel's bankers. Since he is her grandfather, he might be able to persuade them to illuminate the situation."

"I have no doubt he will succeed in doing just that," Trask replied dryly.

The two men subsided into a companionable silence, listening to the gentle creaks and moans of the old house as it settled in for the night.

"So, what else has been happening back here?" Trask eventually asked, idly swirling the brandy in his crystal tumbler.

"Chaos," replied Silverton.

"Do tell." His friend grinned back at him.

Silverton rose from his chair and began to slowly circle the library. A gnawing restlessness made it impossible for him to sit for any length of time. Even though Meredith was safe, at least for now, he knew anxiety would continue to eat at him until he eliminated the threat against her.

"I had the kitchen torn apart. It was necessary to tell Cook, the housekeeper, and my butler what really happened—Cook was outraged at the very notion that her food made Meredith ill. And it would be difficult to explain why no one else got sick."

Silverton shook his head, recalling the looks of horror on the faces of his senior staff when he revealed that Meredith had been poisoned. "We inspected and disposed of any food or drink not in sealed containers, or under lock and key. All the dishes were scrubbed, all the open liquor discarded. Although there seemed to be no trace of poison anywhere but in the original pitcher of lemonade, it seemed a wise precaution."

He continued his restless circle of the room, forcing Trask to swivel in his seat to follow him.

"What did you tell the others?"

"That something had gone off, but that Cook was unsure of what it was. My mother, of course, greatly objected to the upset and inconvenience to her daily routine, although one wonders how she was actually affected. She let me know in very clear terms that she held Meredith to blame for all the fuss and bother, as she called it."

"Imagine my surprise," Trask replied, his upper lip curling in contempt.

Silverton didn't answer. His mother's atrocious behavior had shocked him, even though he had thought, after all these years, he had grown impervious to her selfishness.

"Really, Stephen," Lady Silverton had complained that first day when dinner had been delayed, "that young woman creates a great deal of turmoil. How dare she put everyone to such trouble? I don't know when we are going to eat tonight, and the servants are in such an uproar I swear it will be a miracle if I don't get the headache."

Silverton had barely managed to contain his temper, already stretched to its limits by the worst day of his life. His anger must have been clearly written on his face, because his mother had taken a hasty step away from him before he even opened his mouth.

"She almost died, ma'am," he had said in a tightly controlled voice. "Would that have pleased you?"

Her eyes had widened in horror, and she had babbled her apologies, assuring her son that no inconvenience was too great for the comfort of their guests. Silverton had broken in with a curt thanks and left her bedroom as quickly as he could. His mother had subsequently done her best to placate him, although her improved behavior had not extended to the servants.

After enduring two days of his mother's domestic mayhem, Silverton had finally escaped by shutting himself up in his library to attend to his correspondence. Only the earl had dared to interrupt his solitude.

"Well," Trask yawned as he stretched his arms over his head, "you have my heartfelt sympathies. I'd love to stay and chat about your mother, but I've had enough for one day. In any event, it seems likely that Welland is at least a hundred miles from here by now. I suggest you contact Bow Street. They may have better luck tracking him down."

"I have already done so."

"Good." Trask yawned again and stood. "Besides, you're like watching a top spin around the room. In my condition, I'm liable to become dizzy."

"Simon."

The earl paused on his way to the door, looking back at Silverton with raised eyebrows.

"Thank you."

Trask nodded brusquely and left the room.

Silverton returned to his desk and attempted to focus on his letter to General Stanton. After a few minutes' struggle, he threw down his pen and sighed. He found it impossible to concentrate. If he didn't see Meredith soon, he would go mad with frustration.

She had not left her room since he had carried her there two days ago. The local physician, Dr. Thatcher, who had served the estate for years, had given her a tincture and ordered her to rest. According to Annabel, Meredith had fallen asleep almost immediately, sleeping through the night and much of the next day. Dr. Thatcher had come again this afternoon, informing his patient that she was recovering nicely and could leave her bed tomorrow.

On hearing the news, Silverton had been overwhelmed with relief, and seized with a growing impatience to be with Meredith again. That feeling had only grown more acute as the day wore on. As he listened now to the chimes of the mantel clock sound the midnight hour, he decided he'd waited long enough.

He pushed back his chair and stood. Striding across the room and out into the great hall, he swiftly climbed the massive oak staircase and turned into the east corridor. Meredith's bedroom was at the very end of the hallway, facing south over the gently rolling slope of the deer park. Silverton told himself he would simply make sure that she was recovering and then leave her alone until morning.

But as he stood outside her door, his hand poised to knock, he knew he lied. He needed to feel her in his arms, to know that she was really safe and that she belonged to him.

Silverton leaned his head briefly against the heavy door, trying to quiet the pounding of his heart. She held such power over him, making him feel like nothing more than a callow youth. And yet the need to claim her in the most elemental and primitive way crashed through his veins, arousing his body in an instant.

Inhaling deeply, he knocked softly on the door, praying that she was still awake. And alone.

After a short pause, he heard her gentle reply.

"Enter."

He opened the door and stepped into the dimly lit room. His eyes flew to the large canopied bed, but it was empty. Closing the door gently behind him, he looked around to find her seated in a comfortable bergère armchair pulled up beside an open window.

For a moment she looked startled, but then her face lit up with a radiant smile. She rose gracefully from her chair as he walked across the room to stand before her.

God, she's so beautiful, he thought.

Meredith wore a delicate lawn nightrail, her generous curves softly outlined by the fine weave of fabric skimming her body. She clutched a wine-colored silk shawl around her shoulders, but it did nothing to disguise the fact that she was naked underneath the gown. Her lustrous hair tumbled down her back, blue-black highlights gleaming in the light cast by a branch of candles on a nearby table.

She looked like a goddess, and not one of the virginal ones, either. Silverton couldn't imagine how he could keep his hands from her lush body. He felt quite certain that he wouldn't even try.

"I am very happy to see you, my lord." Meredith extended a slender hand in greeting. "I have wanted to thank you so much for taking care of me. Indeed, these past few days I have thought of little else."

Even in the flickering light he could see that she blushed, but the look she gave him was open and warm. When he took her hand and raised it to his lips, her blush deepened to a rosy pink.

"I, too, have thought of little else but you, Meredith, these last two days."

With a soft touch, he urged her to sit back down. Glancing around, he grabbed a lap rug that had been folded across an ottoman and draped it around her legs. He pulled the ottoman over to sit in front of her.

Taking her hands in his, Silverton carefully inspected her face. Her eyes were clear, her complexion its usual combination of porcelain and roses.

"How are you feeling?"

"I am well, my lord." She smiled sweetly at him. "The doctor says I can leave my room tomorrow."

"Only if you feel well enough to do so," he gently admonished as he played with her fingers.

She scrunched up her nose. "I think I have slept enough to last me a month. Besides, I am sure the housekeeper and the maids are quite tired of waiting on me."

"They are all happy to do so."

She sat quietly and watched him stroke her fingers. Her smile faltered, and she seemed to hesitate, as if afraid to voice her thoughts.

"What is it, my sweet?" He squeezed her hands gently to encourage her.

Her eyes rose to his, and he was distressed to see a flash of anguish in the silver depths.

"Can you tell me now what happened to me?" she asked.

He sighed and gripped her hands more firmly. "Annabel didn't tell you?"

She shook her head. "She didn't want to worry me. In truth, I think she was too upset to talk about it, so I didn't press her."

He nodded and raised her hands to his mouth, pressing a tender kiss on them before returning them to her lap. "The lemonade was poisoned with cyanide. Dosed, we feel sure, by the footman who brought the drink out to the meadow."

The blood drained from her face. "Why didn't it kill me?"

Silverton had to close his eyes against the rage that threatened to seize him whenever he thought of how close she had come to death. He took a moment to bring his emotions under control. "Fortunately, the man proved to be inept. He put too much in the pitcher, making it so bitter that you were able to taste it. Thank God you drank as little as you did."

She shook her head impatiently. "I don't understand. Why would anyone want to poison me?"

"Not you, my love," he said quietly, trying to soften the blow. "Annabel."

Meredith's eyes grew wide for a moment, before narrowing into angry slits. "Uncle Isaac!" She practically spat his name.

"I'm afraid so, although we don't, as yet, have any evidence to prove it."

"Tell me what you've done."

In spite of himself, Silverton had to repress a smile. Meredith sounded so imperious that she really did remind him of Aunt Georgina. He had half expected her to fall apart when he told her the truth; of course, he should have known better. -

He related the events that had occurred over the last few days, including the likelihood that Welland had met her uncle and cousin in Aylesford. She listened intently, interrupting once or twice to clarify a point. When he told her the trail had gone cold, a fierce scowl wrinkled her brow.

"This is simply intolerable," she exclaimed, wrapping her shawl tightly around her body. She was angry, but he could see her begin to shiver. Despite her brave demeanor, she was obviously frightened.

"Surely there must be something we can do. Can you not go to the magistrate and swear out a warrant on my uncle?"

"We need some hard proof, my love, before we can do that.

All we have right now is a vague description from an innkeeper, and a missing footman."

"What about his threat to incarcerate Annabel in an asylum?"

He shook his head. "Your uncle would simply say he was acting on the advice of her doctor. He is, after all, her legal guardian."

Meredith fumed silently, an angry flush staining her cheeks. "But you are the Marquess of Silverton!" she finally blurted out. "Surely the magistrate will listen to you."

"On an attempted murder charge, even a marquess needs evidence that will stand up in a court of law." He smiled ruefully at her. "I'm sorry, Meredith. You mustn't think I'm doing nothing about it, but for the moment I must wait for some answers from London. I know it's very difficult, but try to be patient."

She subsided into her chair with a grumble. "It's very hard to be patient when one has been poisoned."

He instantly felt a stab of guilt. "I know, my sweet, and I am a brute to lecture you so. Surely you know I will do everything in my power to protect you and Annabel." He stroked her cheek, and the rebellious look on her face vanished. Her eyes turned soft and smoky.

"I know," she whispered.

He leaned forward on the ottoman, brushing back the glossy hair that tumbled around her shoulders. "You must forgive me for not taking better care of you," he murmured. "If anything had happened to you . . ."

She placed her fingers on his lips. "But you were there. You did take care of me, and I am fine."

At the touch of her warm hand on his mouth, all his senses flared to life. "Meredith," he said hoarsely, "you must believe me . . ."

"Hush," she murmured. She placed her smooth, fine-boned

hands on his face and pulled him down so that their mouths almost touched.

"No more talking," she said. Her lips parted, meeting his in the sweet, hot kiss he had been dreaming about for the last two days.

Chapter Twenty-Five

As Silverton's hands closed around her shoulders, Meredith pressed herself against him, desperate to assuage the powerful yearning that possessed her, body and soul.

When she had been so ill in the woods, overwhelmed with nausea and fear, only the feel of his strong arms about her had made it bearable. His strength had sliced through her terror, and on a level deeper than thought, she had known he would keep her safe.

Her memories after their return to the house were disjointed—cries of alarm, servants rushing past them as Silverton carried her up the stairs, Annabel holding a cool cloth to her burning forehead. But what she remembered most was the emptiness inside after Silverton gently placed her on the bed and stepped away, allowing his housekeeper to tend her. She would never forget the tortured look on his face when the older woman shooed him from the room. If Meredith had been able to speak, she would have begged him not to leave her.

But now he was here, and she wouldn't let him leave again until she showed him how much she loved him.

She hesitantly touched her lips to the edge of his mouth. He instantly took control of the tentative kiss, sliding his tongue across her lips and into her mouth. The taste of him made her head spin. She remembered the flavor of brandy and smoke, and a heat she had secretly craved since the first time he had kissed her.

Silverton broke the kiss, wrapped his arms around her and pulled her to her feet. The movement brought her into sharp contact with his erection; she gasped at the thick, hard feel of it against her stomach. Her breasts slid across the brocade of his waistcoat, and she reveled in the slippery, satin feel of it. Meredith couldn't help squirming in his arms as she tried to ease the ache of her puckered nipples against his hard body.

Silverton growled low in his throat. He unexpectedly broke from her, lifting his head to stare into her face. His skin— already tan—flushed a deeper bronze, and his eyes glittered with a fire that made her knees tremble and weaken. She would have slithered to the floor if he had not been holding her so securely.

He took a deep breath and put her slightly away from him. "Meredith," he murmured in a husky voice, "are you sure this is what you want?"

His cobalt eyes raked her body with a dark intensity. He stroked her hips through the thin fabric of her nightrail, his long fingers sending waves of heat coursing between her legs.

"Once we start this, there is no going back, for either of us." His voice held a dark note of warning, bringing her eyes up to meet his.

There was no trace of a smile on his face. In fact, he looked almost savage, and she sensed that he struggled to keep his emotions tightly leashed. She experienced a flash of trepidation at the thought of what would happen to her once she surrendered to his arousal.

But as Silverton's blazing eyes searched her face, Meredith suddenly found herself swept away by an unfamiliar sense of joy. Since the day she had met him, Silverton had only ever protected and cared for her. Even now, after everything that had led them to this moment, he still offered her the opportunity to step back.

Meredith leaned into him, acutely aware of the coiled tension in his muscles, the rapid rise and fall of his chest. Her desire to say yes—to give in to all that masculine energy—was so powerful she could hardly breathe.

Unable to speak past the tightness in her throat, she raised her head and nodded, hoping the look on her face conveyed the depth of her own desires. It must have done so, because a smile lifted the corners of his mouth, and the hard look around his eyes began to ease.

"Come with me, darling." He took her hand and led her to the ornate, satin-draped canopy bed.

Her legs felt boneless, but she managed to follow him without stumbling over her own feet. Silverton turned her to face him, plucking the silk shawl from her suddenly nerveless hands. He grasped the hem of her nightrail and slowly pulled it up to her waist. She closed her eyes, not yet brave enough to meet his gaze. As the material rustled over her head she heard him expel his breath in a slow hiss.

"God, Meredith," he said hoarsely, "I really don't know how I managed to keep my hands from you all this time. You are perfect."

The tone of his voice as much as his words encouraged her to peek up at him. His eyes were glittering with the same intensity as before, but his smile now held a warmth that eased her trepidation.

She met his gaze with a smile of her own, knowing that she would trust him with every last secret of her soul. "What do you want me to do?" she asked, desiring at this moment only to please him. To her surprise, he shook his head and laughed softly.

"My darling girl," he said, his face lighting up with amusement, "for once you are to do nothing but lie back and enjoy yourself. Do you think you'll be able to do that?"

Meredith wrinkled her brow. "Well, I'll try, but I don't really know what is expected of me." She smiled apologetically at him.

"Don't worry," he reassured her as he helped her climb onto the high mattress. "I know exactly what to do."

Meredith settled against the pillows as Silverton quickly divested himself of his coat and cravat. Her heart hammered in her chest, and she couldn't help but feel a small twinge of fear for what would come next. She took a deep breath, trying to relax, trusting that he would do all he could to ensure her comfort.

It took him just a few moments to shed the rest of his clothing. He was half turned away from her as he stripped out of his breeches. The uneven light thrown by the fire rippled across the muscled contours of his athletic body, polishing his skin to the color of burnished gold. His broad shoulders flexed when he tossed his clothes on a nearby chair.

Meredith's heart melted at the sight of him. In her imagination he was like a large, sleek cat, sheathing his claws only for her. To the world, he was a wealthy and sophisticated aristocrat. But Meredith saw beneath the smooth surface to the elemental man. To her, Silverton radiated intense power and a primitive sense of possessiveness toward everything that belonged to him.

Now she knew that possessiveness included her.

He turned back to the bed, and her mouth suddenly went dry. Meredith had a general idea what to expect, but she experienced a small and very real jolt of alarm at the size of him. She glanced anxiously at his face, wondering if she should say something, although she couldn't imagine what.

Fortunately, her common sense quickly began to reassert itself. Meredith reminded herself that men and women had been engaging in relations since the time of Adam and Eve. Most certainly nature had designed her to accommodate him, even though he did seem very large.

She welcomed him into bed with a hesitant smile, pushing

back the gold satin coverlet and fine linen sheets as he climbed in beside her. Silverton murmured his satisfaction as he pulled her into his arms, gently pinning her lower body to the mattress with his legs.

"My sweet, you can't imagine how long I have been wanting to do this."

"Actually," she confessed, "I think I can."

He laughed softly and then brought his mouth down onto hers. She sank into the pillows, shuddering with pleasure as he skimmed a hand over her breasts and down to her waist. He slipped his other arm under her back, holding her still as he nuzzled her cheek, beneath an ear, and down to her neck.

The restless sensation she had experienced once before grew within her as he kissed his way to the base of her throat and across the top of her breasts. When his tongue dragged slowly over her nipple, she whimpered with pleasure. The slow ache in the hidden place between her thighs began to intensify, the feel of it building in a moist, hot surge.

Meredith's hands, quite of their own volition, began to roam over his body, stroking up his back and neck to delve into his thick hair. Silverton muttered something against her breast before sucking her pebbled nipple into the wet heat of his mouth.

She stifled a small shriek, jerking her body up off the bed to follow his mouth. He suckled her relentlessly, the rasp of his tongue against her nipple so acutely pleasurable that she could hardly stand it. When he bit down, gently tugging on her swollen flesh, a cry broke from her lips.

He raised his head, eyes blazing down at her. "I can't wait much longer, Meredith." His voice was a deep, feral growl. "You test my patience beyond all endurance."

She groggily lifted her eyes, so dazed by the sensation of his mouth and tongue on her naked body that she barely comprehended what he said. She only knew she would die if he didn't continue.

"Don't stop," she panted, trying to pull him back down. "Please don't stop."

His eyes turned black, and he reached down to push her legs apart. Long fingers trailed over the soft skin of her inner thighs, sending shivers deep inside her. Meredith made no attempt to resist, pulling her knees up to open herself more fully to his touch. He stroked into the damp curls between her legs. She couldn't help squirming against his hand.

"My God, Meredith." He briefly rested his forehead on hers. "You are so hot . . . so wet. You drench my hand with your dew."

She retreated against the pillows, embarrassed by his comment and her body's uncontrolled response to him. But her mortification fled instantly when his hand delved farther between her thighs. He found the small bud hidden there and gently circled it. She wriggled against his hand, moaning as she sought relief from the almost unbearable feeling of tension deep in her womb. Meredith opened her legs even wider, inviting him to do more—to do what he must to bring her relief.

"Yes," he purred against her ear. "You're ready for me, my love."

He shifted over until he lay cradled between her legs, his erection probing the entrance to her body. He gently undulated his hips, sliding his hard length across her little wet bud. Meredith wanted to weep, consumed with an urgent need to be possessed by him, to be his in every way possible. She heard herself plead with him, the words incoherent as she slid her arms around his neck.

"Open your eyes, Meredith," Silverton ordered in a husky voice. "Look at me when I come into you."

She hadn't even realized her eyes were closed, so lost was she in the sensations coursing through her body. He caught her head between his hands and tenderly forced her to look at him. Meredith smiled tremulously into his handsome face, now hard with desire for her, his jaw set like granite. She knew all the love in her heart was reflected back in the brilliance of his gaze.

"I'm ready," she whispered.

He clenched his teeth and slowly penetrated her, pushing relentlessly and deeply into her damp flesh. Meredith gasped in shock at the brutally sharp pain lancing through her sheath as he claimed her.

"Lord Silverton!" Her voice was high and sharp with protest.

He winced, resting on his elbows as he held himself motionless within her. The expression on his face was both regretful and, it irked her to notice, slightly amused.

"I'm sorry, my love," he soothed, but his voice contained a hint of laughter. "I know it hurts."

"A great deal more than I expected," she grumbled, irritated he had neglected to tell her about this part.

"The pain will ease momentarily, Meredith, I assure you." He reached down and grasped her knee, nudging it up to his hips. "Wrap your legs around me, sweetheart."

His voice was thick and dark, and in spite of her discomfort it sent a pulse of heat snaking through her belly. She hesitated for a moment and then complied with his gentle command, wrapping her legs over his muscular buttocks.

The pain between her thighs eased dramatically. Silverton remained propped on his elbows, stroking her tangled hair as he gazed down at her.

"Now stop holding your breath."

Meredith let go the breath she hadn't realized she was holding and loosened her convulsive grip on his shoulders.

"Is that better?" he asked as he smiled at her.

She looked at his face and then let her eyes drift across the hard, perfect body looming over her. Meredith suspected that if she were a weaker woman, she would have swooned from the overwhelming nature of their physical intimacy. Trapped beneath him as she was, she had never felt so vulnerable in her life. But she knew with an unshakeable conviction he would never willingly hurt her again, especially now he had claimed her for his own.

Meredith felt joy pulse through her again as she realized that, for the first time in her life, she truly belonged to someone and he belonged to her. She relaxed and allowed herself to sink into the soft mattress, luxuriating in the feel of his body covering hers. She smiled up at him.

"Oh, yes, my lord." The husky purr didn't even sound like her. "That is a great deal more comfortable."

He bent his head to nibble her mouth before feathering light kisses across her cheeks. "I'm so glad," he whispered in her ear. He slowly began to move his hips against her.

Her residual pain faded away as the sensual stroke of his arousal ignited the heat between her legs. She pushed up against him, loving the feel of her erect nipples brushing through the coarse hair on his chest.

"Meredith!" he groaned, dipping his head briefly to suck the beaded nub into his mouth. She tilted her pelvis against him, instinctively trying to relieve the growing ache between her thighs.

He withdrew almost fully from her body, and then pushed heavily back into her—the stroke harder now—but with the same slow rhythm that twisted her insides into a tight heat. She fell back onto the pillows, forcing her drooping eyelids open to look at him. Silverton gazed back with an expression that was both fierce and heartbreakingly tender. She reveled in the sense that he so thoroughly dominated her, quivering at the sight of his body moving over her, the feel of his thick hardness sliding inside her.

An unfamiliar weakness began to invade her limbs, captivating her with a delicious sense of enervation as her hips rose to meet his languid strokes. Meredith had imagined their first joining as breathless and wrenching. Instead, she felt herself melting beneath him in a luxurious swirl of acute sensation.

She slowly arched into him, dizzy with the joy of it, the feel of his utterly masculine body pressing her woman's softness into the cool linen sheets. Enveloping her so completely she thought she *might* actually swoon from the sheer physical pleasure of the act.

Silverton bent to capture her lips as he began to thrust more quickly and powerfully into her body. She cried out softly in surprise as the tip of his erection nudged her womb.

"God, Meredith," he moaned into her mouth, "I want to devour you."

The tight heat coiled unbearably within her, and she heard herself pleading once more for release. He reached a hand down, found the little bud nesting in her drenched curls, and gently rubbed it. Her climax suddenly burned through her. The sweet fire poured through her trembling limbs as he continued to drive into her.

She could feel the soft flesh of her sheath contract around him, as if to draw him more deeply into her. He cried out her name as he thrust—hard—one last time. He buried his face in her neck, wrapping his arms tightly around her shoulders as he ground his hips in a shuddering release.

For several seconds, the only sound in the room was the gasping of their mingled breaths.

Then Meredith curled tightly around him and surprised herself by bursting into tears. She could hardly believe it, but her heart had finally torn free of the terrible loneliness that had plagued her for as long as she could remember. She was no longer alone.

Her emotional outburst had startled him. Silverton had barely caught his breath when Meredith had buried her face in his chest and started to weep. Given her passionate response to him only moments ago, he felt relatively certain his lovemaking was not the cause of her distress. But when he had gently prompted her to tell him why she cried, she had simply huddled close and sobbed even harder.

He had petted and soothed her, of course, murmuring soft love words as he rocked her in his arms. She managed to hiccup out a few broken sentences, claiming only that she was exhausted by the events of the last few days. And although he suspected there was more to it than that, he decided to leave any questions for a later, less emotional time.

Instead, he had stopped her tears by rolling her onto her back and making love to her once more. She had caught fire with a sweet ardor that drove him wild. Silverton knew he could never get enough of her.

The intensity of their lovemaking had not surprised him. He had always known Meredith held great passion within her. Indeed, nature would not have made her so lush if it had not intended her to respond sexually to the right man.

And Silverton knew beyond all doubt he was that man.

As far as he was concerned, it was only a short matter of time before she became his wife. No other man would ever enjoy the pleasure of her intimate companionship, the sweet generosity of her sensuality, or the riches of the body that currently rested under his hand.

Meredith had surrendered heart and soul to him, and he would never let her go. She had truly astonished him by holding nothing back, boldly initiating their lovemaking and sweeping aside his worries that he might hurt her. More than that, when finally sheathed inside her, he had experienced a sense of rightness and belonging he had never felt before.

Silverton knew full well the value of such a gift, and no one would prevent him from claiming it. As soon as he secured her promise to marry him, he would leave for London and obtain a special license.

Of course, he had another equally compelling reason to return to London. Silverton had written to his private secretary, instructing him to contact Bow Street and begin an investigation into the attempt on Meredith's life. He felt a driving urgency to run Isaac and Jacob Burnley to ground. As long as Meredith and Annabel remained unmarried, Silverton could not completely protect them. Fortunately, Robert and Annabel's betrothal announcement had already been sent to the papers, and soon they would all be returning to Stanton House to prepare for the nuptials.

As to what should happen to Isaac and Jacob Burnley when he *did* finally run them to ground, all Silverton knew for sure was that the sisters shouldn't be subjected to the scandal of a public trial. Whatever he decided to do, however, he needed real evidence in hand to prove a murder plot against Annabel. Trask had written his business contacts in Bristol, hoping to scare up information on the Burnley family's finances, and Silverton intended to speak to Annabel's bankers in London himself. He sincerely hoped those sources could shed some light on the convoluted, dangerous situation, and soon.

The thought of bankers and money reminded him of the question he had intended to ask Meredith a few hours ago. He glanced down at the profusion of shiny black curls tumbled across his chest and gently nudged the warm softness that lay cuddled in his arms.

"Meredith, are you awake?"

"Hmmm . . . ," she murmured, sounding very content and very sleepy. He smiled, well satisfied with the state he had reduced her to.

"If something were to happen to Annabel, who would inherit her fortune?"

She stirred against him. "I would," she yawned.

He lapsed into silence. After a few moments, he felt her body begin to stiffen as she slowly came fully awake. There was a long pause, and then she exclaimed, "Oh . . . Jacob!"

"Yes," he replied. "Jacob indeed."

Chapter Twenty-Six

Silverton's boots rang out on the yellow ironstone floor as he crossed the Abbey's entrance hall and strode down the wide gallery leading to the morning room. Contentment flowed through his veins, and he felt happier than he could ever remember.

Meredith loved him. Whatever problems stood in the way of their marriage, he knew he could resolve them. The only thing that nagged at him was her refusal last night to discuss a wedding date. Her qualms obviously stemmed from her fears about his family's reaction to their impending betrothal, but, with the exception of his mother, Silverton confidently believed those closest to him would wholeheartedly approve of his bride.

He had left Meredith's bed at dawn, reluctantly pulling himself from her arms in spite of her sleepy protests. It had killed him to leave her. She looked so beautiful, her midnight hair tousled on the pillow, her body warm and flushed from a night of lovemaking. But the house would soon begin to stir, so he had simply brushed his lips across her kiss-swollen mouth and told her he would see her after breakfast.

Too restless to go back to bed, Silverton had dressed, met with his land agent, and visited the stables to check on a new foal. The ladies, as usual, had risen hours later and had just adjourned to the morning room after a leisurely breakfast.

As he walked down the tapestry-hung gallery, he smiled to himself, wondering what Meredith's reaction to him would be this morning. She was dignity personified, and last night he had coaxed her into some very undignified positions. For a virgin, she had taken to the act of lovemaking like a bird to flight.

He forced himself to banish the image of her naked body from his brain, having no desire to face a roomful of people with an idiot's grin on his face.

The door to the morning room stood open, the quiet chatter of feminine voices drifting into the corridor. He paused on the threshold of the cheerful, sun-lit parlor, searching the room for Meredith.

She sat on a low divan, clad in a simple, cream-colored muslin dress that emphasized her lush beauty more than the most elegant evening gown ever could. Glossy tendrils of hair tumbled from a knot on top of her head, caressing the soft skin of her neck and shoulders. Her lips were deep cherry and slightly swollen, stained crimson not by cosmetics but by his devouring kisses. Just looking at her mouth made him want to drag her back up to her room, yank her clothes off, and start all over again.

Silverton took a deep breath, clamping down on the surge of lust that threatened to expose him to the scrutiny of his family and friends. He schooled his face appropriately and walked into the room to greet the other members of the party.

Lady Silverton reclined in an overstuffed armchair opposite Meredith, her embroidery thrown to the side as she languidly fanned herself with an exquisite and, he knew, very expensive fan of ivory and lace. Annabel and Robert were seated in front of the pianoforte at the opposite end of the morning room, totally engrossed in each other as usual. And Trask sat on a padded bench in one of the window alcoves, impatiently tapping a riding crop against his boots as he scowled at the room in general.

Silverton crossed to his mother, took her hand, and carried it to his lips. "Good morning, Mother. I hope you slept well last night?"

"As well as anyone can in this heat." She sighed as she reached up to pat his cheek. "How did you sleep? Did the heat bother you?"

"I also found it hot, but it didn't seem to trouble me," he said, letting a hint of laughter creep into his voice.

Meredith's head jerked up, her cheeks blushing to a rosy hue. He bowed to her and to Sophia, who also sat on the divan, encompassing them both with his smile.

"Good morning, ladies. How are you today?"

Meredith glanced shyly up at him, her eyes shining with an ardent glow. That innocent but sensual look made him want to puff out his chest and roar.

"I am well, sir. Thank you," she replied, her calm voice at odds with the flustered-but-happy expression on her face.

"Blast!" muttered Sophia, ignoring him as she struggled with her embroidery.

Silverton grinned. Like his mother, Sophia hated needle-work. But unlike his mother, who preferred to gossip or simply lie about, Sophia would rather be in motion, riding about the countryside in her little phaeton, checking on the tenants or discussing improvements to the parish with the vicar's wife.

"Sophia," Lady Silverton admonished, frowning severely at her niece, "it is most unseemly to use such unladylike language."

Trask glanced over from the window and snorted, the noise suggesting that Sophia's unladylike behavior was her natural state of existence. The girl's eyes slid over to the earl, narrowing thoughtfully for a moment before she looked back down at her work.

"Yes, Aunt Alexandra," Sophia replied meekly.

Silverton returned his attention to Meredith, whose cheeks turned an even brighter pink under his steady gaze. She bent diligently over her needlework, but her hand trembled slightly as she pulled at a thread. It pleased him that she could not control herself in his presence, even though she obviously wanted to.

As much as he wanted to stand about all day and stare at her, Silverton had work to do. Tonight would come soon enough, and then he would have Meredith all to himself again, he vowed.

Out of the corner of his eye he saw his mother sit bolt upright in her chair, her startled gaze fixing intently on Meredith. Silverton fought the urge to grind his teeth, resigning himself to the inevitable. His mother clearly had the scent and, if left to her own devices, would cause him no end of trouble. He resolved to speak to her about Meredith after lunch.

As he walked from the room, he looked over his shoulder at the earl, who still lounged in the alcove. "Well, Trask, are you ready to go, or shall we just sit about with the ladies all day?"

"I've been ready for hours," growled his friend, joining him by the door. "As well you know."

Silverton smiled wryly before turning back to the room. "Mother, Simon and I are riding over to the north farm to inspect the new bridge. We'll be back in time for luncheon."

Sophia looked up eagerly from her stitching. "Silverton, while you are out that way, you might think to check on Jonas Cooper. He fell from a ladder and broke his leg. Dr. Burns says it will be several weeks before he walks again."

She tapped her index finger to her cheek as if to remind herself of something. "Oh, and please ensure that the cattle hauling the stones for the bridge are adequately watered. I passed by the site yesterday, and I thought the poor things looked very hot and labored."

Silverton laughed. Sophia had a marked inclination to treat him like a simpleton, a trait he found rather endearing.

Before he could reply, however, Trask snapped at her in an irritated voice.

"Really, Sophia, I'm sure Silverton knows his own business. And may I point out, those concerns belong to the lady of the house, not you."

Lady Silverton's eyes widened in alarm, as if the earl expected her to jump up and immediately begin caring for all the sick and injured on the estate, including the overworked animals.

Sophia carefully folded her needlework before answering him. "My lord, I'm simply assisting my aunt in her very substantial duties here at Belfield Abbey. I don't understand why you should object to that."

"Because," Trask retorted, "it's not your place to do so. Why can't you just concentrate on your embroidery and music like other proper young ladies?"

Instead of answering him, Sophia lifted her eyes to the ceiling and gave an almost imperceptible shake of her head.

"Sophia, did you just roll your eyes at me?" The earl looked outraged.

She blinked at him, the picture of wounded innocence. "Why, my lord, how could you imagine I would ever have the nerve to show you such disrespect?"

Lady Silverton clucked her tongue at her niece. Trask opened his mouth, looking as if he would argue with the girl, but then seemed to realize how ridiculous the situation had become. He glared at her instead as he walked to the door. Sophia returned his fiery look with a vague smile, although her cheeks turned very pink.

His interest piqued, Silverton looked from Sophia's blushing countenance to Trask's stony expression as his friend brushed past him and out the room. He followed him along the gallery. Trask seemed to be muttering something under his breath.

"Pardon me, Simon," he asked politely. "What did you say?"

Trask threw him an impatient look as he slowed to walk beside him. "Nothing," he replied abruptly.

Biting back a smile, Silverton paused and then commented innocently, "Lovely girl, Sophia, wouldn't you agree?"

"Shut up, Silverton," retorted his friend as he stomped through the entrance hall and out the front door.

Silverton grinned, more thankful than ever that he would soon be a married man.

Meredith's pulse finally began to slow when Silverton and Lord Trask left the morning room. She had hardly dared lift her head for fear of exposing her feelings in front of his mother.

Silverton loved her! He had said so last night, and then proceeded to demonstrate it in more ways than she could ever have imagined. Their lovemaking had seared a brand on her heart, and Meredith knew without a doubt she belonged to him forever. She still feared the censure of his family and friends, of course, but she hoped his love would give her the courage to face their disapproval.

For today, though, she must act as if nothing had happened between them. She and Silverton still faced many challenges—Annabel's safety, for one—and Meredith refused to even consider her own future until her sister's happiness and security were assured. Silverton hadn't liked it, but Annabel must come first.

Across from her, Lady Silverton sighed and finally stopped pretending to work on her embroidery. She fussed briefly with the material before stuffing it back into an elaborately woven workbasket.

"Well, my dears," the older woman trilled, "I must write some letters to London before the morning grows any later. Meredith, I'd like to pick some roses in the garden to replace the blooms in the Great Hall. I find they fade so quickly in this heat." The marchioness rose gracefully from her chair. "Would you be so kind as to join me to hold the basket while I clip?"

Meredith blinked, astonished by the request. Lady Silverton much preferred Annabel's company to hers, but perhaps the marchioness was reluctant to disturb the young lovers. She swallowed a groan, struggling to conceal her dismay.

"Of course, your ladyship. Whenever you desire."

"Shall we say in an hour, then? I will meet you out in the rose garden." Lady Silverton graced Meredith with a charming smile before rustling from the room in a flutter of delicate silks.

Meredith repressed the impulse to grumble, and glanced at Sophia. The girl looked harassed, wrestling with her needle and repeatedly pushing her glasses up her nose.

"Can I assist you?" Meredith asked gently.

Sophia jumped slightly in her seat and then bent her head to apply herself diligently to her work.

"Oh, no, thank you, Miss Burnley. I'm fine." She smiled apologetically.

Sophia's cheeks were very flushed, and Meredith thought she spied the glimmer of a tear in the girl's eye. They stitched in silence while Meredith pondered the little scene that had occurred between Sophia and the Earl of Trask.

"How long have you known Lord Trask?" she eventually asked, trying to sound as if she were just making casual conversation.

"Forever," came the terse answer.

Meredith wrinkled her brow as she reflected on the girl's behavior. She had often noticed that Sophia's eyes were in the habit of following the earl whenever he was in her company.

"And you know him very well, I believe?" Meredith gently prodded.

Sophia glanced over at Robert, still at the pianoforte with Annabel, laughing with her as they stumbled through a new piece of music.

"They can't hear us," Meredith said dryly. "I doubt there is little we could do to distract them, in any event."

"I'm sure you're right," grimaced Sophia, who gazed at her brother with an expression of affection mingled with sadness. It suddenly occurred to Meredith that she was not the only one who would soon lose the company of a beloved sibling. Sophia and Robert were very close, and no doubt the girl would feel keenly the change in circumstances after her brother married Annabel.

Meredith waited patiently for her to answer the query about Lord Trask. Finally, Sophia glanced up with a crooked smile.

"Perhaps I know him too well," she said in a gruff tone. "You see, he has been almost part of my family since I was a child. When I was twelve years old he pulled me out of a lake after I tumbled from a boat. Ever since then he has treated me as a little sister." The crooked smile faded away. "Unfortunately, he never even looks at me now except to reprimand me or bite my head off. It's most annoying."

She stared grimly at the fabric that had fallen unheeded into her lap. Meredith cast about in her mind for something to say that might console the girl. Before she could think of anything, Sophia shrugged her shoulders and smiled ruefully at Meredith.

"And why should he not treat me so?" she said with a self-deprecating laugh. "I'm sure he finds me a great nuisance, but tolerates me for Silverton's sake. It's only to be expected. After all, he has known me for so long."

Sophia began to rummage busily around in her workbasket, clearly signaling her desire to end the conversation.

Meredith lapsed into silence and returned to her stitching, profoundly grateful that her own days as a spinster were finally coming to an end.

Meredith wandered aimlessly about the rose garden, down the gravel path to the pergola, and back round to the steps of the terrace. Every minute or so she glanced at the doors to the drawing room, waiting for Lady Silverton to appear.

The marchioness was already a half hour late. During that seemingly endless span of time, Meredith convinced herself that Lady Silverton had guessed that she and her son were all but betrothed. If that were the case, then the thought of facing her future mother-in-law alone made her blood run cold, in spite of the day's heat.

Meredith took a shuddering breath and spun on her heel, pacing back to the steps of the terrace. As the minutes ticked by, she grew increasingly anxious. And, she had to admit, she was annoyed with Silverton for putting her in this horrible position in the first place. Why hadn't he warned her that his mother knew about them?

The French doors to the drawing room swung open, and Lady Silverton floated across the terrace. Following closely behind was a nervous-looking young maid carrying a large straw basket.

"My dear Meredith," purred the marchioness, "do forgive me for keeping you so long in the hot sun. Indeed, my dear, you should not be out here without a hat. You are already turning a most unbecoming shade of red."

Lady Silverton inspected her with a critical eye before motioning imperiously to the maid. "Give the basket to Miss Burnley, and go up to her room and fetch her bonnet."

"Oh, your ladyship, that won't be necessary." Meredith smiled and gently waved the maid away from her. "I'll just run up and fetch it myself. It won't take me but a moment."

"My dear girl, don't be so foolish," Lady Silverton exclaimed, raising her eyebrows from under the brim of her huge gauze-trimmed hat. "That's what servants are for."

She dismissed the maid with a flick of her hand. The young girl scurried up the steps of the terrace and fled into the safety of the house.

Meredith groaned inwardly, acutely aware that she had

once again displayed an inappropriate regard for a servant's well-being. It was the kind of behavior Lady Silverton loathed. She sighed as she followed the marchioness into the garden, steeling herself for what she suspected would be a most unpleasant conversation.

But to her surprise, the older woman began to chat amicably about her acquaintances in the city. She clipped roses and dropped them in the basket Meredith held out for her, all the while relating several amusing incidents that had occurred at the end of the Season.

A few minutes later the maid dashed out of the house, clutching Meredith's best summer bonnet tightly in her fist. Lady Silverton frowned, her eyes narrowing ominously, but she apparently decided not to lecture the girl for crushing the brim of the hat. Instead, she curtly dismissed her and led Meredith deeper into the garden, away from the terrace.

"Really, it is a great shame that careless girl ruined your hat. Most of these country servants are just too stupid to train properly."

"Oh, my lady," Meredith began, "I'm sure she—"

"My dear," Lady Silverton ruthlessly interrupted her, "you mustn't ever excuse the help, or allow them to repeat a mistake. If you do, they will be sure to take advantage of you."

She bent gracefully and clipped another rose, tossing it into Meredith's basket.

"You should realize, Meredith, you are at a disadvantage with the servants. I'm sure they know your background is only somewhat more elevated than theirs. Familiarity with them will only encourage disrespect toward you."

Meredith felt a burning flush creep into her cheeks. Obviously Lady Silverton meant to insult her, but she had to admit she often did prefer the servants to a good number of people she had met in the ton.

The marchioness suddenly flipped up the gauze trim of her

hat, pinning her with a ruthless gaze. Warning prickles flowed down Meredith's spine.

"I only say these things to you, my dear, because you are in such need of guidance," Lady Silverton intoned solemnly. "Since you are without a mother, I feel it only appropriate that I try to set you on a proper course of conduct."

Meredith's heart sank as she waited for the blow to fall. The marchioness studied her with a hooded expression and bent to clip another rose.

"I know you will wish me to speak frankly, Meredith. It has become clear to me that my son intends to make you an offer. While this situation is not what his family wished for him, he is a man full grown and will make his own decisions."

Meredith adopted what she hoped was an impassive expression, even as she sensed the four horsemen of the apocalypse bearing down on the rose garden at Belfield Abbey.

"I suppose I should not be surprised," sighed Lady Silverton. "My son finds you . . . intriguing. You are certainly not what he is used to. But even though I am his mother, I cannot be blind to certain faults in his character, and I would be remiss in my duties not to warn you of them. Silverton is easily bored. You must expect that his attentions to you will eventually begin to wander. His interest in any woman, you know, is never fixed for more than a few months at a time. Everyone is aware of that."

Meredith acknowledged bleakly that Lady Silverton had an uncanny ability to find just the right spot to insert her blade. She wanted to deny what she heard, but a voice in her head whispered darkly that her ladyship was likely correct. Who was she to capture the love of a man like the Marquess of Silverton?

"You mustn't worry too much about that, my dear," Lady Silverton added, her eyes glittering like frost. "Silverton will always be the most punctilious of husbands. He is never vulgar, and he would never expose you to any kind of mortification. But you have lived such a sheltered life, and how could you know that men like my son have other needs—needs their wives are not able to fulfill."

The marchioness gave a delicate shudder. "Nor should they. A lady should never have concourse with the baser appetites of men. And men should only indulge in those appetites with a different kind of woman."

Meredith swallowed a gasp of dismay. What did it say about her—and what Silverton might think of her—that she had so thoroughly enjoyed their lovemaking last night? Was it even remotely possible what his mother said about him was true?

Lady Silverton turned and began to stroll back toward the house. Meredith stumbled after her, even though she wanted to drop the basket laden with roses and escape into the dense woods.

The older woman glanced at Meredith over her shoulder. "A good wife never questions her husband's activities, of course," she said, intent on her gruesome lecture. "As the Marchioness of Silverton, it is your duty to present him with an heir, run his household, and entertain his friends and relations in the ton. You must always maintain an air of decorum and gentility that keeps you above reproach, and above any hint of scandal."

Lady Silverton stopped at the foot of the terrace, smiling graciously. "If you can do all that, Meredith, then I am convinced you will be an acceptable choice for my son."

The marchioness reached over and stroked her wrist. Meredith felt as if an asp had just wound its way around her heart. Perspiration began to trickle down her back.

"I know it will be difficult at first, my dear." Lady Silverton's smile seemed etched in glass. "But I will be constantly at your side to assist you. It will be so lovely to have another woman in the house, especially on those nights when Silverton is busy with his friends, doing whatever it is that men do with their time."

Meredith's stomach began to churn, almost as if she had

been poisoned again. In all the excitement of the last twenty-four hours, it had never occurred to her that she and Silverton would be living with his mother.

The marchioness withdrew her hand from her wrist and lifted the delicate skirts of her gown as she walked up the steps of the terrace.

"Don't stay out in the sun too much longer, my dear. You are ruining your complexion." Lady Silverton blew her a kiss and floated through the French doors, disappearing into the house.

Meredith gazed blankly out into the rose garden, all but unconscious of the heavily scented air and the sharp buzz of the honeybees as they zoomed from bush to bush. The minutes passed, but she seemed unable to force her limbs to move.

As she stood there, her heart turning to stone, she heard masculine voices coming from the direction of the stables. A moment later, Silverton and Lord Trask rounded a large yew hedge. They strode together up the gravel path that led through the rose garden and up to the terrace where she waited.

Silverton looked up at her and smiled, his gaze warm with affection and laughter. Meredith stared at him for a few seconds, then dropped the basket full of roses and fled into the house.

Chapter Twenty-Seven

Meredith carefully folded her paisley shawl and placed it in the trunk at the foot of her bed. She and Annabel were leaving for London in the morning to meet with the dressmaker who would design her sister's wedding clothes.

Meredith's last evening at Belfield Abbey had been a nightmare as she tried to conceal the turmoil afflicting her spirit. She had managed to evade Silverton all day, although she knew she couldn't avoid him much longer.

He was furious with her, of course. After fleeing from him in the garden, Meredith had stayed in Annabel's room for the rest of the afternoon. Then she had slipped away right after dinner, before the men could join the ladies for tea in the drawing room.

Lady Silverton had smiled beatifically when Meredith had asked to be excused in order to finish her packing.

"Certainly, my love," she had murmured, giving Meredith her hand. "I will see you later this week in London. You must come to tea as soon as I am back in town. We have so much to talk about, don't we?"

Meredith shuddered just thinking about the malicious gleam in the marchioness's eyes. She knew full well the other woman had manipulated her, but that provided little consolation against the brutal certainty that marriage to Silverton would be disastrous. As much as she longed to deny it, Meredith knew she would never be at home in the world of the ton.

She sat on the bed and stared listlessly at the small pile of gloves on top of the coverlet. One of the maids had packed most of the contents of her trunks, but Meredith had finally dismissed the young girl, unable to bear her nonstop prattle. Her chest tightened with pain whenever she thought of the heartbreaking conversation that lay ahead of her.

She glanced over at the ornately figured silver clock on the mantel. It was almost midnight. Silverton would no doubt come barging into her room at any minute. She supposed the sensible thing to do would be to lock her door and not talk to him until they had all returned to London. But Meredith had already decided she might as well cut her heart out now and get it over with.

As she expected, her door swung open a moment later without even the barest hint of a knock. Silverton closed it behind him, twisting the key in the lock before turning to face her.

Meredith swallowed in dismay at the hard, angry expression on his face. Two long strides brought him to the bed, and he observed her in stony silence as she slowly came to her feet. He had discarded his coat and waistcoat, his shirt already open at the throat and chest. She found the sight of all that bronzed skin covering broad muscles distinctly unnerving.

"Good evening, my lord. I've been expecting you." Her voice was shockingly calm—a miracle, she thought, given how furious he looked.

"Yes, Meredith, I'm sure you have." His eyes skated over her figure. If possible, his gaze grew even colder.

Although she wore a thin lawn nightrail, she had wrapped herself in a voluminous robe that effectively covered every inch of her body. She had also scraped her hair into a painfully tight braid that fell down her back. Meredith thought she only needed a fusty old mobcap and spectacles to transform her into the old maid she was destined to become.

"What in hell have you done to your hair?" Silverton demanded.

Meredith slid around him to the other side of the bed. She desperately needed to put some distance between them.

"Lord Silverton," she began, determined to take control of the situation, "I'm sure you are wondering . . ."

"Yes, Meredith, I am wondering. I'm wondering why you would choose to act like the ninnyhammer I know you are not, especially after what happened between us last night. It seems impossible to me that you could be having second thoughts, given that you chose to relinquish your innocence to me. Or," he asked sardonically, "did I somehow misinterpret what took place here?" He gestured to the bed as he stalked around it to join her.

Meredith's face bloomed with an intense heat. "N-no my lord," she stammered as she recalled all the things he had done to her last night. "You did not misinterpret what happened between us."

Some of the blazing heat seemed to fade from his eyes. He gently cupped her cheek. Meredith had to fight an overwhelming desire to nestle her face into his hand.

"Then tell me what's wrong, my love," he urged softly.

Steeling herself, she moved away from him again. He frowned, but didn't follow her.

"Lord Silverton," she began, "I will always be profoundly honored by your generous offer of marriage."

He snorted in derision.

She took a deep breath and continued. "But after careful consideration, I must refuse your offer. The differences between us are too great. I'm convinced that, in time, we would come to realize that marriage between us would be a mistake."

Silverton gave another impatient snort, but she put up her hand to silence him.

"You are too generous to admit it, but you must know how unsuited I am to be your marchioness. Eventually you would comprehend this, even though your kindness would prevent you from ever acknowledging my lack of suitability."

He blinked, clearly startled by her words. Silverton's angry expression faded as he shook his head in rueful denial. He looked so sympathetic that Meredith had to fight back a rush of tears. She turned from him, determined not to cry.

"I, however, am all too aware of my own inadequacies, and I couldn't bear to disappoint you."

"Meredith." He grasped her shoulders, bringing her around to face him. "Didn't last night show you how well suited we are to each other?" He slid his hands down to her elbows. "There is no other woman I can ever imagine having in my home or my bed."

Meredith looked up into his eyes; she saw only tenderness and honesty in his gaze. Clearly she had to save him from himself, she thought wretchedly, even though it meant slicing her own heart in two.

"As I said, you are generous, my lord. But the life you envision for me is not the life I wish for myself." She tugged away from his grasp. "After Annabel is married I will return to the country. Our time together will always be precious to me, but, I assure you, I am most content to return to my former existence. In fact, I prefer it." She squeezed her eyes shut, certain that God would strike her dead for telling such dreadful lies.

When Meredith opened her eyes, the kind expression on Silverton's face had vanished. In fact, he now looked positively menacing, and she couldn't help retreating a few steps.

"And what will you do when you go back to Swallow Hill, Meredith? Will you marry some local squire who will surround you with a passel of squalling brats? Or do you so long for your barren spinster's life that you reject the offer of a man who honestly professes his love for you?"

She froze while he shook his head at her.

"It's strange," he said bitterly, "but I never took you for a coward. Apparently, I was wrong."

Meredith jerked back, more stung by his words than she could have imagined. She drew herself up to her full height.

"Lord Silverton, I'm sure I do not deserve your insults. If you're not willing to discuss this matter in a rational fashion, then I must ask you to leave my room. We can continue this conversation when we have both returned to London."

The anger in his eyes slowly transmuted into something else. Meredith felt a warning chill shoot up her spine as his lips parted in a slow smile—the one that always made her knees grow so weak. She forced herself to move away from him, but he matched her step for step.

"As a matter of fact, Meredith, I'm not feeling rational at all. And I would like to point out this is my house, not yours. I have no intention of going anywhere."

"My lord," Meredith quavered. She swallowed, taking one more stab at fending him off. "When your mother and I spoke this morning . . ."

Silverton laughed. The unexpected, husky sound caused her heart to beat erratically against her breastbone.

"My sweet, there are two words no man wants to hear when he is about to make love to his woman, and they are, *your mother!*"

"But I'm not your woman," she protested.

"After last night you are most certainly my woman."

He advanced toward her with a dangerous gleam in his eye. Meredith retreated again, but he continued to stalk her across the room until she found herself backed against the wall. He quickly pinned her by placing his hands on either side of her shoulders as he pressed his lower body against her. With a sense of shock, she registered the heavy length of his arousal through her nightclothes.

"I'm not letting you go, so you might as well get used to

it," he said harshly, dropping his head to nuzzle the sensitive skin beneath her ear.

Meredith whimpered, unwilling to surrender but unable to help herself. She grew weak when he touched her like this, and she loved him too much to deny herself one last night in his arms. Their passion could not change the future, but, for now at least, she would not refuse him. She flattened her hands against the wall, turning her head to meet his lips in a breathless kiss.

Silverton groaned with satisfaction as his tongue surged into her mouth. Meredith's legs shook with the intensity of his response, but he held her up by pressing his strong thighs into her body. His hands reached down to untie her robe, quickly stripping the garment away from her.

Pulling slightly back, Silverton let his eyes roam over her breasts, only thinly veiled by her nightrail. He gently traced the delicate lace collar that framed her shoulders.

"Don't you know you can drive a man insane wearing something like this?"

"I didn't wear it with you in mind," she whispered. The roughness in his voice made her insides melt with longing.

"Are you sure about that?"

Silverton licked the throbbing pulse at the base of her neck. He kissed his way down the collar of her nightrail, hot breath through lace, before pulling her nipple into his mouth. The feel of his tongue rasping wetly through the fabric both irritated and excited her body in a way she didn't understand. She shifted restlessly, captivated by the sight of his head at her breast, suckling her plump curves.

Meredith choked back a protest when his mouth left her, but he paused only to lift her nightrail away from her body. She watched in a daze as the filmy material drifted to the floor. Silverton's large hands flexed around her waist, and the scalding heat of his tongue once again found her breasts. He laved the nipples until they pebbled into stiff little buds. She moaned again, arching into him as she sought relief from the intoxicating ache that flowed across her skin.

Suddenly, he slid down her body, kneeling on the floor in front of her. She almost stumbled when he released her, grabbing his shoulders to keep from falling. His hands moved to her hips as he gently pushed her back against the wall.

"What . . . what are you doing?" Meredith gasped.

"Trust me, sweetheart," he murmured.

A small shriek escaped her lips when he pressed a moist kiss to the tender cleft between her thighs. Apparently satisfied with her reaction, he used his tongue to gently probe and tease the sensitive flesh that lay hidden in her nest of curls. Just when Meredith thought she would dissolve under the sensual assault, Silverton slowly pushed a finger into her damp sheath, all the while continuing to lick her quivering softness. She felt her knees begin to crumple.

"My lord!" she finally managed in a strangled voice.

"Meredith," Silverton murmured before kissing her throbbing bud, "call me Stephen."

"Oh, I couldn't possibly do that," she responded automatically. "That wouldn't be proper."

Silverton stopped licking her, and she froze, suddenly realizing how absurd their conversation was, given that his head rested between her legs. He looked up at her.

"Oh, really," he replied, one eyebrow arching up. Then he returned to his task, and her insides begin to tremble from the soft but relentless pressure of his tongue.

"Stephen!" she cried a moment later as she clutched at his shoulders to maintain her balance.

"That's better," he growled.

She suddenly caught sight of herself in the large pier glass that hung next to her dressing table. Her pale skin glowed ivory against the red cotton damask that covered the walls. Candlelight glinted off Silverton's golden hair as she watched him nuzzling between her thighs. His hands, bronzed by the sun, looked large and powerful as they held her against the wall.

Meredith felt a strange disorientation as she gazed at their reflection in the mirror. The sight of his broad shoulders between her legs, the feel of his scalding mouth branding her body as he licked that most secret part of her—all sensation coalesced until her head swam from the intensity of his lovemaking.

She started a slide to the floor, but he gripped her hips firmly and held her in place.

"Stephen!" she implored breathlessly. He looked up, a fierce lust darkening his blue eyes to indigo.

Silverton flexed his long fingers as he gentled his grasp on her hips. He began once more to tease the tight, hidden bud, stroking through the tangle of curls with a steady lap of his tongue. A piercing warmth unfurled deep inside her sheath as an unbearable tension burgeoned in the place where he worked his mouth. Just then, he slid a hand between her thighs and slowly pushed two fingers into her now-drenched passage.

She cried out as she arched her back, shoulder blades pressing into the wall as tremors rippled out from her core and down into her legs. Her lungs seized as a cataclysmic wave of pleasure raced through her body.

Meredith panted, closing her eyes, welcoming the velvet darkness as the ripples faded and her racing heart began to slow. A trembling weakness invaded her limbs. She would have collapsed if Silverton hadn't held her up with a big hand splayed across her stomach.

She felt him stand, his hands gliding from her hips to her waist as he carefully supported her. Her lids fluttered up. He gazed at her through narrowed eyes. A look of savage possession turned his handsome features into those of a warrior.

Meredith dropped her head weakly on his chest. "My lord," she muttered, "you are a very wicked man."

His lips brushed the top of her head, and then he picked her up as easily as if she were a small child. "I'm glad you think so," he replied as he carried her across the room to the bed.

Silverton set her carefully on the edge of the mattress. He reached behind and pulled her braid around to rest on her chest. His clever fingers quickly began to unravel the entwined strands of hair. Meredith sat quietly, breathing a sigh of relief as he pulled her locks free of the tight confines of the braid. When her black curls were loose once more, tumbling around her shoulders, he raked his fingers through her hair and gently massaged her scalp. She moaned with pleasure as she leaned against him.

"Don't do that to your hair again," he ordered in a hard voice.

Meredith nodded in mute agreement.

Apparently satisfied with her appearance, he removed his shirt, never taking his eyes from her body as she sat naked amidst the bed linens. He yanked off his boots and quickly stepped out of his breeches. When he turned fully to her, she could see that he was intensely aroused. Meredith couldn't help trembling with a volatile mixture of trepidation and excitement.

What demons had she unleashed when she had refused his proposal and tried to push him away? No one ever said no to Silverton. She had not only hurt him by refusing his offer of marriage, she knew she had wounded his pride as well.

He climbed onto the bed, pulling her underneath him and crushing her into the mattress. Pushing her legs wide, he came in, plunging hard and deep. She rose up to take all his length inside her, clinging to him with a desperate need to possess him as he possessed her. He thrust in a relentless rhythm that quickly stoked the growing heat inside her womb.

Without warning, Silverton bent and nipped her shoulder, and the sudden flash of pain shot through her body and deep into her sheath, where his thick sex ruthlessly claimed her. She knew he was marking her for his own, and a primitive part of her thrilled to his loss of control and his masculine need to dominate her.

His hands reached under her bottom, tilting her hips so he could drive more heavily into her. Meredith panted with an almost unbearable excitement, her fingers kneading his muscular buttocks as she tried to pull him closer with every hard thrust. She could feel tension building, a fullness in her swollen flesh giving her such intense pleasure that part of her wished it would never come to completion.

But just when she thought she would scream if she didn't soon find her release, Silverton slid his arms more tightly around her and rolled over onto his back. He pushed her up into a sitting position as she found herself straddling his hips. Her mouth fell open in surprise at the unexpected change in position. Meredith froze, not sure what to do next.

Silverton's eyes glittered, and his mouth curled into a purely wicked, utterly male smile. His hands began to roam over her body, stroking her breasts, pinching her nipples, caressing her thighs. His fingers slid down through her drenched curls, teasing her exquisitely sensitive bud, playing with the wet flesh where they were joined.

Meredith's insides melted like hot syrup. Her head dropped back, a moan escaping her lips as she began to undulate against the huge erection piercing her body. Silverton muttered harsh words that she didn't understand, pushing her thighs even wider as he surged beneath her.

Although she was on top of him, seemingly dominant, Meredith felt totally exposed—open and vulnerable to his rampant desire. It excited her beyond anything she had ever experienced before.

Pushing against him, she rose desperately through a building spiral of need, wanting but not able to achieve release. She leaned forward, pressing her lips to his mouth, trying to communicate her urgency in a heated kiss. He grasped her head and held it still while he explored the silkiness inside her mouth, probing her hard with his tongue. She whimpered helplessly, overwhelmed by a burning desire to reach a completion only he could give her.

He broke the kiss and nudged her back into a sitting position. "I know, my love," Silverton panted, his own face marked with a harsh need. "You're almost there."

Slipping his hand back to the joining of their bodies, he gave one final stroke to her hooded flesh. Then he pressed a finger just inside the rim of her sheath, alongside his own erection.

It was too much. She was too full, and she finally convulsed around him. Meredith twisted the bedclothes in her fists, crying out as a glorious climax raced through her veins, turning her into liquid fire.

As she gave herself over to the heated release, Silverton flexed his hips and drove himself into her one last time, his shoulders coming off the mattress as he surged against her womb. A long, deep groan rose in his throat as his sex pulsated, spilling his seed deep within her.

Meredith collapsed in a heap onto his chest, nestling her face into his throat. His rapid pulse beat against her cheek. He wrapped trembling arms around her body, pulling her securely against him.

Much later, Meredith rested in his arms, listening to the strong, regular beat of his heart. Never had she felt so safe or so loved. But she knew it to be a false security that could never survive the light of day or the cruel regard of his family and friends. She clung to Silverton with all the love and despair she had within her, knowing he was only a temporary refuge against the emotional tempests swirling endlessly in her soul.

Meredith wept silently with the certain sorrow that she would always be alone.

Chapter Twenty-Eight

Silverton leaned his shoulders against the oak banister of the central staircase, observing the bustle in the entrance hall of the Abbey as the travelers prepared to depart. Trask was already outside and mounted on his huge dappled gray, impatient, as always, to be on his way. The earl had agreed to escort Meredith and Annabel back to London, and only that fact enabled Silverton to allow them to leave without him.

That, and the armed grooms who would also accompany the carriage on its short journey to the city.

Silverton cursed the reasons that kept him an extra day in Kent, but he could no longer delay the impending confrontation with his mother. After that, however, he wouldn't rest until he had run Isaac and Jacob Burnley to ground.

In the meantime, he had to stand by and watch the woman he loved—a woman in danger—ride away from him. The possessive part of his nature howled in his ear to keep Meredith by his side. He had both right and obligation to protect her, and he resented ceding those rights to others, even for one day. Fortunately, Trask was more than a match for any dangers they might face on the road, and the actual risk of anything happening, Silverton believed, was slight. He doubted Isaac Burnley would try to hurt Annabel again, especially since he must have realized by now that his first attempt had failed. Still, Silverton had no intention of taking any chances.

He glanced up as Robert dashed by him, directing one of the servants on the correct placement of Annabel's numerous bandboxes. The boy's enthusiasm, and his concern for his fiancée's well-being, brought a reluctant smile to Silverton's lips. His cousin had changed a great deal since his engagement to Annabel, seeming to grow into a man almost overnight.

Of course, Silverton thought with more than a touch of bitter irony, he too was a changed man since falling in love with Meredith. And if he didn't take care, she would likely drive him barking mad as he struggled to understand why she had changed her mind once again.

He glanced over at Meredith, who stood by her sister, tight-lipped and as still as a marble statue. Her demeanor was in marked contrast to that of Annabel and Sophia, who chatted and laughed merrily with each other. Silverton studied her carefully as she stared down at the patterns in the ironstone floor, deep in thought and oblivious to the cheerful chaos that swirled around her.

And, apparently, oblivious to him.

He tried to suppress a growing sense of exasperation. What a fool he had been to think he could impose his will on her, sexual or otherwise. Meredith had responded to him last night with a desperate ardor, but he realized now that her passionate response was more akin to a farewell than to a capitulation.

"We're ready to go!"

Robert's cheerful call from the open doorway jogged Silverton from his frustrated musings. Meredith also started, her eyes flying over to meet his before darting away again. She followed Annabel and Sophia outside, waiting silently for Robert to hand the two girls into the traveling coach.

As Silverton came up behind her, he saw Meredith draw in a tremulous breath as she turned to offer him a gloved hand. She refused to look at him.

"Good-bye, my lord. We are most grateful for everything you have done for us. Please extend my gratitude to your mother for her hospitality."

He held fast when she tried to pull away, forcing her to raise her eyes to his face. One look in the anguished depths told Silverton everything he needed to know.

"I'll follow you up to London tomorrow," he said quietly, so the others wouldn't hear. "We'll talk then about what is troubling you."

She tugged again, but he refused to let go. He turned over her hand and raised it to his lips, brushing a gentle kiss on the exposed skin above her glove. Meredith closed her eyes, her mouth trembling. Relief washed through him at this small display of emotional vulnerability. For the first time all morning, Silverton breathed more freely.

"Don't worry, love." He bent his head to murmur in her ear as he escorted her to the steps of the carriage. "All will be well."

She shook her head but managed to give him a smile even though her eyes were bright with unshed tears. Silverton had to repress the urge to sweep her into his arms, carry her to his bedroom, and love her until she knew beyond all doubt that she belonged to him—irrevocably and forever.

The time for that would come soon enough, he vowed to himself, as soon as he whipped any and all interfering relatives back into line.

The door to the carriage slammed shut. Robert, Annabel, and Sophia waved their good-byes, and the vehicle moved forward.

"I'll see you in London," Trask called as he cantered by, followed closely by the armed grooms.

Silverton raised his hand and watched the carriage until it disappeared down the long drive, rolling quickly into the dense woods flanking the estate. He then spun on his heel and strode through the massive oak doors into the house. As he moved past his butler, Deacon, he barked a question over his shoulder.

"Has Lady Silverton left her room yet?"

"No, my lord. The maid has just brought her ladyship her morning chocolate," Deacon replied. His barely arched eyebrows indicated disbelief that his master could even ask such a question.

"Well, then, I suppose she'll be in for a surprise," Silverton retorted as stalked to the stairs that led to his mother's apartments.

Meredith counted the chimes of the clock out in the hallway. Only nine o'clock, but already the evening seemed endless. She blinked repeatedly, her eyes gritty from an annoying combination of repressed tears and lack of sleep.

The departure from Kent yesterday had depressed her more than she thought possible. She had struggled not to cry when Silverton kissed her wrist before handing her into the carriage. That simple gesture had almost broken her resolve as she struggled against a terrible desire to surrender to his masculine protectiveness.

Luckily, she had managed to restrain the impulse. Meredith bleakly congratulated herself on her willpower in the face of such overwhelming temptation.

What had taken almost as much discipline, though, was containing her frustration with her lighthearted companions on the trip back to London. Robert's spirits, in particular, were so ebullient that Meredith had wanted to box his ears. Only Annabel had noticed her grim silence, casting numerous worried glances her way. Fortunately, her sister had been sensible enough to leave her alone, both yesterday and today. Meredith couldn't bear to talk about Silverton and had avoided mentioning his name as much as possible.

She sighed, pushing away the bills that had accumulated

on her desk during their trip to the country. The numbers seemed to swim before her eyes, and she knew it was pointless to do any more work until she got some sleep.

Sleep, Meredith thought gloomily, was not likely to occur anytime soon.

She jumped in her seat when a firm knock sounded on the door of their townhouse. Silverton, no doubt, finally coming to call. Meredith had been expecting him all day with an exhausting combination of breathless anticipation and crushing dread. Rising from her desk, she scrubbed her suddenly damp palms with her handkerchief. She shook the skirts of her light cambric gown and quickly checked her reflection in the mirror that hung over the fireplace.

A quiet tap sounded on the door of her study. Meredith had to clear her throat twice before she could bid the footman to enter.

"Lord Silverton begs leave to see you, Miss Burnley," Peter said as he bowed her visitor into the room.

"Thank you, Peter," she replied, inwardly cursing the slight tremor in her voice.

The door shut. She stood awkwardly by her desk, too nervous to move forward and greet him. Silverton did not move from his position by the door. Instead, he crossed his arms over his chest and carefully studied her through narrowed eyes. His stance did nothing to assuage her anxiety.

His face was inscrutable, almost grim, she thought. As he allowed the silence between them to lengthen, Meredith fought the urge to shift under his gaze like a disobedient child—and not just because he observed her with such a critical eye.

He was dressed in severe but elegantly cut evening attire, the stark black coat hugging his broad shoulders and emphasizing the athletic strength of his physique. Silverton was so handsome, so powerfully *male*, that Meredith felt dizzy just looking at him. She wondered, not for the first time, how he had managed to evade the marital machinations of so many determined debutants. It seemed impossible that he had waited so many years before choosing a wife, before choosing *her*.

Unable to bear the silence any longer, Meredith dropped a proper little curtsy. "Good evening, my lord. I have been expecting your call."

Silverton smothered a curse, closing the space between them so quickly that she gasped. He grabbed her by the shoulders and pulled her into his arms.

"Meredith," he growled, "don't be such a goose."

His mouth covered hers in a kiss so consuming that her legs nearly gave out beneath her. For a long moment she felt herself melting into his rough embrace, her treacherous body now so obviously conditioned to respond to his touch. But then she fought her instincts, dragging her mouth from his to pull away.

"Please, my lord! You mustn't do that anymore."

Silverton muttered some more curses under his breath, but he didn't try to hold on to her.

"Meredith, you try my patience exceedingly." He took a deep breath, his broad chest expanding as he clearly struggled to control himself. Taking her hand in a gentle clasp, he led her over to a chair by the fireplace.

"All right, my love. You may tell me, once again, why you cannot marry me, and I will tell you, once again, why you can."

In spite of her aching heart, Meredith almost laughed at the aggrieved tones of aristocratic exasperation in his voice. She knew it still astonished him that anyone dared to defy him, especially the woman he chose to be his bride.

Rather than sitting, Silverton planted himself firmly before her, arms crossed over his chest, legs apart in a dominating stance. Apparently, he intended to be difficult.

"You know I cannot marry you," Meredith began, deciding a firm and direct approach would be best.

"I know nothing of the sort."

"My lord, surely you comprehend the many obstacles to our marriage! Your mother's objections, for instance . . ." Silverton rolled his eyes to the ceiling. She bit her lip. "Your uncle, General Stanton, will also object to—"

"No, he won't," he interrupted. "My uncle has come to greatly admire you. And you know that Aunt Georgina cares for you as much as she does for Annabel."

"Be that as it may," Meredith forged on before he could say anything else, "you are more aware than anyone of the many responsibilities of the Marchioness of Silverton. I'm not suited to fulfill that role, and there is little doubt in my mind that most of your friends and family would agree."

He glowered at her. "You are perfectly capable of being an excellent marchioness. I have seen ample evidence of that."

"The issue is not whether I *am* capable of being the marchioness," she persisted, resisting the urge to clench her teeth, "but whether I *can* do it. Do you understand the difference?"

"No. And I don't think you do, either. Besides, you would not just be the marchioness. You would be my wife. Did we not agree we both want that?"

Meredith's temper began to shred at his refusal to listen to her. "It's simply impossible! Why can't you see that?" Jumping up from her seat, she paced to the window and back. She felt light-headed with agitation and fatigue, and furious with him for being so obstinate.

Silverton, on the other hand, now seemed to be in complete control of his emotions, watching her with an impassive expression on his face. That angered her even more. Her heart pounded so hard she feared it would leap from her chest.

"You just don't want to understand!" she flung at him. "I have tried to explain this already. Marriage for us would be disastrous. We are too different—our lives are too different. *This* is where you belong. *This* is what is right for you. London, the ton, and all the rest of it."

She stopped pacing to fling her arms out wide, as if to

encompass the entire city and his life there. "All this is your world, not mine. It is what you want. You are respected and admired by those who belong here. You are one of them."

Meredith swallowed around the painful constriction in her throat. Her words tasted like ashes. "I don't belong in London—in your world—and you know it. Unlike you, I don't want it. You shouldn't make me have to explain it," she exclaimed bitterly. "You know perfectly well what a failure my Season has been."

Silverton frowned and shook his head at her.

At his disapproving gesture, something inside of her snapped. She was so tired of others, even him, telling her how she should feel. Suddenly, it all poured out of her, like a spring torrent breaching a riverbank. Her anger, her resentment. Her amazed disappointment in so many of the people she had met. Her fruitless struggle to understand the opaque world he lived in, until she hardly knew who she was anymore.

She paced back and forth across the study, holding nothing back, telling him everything she had thought and felt these last few months. How she hated the ton, how much the whispers, the cutting glances, the cruel laughs wounded her spirit. How she felt as if she were always being measured to some invisible standard. How her failure to meet that standard created anxieties she hadn't even known existed until coming to London.

While all the poison flowed out of her, Silverton never moved. Only his eyes followed her restless movements about the room as her emotional torrent poured forth, as she demanded that he understand.

Finally, she ran out of words. Meredith stumbled to a halt by the window, trying to calm her heaving breath, appalled that she had revealed so much. She stole a glance at Silverton, who looked at her so sympathetically she wanted to cringe. What in God's name had come over her? How could she have been so foolish as to reveal all that ugliness to him?

"Don't look at me like that!" she blurted out, turning her head away. Meredith hated how bereft she sounded, but her voice no longer seemed her own.

Silverton bowed his head and frowned at the floor, either pondering her words seriously this time or simply giving her the chance to recover herself. It seemed forever before he lifted his head to speak. When he did, his deep voice pierced her to the depths of her soul.

"Meredith, I understand your fears, I truly do. But I do not foresee one obstacle we cannot overcome together. You would be the Marchioness of Silverton, my wife. Who you are, your place in the world, would never be in question. With me by your side, no one would dare challenge you."

Meredith fought a desperate impulse to give in. She wanted so much to believe they were capable of transcending the cold banalities of the fashionable world.

Unfortunately, his hesitation in those moments before he replied to her illuminated more than he probably realized. Clearly, Silverton had made a calculated decision to dismiss her concerns. He wanted her for his wife, and he would drive over whatever obstacles stood in his path.

But Meredith couldn't bring herself to ignore his mother's censure or the disapproval of his friends. Nor could she promise she would ever move comfortably in the ton. More than anything, she feared he would come to regret their union, and she couldn't bear the thought of losing his love or his respect. Or of losing hers for him.

Meredith finally admitted to herself that sleeping with Silverton was the worst mistake of her life. *No*, she silently amended, stealing a look at him. *The worst mistake would be to marry him.*

"No, Meredith, it would not be a mistake to marry me."

She gasped, stunned by his perception. How could he read her thoughts so easily? She gazed into his eyes, which looked back at her with avid tenderness. She felt a tear slide down her face, born of fatigue and an anguished desire to ignore her doubts and give him what he wanted.

"Come and sit beside me, my sweet." He reached for her, coaxing her away from the window to sit on the comfortable velvet sofa. Wrapping a strong arm around her shoulders, he brushed the dampness away from her cheek. She was so tired she allowed herself to lean into him, sighing with a kind of brokenhearted relief.

"Meredith, do you love me?"

She lifted her head from his shoulder, stung that he could even ask her the question. "You know I do!"

"Then listen well, my love. All those things that concern you—my life in London, the Season, the endless round of boring and pointless parties— they mean almost nothing to me anymore, especially if you are not in my life."

She stared mutely back at him, but he must have seen the skepticism on her face. He frowned thoughtfully for a few moments and then appeared to reach a decision.

"Meredith, when I was young—not much more than a boy— I fell in love."

She blinked in surprise, both at his words and at his clipped tone. His furrowed expression relaxed into a wry smile, but his voice still held a touch of acid.

"Madly in love, in fact," he continued, "or at least I thought so at the time. She was an enchanting little slip of a thing named Esme Newton. I was convinced she returned my feelings, and had every intention of asking her to marry me."

Meredith felt a sharp little stab of jealousy toward the petite and, she was certain, blond Esme Newton. But at the somber look on Silverton's face, she felt her petty anger fade away. Her hand slid across his hard thigh to grasp his fingers in a comforting grip.

"What happened?" she ventured.

"Much to my surprise, she fell in love with someone else, someone I knew very well."

"A friend?"

He hesitated. "At the time, yes."

There was no mistaking the brooding resentment in his voice. Part of her wished him to stop, not wanting to hear the story of bitterness and lost love, but Meredith knew he was telling her something important.

"What happened?"

He shrugged his shoulders, looking down at her fingers intertwined with his. "Nothing, really, which makes the whole sorry tale so foolish. Esme and I obviously didn't marry, nor did she marry . . . my friend. He went off to join Wellington's army and came back a war hero several years later. Esme became the wife of a Scottish earl, rarely coming down to London after her marriage. As far as I know, she has always been content with her choice."

Silverton raised his eyes to hers, and her nerves jumped at the fierceness reflected there. "I, however, allowed myself to become bitter and cold, never wishing to love again. And I believed I never would, until we met. You rescued me, Meredith, from my own stupidity and selfishness."

His admission melted her heart. She knew how it must have cost him—so proud and in control as he always was—to reveal the pain of his youthful infatuation. Meredith also sensed he held his emotions in check, especially those regarding the betrayal of his friend. But instead of pressing for answers, she simply stroked the back of his hand, trying to convey comfort and love with her touch.

He smiled at her, and the warmth returned to his voice. "The point is, my love, I am no longer that callow youth. I am a man, and know exactly what I want. I want a wife to cherish, and children to protect and care for until they are old enough to have families of their own. That is what I wish for my life. That is what I desire with you."

She drew in a shuddering breath, searching his face. She saw truth in his expression, heard it in the tone of his voice.

Silverton carefully took her face between his hands, gazing at her with eyes as clear, deep, and blue as the sky on a hot summer morning. Meredith had the oddest feeling he comprehended everything about her, and that she didn't have to say another word.

"Meredith, before I met you I was . . . adrift. I understood my purpose in life, my duty to my family, and my responsibilities to the title and estate. But I could never really seem to *feel* it, to know it in my heart, as I should."

His firm lips brushed her forehead, and another stone in the wall of her resistance tumbled to the ground.

"All that changed when I met you. I have the chance to become the man I should be, thanks to you. You are the kindest, most loving person I have ever known. I need you more than you will ever realize."

Meredith looked up into his dear face, and what she saw there both terrified and exhilarated her. She felt something new and unexpected stir within her. It took her a moment to recognize it as the dawning of hope.

"Really?" In spite of herself, she couldn't keep a little doubt from creeping into her voice.

"Meredith!" Now his tone was an impatient growl. "I love you. That will never change, I promise."

The wall crumbled to dust, but then an alarming thought flashed unbidden into her mind.

"But what about your mother?" she blurted out.

He sighed as his arms tightened around her. "My sweet, I am truly sorry my mother has caused you such distress. I can assure you, however, she will raise no further objection to our marriage."

From the look on his face, she suspected that Silverton had given the marchioness very little choice in the matter. Meredith knew she should regret coming between mother and son, but where Lady Silverton was concerned she found it difficult to muster up more than a twinge of guilt.

"Would we have to live with her?" she asked hesitantly, not wanting to offend him. "At least, all the time?"

"Good God," he replied, looking more than slightly appalled. "Of course not. We would certainly live separately from her while in London. As for Belfield Abbey, my mother only visits twice a year, and almost never comes to my estates in the north."

Meredith slowly, very slowly, allowed herself to relax into his arms. Silverton smiled—a trifle smugly, she thought—as a knowing gleam lit his eyes.

"It may also interest you to know," he added, "that I much prefer the country to the city. You mustn't assume that you know everything about me, my sweet. I would rather spend all my time at Belfield Abbey or in the north, mucking about in the dirt like the dull farmer I really am."

"My lord," Meredith protested, stunned by the absurd vision of Silverton covered in mud, "I find that difficult to accept."

"Well, you'd better accept it, because you're about to become a farmer's wife." Bending his head, he captured her mouth with a searing possession. She melted into his arms as he pressed hungry, open-mouth kisses against her lips. Silverton's arms slid around her back, one hand reaching up, fingers threading through her hair. He gently pulled her head back as his tongue traced a fiery trail down her throat.

Passion and relief poured through her veins like an elixir, sweeping aside fatigue and sorrow. A tiny voice in her head still murmured that trouble lay before her, but Meredith had finally come to the end of her resistance. For now, at least, she would put her trust and confidence into Silverton's capable hands.

He nuzzled her ear before looking up to study her as she lay in his arms. His eyes glittered with a soul-stealing desire.

"I trust I have finally answered all your doubts." His husky voice sent shivers down her spine.

She nodded, so dazzled she couldn't speak. He pressed one

more impossibly masterful kiss on her lips and then sat up straight, bringing her with him.

"I have something for you." He reached into his waistcoat and pulled out a small velvet bag, tipping the contents into his hand.

"It was my grandmother's," he said softly.

Meredith opened her eyes wide as a tumble of gold slid from the bag into his palm. It was a very old, very beautiful mesh bracelet. Gold filigree threads in a delicate weave shimmered in the candlelight. Studded at random intervals along the band were small, glittering emeralds and cabochon opals that gleamed a milky white. She raised her eyes to his in awe.

"It's beautiful," she breathed. "But much too fine for me!"

Silverton cast his gaze heavenward again, as if imploring the gods for patience. Pushing up the ruffled trim of her long sleeve, he fastened the bracelet securely around her wrist. Meredith held it up to the light, fascinated by the play of colors that seemed to emanate from deep within the stones. She threw her arms around his neck and pressed a kiss on his jaw.

"Thank you, my lord. I will cherish it always."

He smiled and wrapped his arms about her, returning her eager display of gratitude. "Meredith, you really must call me Stephen. At least when we're alone."

"Yes, Stephen," she replied absently as she returned her gaze to the bracelet. She stroked it lovingly with one finger, thinking that she would never own anything so wonderful or precious if she lived to be a hundred.

"Now," Silverton said in an amused voice, "perhaps we could discuss the date of our wedding."

She jerked her head up as reality came flooding back.

"Oh, my lord—Stephen—do we really have to talk about this now? It's been such a long day." She gave him a wavering smile, trying to remove the sting of rejection from her words, but she was simply too tired to argue with him anymore.

He started to look grim again. She placed her hand on his sleeve and massaged the corded muscle that lay under the fine broadcloth of his coat.

"There is so much to do for Annabel's wedding. Don't you think seeing her safely bestowed is the most important thing right now? We have plenty of time to discuss our own marriage later." She batted her eyelashes at him, hoping he would respond to a display of feminine wiles.

Silverton looked ready to dispute the matter, but after examining her face through narrowed eyes, he capitulated. "All right, my love. Annabel and Robert will be married by the end of the month. I suppose I can wait till then."

She sighed in relief. One side of his mouth quirked up wryly.

"Meredith, you worry too much."

"I know," she replied solemnly. "I have always found it a most vexing trait."

He laughed. "Well, we have to see what we can do to change that." He dropped a soft kiss on her lips before standing and pulling her to her feet.

"As much as I want to stay," he murmured huskily, "I think you need your sleep more than you need lovemaking."

Silverton grinned like a schoolboy at her undoubtedly shocked expression. He raised both her hands to his mouth and pressed them, one after the other, to his lips. "Rest, sweetheart. I will see you in the morning."

He strode to the door, gave her one last, lingering look, and left the room.

Meredith sighed and sank back down onto the sofa. Her emotions were a jumble. Part of her still believed she was making a mistake, but if Silverton wanted to marry her in a month's time, she would find the courage to be the best wife possible. In any event, she thought ruefully, it certainly seemed that he wouldn't take no for an answer.

"Meredith?"

She looked up as Annabel peeked into the room.

"Was Lord Silverton just here?" the girl inquired innocently.

Meredith tried to frown severely at her sister. "You know exactly who it was."

Annabel plumped down beside her on the sofa. "Well, I certainly hope you have made up with him. You've been moping around for two whole days now, and anyone can see it's because you've been foolish enough to resist him."

"Annabel!" gasped Meredith.

Her sister's eyes suddenly grew round with excitement. "Did he give you that bracelet?" she squeaked, grabbing Meredith's arm. "It's the most beautiful thing I've ever seen."

"I know," Meredith breathed as she returned her gaze to the glittering piece. "I shouldn't have accepted it, but I just couldn't seem to help myself."

Annabel's eyes grew solemn. "He loves you, doesn't he?"

"He does, but is that enough?"

"Dearest!" Annabel threw her arms around her. "Of course it's enough. It's everything!"

Meredith returned her sister's enthusiastic hug. If Annabel was so happy for her, then perhaps she had made the right decision after all. The girl might be young, but she had a perception and wisdom Meredith had learned to trust long ago. She laughed nervously, finally allowing herself to feel the restless happiness she had been holding at bay for the last half hour.

Annabel opened her mouth, no doubt to ask a thousand questions, when she was interrupted by a loud knock on the front door.

"Now who could be calling at this time of night?" Meredith wondered as she got to her feet.

Annabel shrugged. "I haven't a clue, unless it's Robert. He apparently needs to see me at least three times a day."

Meredith was about to make a sarcastic reply, but she froze instead when she heard the sound of raised voices and breaking glass. Annabel leapt up and rushed over to grab her arm.

"Meredith," her voice quivered with anxiety. "You don't think . . ."

They heard heavy footsteps rushing up the steps and down the hallway. The door to the study flew open.

Isaac Burnley strode into the room, followed closely by his son Jacob. Both men wore heavy greatcoats, with thick mufflers around their throats. Meredith and Annabel shrank back against the sofa as their uncle advanced relentlessly toward them.

"My dear nieces," he snarled, his lips stretched back in a feral grin. "Did you really think you could avoid me forever?"

Chapter Twenty-Nine

"Why didn't you tell me before?" Robert demanded in a hostile voice.

Silverton ignored his cousin as he banged loudly on the front door of Meredith's townhouse on Hill Street. He had been hammering the knocker against the door for five minutes now, and no one had answered. It was only ten in the morning. Even if Meredith and Annabel were out—unlikely, at best—one of the servants would have answered by now.

"Stephen!" Robert poked him hard in the arm. "How could you have kept this from me? Didn't you think I'd want to know Annabel was in danger?"

Robert, of course, referred to the fact that he had been kept in the dark about the failed attempt to poison Annabel. Silverton had only told his cousin of the plot this morning, after picking him up on his way to Hill Street.

He spun on his heel and rushed down the front steps, running for the entrance to the laneway that ran behind the row of townhouses. Robert and Silverton's groom, Simmons, followed closely behind.

"I'm sorry, Robert," Silverton flung back over his shoulder. "Annabel and Meredith didn't want to worry you or the rest of the family. We thought it best to keep it to ourselves until we had real proof of the attempt on her life."

Robert raced to catch up with him. "I'll wager my horse you told Trask, though, didn't you?" he retorted bitterly.

Silverton slid to a halt at the entrance to the laneway. He grabbed his cousin by the shoulders and finally looked into the boy's pale face. "I'm sorry, Robert, I truly am. But I needed his help. Please forgive me for offending you, but can we stop arguing for the moment and find out why no one answers the door at your fiancée's house?"

Robert jerkily nodded his head. Silverton understood that part of his cousin's anger sprang from the fear that something terrible had happened to Annabel and Meredith. He shared that fear, and he cursed himself now for assuming the sisters would be safe once they returned to the city.

After leaving Meredith last night Silverton had gone to Lady Mountley's ball, the last big social event before the ton decamped from town for the summer. He was in no mood for socializing, but Trask had sent a missive earlier in the day informing him that he would be at the ball. The earl had, apparently, discovered important information regarding the Burnleys' finances.

Silverton found Trask in the card room. As soon as the earl spied him, he threw down his cards and rose from the table. Ignoring the protests from the other players, Trask led the way out to Lady Mountley's terrace.

"Is it as bad as we feared?" Silverton asked without any preamble.

"Worse," Trask grimaced. "Isaac Burnley is completely bankrupt. My sources in Bristol tell me their wool factory has been struggling for some years, and probably never recovered from the financial crisis in 1811. When the trade began to move north, they lost most of their remaining business. Burnley then tried to recover his losses by investing on the Exchange with money he didn't have. Those investments went bad sometime in the new year, which precipitated the final destruction of the family fortune."

"The timing is just about right then," mused Silverton. "The Burnleys appeared at Swallow Hill in February, which, coincidentally, was the same time that Annabel suffered a relapse of her illness. I think they were drugging the girl in order to justify her incarceration in a madhouse."

"Have you received any information from the runner yet?"

"No. I just returned to London this afternoon. I sent a note around to Bow Street requesting him to report first thing tomorrow."

Trask nodded brusquely. "Let me know what else I can do."

The earl had returned to his card game, and Silverton had returned home to ponder the information his friend had provided.

Now Silverton couldn't believe he had waited till morning to act. He should have returned immediately to Hill Street, pulled Meredith and Annabel from their beds, and brought them to the safety of his mansion in Grosvenor Square. As he raced into the laneway, he devoutly prayed that his own lapse in judgment wouldn't separate him from Meredith forever.

The three men dashed past high walls and iron gates, splashing heavily through the mud and debris that collected in the alleyway. Silverton counted back entrances, then yanked open the gate to the small garden behind Meredith's house. He strode swiftly to the basement door. It was flung wide open against the wall of the house.

Bloody hell. Fear clutched at his chest, making him breathless.

He pelted down into the kitchen. It was empty, and a shambles—chairs overturned, crockery smashed on the floor, the table askew against the wall.

"Robert, Simmons!" He gestured impatiently at the two

men gaping in the doorway. "Go upstairs and see what you can find."

Simmons brushed past him and headed for the front of the house. Robert, however, seemed paralyzed, his breath coming in short, sharp exhalations as the blood drained from his face.

"Robert," Silverton urged quietly. "Go up to Annabel's bedroom."

The boy's eyes darkened with anguish, his body still unable to move. Silverton knew he was afraid of what he would find upstairs.

He gripped Robert's shoulder. "I promise you, she is fine. Isaac Burnley will not hurt her. He needs her too much."

His cousin nodded and hurried from the room.

Silverton was about to follow when he heard pounding in a corner of the basement. Wheeling about, he saw a cramped set of stairs leading down to the cold cellar.

"Who's in there?" he commanded in a loud voice.

"It's Peter, sir, the footman," came the muffled reply.

Silverton searched the floor and quickly found a key that had obviously been flung in the corner. He unfastened the lock and wrenched the door wide, gasping at the vision that met his eyes.

Peter, Mrs. Biggs, and a young scullery maid stood blinking in the light that flooded down from the kitchen. They were disheveled, dirty, and, from the distraught looks on their faces, appeared to have been locked away in the dark for hours. Silverton extended his hand and helped the women up the steps to the kitchen. The young maid was crying, and Mrs. Biggs flapped her immense apron in distress, causing billows of dust to waft up from the garment.

"Oh, my lord," she keened, "those evil villains took away my poor lambs, they did, and there weren't nothing we could do to stop them!"

Silverton's gut clenched as his eyes roamed over the

bruises on Mrs. Biggs' cheek. Peter was in even worse shape, with a cut lip and two purple and swollen eyes.

"We tried, my lord." The footman wrung his hands in distress. "But there were too many of them—five or six, at least. And there were just the three of us, seeing as Miss Noyes and Agatha were not returning until today, and Ruddle off visiting his sister in the country. I'm sorry, my lord. Those young ladies were my responsibility, and I let you down."

Silverton led Mrs. Biggs to the kitchen table, picking up a chair and gently pushing her into it. He glanced over at the footman and shook his head.

"No, Peter, the fault is mine. I should have anticipated this and not allowed them to return to the house."

Robert and Simmons reentered the kitchen in time to hear the last part of the conversation. Silverton looked a quick question at them. His cousin stared back, his boyish face expressing a searing combination of fear and reproach.

Robert had always idolized him, and to know that he had failed him so miserably was almost more than Silverton could bear. He had failed them all. He thought he had anticipated every circumstance, but his own arrogance had blinded him to the desperate stupidity of Isaac and Jacob Burnley.

"What did you find?" Silverton directed his question to Simmons.

"The furniture in the study is all in a tumble, my lord," replied the man, shaking his head. "It looks to me like the young ladies were taken there."

"They were in the bedrooms, too." Robert finally found his voice, although it was hoarse with distress. "The drawers are pulled open, and some of their clothes appear to be gone."

Silverton shut his eyes, nodding to himself. A bloody rage shifted behind his closed lids, but he forced himself to grasp the reins of his temper and calmly analyze the situation.

"Peter," he said, opening his eyes and turning to the footman. "What time did they force the house last night?"

"Shortly after you left, my lord, just after ten o'clock. They were on me in a second, and dragged me right back to the kitchen with Mrs. Biggs and Maddie."

"Aye, and I gave one of those devils a good wallop with my rolling pin," cried the cook. "I vow he didn't walk out the front door on his own two legs."

"I know you did everything you could, Mrs. Biggs," Silverton tried to smile at her.

"It weren't enough!"

The sturdy woman burst into tears, throwing her dirty apron over her face. Silverton's aching heart empathized with Mrs. Biggs's tortured sense of failure.

"And to the best of your knowledge," he grimly asked Peter, forcing himself to ignore the weeping women, "when did the Burnleys actually leave the house?"

"Can't have been more than twenty minutes or so after they seized us, your lordship. Those men knew what they were about. They had us down in the root cellar so fast that my head was like to spin off, what with the beating they gave me and all. The house went quiet just a few minutes after that. We screamed and yelled, but heard not a single thing until you let us out just now."

"Twelve hours head start . . . ," murmured Silverton. "Did you happen to see how many carriages they had with them?"

"Two, my lord. We had quite a tussle, but I saw them in front of the house as plain as day."

Silverton bowed his head as he calculated the lost time, the distance the carriages must have traveled, and all the complications of a rescue attempt.

"What are we going to do, Stephen?" implored Robert.

Silverton looked up. Everyone in the room stared at him with expressions of mingled anxiety and hope. They clearly expected him to know what to do. He could not afford to fail them again.

"Simmons, go now and find Lord Trask. Check his home

first. If he is not there, then try him at White's, but do not give up until you find him. Tell him to meet me at Silverton House in an hour, with his curricle and fastest horses. We'll be driving almost to Bath."

"Yes, my lord." Simmons disappeared through the back door.

"Peter."

"Aye, my lord?"

"Get cleaned up and follow us home. We'll be leaving in an hour."

"What can I do, my lord?" inquired Mrs. Biggs with a huge sniffle.

Silverton patted her shoulder. "You can best help by setting the house to rights, Mrs. Biggs. Your mistresses will be tired when they return home, and I want them surrounded by their usual comforts."

A beefy hand stretched out and grasped his sleeve. "Do you promise to bring them back, my lord?"

"Yes, Mrs. Biggs," he said, knowing he would succeed or die trying. "I promise."

"Right you are then." She nodded once and got to her feet. "Good luck to you, my lord."

Silverton motioned to Robert and stalked down the hallway to the front door. He threw it open and ran down the steps to his waiting curricle.

"Stephen, old man." His cousin hurried after him. "Where in God's name are we going? We can't just dash off and hope we'll stumble across their trail, can we?"

Silverton leapt up onto the high perch and waited for Robert to climb after him. As he took the ribbons into his hands, Silverton thought back to the conversation he'd had with the Bow Street runner earlier this morning. The runner had not been able to discover the whereabouts of the man who had poisoned Meredith, but he had unearthed a nugget of information that was now infinitely more valuable, given the change in circumstances.

"Try not to worry, Robert. I'll explain everything once we're on our way." Silverton urged the horses into a quick trot. "But I assure you, I know exactly where to look for them. And this time, Isaac and Jacob Burnley will not escape."

Meredith stumbled down the steps of the carriage, following Annabel across a dirty yard paved with broken flagstones. She looked blearily up at the windblown sky, trying to shake off the effects of the drug she had been forced to drink the night before. As far as she could tell, it was around midday, although thick clouds had hidden the sun since dawn.

The carriage had traveled through the night, causing her to lose all sense of time many hours ago. She had thought the nightmarish journey would never end. Not that Meredith could remember much of it—just flashes of panic whenever she surfaced from her unnatural sleep to catch Jacob staring at her from the opposite bench of the coach. Once or twice he had reached out to touch her, but she had shrunk back against Annabel, turning her face away from him. Later, near dawn, she had forced herself to look at her cousin. In the dim light of the travel lamps, Jacob had appeared as evil as any monster that Meredith could have conjured up in a painting.

Annabel, fortunately, had slept most of the night. At first Meredith had been terrified the dose of laudanum Isaac had poured down her sister's throat had been too much. It wasn't, and she was grateful Annabel had been spared the realization of what was happening to them, at least for a few hours.

Meredith felt Jacob's hand against the small of her back, pushing her toward an open doorway. As she crossed the yard she looked up at the old house looming before her. It was a low, rambling building roofed in gray slate, grown dingy with age. Tall chimneys rose against the iron gray sky but, despite the day's chill, no smoke crept up to hint of any welcoming fires. The windows were latticed and covered in soot, emitting no light. The whole effect of the place was one of dirtiness and disrepair.

And, Meredith thought bleakly, of despair. She needed no one to tell her that Isaac Burnley had brought them to a madhouse, as he had sworn to do those many weeks ago.

She almost tripped over the uneven threshold of the door, but Jacob grabbed her elbow to steady her. Even though her head swam and she struggled against a feeling of lassitude, Meredith shook him off. The touch of his hand, even through multiple layers of clothing, made her skin crawl.

Isaac walked ahead of her, propelling Annabel down a dim, low-pitched passageway to the back of the house. Her sister tried to look over her shoulder at Meredith, but her uncle gripped her arm and dragged her along.

"I'm right behind you, my love, don't worry," Meredith called out in a raspy voice.

Jacob uttered a deep laugh that sounded like an animal growling. "Worry about yourself, Meredith. We'll take care of Annabel."

A door on the right side of the passage suddenly opened, and a severe looking woman in a rusty-colored bombazine dress emerged to greet Isaac.

"We have been waiting for you, Mr. Burnley," she said. "Everything is ready."

Meredith halted next to Annabel. She reached over and took her sister's hand. The girl looked up, her eyes huge and pitch-black with fear and the lingering effects of the drug.

"Mrs. Jukes, take this one and lock her up," Isaac ordered, shoving Annabel into the woman's arms.

"What are you doing?" gasped Meredith, as she struggled to hold on to her sister. "Uncle Isaac, are you insane?"

"Meredith!" cried Annabel. "Don't let them take me!"

Tears streamed down Annabel's face as Mrs. Jukes tried to wrestle her away from Meredith. A hulking man with a misshapen nose appeared as if from nowhere and grabbed the girl around the waist, lifting her backward through the door.

"No!" screamed Meredith as she struggled to reach her sister. Jacob's arm wrapped around her chest, as hard as an iron bar, squeezing all the air from her lungs. Black dots swam across her vision.

The door to the room slammed shut, and Annabel was gone. Meredith sagged back against her cousin's body as the fight drained out of her. She was stunned—her mind completely unable to comprehend the terrible thought that she might never see her sister again. Suddenly, her feet left the floor as Jacob picked her up to carry her down the passage.

"Let me down," she choked out as she pushed her hands against Jacob's chest.

He laughed. "You'll fall flat on your face if I do. Don't worry, sweet cousin. You'll see your sister again, as long as you do what we say."

Meredith stopped struggling. Jacob was too powerful, and she needed to conserve her strength if she had any hope of saving Annabel's life. The most important thing was to keep the girl alive until Silverton could find them.

At the thought of her fiancé, her eyes filled with tears. She had clung to his image as a bulwark against the terror that had threatened to overwhelm her during the long night. Meredith surreptitiously fingered the cool mesh of the gold bracelet still encircling her wrist. It had become a talisman during the seemingly endless journey; as long as she wore it, she could believe Silverton would rescue them from this living hell. It was proof of his love and his promise to keep her and Annabel safe.

Jacob carried her into a low-ceilinged room, lit dimly by a lamp and a smoking fire in a small grate. The grimy windows filtered out most of the weak light from the overcast day.

Isaac stripped off his gloves before tossing his greatcoat over the back of an old-fashioned high-back chair. "Put her down," he ordered.

Jacob set her on her feet. Meredith stumbled slightly and grabbed the edge of a table that stood in the center of the room.

Her cousin laughed. "I told you that you would fall."

Meredith ignored him. Drawing herself up, she pushed her tangled hair from her forehead and faced her uncle. "What do you intend to do now?" Her voice was as cold as she could make it.

Isaac snorted as he reached for a tankard of ale that had been placed on the table. He handed it to his son and took a second one for himself.

"Always playing the lady of the manor, eh, Meredith?" her uncle sneered. "Well, you best realize that no bloody aristocrat will come to your rescue this time, my girl. If you want to see your sister alive again, you'll do exactly as I tell you."

Meredith gripped the edge of the table even harder, staring back at Isaac with every ounce of loathing in her soul. His eyes swept over her face.

"You'll do what I say," he said with a casual cruelty, "or your sister will be dead by morning."

His coarse features looked positively demonic in the shadows cast by the lamp. Meredith tasted the bitter memory of the drug on her tongue and knew her uncle would do exactly as he threatened. She took a deep breath and stiffly nodded her head.

"Sit," said Isaac, grabbing a chair and shoving it toward her.

Meredith sat, warily looking back and forth between her cousin and uncle.

Isaac lounged against the table. "You'll do everything we say, Meredith, because we have nothing to lose. You always wondered why Nora and I came to Swallow Hill, didn't you? We had to. I lost my business—everything I owned—at the end of last year. Nothing remains of the great Burnley fortune," he said bitterly, "except, of course, for the inheritance left to you by your father. The creditors have been hounding us for months, and if we don't give them something soon, it's debtor's prison for us. That, or the continent."

Meredith felt her mouth gape open, but she managed to hold her tongue.

Isaac laughed harshly. "You didn't think we moved there because of familial devotion, did you? I can't stand the sight of you, you arrogant bitch! And your sister is so weak it would do the world a favor if I let her rot in this hellhole until she died."

Meredith swallowed the bile that rushed into her throat. If someone had placed a pistol in her hand at this moment, there was little doubt in her mind she would have shot her uncle.

"Of course, we did try to poison your sweet sister down in Kent, but I suppose you already know that. Jacob was very distressed when you almost died and ruined all our plans, weren't you, my boy?"

Meredith looked over at her cousin, surprised to see him gazing at his father with ill-concealed hatred. She knew it was too much to hope that Jacob would turn on Isaac, but perhaps she could use his animosity to some advantage.

"Of course, that's all in the past now, isn't it?" Isaac mused. "We may not get Annabel's money, but we'll get enough to survive on, and then some." He looked over at his son. "And you'll finally get what you've been lusting after all these years, won't you, Jacob?"

Meredith saw the greedy triumph in her cousin's eyes, and the faint hope she had been harboring died within her. Isaac clearly intended to give Jacob exactly what he wanted.

"What must I do?" Meredith asked around the lump in her throat.

"It's simple, really," explained Isaac with a grin that turned her blood to ice water. "You marry Jacob. As a wedding present, Annabel will give the ownership of Swallow Hill to you. It's a nice, tidy estate and should fetch a high enough price to pay off the rest of our creditors. Your fortune is not as great as Annabel's, but fifteen hundred a year is better than exile on the continent. Your sister may have slipped out of our hands, but I assure you, Niece, I will never let you go."

"You *are* mad!" Meredith cried, no longer able to contain her loathing. "Annabel's family will find us, and you'll be put on trial for attempted murder and kidnapping. How could you ever imagine I would agree to this?"

"Oh, but they won't find her," vowed Isaac softly. "They won't find either of you. You'll both simply disappear, and so will we. Do you actually think anyone knows where you are? I've been much too careful for that."

"But even if I were to agree to marry Jacob, Annabel will never remain silent," Meredith argued desperately. "The Stantons will not allow you to use us in this way."

"That's where you're wrong, Meredith," Jacob finally interjected. "By the time the Stantons know what's happening, you'll already be married to me. Do you really think the great general will see the family name tarred by a scandal like this? What will you try to do—divorce me? Charge us for kidnapping? The Stantons won't allow Annabel to be dragged into the middle of a trial, and you know it. After all"—his laugh was a guttural bark—"she's a very fragile girl. They'll be only too happy to keep their mouths shut, as long as they get their precious granddaughter back in one piece."

Jacob reached over and stroked her cheek. Meredith flinched away from him.

"Besides," added Isaac, pushing up from the table, "I'm Annabel's guardian. You'll never be able to prove murder, and if I see fit to place Annabel in a madhouse, that's my legal right. I already have a doctor who will swear to her insanity. In fact, this is his asylum. You remember Dr. Leeds from Bristol, don't you? No, Meredith. Those proud bastards the Stantons will be only too happy to avoid the scandal, and Annabel will be only too happy to give you Swallow Hill. We all know she'll do anything to please you."

Meredith could hardly breathe, a misery as heavy as death crushing her chest. She could see no escape from this nightmare, at least not before Silverton could find them.

Jacob chuckled, almost as if he could read her thoughts. "As for you, my sweet, did you really think the Stantons would give a damn about you? To them, you're nothing but a shopgirl. They'll probably be grateful I took you off their hands, since you'll no longer be able to embarrass them."

Meredith thought of the promises Silverton had made to her last night and felt something shrivel within her soul. She looked into the long passage of years stretching before her— a life bound inextricably to the people she hated most. She thought of the endless torture of nights in Jacob's bed and knew she would prefer death to such an existence.

But it was not just her own life she was responsible for. There was Annabel. Meredith would do anything to save her sister, including consigning herself to a marriage that would utterly destroy her.

A sense of dull resignation crept over her. She closed her mind to the terrifying vision of a ruined life and focused on the present. Meredith would live only for this moment, and right now what she needed to do was save Annabel.

She lifted her head and tried to force the words of submission from her throat. But she couldn't speak. Meredith grasped the arms of the chair, took a deep breath, and tried again. Still the words would not come.

Jacob's face twisted with anger. He reached down and yanked her up from the chair. "Perhaps you need a little encouragement," he leered.

He covered her lips in a suffocating kiss. She managed to get one arm free, raking her nails down his face. Jacob screamed, drew his arm back, and struck her hard across the face. Meredith fell to the floor, her ears ringing in pain, her face throbbing as she fought the black tide that threatened to pull her under. She dimly heard the chair scraping against the floor and braced herself for the blow that was sure to follow.

"Stop it, Jacob," barked Isaac. "We don't want the preacher to see any marks on her face. Lock her up with Annabel for the rest of the day. Maybe a little time spent in the madhouse will help the fool come to her senses."

Cruel hands pulled her up and began to drag her to the door. An iron claw wrapped itself around her wrist. "What's this?" snarled Jacob.

Meredith cried out as Jacob found the bracelet concealed under her sleeve. She struggled to break free, but he managed to unclasp the band and hold it up to the light.

"Now that's a pretty little trinket," he breathed harshly. "Is it a gift from Silverton? Have you already opened your legs for him, my sweet little cousin? It looks as if you won't be coming to my bed a virgin, after all. That should make things more interesting, at least for me."

Meredith barely heard a word he said. The black wave that had been threatening to drown her finally crashed through her remaining barriers of self-control. The voices faded away as she surrendered to a pitiless void of despair.

Chapter Thirty

"Meredith, are you awake?"

Annabel's whisper intruded on Meredith's consciousness, rousing her from the twilight state she had drifted in during the last few hours.

"Yes, dear, I'm awake."

She stirred on the filthy straw mattress slung across a rickety wooden bed frame, the only piece of furniture in the tiny room. Annabel huddled against her side, arms wrapped tightly around her waist. Meredith ducked her head to inspect the girl's face in the dismal light, praying that her sister had recovered from her earlier bout of hysterical tears.

Meredith had been in a half-swoon when Jacob carried her into the wing of the madhouse where Annabel had been incarcerated. At first, she had thought herself trapped in the throes of a nightmare. It took several moments to understand that the screams emanating as if from the very walls were the cries of the asylum's inmates.

The smells were even worse than the noise. The odor of unwashed bodies and filthy privies so overwhelmed her that Meredith feared she would faint a second time. Refusing to make herself so vulnerable again, she closed her eyes and breathed through her mouth to steady her spinning head.

Jacob suddenly stopped, and Meredith heard a loud rattling of keys. She opened her eyes, noticing for the first time that Mrs. Jukes preceded them. The severe-looking woman opened a door, and Jacob carried her through it. Annabel was huddled on a decrepit bed shoved up against the wall of the otherwise empty room. As soon as she saw Meredith, she launched herself up from the mattress.

"Meredith!" she shrieked, flying toward her.

Mrs. Jukes grabbed the girl by the arms and forced her back to the bed.

"What have you done to my sister?" Annabel sobbed.

"If you know what's good for you, my girl," Mrs. Jukes said in a cold voice, "you'll best keep quiet. If you don't behave yourself, we'll have to put you in restraints. A fine young miss like yourself shouldn't be making such a fuss, now, should she?"

"Annabel, I'm fine," Meredith gasped, terrified Mrs. Jukes would carry out her threat.

"You won't be for long if you don't do what you're told," Jacob warned as he dumped her down on the bed beside her sister. "I'll be back for you later, Meredith. Think on what my father said, or you and Annabel won't see the dawn of another day."

Jacob and Mrs. Jukes left the room. The door slammed shut, plunging the tiny cell into a shadowed gloom.

"I was so afraid I would never see you again," Annabel wept as Meredith pulled her into her arms.

"I know, dear. I'm here now. Don't cry. I won't let anyone hurt you." Meredith rocked her sister back and forth as the girl cried hysterically in her arms.

Eventually, the shattering sobs tapered off into the occasional hiccup, and Annabel fell into a deep sleep. Meredith held her for hours, trying to gauge the passage of time as the dim light faded through the small, iron-barred window set high up in the stone wall of their prison.

Eventually, worn out by her own anxious vigil, she had fallen into a restless doze.

Now, as Meredith sat up on the creaky bed, she struggled against the lassitude that clouded her mind. As she gazed blearily at the unfamiliar surroundings, she suddenly experienced a brief flash of disorientation and then panic. Night had fallen, and Silverton had not come. She knew that Jacob could return at any moment, and, when he did, she would have no choice but to do as he wished. If she didn't, her cousin and uncle would kill them both.

"How long do you think they'll leave us in here?"

Meredith stroked her hands over Annabel's tangled hair, her heart breaking at the quaver in her sister's voice. "I don't know, darling. Perhaps not much longer."

Annabel shifted on the bed, turning to look directly into her eyes. Meredith was startled by the unwavering resolve in her sister's gaze.

"Don't worry, Meredith." Annabel's voice was much stronger than it had been even a moment ago. "Lord Silverton and Robert will find us, I know they will."

Meredith could only nod her head, silenced by the misery threatening to consume her. If she could only keep Annabel safe, Silverton would eventually rescue them. She knew he would not rest until he found them.

But she also knew that help would come too late for her. Jacob would undoubtedly force her into marriage this night, and bed her immediately afterward. Even Silverton could not extend his love to a woman who had been despoiled by another man, nor tolerate the scandal of a divorce. His family wouldn't permit it, and, for Annabel's sake, neither would she.

Meredith struggled to accept the crushing weight of despair bearing down on her spirit. The sooner she purged her love for Silverton from her heart the better, since it would only torture her to madness. That part of her life was dead to her now, and she must look unflinchingly to the future, however terrible it might be. Annabel was all that mattered, and Meredith would do whatever was necessary to save her life.

Her sister suddenly moved to the edge of the bed. "I think I hear something."

Meredith heard it too, the sound of heavy footsteps moving rapidly toward them. A key was inserted in the lock and the door swung open, rusty hinges screeching in protest. She stood and faced the door, pulling Annabel up beside her. Jacob, Mrs. Jukes, and the man with the misshapen nose crowded into the room. Meredith froze when she saw the ugly man carried a pistol.

Jacob's face appeared satanic in the fitful light cast by Mrs. Jukes's lantern. "Well, Meredith? Have you made your decision?"

Annabel jerked her head, her eyes widening in alarm as she stared at her sister. "What is he talking about, Meredith? What decision?"

"It's all right, dear," Meredith murmured as she gazed steadily at Jacob. "Everything will be all right. You'll be away from this place soon enough."

Her cousin's mouth stretched into a triumphant sneer. "I'm pleased you made the right decision. Father always said you were no fool, and he was obviously right." He grabbed her arm. "Now say good-bye to Annabel. It may be some time before you see her again."

"No!" Annabel wrapped her arms around Meredith's waist, clinging to her with desperate hands. Mrs. Jukes darted forward to pull her away.

"Don't you touch her," Meredith warned as she tightened her arms around her sister.

Jacob shook his head at the asylum keeper. Mrs. Jukes frowned but stepped back.

Meredith cradled Annabel's face in her hands, staring into her sister's anguished eyes. "Annabel, you must listen to me.

I know what I'm doing. No one will harm you, and you'll be returning home very soon."

Her sister's lips quivered as she struggled not to cry, but tears dripped down her cheeks anyway. Meredith was very certain her own heart was shattered beyond repair.

"I will see you soon enough," she said, tenderly brushing the tears from Annabel's face. "I promise." She cast a glance over her shoulder at the group by the door. "Is that not right, Jacob?" Her voice contained a note of challenge her cousin could not fail to understand.

Jacob glowered at her for a moment before impatiently nodding his head. "Aye, you'll see each other soon enough."

Meredith inwardly sighed with relief. She needed to keep her sister from finding out the truth. If Annabel knew, she would fight it, and Meredith was terrified Mrs. Jukes would put the girl in restraints or worse.

"Do you promise?" Annabel's voice broke.

"Darling, I promise!" Meredith hugged her fiercely, only letting go when Jacob's hand came down heavily on her shoulder. She allowed him to steer her from the room, not daring to look back at Annabel's tear-streaked face. Meredith could not bear the pain she knew she would see in the girl's eyes.

Jacob towed her quickly down the dingy passage. Meredith suddenly dug in her heels, forcing him to stop.

"Don't try your luck, Meredith," he rasped, tugging at her arm.

"I will do everything you wish of me," she replied calmly, even though she felt her legs would collapse at any second. "But you must give me your word as my cousin, as the friend of my youth, that you will do as you promise—that you will release Annabel unharmed."

He scowled at her, but she thought a hint of uneasiness and possibly even shame darkened his coarse features.

"I said she would be unharmed if you marry me. She will be returned to London in the morning."

He started to pull her down the hall, but Meredith resisted. "Even if your father doesn't wish it?" she challenged.

He rounded on her so quickly that she almost staggered from the shock.

"Blast you, I told you, didn't I?" He pressed her body back against the wall, leering at her as he did so. *"If* you do everything I say, and I mean everything, then Annabel will be released unharmed."

Meredith swallowed a rush of saliva, sickened by the feel of his huge body pushing against hers. She nodded quickly.

"Good," he grunted, marching her to a set of stairs at the end of the passage. He hurried her down to a landing, which branched out into two separate hallways. The old house was like a rabbit warren, ramshackle and poorly lit. As Jacob hustled her along after Mrs. Jukes, Meredith tried desperately to memorize the way back to Annabel's room.

The hallway branched again, and she recognized the passage leading to the front of the house. As they reached the end of the hall, a door swung open and light spilled out into the passage. Isaac stood framed in the doorway.

"What took you so long?"

Jacob ignored his father as he pushed Meredith into the room. It was the same parlor as before, but now it was brightly lit with two brass lanterns, and a roaring fire had been built up on the hearth.

"Well?" growled Isaac.

Jacob grinned at his father.

Isaac laughed. "Well, girl, I'm glad to see you've come to your senses. In the morning, Annabel will sign over the ownership of Swallow Hill to you. As her guardian, I will approve the transaction. Then we'll put her in a coach and send her back to London."

"Why does she have to wait till tomorrow?" demanded Meredith. "Why not do it tonight?"

Isaac tsked and shook his finger at her in a horrible parody of an affectionate uncle. "Now, now, my dear. We wouldn't want to deprive you and Jacob of your wedding night, would we? Must have things tied up properly before we send Annabel on her way."

Jacob's eyes ran hungrily over her body, and Meredith's last faint hope burned away in the black smoke of his gaze. She looked into the fire, trying to control the roiling pain in her stomach.

"Mrs. Jukes." Isaac spoke harshly. "Where is the parson? He should have been here by now."

"My apologies, sir." The woman shrugged her shoulders. "He sent a boy around not twenty minutes ago to tell me he would be late. Reverend Caine is attending a deathbed. The boy said that old Mr. Tyler would not live out the hour."

Isaac snorted loudly, obviously frustrated.

"How . . ." Meredith cleared her throat and started again. "How will Jacob and I be able to marry so quickly?"

"Not to worry, dear Niece," Isaac sneered. "We obtained a special license before we left London. All you need do is convince the good parson that you wish to be married. In fact," he laughed, "you'll tell the man you simply can't wait a moment longer to be Jacob's wife, won't you?"

Jacob joined in the laughter. Meredith swallowed again, afraid she would soon be sick all over the floor. Her uncle abruptly stopped laughing and ran a disapproving eye over her figure.

"The parson will think something's amiss if you come to your groom looking like a trollop. Go with Mrs. Jukes and clean yourself up."

There was obviously nothing she could do to fight them. Resigned, Meredith was about to follow the other woman from the room when she caught the sound of raised voices from the front of the house. There was a distant crash, and then a door farther down the hallway slammed shut.

"What the hell was that?" Isaac's head snapped back at the noise.

Mrs. Jukes gaped at the two men. "I haven't a clue, sir. We are only expecting the parson. There are no other patients arriving tonight."

Isaac snatched up the lantern from the table and headed for the door. "Jacob, keep an eye on your cousin. Don't let her out of the room. You"—he jerked his head at Mrs. Jukes—"come with me."

He strode from the room. Jacob gazed uneasily after his father and then began rummaging for something in his coat pocket.

Praying to herself that her cousin would remain distracted, Meredith began inching toward the door. Jacob glanced up, cursed, and crossed the room in a flash. He wrapped his fingers around the back of her neck in a punishing grip. She gasped at the pain, her eyes flooding with moisture.

"Where the hell do you think you're going?" He pushed her across the room to the one of the ladder-back chairs.

"Sit down and shut up, Meredith, or I swear you'll regret it for the rest of your life."

He was about to shove her down on the hard wooden seat when there was a pounding of footsteps out in the hall, and the door to the parlor suddenly flew open. Silverton strode into the room, looking as grim and hard as any battle-scarred warrior. He was clad in a dusty greatcoat and mud-splattered boots. His head was uncovered, his hair tousled and damp.

When Meredith saw the expression in Silverton's eyes, her heart took a great leap in her chest. They were like windows into hell—but it was a hell encased in thick sheets of impenetrable ice rather than the blazing fires of the damned. He calmly raised his right hand and pointed a large pistol at Jacob's head.

With startling speed, Jacob lurched back and pulled Meredith in front of him. He gripped her tightly from behind as Silverton slowly advanced toward them. She heard more noise out in the hall, and then Robert burst into the room. He froze as he took in the scene that met his eyes.

Jacob dragged Meredith behind the table, away from Silverton.

"Let her go." Silverton's voice was soft and deadly.

Jacob's hand clenched her wrist so tightly that Meredith feared her bones would snap. Silverton continued his predatory stalk across the room as her cousin pulled her farther around the massive wooden table.

Robert's eyes darted into the corners. "Meredith," he gasped, "where is Annabel?"

She clawed frantically at Jacob's fingers, trying to release the unbearable pressure on her wrist. "Down the hallway to the right and up the stairs to the landing," she cried. "Go right again to the end of the passage. Annabel is there."

Robert spun around and dashed out the doorway. She heard him call to someone, ordering the person to follow him.

Jacob held Meredith in front of him as he edged around the other side of the table and moved toward the door. She hung heavily against him, trying to slow him down.

Silverton kept his pistol trained at Jacob's head.

"Shoot and you'll hit her," Jacob rasped.

Silverton hesitated. He dropped the pistol into the pocket of his greatcoat.

"Let her go, Burnley," he said, his voice completely devoid of emotion. Meredith shivered at the sound of it. "Let her go now, or I'll kill you."

Jacob's hoarse laugh reverberated off the low ceiling. "Meredith belongs to me, you bastard. Before this night is out, she'll be damaged goods. No man but me will ever want her again, I'll make certain of that."

Jacob's face was congested with blood, his eyeballs

protruding from his sockets. But Silverton might as well have been carved from granite for all he responded to the other man's taunts.

Jacob jerked Meredith to the door. His hand squeezed her arm so tightly she could feel the bones shift beneath her skin. She choked, her breath seizing with the pain that exploded up to her shoulder.

As she saw rage flash across Silverton's face, Meredith decided that she'd had enough. Twisting around, she grabbed her cousin's arm. She bent her head and sank her teeth into his wrist, biting him as hard as she could. Jacob roared, cuffing her on the side of the head with his other hand. Meredith's vision blurred as she crumpled to her knees.

Silverton launched himself across the room at Jacob. All three of them went down in a tangle of flailing limbs, and Meredith was thrown backward with stunning force into the wall. She collapsed onto the floor, gasping painfully as she tried to suck air into her lungs. Rolling out of the way of the struggling men, she groped her way up the wall and pushed herself to her feet.

Silverton had somehow managed to regain his feet as well, dragging Jacob up with him. His left fist smashed into her cousin's face and blood spurted from the other man's mouth.

It was a devastating punch. Jacob swayed but remained standing. Staggering to the side, he swung powerfully at Silverton, who ducked just before the blow connected. Jacob lashed out again. Silverton jerked his face out of the way, but this time her cousin's massive fist landed solidly on his shoulder. He fell back into the table, and Jacob threw himself on top of him. They crashed to the floor.

Meredith watched, terrified, as the two men rolled over the uneven floorboards. Jacob was a brute, outweighing Silverton by almost two stone. If he got the upper hand, Meredith was sure he would kill the man she loved.

She cast her eyes about frantically for a weapon. Spying a

large brass candlestick on the fireplace mantel, Meredith ran across the room. She flung the lit candle into the fire and rushed back to the rolling bodies on the floor. Jacob heaved himself on top of Silverton, trying to wrap his beefy hands tightly around his neck. Silverton gasped for air but was still able to free an arm and push the heel of his hand against the other man's chin.

As Jacob's head snapped back under the force of Silverton's hand, Meredith slammed the candlestick into the back of her cousin's skull. He collapsed, blood pouring freely from the wound she had inflicted on his head.

The room was silent but for the sound of heavy breathing. Silverton pushed Jacob's body from him and slowly sat upright, coughing as he gingerly rubbed his throat. Meredith stood frozen, the candlestick dangling from her hand. From what seemed a very great distance, she noticed a few strands of bloody hair stuck to the brass.

"Is he dead?" she asked in a strangled whisper.

Silverton put his hand to Jacob's throat to feel for a pulse. After a moment, he shook his head. He looked up at her, and the edges of his mouth began to lift in a ragged smile.

"Thank you, my love," he murmured in a raspy voice. "Your cousin is a very large man."

The sound of his voice released her from her paralysis. She gave a small cry, dropped the candlestick, and threw herself onto the floor and into his arms. Meredith sobbed against his chest as he rocked and soothed her, just as she had done for Annabel only a short time ago.

At the thought of her sister, she jerked up, alarm tightening every muscle in her body.

"Annabel!" she gasped. "We must find her."

Silverton grimaced as he helped her to her feet. "Robert and Peter have already gone to look. Show me where they were holding her."

She was momentarily distracted by the pale and drawn

set of his face. "You're hurt!" she exclaimed. "What did he do to you?"

Silverton winced as he touched his shoulder. "Nothing but a little bruising, my love. Don't concern yourself."

He put his arm around her to lead her from the room when Trask and two other men strode through the door. Meredith vaguely recognized the strangers as two of Silverton's grooms.

"Well?" asked Silverton.

The earl smiled grimly as he wiped blood from an ugly looking cut on his cheek. "Isaac Burnley and his companions are trussed up in one of the rooms off the stables. Simmons is standing guard with a pistol. Not that Burnley is in any condition to notice such details."

Meredith expelled a shaky breath of relief at the news of her uncle's capture.

"What about him?" The earl jerked his head at Jacob's motionless form on the floor.

"Meredith brained him with a candlestick."

Trask laughed. "I'm glad to hear it." He motioned to the grooms, who picked up Jacob and lugged him from the room.

"Miss Burnley." The earl made her a small bow. "I am greatly relieved to see you in one piece."

"So am I," she replied fervently, "but we must go to Annabel."

There was a quick, light step out in the hall. "Meredith!"

A moment later and Annabel was in her embrace. Robert walked in right behind her and went to stand by Silverton and Trask. Meredith wrapped her arms around her sister, vowing irrationally to herself that she would never let the girl out of her sight again.

After a moment, Annabel sniffed loudly and very inelegantly, and lifted her head to smile mistily at Meredith. "I told you Silverton and Robert would find us, didn't I?"

Meredith looked over her sister's head at the three men standing by the door, each one of them blinking rapidly, as if their eyes bothered them. Silverton surreptitiously rubbed his cheek.

Something effervescent started to bubble up within her, almost like champagne, but so much more wonderful that Meredith couldn't even put a name to it. A laugh began to prickle in her throat as she studied the battered, dirt-covered man who had risked his very life to save her. Silverton gazed back at her with such longing that her laughter was silenced with a joy so enormous it almost terrified her. All at once her spirit broke free, shattering the chains of doubt and fear that had gripped her soul for so many long, lonely years.

Meredith hugged Annabel tightly in her arms. "Yes, my love," she replied, almost to herself. "Yes, you did tell me he would find us. And he did!"

Epilogue

She felt smothered. The darkness overwhelmed her, and the only sound she heard was the rapid beating of her own heart. Meredith whimpered, shrinking from the terror hovering at the edge of her consciousness.

She sensed movement even before the small sound from her lips faded away. Something big wrapped itself around her, cocooning her in a warmth that drove away the lingering remnants of fear. She relaxed, free to float up out of the darkness, swimming toward a gentle light glimmering just out of reach.

Meredith woke up. She blinked her eyes in the soft morning light beginning to illuminate her bedroom at Swallow Hill. A heavy weight pressed along the length of her body, enveloping her in a reassuring embrace. As she came fully awake, she realized the comforting heat came from a large male body sprawled on top of her. A golden head rested on her breast, a strong arm was thrown across her hips, and a long leg pinned her lower limbs to the mattress.

Meredith's heart constricted and then expanded with the startling joy of waking up in her own bed with Silverton on top of her. She lay quietly for a few moments, sifting through the glorious but unsettling emotions that rushed to greet her with the new dawn and her new life.

Moving cautiously so as not to rouse him, Meredith raised her left wrist into an errant sunbeam, catching the morning light on her emerald and opal bracelet. She had refused to take it and her wedding gift—a matching necklace—off last night. Silverton, however, had not seemed to mind that she had wanted to wear her jewelry to bed. In fact, he had been quite taken with the idea of his new bride clothed in nothing more than precious stones and metals. Meredith still couldn't help blushing whenever she thought of his enthusiastic response to her lack of attire.

She idly twisted her wrist, watching the light sparkle on the jewels and on the single, perfect emerald set in the gold band on her left hand. As much as she loved her wedding ring and her necklace, no piece of jewelry would ever mean so much to her as the bracelet. It had served as a precious link to Silverton during her and Annabel's hideous ordeal.

On that terrible night two weeks ago, Silverton had been eager to remove the sisters from the scene of their captivity. Both Meredith and Annabel were exhausted, and no one had relished the thought of the long trip back to London. After a hurried consultation with Robert and Trask, Silverton had decided they should drive to Swallow Hill, which could be reached in less than two hours. Meredith had insisted that two footmen ride ahead to warn the servants and to ensure that Nora Burnley had departed the estate before they arrived.

Meredith and Annabel emerged from the dank asylum into the clean air of a cloudless and star-filled night. The storm that had threatened earlier in the day had dissipated before a bracing wind that swept everything before it. Torches flickered in the courtyard as the grooms hurried to prepare the traveling coach for their departure.

Meredith started to climb into the carriage when she remembered that she had not yet reclaimed her bracelet. Coming to a sudden halt, she pleaded with Silverton to fetch it for her immediately. He was impatient to be gone, however, and would only promise to send one of the footmen to retrieve it.

Meredith stubbornly refused to take another step. Silverton finally spun on his heel and, muttering to himself, stalked over to the barn where Jacob and Isaac were being held.

He returned to her shortly thereafter, his face set and grim. When Meredith asked him what had transpired, he simply shook his head and handed her the bracelet. She threw her arms around his neck and planted a grateful kiss on his cheek. Silverton had allowed a tiny smile to touch his lips as he returned her embrace, apparently satisfied with the reward for fulfilling his lady's request.

Now Meredith lay quietly in her bed, gazing at the bracelet and trying not to think too hard about the cousin and uncle who had betrayed her. Try as she might, though, she was unable to repress a small, bitter sigh. Silverton moved his head against her breast as his arm tightened around her hips. She wriggled under his weight.

"My lord, you are squashing me," she whispered, not sure if he was awake.

She felt a moist puff of warm air against her nipple as he blew out a small but exasperated breath.

"Meredith, when are you going to stop calling me my lord?"

"When you stop squashing me."

He rolled over and onto his back, winding one arm around her waist and pulling her to his side. She snuggled against him, resting her head on his shoulder as she stroked the smooth muscles of his broad chest.

Meredith had never felt so cherished or so safe. But she still couldn't seem to let go the dark memory of Jacob and the searing hatred he had revealed to her.

"Why does it still trouble you, my love?"

She tilted her head up to look at her husband, startled as always by his uncanny ability to read her thoughts. His cobalt eyes were gentle, and she couldn't help reaching up to stroke his firm jaw, rough with early morning bristle. He caught her hand and pressed it to his lips.

She sighed again as she snuggled closer to his warmth. "I know it's foolish, but I can't help thinking about it."

Silverton settled her more comfortably into the crook of his arm. "You're safe now, sweetheart." He tilted her chin up and dropped a soft kiss onto her lips. "I promise. They can never hurt you again."

Trask and his servants had swiftly bundled Jacob and Isaac on board one of the earl's merchant ships bound for New South Wales. Silverton had believed the sooner they left the country, the better. Surprisingly, only Annabel had protested the plan, outraged that her uncle and cousin would escape the full wrath of the law. But Robert had eventually convinced his fiancée that penniless exile was far preferable to the scandal of a public trial, particularly for the sake of General and Lady Stanton. Annabel grudgingly agreed, and the Burnleys had shipped out from Bristol under close guard, never to be seen again.

"You don't think they'll ever try to come back, do you?" Meredith hated to even ask that question, but the idea had haunted her dreams for the last two weeks.

"If they do, they're dead men," her husband responded in a casual voice that she found rather chilling.

He said nothing more, and Meredith assumed his reticence signaled the end of the discussion about her criminally inclined relatives. She let the matter drop. After all, it was her first morning as a married woman, and she really should make an effort to find a more cheerful topic of conversation. Meredith tried to absorb once more the idea that she was the new Marchioness of Silverton and that the man lying next to her would be there every morning for the rest of her life.

"Sometimes I think I don't deserve to be this happy." The words popped out of her mouth before she could stop them.

Silverton turned on his side to look at her, his lips parting slightly as if in disbelief. Meredith could think of nothing to say that would justify her remark, so she smiled apologetically instead. He groaned and dropped his head back on the pillow, his eyes rolling up to the ceiling. She had a sneaking suspicion he sought patience from the heavens.

"Well, it's true," she defended herself. "It just seems to be the way I think."

He moved swiftly, rolling her onto her back and coming down heavily on top of her. "Meredith, I told you once before—you are the best person I've ever known. You deserve everything I can give you, and more. What will it take to convince you?"

She studied his narrowed eyes, pretending to seriously ponder the question.

"Well . . . I suppose you'll simply have to show me." Meredith wrapped her arms around his neck. "Preferably when we're alone." She nuzzled his mouth with her lips. "Like we are now."

A passionate heat flared in his eyes, and for the next little while she knew nothing but the feel of his mouth and hands roaming over her body. In less time than she could have imagined, he brought her panting to ecstatic completion, any tiny doubts still lingering in her heart obliterated in the dazzling fire that blazed between them.

When they again rested in each other's arms, rather more breathless than they had been before, Meredith suddenly remembered a question she had meant to ask him yesterday.

"Stephen?"

"Hmmm?"

"How did you manage to convince your mother to behave so beautifully at our wedding?"

She felt rather than heard the low rumble of laughter in his chest. "Oh, her impeccable behavior might have something to do with the new townhouse I promised to build her in London."

Meredith gave a small snort. "I should have known it had nothing to do with me."

"Don't despair, my love. You have, after all, achieved a great victory in bringing the general so thoroughly around to your side. I only wish you could have heard the thundering lecture he gave my mother when she tried to complain to him about our marriage."

Meredith still found herself amazed by the general's impassioned defense. He *had* softened to her considerably after Lady Stanton's illness, but now he seemed to regard her in much the same light as he did Annabel. He had been greatly affected by the kidnapping and had been almost pathetically grateful to Silverton for rescuing his granddaughter and Meredith.

"He wants me to give him one of my paintings. I must say, I can't imagine that any one of them won't shock him. He has such conservative tastes."

Silverton propped himself up on his elbow, a teasing smile playing around the corners of his lips. "I know exactly which painting to give to him."

She stared back, puzzled by his reaction.

"You know," he prompted. She could hear the mischief in his voice. "Robert suggested it to him several weeks ago when Aunt Georgina was recuperating from her illness. Don't you remember? Your painting of the Minotaur in the maze— the one that Robert said looks just like the general."

Meredith's eyes widened in shock, and then she burst into laughter.

His smile stretched into a grin, and then he was laughing, too. He swooped down and pulled her into his arms. Meredith's laughter continued to build inside her, fed by the sheer joy of the perfect, timeless moment.

The sound of their joy drifted across the room and out through the open window. Meredith heard a swallow's trill exuberantly echo their laughter as the small bird wheeled up from the lavender-scented garden to greet the dawning of the bright August morn.

Summer, she decided as Silverton's mouth covered hers, was surely the happiest season of them all.